Duty

Samuel Smiles

Duty

The present edition is a reproduction of previous publication of this classic work. Minor typographical errors may have been corrected without note, however, for an authentic reading experience the spelling, punctuation, and capitalization have been retained from the original text.

ISBN: 978-1-64799-198-2

PREFACE

TWENTY-FOUR years since, I wrote "Self-Help". It was published three years later, in 1859. The writing of that book was occasioned by an apparently slight circumstance. I had delivered a few lectures at Leeds to some young men, in a place that had been used as a temporary cholera hospital. I endeavoured to point out to them that their happiness and well-being in after life depended very much upon themselves — upon their diligent self-culture, self-discipline, and self-control; and, above all, upon the honest and upright performance of individual duty, which constitutes the glory of manly character. '

The results were more satisfactory than I could have expected. I found that many of these young men, as they grew up into manhood, were chosen to fill positions of trust, responsibility, and usefulness; and some of them were pleased to attribute some measure of their honest success in life to their endeavours to work up to the spirit of the lessons which they had received from their instructor.

I was thus led to prepare the memoranda for a book on the same subject; for books readi much farther than spoken words. I prepared the work in my leisure evening moments, after the hours of business were over. I entitled the book "Self-Help" being able to find no better word to suit the purpose; though mutual help, as well as self-help, was as prominently set forward.

When the book was prepared, I offered the manuscript to a London publisher, but it was declined with thanks. The Crimean war was then raging, and books were almost unsaleable. It was not until after the "Life of George Stephenson" had been published, that I issued "Self-Help" through the kindness of Mr. Murray.

It was received most favourably. I owe my greatest thanks to the reviewers. I believe their reviews have been just. With very few exceptions, they have praised my efforts perhaps more than they deserved. And yet I knew nothing of them, nor they of me.

"Self-Help" was translated and published in nearly every European language; as well as into some of the languages or dialects of India and Japan. In America, the book has been more widely published and read than in Great Britain. But the English author can never know the fate of his book in America, Piracy of English books is protected by American law; and the honest publisher of New York is overwhelmed by the dishonest publisher of Chicago. I cannot understand why the American legislature should be less honest than the governments of France, Germany, and Italy. In all these countries international copyright is freely granted

Thirteen years after the appearance of "Self-Help" during which I had been engaged with other works, I wrote and published "Character." I there endeavoured to fill up the picture of the noble and magnanimous man and woman, and cited numerous examples taken from the lives of the best men and women who ever lived. It seemed to me that this was the best manner of impressing the minds of young people, by giving them invigorating examples of nobility of character. "Some people exclaim," said Isaac Disraeli, "give me no anecdotes of an author, but give me his works; yet I have often found that the anecdotes are more interesting thaji the works." This is the example which I have always pursued. "It is not," said Plutarch, "in the most distinguished exploits that men's virtues or vices may be best discovered, but frequently an action of small note, a short saying, or a jest that distinguishes a person's real character more than the greatest battles or the most important actions."

Five years later, "Thrift" appeared. In that book I assumed the dignity of labour, and urged men to economise in order to secure their independence; to provide for their familles, with a view to the future; to live a clean, sober, and manly life; to avoid the horrible curse of drink, which keeps so many men and women poor; and to raise them up to an elevation of virtue, morality, and religion. I believe that the book has done much good. Since its publication many institutions have been formed for the establishment of National Thrift; and I know, from many correspondents, that thriving Penny Banks have been established where they did not exist before.

Five years after the publication of "Thrift," I now give "Duty," — the last book of the series. I hope it will be as useful as its predecessors. I have, at all events, done my best, according to the faculty that still remains in me. The reader will find, in the following pages, numerous examples given of the best and bravest men and women in the career of well-doing.

Great deeds are great legacies, which work with wondrous usury. By what men have done, we learn what men can do. A great career, though baulked of its end, is still a landmark of human energy. He who approaches the highest point of the supreme quality of Duty, is entitled to rank with the most distinguished of his race.

> "The primal duties shine aloft like stars,
> And charities that soothe, and heal, and bless,
> Are scattered at the feet of men like flowers."

London, November 1880

CONTENTS

Preface iii

CHAPTER I   Duty — Conscience 1
CHAPTER II   Duty in Action 13
CHAPTER III   Honesty— Truth 26
CHAPTER IV   Men Who Cannot be Bought 40
CHAPTER V   Courage — Endurance 53
CHAPTER VI   Endurance to the End — Savonarola 73
CHAPTER VII   The Sailor 87
CHAPTER VIII   The Soldier 107
CHAPTER IX   Heroism in Well-Doing 128
CHAPTER X   Sympathy 146
CHAPTER XI   Philanthropy 163
CHAPTER XII   Heroism in Missions 181
CHAPTER XIII   Kindness to Animals 199
CHAPTER XIV   Humanity to Horses — E. F. Flower 214
CHAPTER XV   Responsibility 228
CHAPTER XVI   The Last 235

CHAPTER I

DUTY — CONSCIENCE

He walked attended By a strong-aidiog champion — Conscience.
                                        Milton

Whatever thy race or speech, thou art the same; Before thy eyes Duty, a constant flame, Shines always steadfast with tuchanging light. Through dark days and through bright.

                                    The Ode of Life

Why, O man, do you vituperate the world? The world is most beautiful, framed by the best and most perfect reason, though to you indeed it may be unclean and evil, because you are unclean and evil in a good world.

                                    Marsilius Ficinus

MAN does not live for himself alone. He lives for the good of others as well as of himself. Every one has his duties to perform — the richest as well as the poorest. To some life is pleasure, to others suffering. But the best do not live for self-enjoyment, or even for fame. Their strongest motive power is hopeful useful work in every good cause.

Hierocles says that each one of us is a centre, circumscribed by many concentric circles. From ourselves the first circle extends — comprising parents, wife, and children. The next concentring circle comprises relations; then fellow-citizens; and lastly, the whole human race.

To do our duty in this world towards God and towards man, consistently and steadily, requires the cultivation of all the faculties which God hath given us. And He has given us everything. It is the higher Will that instructs and guides our will. It is the knowledge of good and evil, the knowledge of what is right and what is wrong, that makes us responsible to man here, and to God hereafter.

The sphere of Duty is infinite. It exists in every station of life. We have it not in our choice to be rich or poor, to be happy or unhappy; but it becomes us to do the duty that everywhere surrounds us. Obedience to duty, at all costs and risks, is the very essence of the highest civilised life. Great deeds must be worked for, hoped for, died for, now as in the past.

We often connect the idea of Duty with the soldier's trust. We remember the pagan sentinel at Pompeii, who died at his post, during the burial of the city by the ashes of Vesuvius, 'some eighteen hundred years ago. This was the true soldier. While others fled, he stood to his post It was his Duty. He had been set to guard the place, and he never flinched He was suffocated by the sulphureous vapour of the falling ashes. His body was resolved to dust, but his memory survives. His helmet, lance, and breastplate are still to be seen at the Museo Borbonico at Naples.

1

This soldier was obedient and disciplined. He did what he was appointed to do. Obedience, to the parent, to the master, to the officer, is what every one who would do right should be taught to learn. Childhood should begin with obedience. Yet age does not absolve us. We must be obedient even to the end Duty, in its purest form, is so constraining that one never thinks, in performing it, of one's self at all. It is there. It has to be done without any thought of self-sacrifice.

To come to a much later date than that of the Roman soldier at Pompeii—When the Birkenhead went down off the coast of Africa, with her brave soldiers on board firing difeu de joie as they sank beneath the waves, the Duke of Wellington, after the news arrived in England, was entertained at the Banquet of the Royal Academy, Macaulay says, "I remarked (and Mr. Lawrence, the American Minister, remarked the same thing) that in his eulogy of the poor fellows who were lost, the Duke never spoke of their courage, but always of their discipline and subordination. He repeated it several times over. The courage, I suppose, he treated as a matter of course."

Duty is self-devoted. It is not merely fearlessness. The gladiator who fought the lion with the courage of a lion, was urged on by the ardour of the spectators, and never forgot himself and his prizes. Pizarro was full of hardihood. But he was actuated by his love of gold in the midst of his terrible hardships.

"Do you wish to be great?" asks SL Augustine. "Then begin by being little. Do you desire to construct a vast and lofty fabric? Think first about the foundations of humility. The higher your structure is to be, the deeper must be its foundation. Modest humility is beauty's crown."

The best kind of duty is done in secret, and without sight of men. There it does its work devotedly and nobly. It does not follow the routine of worldly-wise morality. It does not advertise itself. It adopts a larger creed and a loftier code; which to be subject to and to obey, is to consider every human life, and every human action, in the light of an eternal obligation to the race. Our evil or our careless actions incur debts every day, that humanity, sooner or later, must discharge.

But how to learn to do one's duty? Can there be any difficulty here? First, there is the pervading, abiding sense of duty to God. Then follow others: — Duty to one's family; duty to our neighbours; duty of masters to servants, and of servants to masters; duty to our fellow-creatures; duty to the State, which has also its duty to perform to the citizen.

Many of these duties ate preformed privately. Our public life may be well known, but in private there is that which no one sees — the inner life of the soul and spirit. We have it in our choice to be worthy or worthless. No one can kill our soul, which can perish only by its own suicide. If we can only make ourselves and each other a little better, holier, and nobler we have perhaps done the most that we could.

Here is the manner in which an American legislator stood to his post:—

An eclipse of the sun happened in New England about a century ago. The heavens became very dark, and it seemed by many that the Day of

2

Judgment was at hand. The Legislature of Connecticut happened then to be in session, and on the darkness coming on, a member moved the adjournment of the House, on which an old Puritan legislator, Davenport of Stamford, rose up and said that if the last day had come, he desired to be found in his place and doing his duty; for which reasons he moved that candles should be brought, so that the House might proceed with its business. Waiting at the post of Duty was the maxim of the wise man, and he carried his motion.

There was a man of delicate constitution, who devoted a great deal of his time to philanthropic work. He visited the sick, he sat by them in their miserable homes, he nursed them and helped them in all ways. He was expostulated with by his friends for neglecting his business, and threatened with the illness he was sure to contract by visiting the fevered and the dying. He replied to his friends with firmness and simplicity, "I look after my business for the sake of my wife and my children, but I hold that a man's duty to society requires him to have a care for those who are not of his own household."

These were the words of a willing servant to duty. It is not the man who gives his money that is the true benefactor of his kind, but the man who gives himself. The man who gives his money is advertised; the man who gives his time, strength, and soul, is beloved. The one may be remembered, while the other may be forgotten, though the good influence he has sown will never die.

But what is the foundation of Duty? Jules Simon has written a valuable work, Le Devoir, iii which he makes duty depend upon liberty. Men must be free in order to perform their public duties, as well as to build up their individual character. They are free to think; they must also be free to act. At the same time liberty may be used to do evil rather than to do good. The tyranny of a multitude is worse than the tyranny of an individual. Thoreau, the American, says that modem freedom is only the exchange of the slavery of feudality for the slavery of opinion.

Freedom, enjoyed by all men alike, is a late idea in history.[1] In remote ages, men who were so-called "free" possessed the right of being served by slaves. There was slavery in the state, and also in the family. It existed in

---

[1] The feeling that labour is not an honourable ocaipation is but a survival of the old pagan and feudal times, when the plough was left to the slaves, and only the villeins hoed the com. The Roman definition of gentility was gentem habent soli cujus parentes nemini servierunt — "those only are genteel whose ancestors have never served." The idea prevalent in the North American Republic, according to which slave blood, in even the extremest branch contaminates, is decidedly of Roman origin. "Dear German peasants," says Heine, " go to America; there you will find neither princes nor nobles; all men are equals, with the exception, in truth, of a few millions who have a black or a brown skin, and are treated like dogs. He who has the least trace of negro descent, and betrays his origin no longer in colour, but in the form of his features, is forced to suffer the greatest humiliations. . . . Doubtless many a noble heart may there in silence lament the universal self-seeking and unrighteousness. Would he, however, strive against it, a martyrdom awaits him which surpasses all European conception."

republics as well as in monarchies. The elder Cato, the greatest economist of Republican Rome, enforced the expediency of getting rid of old slaves to avoid the burden of their maintenance. The sick and infirm slaves were carried to the island of -sculapius, in the Tiber, where they were suffered to die of disease or of hunger. In Imperial Rome, the Populus Romanus was dependent upon charity. In England also, when slavery was abolished, and when the poor were no longer fed by the charity of the monasteries, a poor law was established, which was only a compensation for the loss of liberty.

There is a stronger word than Liberty, and that is Conscience. From the beginning of civilisation the power of this word has been acknowledged. Menander, the Greek poet, who lived three hundred years before Christ, duly recognised it. "In our own breast," he said, "we have a god — our conscience." Again he says, "Tis not to live, to live for self alone. Whenever you do what is holy, be of good cheer, knowing that God himself takes part with rightful courage. The rich heart is the great thing that man wants."

Conscience is that peculiar faculty of the soul which may be called the religious instinct. It first reveals itself when we become aware of the strife between a higher and a lower nature within us — of spirit warring against flesh — of good striving for the mastery over evil Look where you will, in the church or without the church, the same struggle is always going on — war for life or death; men and women wrung with pain because they love the good and cannot yet attain it.

It is out of this experience that Religion is born — the higher law leading us up to one whom the law of conscience represents. "It is an introspection," says Canon Mosely, "on which all religion has been built. Man going into himself and seeing the struggle within him, and thence getting self-knowledge, and thence the knowledge of God." Under this influence man knows and feels what is right and wrong. He has the choice between good and evil. And because he is free to choose, he is responsible.

Whatever men may theoretically believe, none practically feel that their actions are necessary and inevitable. There is no constraint upon our volition. We know that we are not compelled, as by a spell, to obey any particular motive. "We feel," says John Stuart Mill, "that if we wished to prove that we have the power of resisting the motive, we could do so; and it would be humiliating to our pride, and paralysing to our desire of excellence, if we thought otherwise."

Our actions are controllable, else why do men all over the world enact laws? They are enacted in order to be obeyed, because it is the universal belief, as it is the universal fact, that men obey them or not, very much as they determine. We feel each one of us, that our habits and temptations are not our masters, but we of them. Even in yielding to them we know that we could resist, and that, were we desirous of throwing them off altogether, there could not be required for that purpose a stronger desire or will than we know ourselves to be capable of feeling.

To enjoy spiritual freedom of the highest kind, the mind must have been awakened by knowledge. As the mind has become enlightened, and conscience shows its power, the responsibility of man increases. He submits himself to the influence of the Supreme Will, and acts in conformity with it — not by constraint, but cheerfully; and the law which holds him is that of Love. In the act of belief, implying knowledge and confidence, his humanity unfolds. He feels that by his own free act, his faith in and his working in conformity to the purpose of a Divine Will, he is achieving good and securing the highest good.

"Man without religion," says Archdeacon Hare, "is the creature of circumstances; but religion is above all circumstances, and will lift him up above them." And Thomas Lynch, in his Theophilus Trinal, says, "Till fixed, we are not free. The acorn must be earthed ere the oak will develop. The man of faith is the man who has taken root — taken root in God; our works prove our heart — our heart in God." In the New Testament we find, "Where the Spirit of the Lord is, there is liberty." And Cowper:

"He is the freeman whom the truth makes free
And all are slaves beside."

Where there is no such acknowledgment of Divine law, men act in obedience to sense, to passion, to selfishnesis. In indulging any vicious propensity, they know they are doing wrong. Their conscience condemns them. The law of nature cries out against them. They know that their act has been wilful and sinful. But their power to resist in the future has become weakened. Their will has lost power and next time the temptation offers, the resistance will be less. Then the habit is formed. The curse of every evil deed is, that, propagating still, it brings forth evil.

But conscience is not dead. We cannot dig a grave for it, and tell it to lie there. We may trample it under foot, but it still lives. Every sin or crime has, at the moment of its perpetration, its own avenging angel. We cannot blind our eyes to it, or stop our ears to it "Tis conscience that makes cowards of us all" There comes a day of judgment, even in this world, when it stands up confronting us, and warning us to return to the life of well-doing.

Conscience is permanent and universal. It is the very essence of individual character. It gives a man self-control — the power of resisting temptations and defying them. Every man is bound to develop his individuality, to endeavour to find the right way of life, and to walk in it. He has the will to do so: he has the power to be himself and not the echo of somebody else, nor the reflection of lower conditions, nor the spirit of current conventions. True manhood comes from self-control — from subjection of the lower powers to the higher conditions of our being.

The only comprehensive and sustained exercise of self-control is to be attained through the ascendency of conscience — in the sense of duty performed. It is conscience alone which sets a man on his feet, frees him from the dominions of his own passions and propensities. It places him in relation to the best interests of his kind. The truest source of enjoyment is found in the paths of duty alone. Enjoyment will come as the unbidden sweetener of labour, and crown every right work.

At its fullest growth, conscience bids men do whatever makes them

5

happy in the highest sense, and forbear doing whatever makes them unhappy. "There are few if any among civilised people," says Herbert Spencer, "who do not agree that human well-being is in accordance with the Divine Will. The doctrine is taught by all our religious teachers; it is assumed by every writer on morality: we may therefore safely consider it an admitted truth."

Without conscience, a man can have no higher principle of action than pleasure. He does what he likes best, whether it be sensuality or even sensuous intellectual enjoyment. We are not sent into the world to follow our own bent — to indulge merely in self-satisfaction. The whole constitution of nature works against this idea of life. The mind ought never to be held in subjection to the lower parts of our nature. There can be no self-sacrifice, no self-denial, no self-control, — except what may be necessary to avoid the consequences of human law.

A race so constituted, with intellect and passions such as man possesses, and without the paramount influence of conscience to govern their deeds, would soon be consigned to utter anarchy, and terminate in mutual destruction. We partly see the results already, in the mad riot in human life which has recently prevailed among the Nihilists in Germany and Russia, and the fire and destruction of the Communists' war in Paris? Such a principle prevailing throughout society, can lead to nothing else than utter demoralisation — individual, social, and national.

The only method left is to recall men to their sense of Duty. The task of our fathers has been to conquer right; be it the task of this generation to teach and propagate duty. Give justice also, — justice, which is the splendour of virtue; and benevolence, its companion. There is a sentence in the Evangelists which comes back to us without ceasing, and which ought to be written on every page of a book of morality, — "Do unto others as ye would that they should do unto you." "In life," says Wilhelm von Humboldt, "it is worthy of special remark, that when we are not too anxious about happiness and unhappiness, but devote ourselves to the strict and unsparing performance of duty, then happiness comes of itself, — nay, even springs from the midst of a life of troubles and anxieties and privations."

"What is your duty?" asks Goethe. "The carrying out of the affairs of the day that lies before you." But this is too narrow a view of duty. "What again," he asks, "is the best government? That which teaches us to govern ourselves." Plutarch said to the Emperor Trajan, "Let your government commence in your own breast, and lay the foundation of it in the command of your own passions." Here come in the words, self-control, duty, and conscience. "There will come a time," said Bishop Hooker, "when three words, uttered with chastity and meekness, shall receive a far more blessed reward than three thousand volumes written with the disdainful sharpness of wit."

It is well for the soul to look on actions done for love, not for selfish objects, but for duty, mercy, and loving-kindness. There are many things done for love, which are a thousand times better than those done for money. The former inspire the spirit of heroism and self-devotion. The latter die with the giving. Duty that is bought is worth little. "I consider," said Dr. Arnold, "beyond all wealth, honour, or even health, is the attachment due to noble souls; because to become one with the good, generous, and true, is to be in a manner, good, generous, and true yourself."

Every man has a service to do, to himself as an individual, and to those who are near him. In fact, life is of little value unless it be consecrated by duty. "Show those qualities then," said Marcus Aurelius Antoninus, "which are altogether in thy power, — sincerity, gravity, endurance of labour, aversidn to pleasure, contentment with thy portion and with few things, benevolence, frankness, and magnanimity."

The greatest intellectual power may exist without a particle of magnanimity. The latter comes from the highest power in man's mind — conscience, and from the highest faculty, reason, and capacity for faith — that by which man is capable of apprehending more than the senses supply. It is this which makes man a reasonable creature — more than a mere animal. Mr. Darwin has truly said "that the motives of conscience, as connected with repentance and the feelings of duty, are the most important differences which separate man from the animal."[2]

We are invited to believe in the all-powerful potency of matter. We are to believe only in what we can see with our eyes, and touch with our hands. We are to believe in nothing that we do not understand But how very little do we absolutely know and understand! We see only the surfaces of things, "as in a glass darkly." How can matter help us to understand the mysteries of life? We know absolutely nothing about the causes of volition, sensation, and mental action. We know that they exist, but we cannot understand them.

When a young man declared to Dr. Parr that he would believe nothing he did not understand, "Then, sir," said the doctor, "your creed would be the shortest of any man whom I ever knew." But Sydney Smith said a better thing than this. At a dinner at Holland House, a foreigner announced himself as a materialist. Presently Sydney Smith observed, "A very good soufflet this!" To which the materialist rejoined, "Oui, monsieur; il est ravissant!" "By the way," replied Smith, with his usual knock-down application, "may I ask, sir, whether you happen to believe in a cook?"

We must believe a thousand things that we do not understand. Matter and its combinations are as great a mystery as Life is. Look at those numberless far-off worlds majestically wheeling in their appointed orbits; or at this earth on which we live, performing its diurnal motion on its own axis, during its annual circle round the sun. What do we understand about the causes of such motions? What can we ever know about them, beyond the fact that such things are?

"The circuit of the sun in the heavens," says Pascal, "vast as it is, is itself only a delicate point when compared with the vaster circuit that is accomplished by the stars. Beyond the range of sight, this universe is but a spot in the ample bosom of nature. We can only imagine of atoms as

---

[2] Descent of Man vol. i. chap. ii.

compared with the reality, which is an infinite sphere, of which the centre is everywhere, the circumference nowhere. What is man iti the midst of this infinite? But there is another prospect not less astounding; it is the Infinite beneath him. Let him look to the smallest of the things which come under his notice-a mite It has limbs, veins, blood circulating in them globules in that blood, humours, and serum. Within the enclosure of this atom, I will show you not merely the visible universe, but the very immensity of Nature. Whoever gives his mind to thoughts such as this, will be terrified at himself — trembling where Nature has placed him — suspended, as it were, between infinity and nothingness. The Author of these wonders comprehends them; none but He can do so."

Confucius taught his disciples to believe that Conduct is three-fourths of life. "Ponder righteousness, and practise virtue. Knowledge, magnanimity, and energy, are universally binding. Gravity, generosity of soul, sincerity, earnestness, and kindness, constitute perfect virtue." These words come to us as the far-off echo of the great teacher of ten thousand ages, as his disciples called him — the holy and prescient sage Confucius.

But all these virtues come from the innate monitor Conscience. From this first principle all rules of behaviour are drawn. It bids us do what we call right, and forbids us doing what we call wrong. At its fullest growth it bids us do what makes others happy, and forbids us doing what makes others unhappy. The great lesson to be learnt is, that man must strengthen himself to perform his duty and do what is right, seeking his happiness and inward peace in objects that cannot be taken away from him. Conscience is the conflict by which we get the mastery over our own failings. It is a silent working of the inner man, by which he proves his peculiar power of the will and spirit of God.

We have also something to learn from the noble old Greeks as to the virtue of Duty. Socrates is considered by some as the founder of Greek philosophy. It was his belief that he was specially charged by the Deity to awaken moral consciousness in men. He was born at Athens 468 years before Christ. He received the best education which an Athenian could obtain. He first learnt sculpture, in which he acquired some reputation. He then served his country as a soldier, according to the duty of all Athenian citizens. The oath which he took, in common with all other youths, was as follows: — "I will not disgrace the sacred arms entrusted to me by my country; nor will I desert the place committed to me to defend."

He displayed much fortitude and valour in all the expeditions in which he was engaged. In one of the engagements which took place before Potidaea, Alcibiades fell wounded in the midst of the enemy. Socrates rushed forward to rescue him, and carried him back, together with his arms. For this gallant performance he was awarded the civic crawn as the prize of valour — the Victoria Cross of those days. His second campaign was no less honourable. At the disastrous battle of Delium he saved the life of Xenophon, whom he carried from the field on his shoulder, fighting his way as he went He served in another campaign, after which he devoted himself for a time to the civil service of his country.

He was as brave as a senator as he had been as a soldier. He possessed that high moral courage which can brave not only death but adverse opinion. He could defy a tyrant, as well as a tyrannical mob. When the admirals were tried after the battle of Arginusse, for not having rescued the bodies of the slain, Socrates stood alone in defending them. The mob were furious. He was dismissed from the Council, and the admirals were condemned.

Socrates then devoted himself to teaching. He stood in the market-places, entered the workshops, and visited the schools, in order to teach the people his ideas respecting the scope and value of human speculation and action. He appeared during a time of utter scepticism. He endeavoured to withdraw men from their metaphysical speculation about nature, which had led them into the inextricable confusion of doubt "Is life worth living?" was a matter of as much speculation in these days as it is in ours. Socrates bade them look inwards. While men were propitiating the gods, he insisted upon moral conduct as alone guiding man to happiness here and hereafter.

Socrates went about teaching. Wise men and pupils followed him. Aristippus offered him a large sum of money, but the offer was at once declined. Socrates did not teach for money, but to propagate wisdom. He declared that the highest reward he could enjoy was to see mankind benefiting by his labours.

He did not expound from books; he merely argued. "Books," he said, "cannot be interrogated, cannot answer, therefore they cannot teach. We can only learn from them what we knew before." He endeavoured to reduce things to their first elements, and to arrive at certainty as the only standard of truth. He believed in the unity of virtue, and averred that it was teachable as a matter of science. He was of opinion that the only valuable philosophy is that which teaches us our moral duties and religious hopes. He hated injustice and folly of all kinds, and never lost an occasion of exposing them. He expressed his contempt for the capacity for government assumed by all men. He held that only the wise were fit to govern, and that they were the few.

In his seventy-second year he was brought before the judges. The accusers stated their charge as follows: Socrates is an evil-doer, and corrupter of the youth; he does not receive the gods whom the state receives, but introduces new divinities. He was tried on these grounds, and condemned to die. He was taken to his prison, and for thirty days he conversed with his friends on his favourite topics. Crito provided for him the means of escaping from prison, but he would not avail himself of the opportunity. He conversed about the immortality of the soul,[3] about courage, and virtue, and temperance, about absolute beauty and absolute good, and about his wife and children.

He consoled his weeping friends, and gently upbraided them for their complaints about the injustice of his sentence.

---

[3] "If death," he said, "had only been the end of all, the wicked would have had a good bargain in dying, for they would have been happily quit, not only of their bodies, but of their own evil, together with their souls. But now, inasmuch as the soul is manifestly immortal, there is no release or salvation from evil, except the attainment of the highest virtue and wisdom. "—Jowett's Dialogues of Plato i. 488.

He was about to die. Why should they complain? He was far advanced in years. Had they waited a short time, the thing would have happened in the course of nature. No man ever welcomed death as a new birth to a higher state of being with greater faith. The time at length came when the gaoler presented him with the cup of hemlock. He drank it with courage, and died in complete calmness, "Such was the end," said Phædo, "of our friend, whom! may truly call the wisest and justest and best of all the men whom I have ever known."

"After ages have cherished the memory of his virtues and of his fate," says Mr. Lewes; "but without profiting much by his example, and without learning tolerance from his story. His name has become a moral thesis for schoolboys and rhetoricians. Would that it CQuld become a Moral Influence!"[4]

Socrates wrote no books. Nearly all that we know of him is derived from his illustrious disciples, Plato and Xenophon, who have embalmed the memory of his actions, lessons, wrongs, and death. Plato lived with him for ten years, and afterwards expounded his views in the famous "Dialogues "; but in these dialogues it is difficult to know which is Plato and which is Socrates. After they had been separated by death, Plato, in his fortieth year, travelled into Sicily. He there became acquainted with Dionysius I., the Tyrant of Syracuse. Owing to a difference of opinion about politics, for Plato was bold and free in his expressions about liberty, the tyrant threatened his life. Dion, his brother, interceded for him, and his life was saved; but he was ordered to be sold as a slave. He was bought by a friend, and immediately set at liberty.

Plato returned to Athens, and began to teach. Like his master, he taught without money and without price. It is not necessary to follow his history. Suffice it to say, that he devoted himself to the inculcation of truth, morality, and duty. He divided the four cardinal virtues into (i) Prudence and wisdom; (2) Courage, constancy, and fortitude; (3) Temperance, discretion, and self-control; and (4) Justice and righteousness. He assumed this division of virtue as the basis of his moral philosophy. "Let men of all ranks," he said, "whether they are successful or unsuccessful, whether they triumph or not — let them do their duty, and rest satisfied." What a lesson for future ages lies in these words!

Plato devoted the end of his days to the calm retirement of his Academy. The composition of the "Dialogues," which have been the admiration of posterity, was the cheering solace of his life, and especially of his declining years. He has been called the Divine Plato. His soul panted for truth. This alone, he said, should be man's great object. Like his master, he connected with Supreme Intelligence the attributes of goodness, justice, and wisdom, and the idea of direct interposition in human affairs. He disliked poetry as much as Carlyle.[5] The only poetry he ever praises is

---

[4] Biographical History of Philosophy i 213 (first edition).

[5] Carlyle says, "If you have anything profitable to communicate to men, why sing it f That a man has to bring out his gift in words of any kind, and not in silent divine actions which alone are fit to express it well, seems to me a great misfortune for

moral poetry, which is in truth verified philosophy. Let it be remarked that he lived about four hundred years before Christ Coleridge speaks of him as the genuine prophet of the Christian Era; and Count de Maistre was accustomed to say of him, "Let us never leave a great question without having consulted Plato."

The New Testament gives a glorified ideal of a possible human life; but hard are his labours who endeavours to keep that ideal uppermost in his mind. We feel that there is something else that we would like to do, much better than the thing that is incumbent upon us. But the Duty is there, and it must be done, without dreaming or idling. How much of the philosophy of moral health and happiness is involved in the injunction — "Whatsoever thy hand findeth to do, do it with all thy might." He that does his best, whatever his lot may be, is on the sure road of advancement.

It is related of one, who in the depths of his despair cried, "It is of no use to be good for you cannot be good, and if you were, it would do you no good." It is hopeless, truthless, and faithless, thus to speak of the goodness of word and work. Each one of us can do a little good in our own sphere of life. If we can do it, we are bound to do it. We have no more right to render ourselves useless than to destroy ourselves.

We have to be faithful in small things as well as in great We are required to make as good a use of our one talent as of the many talents that have been conferred upon us. We can follow the dictates of our conscience, and walk, though alone, in the paths of duty. We can be honest, truthful, diligent, were it only out of respect for one's self. We have to be faithful even to the end. Who is not struck with the answer of the slave, who, when asked by an intending purchaser, "Wilt thou be faithful if I buy thee?" "Yes," said the slave, "whether you buy me or not."

In the description of a sermon preached to the working classes by the late Dr. Macleod, in the Barony Church of Glasgow, it is said that he made a grand stand for Character. From the highest to the lowest that was the grand aim to be made. He said that "the most valuable thing that Prince Albert had left was Character. He knew perfectly well that many very poor people thought it was impossible for them to have a character. It was not true; he would not hear of it. There was not a man or woman before him, however poor they might be, but had it in their power, by the grace of God, to leave behind them the grandest thing on earth. Character; and their

---

him. It is one of my constant regrets in this generation, that men to whom the gods have given a genius (which means a light of intelligence, of courage, and all manfulness, or else means nothing) will insist, in such an earnest time as ours has grown, in bringing out their Divine gift in the shape of verse which now no man reads entirely in earnest." On the other hand, Mr. Matthew Arnold, in his Introduction to The English Poetry says that our race, as time goes on, will find an ever surer and surer stay in Poetry, "There is not a creed which is not shaken, not an accredited dogma which is not shown to be questionable, not a received tradition which does not threaten to dissolve. Our religion has materialised itself in the fact, in the supposed fact, it has attached its emotions to the fact, and now the fact is failing it. But for poetry the idea is everything; the rest is a world of illusion, of divine illusion."

children might rise up after them and thank God that their mother was a pious woman, or their father a pious man."

Character is made up of small duties faithfully performed, — of self-denials, of self-sacrifices, of kindly acts of love and duty. The backbone of character is laid at home; and whether the constitutional tendencies be good or bad, home influences will as a rule fan them into activity. "He that is faithful in little is faithful in much; and he that is unfaithful in little is unfaithful also in much." Kindness begets kindness, and truth and trust will bear a rich harvest of truth and trust. There are many little trivial acts of kindness which teach us more about a man's character than many vague phrases. These are easy to acquire, and their effects will last much longer than this very temporary life.

For no good thing is ever lost. Nothing dies, not even life, which gives up one form only to resume another. No good action, no good example, dies. It lives for ever in our race. While the frame moulders and disappears, the deed leaves an indelible stamp, and moulds the very thought and will of future generations. Time is not the measure of a noble work; the coming age will share our joy. A single virtuous action has elevated a whole village, a whole city, a whole nation. "The present moment," says Goethe, "is a powerful deity." Man's best products are his happy and sanctifying thoughts, which when once formed and put in practice, extend their fertilising influence for thousands of years, and from generation to generation. It is from small seeds dropped into the ground that the finest productions grow; and it is from the inborn dictates of Conscience and the inspired principle of Duty that the finest growths of Character have arisen. Thus sings Wordsworth of Duty: —

"Stem Lawgiver! yet thou dost wear
The Godhead's most benignant grace,
Nor know I anything so fair
As is the smile upon thy face;
Flowers laugh before thee on their beds.
And fragrance in thy footing treads;
Thou dost preserve the stars from wrong,
And the most ancient heavens are through thee fresh and strong."

12

CHAPTER II

DUTY IN ACTION

Put thou thy trust in God,
In duty's path go on; Fix on His Word thy steadfast eye.
So shall thy work be done.

Luther

Do noble things, not dream them, all day long,
And so make life, death, and that vast forever, one grand, sweet
song.

Charles Kingsley

O worker of the world! to whose young arm
The brute earth yields, and wrong, as to a charm;
Young seaman, soldier, student, toiler at the plough,
Or loom, or forge, or mine, a kingly growth art thou!
Where'er thou art, though earthy oft and coarse.
Thou bearest with thee hidden springs of force.
Creative poyer, the flower, the fruitful strife,
The germ, the potency of life.

The Ode of Life

HE who has well considered his duty will at once carry his convictions into action. Our acts are the only things that are in our power. They not only form the sum of our habits, but of our character.

At the same time, the course of duty is not always the easy course. It has many oppositions and difficulties to surmount. We may have the sagacity to see, but not the strength of purpose to do. To the irresolute there is many a lion in the way. He thinks and moralises and dreams, but does nothing. "There is little to see," said a hard worker, "and little to do; it is only to do it."

There must not only be a conquest over likings and dislikings; but, what is harder to attain, a triumph over adverse repute. The man whose first question, after a right course of action has presented itself, is "What will people say?" is not the man to do anything at all. But if he asks, "Is it my duty?" he can then proceed in his moral panoply, and be ready to incur men's censure, and even to brave their ridicule. "Let us have faith in fine actions," says M. de la Cretlle, "and let us reserve doubt and incredulity for bad. It is even better to be deceived than to distrust."

Duty is first learned at home. The child comes into the world helpless and dependent on others for its health, nurture, and moral and physical development. The child at length imbibes ideas; under proper influences he learns to obey, to control himself, to be kind to others, to be dutiful and happy. He has a will of his own but whether it be well or ill directed depends very much upon parental influences.

The habit of willing is called purpose; and, from what has been said, the importance of forming a right purpose early in life will be obvious. "Character," says Novalis, "is a completely-fashioned will;" and the will, when once fashioned, may be steady and constant for life. When the true man, bent on good, holds by his purpose, he places but small value on the rewards or praises of the world; his own approving conscience, and the "well-done" which awaits him, is his best reward.

Will, considered without regard to direction, is simply constancy, firmness, perseverance. But it will be obvious, that unless the direction of the character be right, the strong will may be merely a power for mischief. In great tyrants it is a demon; with power to wield, it knows no bounds nor restraint. It holds millions subject to it; inflames their passions, excites them to military fury, and is never satisfied but in conquering, destroying, and tyrannising. The boundless Will produces an Alexander or a Napoleon. Alexander cried because there were no more kingdoms to conquer; and Buonaparte, after overrunning Europe, spent his force amidst the snows of Russia. "Conquest has made me," he said, "and conquest must maintain me." But he was a man of no moral principle, and Europe cast him aside when his work of destruction was done.

The strong Will, allied to right motives, is as full of blessings as the other is of mischief. The man thus influenced moves and inflames the minds and consciences of others. He bends them to his views of duty, carries them with him in his endeavours to secure worthy objects, and directs opinion to the suppression of wrong and the establishment of right The man of strong will stamps power upon his actions. His energetic perseverance becomes habitual. He gives a tone to the company in which he is, to the society in which he lives, and even to the nation in which he is born. He is a joy to the timid, and a perpetual reproach to the sluggard. He sets the former on their feet by giving them hope. He may even inspire the latter to good deeds by the influence of his example. Tennyson hits the mark in the following words: —

> O living Will, that shalt endure
> When all that seems shall suffer shock.
> Rise in the spiritual rock,
> Flow through our deeds and make them pure;
>
> That we may lift from out of dust,
> A voice as unto him that hears,
> A cry above the conquered years,
> To one that with us works, and trust,
>
> With faith that comes of self-control.
> The truths that never can be proved.
> Until we close with all we loved.
> And all we flow from, soul in soul."

Besides the men of strong bad wills and strong good wills, there is a

14

far larger number who have very weak wills, or no wills at all. They are characterless. They have no strong will for vice, yet they have none for virtue. They are the passive recipients of impressions, which, however, take no hold of them. They seem neither to go forward nor backward. As the wind blows, so their vane turns round; and when the wind blows from another quarter, it turns round again. Any instrument can write on such spirits; any will can govern theirs. They cherish no truth strongly, and do not know what earnestness is. Such persons constitute the mass of society everywhere — the careless, the passive, the submissive, the feeble, and the indifferent

It is, therefore, of the utmost importance that attention should be directed to the improvement and strengthening of the Will; for without this there can neither be independence, nor firmness, nor individuality of character. Without it we cannot give truth its proper force, nor morals their proper direction, nor save ourselves from being machines in the hands of worthless and designing men. Intellectual cultivation will not give decision of character. Philosophers discuss; decisive men act. "Not to resolve," says Bacon, "is to resolve "— that is to do nothing.

"The right time," says Locke, "to educate the Will aright is in youth. There is a certain season when our minds may be enlarged, when a vast stock of useful truths may be acquired; when our passions will readily submit to the government of reason; when right principles may be so fixed in us as to influence every important action in our future lives. But the season for this extends neither to the whole nor to any considerable length of our continuance upon earth. It is limited to but a few years of our term; and if throughout these we neglect it, error or ignorance is. according to the ordinary course of things, entailed upon us. Our Will becomes our law; and our lusts gain a strength which we afterwards vainly oppose."

The first Lord Shaftesbury, in a conversation with Locke, broached a theory of character and conduct which threw a light upon his own. He said that wisdom lay in the heart and not in the head, and that it was not the want of knowledge but the perverseness of will that filled men's actions with folly, and their lives with disorder. Mere knowledge does not give vigour to character. A man may reason too much. He may weigh the thousand probabilities on either side, and come to no action, no decision. Knowledge is thus a check upon action. The Will must act in the light of the spirit and the understanding, and the soul then springs into full life and action.

Indeed, the learning of letters and words and sentences is not of the importance that some think it to be. Learning has nothing to do with goodness or happiness. It may destroy humility and give place to pride. The chief movers of men have been little addicted to literature. Literary men have often attained to greatness of thought which influences men in all ages; but they rarely attain to moral greatness of action.

Men cannot be raised in masses, as the mountains were in the early geological 'states of the world. They must be dealt with as units; for it is only by the elevation of individuals that the elevation of the masses can be effectually secured. Teachers and preachers may influence them from without, but the main action comes from within. Individual men must exert themselves and help themselves, otherwise they never can be effectually helped by others. "As habits belonging to the body," says Dr. Butler, "are produced by external acts, so habits of the mind are produced by the exertion of inward practical purposes — by carrying them into action or acting upon them — the principles of obedience, of veracity, justice, and charity."

In speaking of Butler, Mr. Stephen, in his recent work says that "his attitude is impressive from the moral side alone; but from that side its grandeur is undeniable. In the 'Analogy,' as distinctly as in the Sermons, the deification of the Conscience is the beginning, middle, and end of Butler's preaching. Duty is his last word. Whatever doubts and troubles beset him, he adheres to the firm conviction that the secret of the universe is revealed, so far as it is revealed, through Morality."

There is little or no connection between school teaching and morality. Mere cultivation of the intellect has hardly any influence upon conduct. Creeds posted upon the memory will not eradicate vicious propensities. The intellect is merely an instrument, which is moved and worked by forces behind it — by emotions, by self-restraint, by self-control, by imagination, by enthusiasm, by everything that gives force and energy to character. The most of these principles are implanted at home, and not at school. Where the home is miserable, worthless, and unprincipled — a place rather to be avoided than entered — then school is the only place for learning obedience and discipline. At the same time, home is the true soil where virtue grows. The events of the household are more near and affecting to us than those of the school and the academy. It is in the study of the home that the true character and hopes of the times are to be consulted.

To train up their households is the business of the old; to obey their parents and to grow in wisdom is the business of the young. Education is a work of authority and respect. Christianity, according to Guizot, is the greatest school of respect that the world has ever seen. Religious instruction alone imparts the spirit of self-sacrifice, great virtues and lofty thoughts. It penetrates to the conscience, and makes life bearable without a murmur against the mystery of human conditions.

"The great end of training" says a great writer, "is liberty; and the sooner you can get a child to be a law unto himself, the sooner you will make a man of him." "I will respect human liberty," said Monseigneur Dupanloup, "in the smallest child even more scrupulously than in a grown man; for the latter can defend it against me, while the child cannot. Never will I insult the child so far as to regard him as material to be cast into a mould, to emerge with the stamp given by my will."

Paternal authority and family independence is a sacred domain; and, if momentarily obscured in troublous times, Christian sentiment protests and resists until it regains its authority. But liberty is not all that should be struggled for; obedience, self-restraint, and self-government, are the conditions to be chiefly aimed at. The latter is the principal end of education. It is not imparted by teaching, but by example. The first

16

instruction for youth, says Bonald, consists in habits not in reasonings, in examples rather than in direct lessons. Example preaches better than precept, and that too because it is so much more difficult. At the same time, the best influences grow slowly, and in a gradual correspondence with human needs.

To act rightly, then, is the safety-valve of our moral nature. Good will is not enough; it does not always produce good deeds. Persevering action does most. What is done with diligence and toil imparts to the spectator a silent force, of which we cannot say how far it may reach. The Rev. Canon Liddon, in his lecture to young men at St. Paul's Cathedral, made an eloquent allusion to Work as the true end of life. "The life of man," he said, "is made up of action and endurance, and life is fruitful in the ratio in which it is laid out in noble action or in patient perseverance. But the physical workers are not the only true workers. The lives of thought do not lie outside this division, for true thought is undemonstrative action. . . To pass life in indolence, in a state of moral coma, is degrading, for life is only ennobled by work."

Noble work is the true educator. Idleness is a thorough demoraliser of body, soul, and conscience. Nine tenths of the vices and miseries of the world proceed from idleness. Without work, there can be no active progress in human welfare. No more insufferable misery can be conceived than that which must follow incommunicable privileges. Imagine an idle man condemned to perpetual youth, while all around him decay and die. How sincerely would he call upon death for deliverance I "The weakest living creature," says Carlyle, "by concentrating his powers on a single object, can accomplish something; whereas the strongest, by dispersing his over many, may fail to accomplish anything."

Have we difficulties to contend with? Then work through them. No. exorcism charms like labour. Idleness of mind and body resembles rust. It wears more than work. "I would rather work out, than rust out," said a noble worker. Schiller said that he found the greatest happiness in life to consist in the performance of some mechanical duty. He was also of opinion that "the sense of beauty never furthered the performance of a single duty." The highest order of being is that which loses sight in resolution, and feeling in work.

The greatest of difficulties often lie where we are not looking for them. When painful events occur, they are, perhaps, sent only to try and prove us. If we stand firm in our hour of trial, the firmness gives serenity to the mind, which always feels satisfaction in acting conformably to duty. "The battles of the wilderness," said Norman Macleod, "are the sore battles of everyday life. Their giants are our giants, their sorrows our sorrows, their defeats and victories ours also. As they had honours, defeats and victories, so have we."

The school of difficulty is the best school of moral discipline. When difficulties have to be encountered, they must be met with courage and cheerfulness. Did not Aristotle say that happiness is not so much in our objects as in our energies? Grappling with difficulties is the surest way of overcoming them. The determination to realise an object is the moral

17

conviction that we can and will accomplish it. Our wits are sharpened by our necessity, and the individual man stands forth to meet and pyercome the difficulties which stand in his way.

The memoirs of men who have thrown their opportunities away, would constitute a painful but a memorable volume for the world's instruction. "No strong man, in good health," says Ebenezer Elliot, "can be neglected, if he be true to himself. For the benefit of the young, I wish we had a correct account of the number of persons who fail of success, in a thousand who resolutely strive to do well I do not think it exceeds one per cent" Men grudge success, but it is only the last term of what looked like a series of failures. They failed at first, then again and again, but at last their difficulties vsnished, and success was achieved.

The desire to possess, without being burdened with the trouble of acquiring, is a great sign of weakness and laziness. Everything that is worth enjoying or possessing can only be got by the pleasure of working. This is the great secret of practical strength. "One may very distinctly prefer industry to indolence, the healthful exercise of all one's faculties to allowing them to rest unused in drowsy torpor. In the long run we shall probably find that the exercise of the faculties has of itself been the source of a more genuine happiness than has followed the actual attainment of what the exercise was directed to procure."

It has been said of a great judge that he never threw a legitimate opportunity away, but that he never condescended to avail himself of one that was unlawful. What he had to do, at any period of his career, was done with his whole heart and soul. If failure should result from his labours, self-reproach could not affect him, for he had tried to do his best.

We must work, trusting that some of the good seed we throw into the ground will take root and spring up into deeds of well-doing. What man begins for himself, God finishes for others. Indeed we can finish nothing. Others begin where we leave off, and carry on our work to a stage nearer perfection. We have to bequeath to those who come after us a noble design, worthy of imitation. Well done, well doing, and well to do are inseparable conditions that reach through all the ages of eternity.

Very few people can realise the idea that they are of no use in the world. The fact of their existence implies the necessity for their existence. The world is before them. They have their choice of good and evil— of usefulness and idleness. What have they done with their time and means? Have they shown the world that their existence has been of any use whatever? . Have they made any one the better because of their life? . Has their career been a mere matter of idleness and selfishness, of laziness and indifference?

Have they been seeking pleasure? Pleasure flies before idleness. Happiness is out of the reach of laziness. Pleasure and happiness are the fruits of work and labour, never of carelessness and indifference.

An unfortunate young man, who felt that his life was of no use whatever in this world, determined publicly to put an end to it. The event occurred at Capron, Illinois, United States. The man had cultivated his intellect, but nothing more. He had no idea of duty, virtue, or religion.

18

Being a materialist, he feared no hereafter. He advertised that he would give a lecture, and then shoot himself through the head. The admission to the lecture and the sensational conclusion was a dollar a head. The amount realised was to be appropriated partly to his funeral expenses, and the rest was to be invested in purchasing the works of three London materialists, which were to be placed in the town library. The hall was crowded. A considerable sum of money was realised. After he had concluded his lecture he drew his Derringer and shot his brains out according to his promise. What a conclusion of an earthly life — crushing red-handed into the presence of his God! The event occurred in August 1868.

Perhaps this horrible deed was the result of vanity, or perhaps to make a sensation. His name would be in the papers. Everybody would be shouting about his courage. But it was cowardice, far more than courage. It must have been disappointed vanity. Sheridan once said, "They talk of avarice, lust, ambition, as great passions. It is a mistake; they are little passions. Vanity is the great commanding passion of all. This excites the most heroic deeds, and impels to the most dreadful crimes. Save me from this passion, and I can defy the others. They are mere urchins, but this is a giant,"

A resolute will is needed not only for the performance of difficult duties, but in order to go promptly, energetically, and with self-possession, through the thousand difficult things which come in almost everybody's way. Thus courage is as necessary as integrity in the performance of duty. The force may seem small which is needed to carry one cheerfully through any of these things singly, but to encounter one by one the crowding aggregate, and never to be taken by surprise, or thrown out of temper, is one of the last attainments of the human spirit

Every generation has to bear its own burden, to weather its peculiar perils, to pass through its manifold trials. We are daily exposed to temptations, whether it be of idleness, self-indulgence, or vice. The feeling of duty and the power of courage must resist these things at whatever sacrifice of worldly interest. When virtue has thus become a daily habit, we become possessed of an individual character, prepared for fulfilling, in a great measure, the ends for which we were created.

How much is lost to the world for want of a little courage! We have the willingness to do, but we fail to do it The state of the world is such, and so much depends on action, that everything seems to say loudly to every man, "Do something; do it do it" The poor country parson, fighting against evil in his parish, against wrong-doing, injustice, and iniquity, has nobler ideas of duty than Alexander the Great ever had. Some men are mere apologies for workers, even when they pretend to be up and at it. They stand shivering on the brink, and have not the courage to plunge in. Every day sends to the grave a number of obscure men, who, if they had had the courage to begin, would, in all probability, have gone great lengths in the career of well-doing.

Professor Wilson of Edinburgh, in teaching his students, always put foremost the sense of duty; moreover, of duty in action. His lectures deeply influenced the characters of those who listened to him. He sent them forth to fight the battle of life valiantly; like the old Danish hero, — "to dare nobly, to will strongly, and never to falter in the path of duty." Such was his creed.[6]

There is a great deal of trimming in the world, for the most part arising from the want of courage. When Luther said to Erasmus, "You desire to walk upon eggs without crushing them, and among glasses without breaking them," the timorous, hesitating Erasmus replied, "I will not be unfaithful to the cause of Christ, at least so far as the age will permit w." Luther was of a very different character. "I will go to Worms though devils were combined against me as thick as the tiles upon the house-tops." Or like St. Paul, "I am ready, not only to be bound, but to die at Jerusalem."

Sir Alexander Barnes said, "One trait of my character is thorough seriousness. I am indifferent about nothing that I undertake. In fact, if I undertake to do a thing, I cannot be indifferent." This makes all the difference between a strong man and a weak man. The brave men are often killed, the talkers are left behind, the cowards run away. Deeds show what we are, words only what we should be. Every moment of a working life may be a decisive victory.

The Pessimists say that work, or the necessity for work, is the enemy of man. On the other hand, M. Caro says:

"An irresistible instinct carries man towards action, and through action towards some unforeseen pleasure, or expected happiness, or imposed duty. This irresistible instinct is nothing less than the instinct of life itself; it explains and sums it up. In the very moment in which it develops the sentiment of being within us, it measures the true worth of being. . . There are the pure joys, which lie in a long-sustained effort in the face of obstacles towards a triumphant end; of an energy first mistress of itself and then of life, whether in subduing the bad wills of men, or in triumphing over the difficulties of science, or the resistances of art — of Work, in short, the true friend and consoler of man, which raises him above all his weaknesses, purifies and ennobles him, saves him from vulgar temptation, and helps him to bear his burden through days of sadness, and before which even the deepest griefs give way for a time. In reality, when it has overcome the first weariness and distaste it may inspire. Work itself, apart from all results, is one of the most lively pleasures.. To treat it, with the Pessimists, as an enemy, is to misconceive the very idea of pleasure. For the workman to see his work growing under his hand or in his thought, to identify himself with it, as Aristotle said (Ethic iv. 7), — whether it be the labourer with his harvest, or the architect with his house, or the sculptor with his statue, — whether it be a poem or a book, it matters not

"The joy of creation more than returns all the pains of labour; and, as

---

[6] When he was canvassing the members of the Town-Council of Edinburgh for their votes, one of them said to him — "I wad like to gie ye ma vote, Mr. Wulson; but I'm feared. They say ye donna expect to be saved by grace." "I don't know much about that, Bailie; but if I am not saved by grace, I am sure that my works won't save me," "That'll do, that'll do; I'se gie you my vote."

the conscious labour against external obstacles is the first joy of awakening life, so the completed work is the most intense of pleasures, bringing to full birth in us the sense of personality, and consecrating our triumph, if only partial and momentary, over nature. Such is the true character of effort or will in action"[7]

A man is a miracle of genius because he has been ' a miracle of labour. Strength can conquer circumstances. The principle of action is too powerful for any circumstances to resist It clears the way, and elevates itself above every object, above fortune and misfortune, good and evil The joys that come to us in this world are but to strengthen us for some greater labour that is to succeed. Man's wisdom appears in his actions; for every man is the son of his own work. Richter says that "good deeds ring clear through heaven like a bell."

Active and sympathetic contact with man in the transactions of daily life is a better preparation for healthy robust action than any amount of meditation and seclusion. What Swedenborg said about vowing poverty and retiring from the world in order to live more to heaven, seems reasonable and true. "The life that leads to heaven," he said, "is not a life of retirement from the world, but of action in the world. A life of charity, which consists in acting sincerely and justly in every enjoyment and work, in obedience to the Divine law, is not difficult; but a life of piety alone is difficult, and it leads away from heaven as much as it is commonly believed to lead to it."

With many people, religion is merely a matter of words. So far as words go, we do what we think right. But the words rarely lead to action, thought, and conduct, or to purity, goodness, and honesty. There is too much playing at religion, and too little of enthusiastic hard work. There is a great deal of reading about religion; but true religion, embodied in human character and action, is more instructive than a thousand doctrinal volumes. If a man possesses not a living and strong will that leads the way to good, he will either become a plaything of sensual desires, or pass a life of shameless indolence.

One of the greatest dangers that at present besets the youth of England is laziness. What is called "culture "amounts to little. It may be associated with the meanest moral character, abject servility to those in high places, and arrogance to the poor and lowly. The fast, idle youth believes nothing, venerates nothing, hopes nothing; no, not even the final triumph of good in human hearts. There are many Mr. Tootses in the world, saying, "Its all the same," "It's of no consequence." It is not all the same, nor will it be all the same a hundred years hence. The life of each man tells upon the whole life of society. Each man has his special duty to perform, his special work to do. If he does it not, he himself suffers, and others suffer through him. His idleness infects others, and propagates a bad example. A useless life is only an early death.

There is far 'too much croaking amongst young men. Instead of setting to work upon the thing they dream of, they utter querulous

[7] Le Pessimisme au XIX, Siecle, Par E. Caro. Paris, 1877

complaints which lead to no action. This defect was noted by Dr. Channing, who lamented that so many of our young men should grow up in a school of despair. Is life worth living? Certainly not, if it be wasted in idleness. Even reading is often regarded as a mental dissipation. It is only a cultivated apathy. Hence you find so many grumbling, indifferent, blasé youths, their minds polished into a sort of intellectual keenness and cleverness, breaking out into sarcasm upon the acts of others, but doing nothing themselves. They sneer at earnestness of character. A lamentable indifference possesses these intellectual vagrants. Their souls, if they are conscious of possessing them, are blown about by every passing wind. They understand without believing. The thoughts which such minds receive produce no acts. They hold no principles or convictions. The religious element is ignored. Their creed is nothing, out of which nothing comes; no aspirations after the higher life, no yearnings after noble ideas or a still nobler character.

And yet we have plenty of intellect, but no faith; plenty of knowledge, but no wisdom; plenty of "culture," but no loving-kindness. A nation may possess refinement, and possess nothing else. Knowledge and wisdom, so far from being one, have often no connection with each other. It may be doubted whether erudition tends to promote wisdom or goodness. Fenelon says it is better to be a good living book than to love good books. A multifarious reading may please, but does not feed the mind St. Anselm said that "God often works more by the life of the illiterate, seeking the things which are God's, than by the ability of the learned seeking the things that are their own."

Here is the portrait which a great French writer has drawn of his contemporaries: — "What do you perceive on all sides but a profound indifference as to creeds and duties, with an ardour for pleasure and for gold, which can procure everything you desire? Everything can be bought — conscience, honour, religion, opinions, dignities, power, consideration, respect itself; vast shipwrecks of all truths and of all virtues! all philosophical theories, all the doctrines of impiety, have dissolved themselves and disappeared in the devouring system of indifference, the actual tomb of the understanding, into which it goes down alone, naked, equally stript of truth and error; an empty sepulchre, where one cannot find even bones."

We are, however, to be redeemed by "Culture." This is a new word,[8] of German origin. Many worship "culture."

It is their only religion. It is intellectual cynicism and scepticism, with a varnish of refinement. The persons who profess it live in an atmosphere

---

[8] Another curious word has come up of late — that of Philistine, Mr. Leslie Stephens says that it is a term of abuse given by prigs to the rest of their species. Schopenhauer gives another definition. "A Philistine," he says, "has no spiritual wants, and it follows that he can have no spiritual pleasures, for the saying is true, ' Il n'est de vrais plaisirs, qu'avec de vrais besoins,' no longing for science or insight for its own sake. No enjoyment of art can animate his drear existence. His pleasures are sensual. The end of his life is to add to the number of his physical comforts."

of exquisite superiority, like that represented by Moliere in "Les Precieuse Ridicules." Nil admirari is their motto. They sneer at the old-fashioned virtues of industry and self-denial, energy and self-help. Theirs is a mere creed of chilling negations, in which there is nothing to admire, nothing to hope for. They are sceptics in everything, — doing no work themselves, but denying the works of others. They believe in nothing, except in themselves. They are their own little gods.

Goethe was the inventor of geist or culture. But the poems of Goethe bring forth no deeds like those of Schiller. The works of Goethe are childless. He was a man who traded in the loves of women — women whom he had attached to him by his powers' of fascination. "When he had no woman in his heart," says his latest biographer, "he was like a dissecting surgeon without a subject He said of Balzac, that each of his best novels seemed dug out of a suffering woman's heart Balzac might have returned the compliment In reference to his early fondness for natural history, Goethe says, — 'I remember that when a child I pulled flowers to pieces to see how the petals were inserted into the calyx, or even plucked birds to observe how the feathers were inserted in the wings.' Bettina remarked to Lord Houghton that he treated women in much the same fashion. All his loves, high and low, were subjected to this kind of vivisection. His powers of fascination were extraordinary; and if, for the purposes of art, he wanted a display of strong emotion, he deepened the passion without scruple or compunction — like the painter engaged on a picture of Christ on the Cross, who, to produce the required expression of physical agony in the model, thrust a spear into his side. The capacity for minute observations, under such circumstances, implies comparative coldness; and we can fancy Goethe, like the hero in 'L'Homme Blasé,' marking with finger on pulse, when the required degree of excitement had been reached, and taking good care to stop short of fever heat .... Goethe tells us frankly that he turned everything in the way of adventure or love affair to account; and that he regarded all that befell him with his female acquaintance from the aesthetic point of view, and found that the most instructive palliative for a mishap or a disappointment was to write about it"[9]

Oh the vain pride of mere intellectual ability! how worthless, how contemptible, when contrasted with the riches of the heart. What is the understanding of the hard dry capacity of the brain and body? A mere dead skeleton of opinions, a few dry bones tied up together, if there be not a soul to add moisture and life, substance and reality, truth and joy. Every one will remember the modest saying of Newton — perhaps the greatest man who ever lived — the discoverer of the method of Fluxions, the theory of universal gravitation, and the decomposition of light, — that he felt himself but as a child playing by the sea-shore, while the immense ocean of truth lay all unexplored before him! Have we any philosophers who will make such a confession now?

"There are truths," said the Count de Maistre, "which man can only

---

[9] Goethe by A. Hayward, Q.C.

attain by the spirit of his heart. A good man is often astonished to find persons of great ability resist proofs which appear clear to him. These persons are deficient in a certain faculty; that is the true meaning. When the cleverest man does not possess a sense of religion, we can not only not conquer him, but we have not even the means of making him understand us." Again, "Sir Humphry Davy said, "Reason is often a dead weight in life, destroying feeling, and substituting for principle only calculation and caution."

But the widest field of duty lies outside the line of literature and books. Men are social beings more than intellectual creatures. The best part of human cultivation is derived from social contact; hence courtesy, self-respect, mutual toleration, and self-sacrifice for the good of others. Experience of men is wider than literature. Life is a book which lasts ones lifetime, but it requires wisdom to understand its difficult pages.

"In our days," says Lady Verney, "there is an indissoluble connection between the ideas of cultivation and reading and writing. It is now only the ignorant and stupid who cannot do both. But fifty years ago, books, except in the highest education, were the exception, and very clever men and women thought out their own thoughts, with very little assistance from anything beyond the Testament. Even among the upper classes reading was not very common among women. 'My grandmother could hardly spell when she wrote, and she read nothing but her livre d'heures' said a Frenchman who was well able to judge, "but she was far more worthy and wise than women are now.'"

In the old times, boys had duty placed before them as an incentive. To fail was to disgrace one's self, and to succeed was merely to do one's duty. "As for the dream," said Hugh Miller, "that there is to be some extraordinary elevation of the general platform of the human race achieved by means of education, it is simply the hallucination of the age, — the world's present alchemical expedient for converting farthings into guineas, sheerly by dint of scouring."

After all, the best school of discipline is home. Family life is God's own method of training the young. And homes are very much as women make them. "The hope of France," said the late Bishop of Orleans, "is in her mothers." It is the same with England But alas! we are distracted by the outcries of women who protest against their womanhood, and wildly strain to throw off their most lovable characteristics. They want power — apolitical power, and yet the world is entirely what their home influence has made it. They believe in the potentiality of votes, and desire to be "enfranchised." But do they really believe that the world would be better than it is if they had the privilege of giving a vote once in three or five years for a parliamentary representative? St. Paul gave the palm to the women who were stayers and workers at home, for he recognised that home is the crystal of society, and that domestic love and duty are the best security for all that is most dear to us on earth.

A recent writer, after describing the qualities which ought to characterise a woman's nature, says, "One might almost fear, seeing how the women of to-day are lightly stirred up to run after some new fashion of faith or of works, that heaven is not so near to them as it was to their mothers and grandmothers; that religion is a feebler power with them; that their hearts are empty of all secure trust and high faith in the beneficence of God's ordinations." The writer is herself a woman.

Before the recent Franco-Prussian war. Baron Stoffel was deputed to report upon the state of opinion and morals in Prussia, as compared with France. In the course of his remarks, he says, "Discipline in the army depends on the discipline of society and private families. The young men in Prussia are trained to general obedience, to respect authority, and above all, to do their Duty. But how can this discipline exist in the French army, when it does not exist in French families? Moreover, look beyond the family circle, at lycèes, schools, colleges, etc. — is anything done to develop among the children respect for their parents, regard for duty, obedience to authority and the law, and above all, belief in God? Nothing, or next to nothing! The consequence is, that every year we introduce into the army a contingent of young men, who, for the most part, are entirely devoid of religious principles and sound morality, and who, from their childhood, have been used to obey no one, to discuss everything, and to respect nothing. And yet there are people who pretend that all at once we can, as soon as they get into the army, inure to discipline these undisciplined and unprincipled youths. These people do not suspect that discipline in the army is nothing but discipline in private life — that is, sense of duty, obedience to appointed superiors, respect for the principles of authority and established institutions.... Artificial discipline once established may last a little time under the pressure of circumstances; but be sure that it will vanish into thin air the moment it is put to the real test" It need scarcely be said that in these words Baron Stoffel proved a true prophet.

Can it be that we are undergoing the same process in England; that the ever-extending tide of democracy is bearing down the best fruits of domestic discipline and moral character? We are a very vainglorious people. We boast of our wealth, our power, our resources, our naval and military strength, and our commercial superiority. Yet all these may depart from us in a few years, and we may remain, like Holland, a rich and a comparatively powerless people. The nation depends upon the individuals who compose it; and no nation can ever be distinguished for morality, duty, adherence to the rules of honour and justice, whose citizens, individually and collectively, do not possess the same traits.

Lord Derby observed in one of his recent speeches: — "An accomplished nobleman said to me the other day, that he thought England had steadily declined in those qualities that make up the force and strength of national character since the day of Waterloo; and though he did not say so in words, yet from his manner and tone I inferred that he thought it was too late to hope for a recovery; that the deluge was coming, and that happy were they who had almost lived their lives, and would not survive to see the catastrophe. Of course, it is possible that such a catastrophe may come; and, given certain conditions, it is certain that it will come."

This is a serious word of warning. Is the deluge really to come, as it did in France a hundred years ago? The late Dr. Norman Macleod said,

"The confusion that exists at this moment, which began soon after the war of '15, and is as eventful as the Reformation, is most oppressive. On the one hand, there is a breaking up of the old forms of thought about everything — social, political, scientific, philosophic, theological In spite of much foolish conceit and sense of power on the part of those who guide the battering rams against the old walls, there is, on the part of many more, a great sense of the paramount importance of truth and duty; which, if rightly considered, would but express faith in God, who is ever on the side of truth. ... As for Scotland, the church of the future is not here. We ignore great world questions. We squabble like fish-women over skate and turbot!"

What spectacle can be sadder than to see men, and even women, passing their lives in theorising and gossiping over the great principles which their forefathers really believed; and by believing which, they secured for their generation the gifts of faith, of goodness, and of well-doing? There are two thoughts, which, if once admitted to the mind, change our whole course of life — the belief that this world is but the vestibule of an endless state of being, and the thought of Him in whom man lives here, or shall live hereafter. We each have the choice of following good or following evil. Who shall say which shall prove the mightier? It depends upon ourselves — on our awakened conscience and enlightened will. Troubles and sorrows may have to be encountered in performing our various duties. But these have to be done, and done cheerfully, because it is the will of God. Good actions give strength to ourselves, and inspire good actions in others. They prove treasures guarded for the doer's need. Let us therefore strengthen our mind, and brace up our soul, and prepare our heart for the future. The race is for Life,

CHAPTER III

HONESTY — TRUTH

There is na workemen
That can bothe vofken well and hastilie.
Tills must be done at leisure parfaitlie.

Chaucer

Gold thou may'st safely touch, but if it stick
Unto thy hands, it woundeth to the quick.

George Herbert

26

The honest man, though e'er so poor.
Is king o' men for a' that.

Burns

Ne quittez jamais le chemin de la virtue et de I'honneur; c'est le seul moyen d'etre hereux.

Buffon

HONESTY and truthfulness go well together. Honesty is truth, and truth is honesty. Truth alone may not constitute a great man, but it is the most important element of a great character. It gives security to those who employ him, and confidence to those who serve under him. Truth is the essence of principle, integrity, and independence. It is the primary need of every man. Absolute veracity is more needed now than at any former period in our history.

Lying, common though it be, is denounced even 6y the liar himself. He protests that he is speaking the truth, for he knows that truth is universally respected, whilst lying is universally condemned. Lying is not only dishonest, but cowardly. "Dare to be true," said George Herbert; "nothing can ever need a lie." The most mischievous liars are those who keep on the verge of truth. They have not the courage to speak out the fact, but go round about it, and tell what is really untrue. - A lie which is half the truth is the worst of lies.

There is a duplicity of life which is quite as bad as verbal falsehood. Actions have as plain a voice as words. The mean man is false to his profession. He evades the truth that he professes to believe. He plays at double dealing. He wants sincerity and veracity. The sincere' man speaks as he thinks, believes as he pretends to believe, acts as he professes to act, and performs as he promises.

"Other forms of practical contradiction are common," says Mr. Spurgeon; "some are intolerantly liberal; others are ferocious advocates for peace, or intemperate on intemperance. We have known pleaders for generosity who were themselves miserably stingy. We have heard of persons who have been wonderful sticklers for 'the truth' — meaning thereby a certain form of doctrine — and yet they have not regarded the truth in matters of buying and selling, or with regard to the reputations of their neighbours, or the incidents of domestic life."[10]

Lying is one of the most common and conventional of vices. It prevails in what is called "Society" Not at home is the fashionable mode of reply to a visitor. Lying is supposed to be so necessary to carry on human affairs that it is tacitly agreed to. One lie may be considered harmless, another slight, another unintended. Little lies are common. However tolerated, lying is more or less loathsome to every pure-minded man or woman. "Lies," says Ruskin, "may be light and accidental, but they are an ugly soot from the smoke of the pit, and it is better that our hearts should be swept clean of them, without our care as to which is largest or blackest."

---

[10] The Bible and the Newspaper, 1878.

"Lying abroad for the benefit of one's country" used to be the maxim of the diplomatist. Yet a man should care more for his word than for his life. When Regulus was sent by the Carthaginians, whose prisoner he was, to Rome, with a convoy of ambassadors to sue for peace, it was under the condition that he should return to his prison if peace were not effected. He took the oath, and swore that he would come back.

When he appeared at Rome he urged the senators to persevere in the war, and not to agree to the exchange of prisoners. That involved his return to captivity at Carthage. The senators, and even the chief priest, held that as his oath had been wrested from him by force, he was not bound to go. "Have you resolved to dishonour me?" asked Regulus. "I am not ignorant that death and tortures are preparing for me; but what are these to the shame of an infamous action, or the wounds of a guilty mind? Slave as I am to Carthage, I have still the spirit of a Roman. I have sworn to return. It is my duty to go. Let the gods take care of the rest" Regulus returned to Carthage, and died under torture.

"Let him that would live well," said Plato, "attain to truth, and then, and not before, he will cease from sorrow." Let us also cite a passage from the Emperor Marcus Aurelius: "He who acts unjustly acts impiously; for since the universal nature has made rational animals for the sake of one another, to help one another according to their deserts, but in no way to injure one another, he who transgresses his will is clearly guilty of impiety towards the highest divinity. And he, too, that lies is guilty of impiety to the same divinity, from the universal nature of all things that are; and all things that are have a relation to all things that come into existence. And further, this universal nature is named Truth, and is the prime cause of all things that are true. He, then, who lies intentionally is guilty of impiety, inasmuch as he acts unjustly by deceiving; and he also who lies unintentionally, inasmuch as he is at variance with the universal nature, and inasmuch as he disturbs the order by fighting against the nature of the world; for he fights against it, who is moved of himself to that which is contrary to truth, for he has received powers from nature, through the neglect of which he is not able now to distinguish falsehood from truth. And, indeed, he who pursues pleasure as good, and avoids pain as evil, is guilty of impiety."[11]

Truth and honesty show themselves in various ways. They characterise the men of just dealing, the faithful men of business, the men who will not deceive you to their own advantage. Honesty is the plainest and humblest manifestation of the principle of truth. Full measures, just weights, true samples, full service, strict fulfilment of engagements, are all indispensable to men of character.

Take a common case. Sam Foote had reason to complain of the shortness of the beer served to him at dinner. He called the landlord, and said to him: "Pray, sir, how many butts of beer do you draw in a month? " "Ten, sir," replied the publican. "And would you like to draw eleven if you

---

[11] Thoughts of Marcus Aurelius Antoninus, Translated by George Long, M.A., pp. 144-5.

28

could?" "Certainly, sir." "Then I will tell you how," said Foote; "fill your measure!"

But the case goes farther than this. We complain of short weights and adulteration of goods. We buy one thing and get another. But goods must sell; if with a profit, so much the better. If the dealer is found out, the customer goes elsewhere. M. Le Play, when he visited England many years ago, observed with great pleasure the commercial probity of English manufacturers. "They display," he said, "a scrupulous exactitude in the quantity and quality of their foreign consignments."

Could he say the same now? Have we not heard in public courts of the depreciation of our manufactures — of cotton loaded with china clay, starch, magnesium, and zinc? We have seen the loading, and therefore know what it is. The cotton becomes mildewed, discoloured, and therefore unsaleable. The mildew is a fungoid which, when developed by moisture, lives and grows upon the starch. China was one of the many marts for English -made cotton. But when the mildew appeared, the trade vanished.

There is a Chinese proverb to the effect that "th conjuror does not deceive the man who beats the gong for him." The Chinaman is as great a deceiver as we are. He puts iron filings into his tea, and water into his silk. He is therefore quite awake to the deceptions of others. "The consequence is," says the British Consul at Cheefoo, "that our textiles have got a bad name, and their place is being supplied by American manufacturers. American drills, though forty per cent dearer, are driving English drills out of the market" We are no longer trusted. The English brand used to be a guarantee of honesty. It is so no longer.

It is the same in India. The English cotton won't wash. When the clay and starch are rinsed out, it becomes a rag. The Indians grow cotton. The Indians are clever workmen, with ingenious, subtle fingers. They can spin an even thread as well as the workwomen of Manchester. Capital has accumulated in India; mills have been built; and the Indians now manufacture for themselves.

All this is well known in the manufacturing districts. It is spoken of at public meetings. Sizing, and starching, and loading cotton cloth with china clay, is known everywhere. Mr. Mellor, M.P., denounced the deception of the adulterating manufacturers. They seem to believe that the consuming inhabitants of the globe are all fools excepting themselves. He mentioned the case of an engineer, who, in crossing the Indian Ocean, was decorating his turban with muslin. "Is that English?" he was asked. "No; it is from Switzerland. The English makes my fingers stick, it is gummy." This is how we are losing our trade. This is how we are encountering bad times.

American cotton goods sell in London, Manchester, and elsewhere, at a fair profit. Indian cotton goods sell in China and Australia; though Bombay twist sells at a higher price than English yams. The local cotton manufacture of India is now equal to the whole home and foreign production of Manchester. Is not this a startling fact? We are now giving our artisans technical education. What will technical education do against wholesale cheating and lying? A young woman buys a reel of cotton marked 250 yards. When she works it out with her skin and bone, she finds it to contain only 175 yards. What can she think of the truthfulness of her countrymen?

The deterioration of the standard of public men, of public morality, and of political principles, is undeniable. When the late Baron Dupin visited England, about sixty years ago, he observed with admiration the courage, the intelligence, and the activity of our commercial men. 'It is not alone the courage, the intelligence, the activity of the manufacturer or merchant which maintain the superiority of the productions and commerce of their country; it is far more their wisdom, their economy, and, above all their probity. If ever, in the British Islands, the useful citizen should lose these virtues, we may be sure that for England, as well as for any other country, notwithstanding the protection of the most formidable navy, notwithstanding the foresight and activity of diplomacy the most extended, and of political science the most profound, the vessels of a degenerate commerce, repulsed from every shore, would speedily disappear from those seas whose surface they now cover with the treasures of the universe, bartered for the treasures of the industry of the Three Kingdoms."[12]

The excuse, no doubt, is the keenness of competition, and the obstacles which the Government throws in the way of freedom of production. The manufacturer is bound hand and foot by restrictive laws. Some of these are excellent; for instance, the law which emancipated women and children from working in coal-pits, and the law which shortened the hours of labour. But it seems that the Factory laws have gone too far. Mr. Kitson recently said at Leeds that through the action of the Factory Acts several industries of the country had been already all but extinguished. Belgium was introducing into this country small sizes of rods in iron and steel, because boys could be employed in their production. All the small engines, which were at one time an important branch of English trade, are now made in France and Belgium. He pointed out that by this means Parliament was extinguishing sundry trades in this country, and then injustice was added by making these trades pay the cost of their own extinction. Another speaker at the meeting said that his firm imported iron castings from Belgium, because they could get them more cheaply than in England, although their works were surrounded by all the mills of Lancashire.

The employer is not only grievously hindered by the law; he is still more grievously hindered by strikes. When trade seems to improve, the men turn out and strike for more wages. Mills are closed, iron-furnaces are damped out, building ceases, and everything is at a standstill. We throw our means and opportunities away; and the foreigner thrives upon our recklessness. It is more than unfortunate — it is ruinous — that workmen should consider their employers as their born enemies.

But what of the quality of the work done by the work-men? Time was when men threw their heart and soul into their work — when they took pride in the quality of their work — in doing that which Chaucer describes

---

[12] The Commercial Power of Great Britain vol. i. Introduction, p. xi

at the head of this chapter — work "must be done at leisure, par-faitlie." But what have we now? Work done scampingly — without skill, without conscience, without industry. Because of this, tunnels fall in, iron bridges give way, and buildings tumble down. Houses are left half-finished, drains are left untrapped, and disease spreads abroad. O careless, thoughtless British workman! What lives you have taken, what families you have made desolate I So that your work is done, you care not how it is done. You have not put your best into it; you have not put yourself into it The work is done anyhow, so that it may pass muster. All this is dishonest and dishonourable. Poor British workman! It is not altogether your own fault. You have been brought up without knowledge. You have been educated without sympathy. You thought the world was against you, whilst it has often sympathised with you.

All bad work is lying. It is thoroughly dishonest You pay for having a work done well; it is done badly and dishonestly. It may be varnished- over with a fair show of sufficiency, but the sin is not discovered until it is too late. So long as these things continue, it is in vain to talk of the dignity of labour, or of the social value of the so-called working man. There can be no dignity of labour where there is no truthfulness of work. "Dignity does not consist in hollowness and in light-handedness, but in substantiality and in strength. If there be flimsiness and superficiality of all kinds apparent in the work of the present day more than in the work of our forefathers, whence comes it? From eagerness and competition, and the haste to be rich."[13]

Even the Polynesians have found us out. When Bishop Patteson was voyaging among the South Sea Islands on his mission of mercy, he found that the natives refused to buy our goods. "A mere Brummagem article," he said, "that won't stand wear, is quite valueless in their eyes. Whatever is given to them, be it cheap or dear, though it cost but a shilling, must be good of its kind For example, a rough-handled, single-bladed knife, bought for a shilling, they fully appreciate; but a knife with half a dozen blades they would almost throw away." So Dr. Livingstone found that the natives of Africa refused to buy English iron, because it was "rotten."

Socrates explained how useful and excellent a thing it was that a man should resolve on perfection in his own line, so that, if he be a carpenter, he will be the best possible carpenter; or if a statesman, that he will be the best possible statesman. It is by such means that true success is achieved. Such a carpenter, Socrates said, would win the wreath of carpentering, though it was only of shavings.

Take the case of Wedgewood, who had the spirit of the true worker. Though risen from the ranks, he was never satisfied until he had done his best. He looked especially to the quality of his work, to the purposes it would serve, and to the appreciation of it by others. This was the source of his power and success. He would tolerate no inferior work If it did not come up to his idea of what it should be, he would take up his stick, break

---

[13] F. R. Conder, C.E., in Good Words,

the vessel, and throw it away, saying, "This won't do for Josiah Wedgewood! "

Of course he took the greatest care to ensure perfection, as regarded geometrical proportions, glaze, form, and ornament He pulled down kiln after kiln to effect some necessary improvement He learned perfection through repeated failures. He invented and improved almost every tool used in his works. He passed much of his time at the bench beside his workmen, instructing them individually. How he succeeded, his works will show.

Another instance of true honesty and courage may be mentioned in the case of a great contractor. We mean Thomas Brassey. Even when scamping was common, he was always true to his word and work. The Barentin viaduct of twenty-seven arches was nearly completed, when, loaded with wet after a heavy fall of rain, the whole building tumbled down. The casualty involved a loss of £ 30,000. The contractor was neither morally nor legally responsible. He had repeatedly protested against the material used in the structure, and the French lawyers maintained that his protest freed him from liability. But Mr. Brassey was of a different opinion. He had contracted, he said, to make and maintain the road, and no law should prevent him from being as good as his word. The viaduct was rebuilt at Mr. Brassey's cost. His life is one of the highest examples we can offer to this generation.

We have had good times and bad times; but the result is always the same. We take little thought of the future. We only economise when we have no more money to spend upon selfish gratifications. An employer at Bradford recently said, — Some five or six years ago, we were in a state of great commercial prosperity. It almost carried the trading classes off their heads. Everybody was becoming rapidly rich, and so bent were they on amassing money, that they seemed to think there would be no end to it. The working classes joined in the prosperity, and they lost their heads as well as those above them. They struck for higher wages, and for a time they got what they desired. They limited production, and urged that the fewer hours they worked, the more money they would get for their labour, and the better they would be off. But then came the period of depression, and no efforts of strikes or unions could stave it off. He urged upon the workmen that if they wished to see a return to better times, they must honestly and faithfully do their duty, and alter their present manner of doing slippery work, and doing as little as possible for their money.

At a conference of working men in Edinburgh, one of the speakers upheld the advantages of strikes. "My theory is," he said, "work as little as you possibly can, and get as high a wage as you possibly can." This theory, if worked out, would produce the entire demoralisation of labour; it would make it idle, inefficient, and disloyal. Another speaker took an opposite view. He said, "the existence of unions for the purpose of striking was immoral in the extreme. The other day, he was going along a street in Edinburgh, when he met a man walking very slowly and easily along. A boy passing, said to him, 'You're taking it very easy the day.' 'It's my master's time,' said the man. The man," he added, "had the idea forced into him

32

that, by the striking system, the master's injury was their benefit; and the effect of the whole sytem was, that a piece of work well done could not be got."

It would be well if the working men could be got to see the position in which they actually stand. They are now competing with the working men all over the Continent and in America. It used to be supposed that the superiority of English labour would overcome all foreign competition. Whatever it may have once been, this is now an utter fellacy. The foreigners have all the advantages of our best machinery, with the latest improvements. They now manufacture machines for themselves. They have learned to work as fast and as well as English operatives. They work on Sunday and Saturday alike. In France they work 72 hours a week, while in this country they work only 56 hours a week. And the wages of the foreign artisans are about 25 per cent less than those in England. The English work turned out is not so good and honest as that of France. How can we maintain competition in the face of these facts? The French and German cotton manufactures come into England free, while ours cannot get into French and German ports without high prohibitive duties. We have lost the monopoly of the trade, which we once possessed, and it is not likely that we can ever regain it Our cotton trade will soon be confined to home supply; and if the articles are not made good and cheap, they will be driven out of use by the French and American fabrics. It will be the same with every other product.

Mr. Holyoake spoke in the right spirit when he rebuked the mistakes of unionism, and expressed his opinion — no doubt that of the elite of the working classes — as to the duty of sympathy and sincerity between master and man. "Recalling to my recollection," he said, "fourteen years' experience as a workman, I say now that were I secured wages for eight hours' daily labour, which would supply a moderate competence before the strength of life was spent, and was I left at liberty to produce the best work I could, so that my pride and taste and character should be in my handicraft, and I had a reasonable assurance of continuing in my situation while I discharged my duties in good faith, I should now prefer that state to any other. I should be the friend of the master; his fame would be my pride, his interests mine. He would have the care and the profit which is the honest due of care, and I should have content and leisure for learning and study."

This nation, no doubt, possesses the best material in the world. We have men who are willing to work and able to work. But we want good work, not scamped work. We have strikers against receiving low wages; but we have no strikers against doing bad work. It is better work, not longer hours, that is wanted. It is dishonest and insincere labour that is discrediting English articles in all of the great markets of the world. "Work," again says Mr. Holyoake, "has small pleasure, because it has little pride. It ought to be impossible for employers to find men who will execute shabby work. It is a sort of crime against the honour of industry, a fraud by connivance upon the purchaser. Nothing shows more plainly the state of honour in artisanship than the fact that we have all sorts of trade unions to come to the support of a man who refuses low wages, but not one union professedly to succour a man who refuses to do dishonest work." Let such a system continue, and all the science and arts schools in the world could not maintain England as a great commercial country.

The same cry comes to us from America. The truth of the proverbial saying, "There is no God west of the Missouri," is everywhere manifest The almighty dollar is the true divinity, and its worship is universal A Sacramento paper says that "Americans are a money-loving and money-making people. They have no Queen or aristocracy to rule them; their aristocracy is money. The lust of wealth overrides every other consideration Fraud in trade is the rule instead of the exception. We poison our provisions with adulteration. We even poison our drugs with cheaper materials. We sell shoddy for wool. We sell veneering for solid wood. We build wretched sheds of bad brick and bad mortar and green wood, and call them houses. We rob and cheat each other all round, and in every trade and business, and we are all so bent on making money that we have not time to protest against even the more palpable frauds, but console ourselves by going forth and swindling somebody else. We pay a very heavy price for our national idiosyncrasy. We are rapidly destroying our national sense of honesty and integrity. In those benighted and slavish countries which are ruled by monarchs, they contrive to live a great deal cheaper, and a good deal better than we can. There, fraud is regarded as criminal, and the impostor, when detected, is punished severely. But those are old fogy countries, who know nothing about liberty. They have no Fourth of July, no Wall Street, no codfish or shoddy aristocracies. They do not recognise the fact that the right to life, liberty, and the pursuit of happiness (which means money), entitles every man to cheat his neighbours, and bars redress."

Strange to say, the Americans are beginning to think that the badness of work, and the unwillingness to do good work, is, to a certain extent, the outcome of the common school system. Everybody is so well educated that he is above doing manual labour. There are no American apprentices, and no American servants. We do not speak without authority. A writer in Scrihners Monthly says "that the Americans make a god of their common school system. It is treason to speak a word against it. A man is regarded as a foe to education who expresses any doubt of the value of it. But we may as well open our eyes to the fact that in preparing men for the work of life, especially for that work depending on manual skill, it is a hindrance and a failure. It is mere smatter, veneering, and cram."

The writer of the article says that the old system of apprenticeship has grown almost entirely into disuse. The boys are at school, and cannot be apprenticed to a trade. Hence most mechanical work is done by foreigners. The lad who has made a successful beginning of the cultivation of his intellect, does not like the idea of getting a living by the skilful use of his hands in the common emplo5rment of life. He has no taste for bodily labour. He gets some light employment, or tries to live upon his wits.[14]

---

[14] If it is asked why there is not a universal effort made for the restoration of the apprentice system, we reply that there is a very ugly lion in the way. A piano-

> "Under a spreading chestnut tree
> The village smithy stands."

So said Longfellow. The village smithy stands there no longer. When General Armstrong, of the coloured college of Hampton, went to the north in search of blacksmiths, he found no Americans to engage. Every blacksmith was an Irishman. And in the next generation of Irishmen, every boy will be so well educated that he will not put his hands to any bodily labour. A New York clergyman possessing a large family (to correct this spreading influence), recently declared from his pulpit that he intended that every lad of his family should learn some mechanical employment, by which, on an emergency, he might get a living. Rich and poor should alike be taught to work, skilfully if possible; for it is quite as likely that the rich will become poor, as that some of the poor will become rich; and that is a poor education which fails to prepare a man to take care of himself and his dependants throughout life.

We have lately been complaining of the badness of trade, but has not much of it happened through our own misdoing? In the arithmetic of the counting-house, two and two do not always make four. How many tricks are resorted to — in which honesty forms no part — for making money faster than others. Instead of working patiently and well for a modest living, many desire to get rich all at once. The spirit of the age is not that of a trader, but of a gambler. The pace is too fast to allow of any one stopping to inquire as to those who have fallen out by the way. They press on; the race for wealth is for the swift. Their faith is in money. It needs no prophet to point out the connection of our distress with the sin of commercial gambling and fraud, and of social extravagance and vanity, of widespread desolation and misery.

"My son," said a father, "ye're gawn out into t'warld; ye may be wranged; but if it comes to that, chet rather than be- cheted." Another said, "Make money, honestly, if you can; but if not, make it" A third said, "Honesty is better than dishonesty; I've tried both." Of course we quote these phrases as being at utter variance with truth and honesty. But it is to

---

maker complained that he could not get men enough to do his work, the reason being that his men belonged to a Society that had taken upon itself to regulate the number of apprentices that he could be permitted to instruct in the business. They had limited the number to one, who was utterly insufficient to supply the demand, and the master was powerless. There was no other way open to him but to import his workmen, already instructed, from abroad. In brief, there is a conspiracy amongst Society men all over the country, to keep American boys out of the useful trades, and industrial education is thus under the ban of an outrageous system, which ought to be put down by the strong hand of the law. It is thus seen that, while the common school naturally turns the great multitudes of its attendants away from manual employments, those who still feel inclined to enter upon them have no freedom to do so, because a great army of Society men stand firmly in the way, overruling employers and employed alike." — Scribna's Monthly Iliustrated Magazine for March 1880.

be doubted whether higher principles of conduct prevail in many of the commercial classes of life. A young man begins business. He goes on slowly yet safely. His gains may be small, but they are justly come by. "A faithful man shall abound with blessings; but he that maketh haste to be rich shall not be innocent: he hath an evil eye, and considereth not that poverty may come upon him."

In large commercial towns, young men are amazed at the splendour of the leaders of trade. They are supposed to be enormously rich. Every door opens to them. They command the highest places in society. They give balls, parties, and dinners. Their houses are full of pictures by the greatest artists. Their cellars are full of wine of the choicest vintage. Their conversation is not great; it is mostly about wine, horses, or prices. They seem to sail upon the golden sea of a great accumulated fortune.

Young business men are often carried away by such examples. If they have not firmness and courage, they are apt to follow in their footsteps. The first speculation may be a gain. The gain may be followed by another, and they are carried off their feet by the lust for wealth. They become dishonest and unscrupulous. Their bills are all over the discount market. To keep up their credit they spend more money upon pictures, and even upon charities. Formerly, greedy and unjust men seized the goods of others by violence. To-day, they obtain them by fraudulent bankruptcies. Formerly, every attempt was open; to-day, everything is secret, until at length the last event comes, and everything is exposed. The man fails; the bills are worthless; the pictures are sold; and the recreant flies to avoid the curses of his creditors.

In one bankruptcy case, over £ 39,000 were stated in the accounts as expenses for orphanages and charities! "I have the authority of the accountant," said a speaker at a meeting of the creditors, "for stating that for four or five years this firm has been purchasing goods to an enormous extent, and flooding the eastern markets, when they were hopelessly insolvent, carrying on a reckless, I will say a gambling, trade for financial purposes, or, in common parlance, to 'raise the wind' The munificent charity of an insolvent estate appears to me ghastly. It reminds me of a remark of our bishop (of Manchester), that there are -some men amongst us who build churches out of part of their ungodly gains to pave their way to heaven."

Who bias not heard of the failure of banks originating in gambling and fraud, with the result of lost fortunes and family reverses amongst all classes of shareholders? Schiller says, "It is daring to embezzle a million, but it is great beyond measure to steal a crown; the sin seems to lessen as the guilt increases." Yet the embezzlement of millions has not been thought extraordinary of recent years. Money has been taken from bank deposits to buy up railway shares, or to buy land in some remote colony, the speculation for a rise often ending in a ruinous fall. Then "the bank broke "and the downfall came, ending in ruin and desolation to a thousand homes. Men have been driven insane, and women have prayed to be delivered from their lives.

"Pity us, God! there are five of us here,
With threescore years on the youngest head,
Five of us sitting in sorrow and fear —
Well for our widowed one she is dead.
Could they not wait awhile? we will not. keep them long;
We could live on so little, too, cheerful and brave,
But to leave the old house, where old memories throng.
For the Poorhouse! oh, rather the peace of the grave!"[15]

Men already rich, but hasting to be richer, throw themselves into wild speculations with the view of making money more rapidly than before. With what result? Only to land them in hopeless bankruptcy. Many instances are at hand to prove this. A rich banker of Tipperary — a radical and a demagogue — got himself returned to Parliament, and in course of time, to quiet him, he was made a Lord of the Treasury. A coronet seemed to gleam before his eyes. But in this he was disappointed. He had launched into Italian, American, and Spanish railways, and lost heavily. Then he began to forge deeds, conveyances, and bills for hundreds of thousands of pounds. His clever but unprincipled schemes failed; his bills were dishonoured; his ruin was imminent. Late at night he entered his study, and took from it a phial of prussic acid. He strayed to Hampstead Heath, drank the poison, and died.

What scenes there were in the streets of Thurles and Tipperary after his death was announced! Old men weeping and wailing for the loss of everything; widows kneeling on the ground and asking God if it could be true that they were beggared for ever. And yet it was true. The banker and Lord of the Treasury had lost the last shilling of his bank, and plunged from fraud into still deeper fraud to recoup his losses, which only served to spread upon those around him a wilder and more hopeless ruin.

One of the last letters that he wrote was to his cousin. He said, "To what infamy I have come step by step, heaping crime upon crime. I am the

---

[15] Dr. Walter C. Smith, the author of these lines, appeared at a meeting at Edinburgh, and said that 'he had received a large number of letters on the subject of the bank failure, and one class of correspondents asked him how he could be ' a converted man ' seeing that he was making so much ado about filthy lucre. The present calamity unhappily involved a great deal of distress to his fellow-men, and for his own part, he had no great sympathy with a religion which had so little sympathy with the sufferings of their brethren. He felt ashamed that such frauds should have been committed among them by men of trust, but he hoped that their dear country would come out of the gloom with its honour unstained, and enter on a career of active industry with an atmosphere purer and healthier than before. He had been asked whether a case of five elderly sisters, about whom many had read, was a real case. It was a real case, and he should never forget the time when he first saw those ladies, nine da3rs after the bank broke. During that time a meal had never been cooked in that house, their clothes had never been taken off their backs, and they had never lain in their beds, they were so bewildered and amazed, vaguely hoping that the good God would come and take them away from the evil that was to follow."

cause of ruin, and misery, and disgrace to thousands. Oh, how I feel for those on whom this ruin must fall! I could bear all punishment, but I could not bear to witness their sufferings. It must be better that I should not live. Oh that I had never quitted Ireland! Oh that I had resisted the first attempts to launch me into speculation! I might then have remained what I was, honest and truthful I weep and weep now, but what can that avail? '16

Nations and states are dishonest as well as individuals. Their condition is to be measured by the state of their 3 per cents. Spain and Greece and Turkey are dishonoured in the commercial world. Spain was killed by her riches. The gold which came pouring into Spain from her vanquished colonies in South America depraved the people, and rendered them indolent and lazy. Nowadays a Spaniard will blush to work; he will not blush to beg. Greece has repudiated her debts for many years. Like Turkey, she has nothing to pay. All the works of industry in those countries are done by foreigners.

Much better things might have been hoped from Philadelphia and the other American States which repudiated their debts many years ago. These were rich States, and the money borrowed from abroad made them richer, by opening up roads, and constructing canals for the benefit of the people. The Rev. Sydney Smith — who lent his money, "the savings from a life's income made with difficulty and privation "— let the world know of his loss. He addressed a remonstrance to the House of Congress at Washington, which he afterwards published. "The Americans," he said,

---

16 "The ignoble love of ease and pleasure," said the Bishop of Peterborough; "the degrading worship of wealth; the demoralising frauds and dishonesties that come of the lust to possess it; the senseless extravagance of luxury that follows too often on its possession; the effrontery of vice that, flushed with pride and fulness of bread, no longer condescends to pay to virtue even the tribute of hypocrisy; the low cynicism that sneers away all those better thoughts and higher aims that are the very breath of a nation's nobler life; and, springing out of these, the strife of interests, the war of classes widening and deepening day by day, as the envious selfishness of poverty rises up in natural reaction against the ostentatious selfishness of wealth; the dull, desperate hate with which those who want and have not, come at last to regard the whole framework of society, which seems to them but one huge contrivance for their oppression; the wild dreams of revolutionary change which shall give to all alike, without the pain of labour and self-denial, these enjoyments which are now the privileged possessions of the few, but which the many long for with a bitter and persistent longing; — these are some of the seeds of evil, which, sown in our own soil and by our own hands, may one day rise up an exceeding great army, more to be dreaded than the invading hosts of any foreign foe. The glare and the glitter of our modem civilisation may hide these from our view for a time; we may fail to see how some of the most precious elements of our national greatness are withering in its heated atmosphere, or what evil things are growing to maturity in the darker shadows that it casts; but they are there nevertheless, and if we heed them not and reform them not, the time may come when we may wish that the sharp and sobering discipline of war— nay, even the terrible trials and sorrows of defeat — had visited us in time to save us from the greater horrors bred of our own sins in times of profoundest ease and peace."

"who boast to have improved the institutions of the Old World, have at least equalled its crimes. A great nation, after trampling under foot all earthly tyranny, has been guilty of a fraud as enormous as ever disgraced the worst King of the most degraded nation of Europe."

The State of Illinois acted nobly, though it was poor. It had borrowed money, like Philadelphia, for the purpose of carrying out internal improvements. When the inhabitants of rich Philadelphia set the example of repudiating their debts, many of the poorer States wished to follow in their footsteps. As every householder had a vote, it was easy, if they were dishonest, to repudiate their debts. A convention met at Springfield, the capital of the State, and the repudiation ordinance was offered to the meeting. It was about to be adopted, when it was stopped by an honest man. Stephen A. Douglas (let his honourable name be mentioned 1) was lying sick at his hotel, when he desired to be taken to the convention. He was carried on a mattress, for he was too ill to walk. Lying on his back he wrote the following resolution, which he offered as a substitute for the repudiation ordinance: —

"Resolved that Illinois will be honesty although she never pays a cent."

The resolution touched the honest sentiment of every member of the convention. It was adopted with enthusiasm. It dealt a death-blow to the system of repudiation. The canal bonds immediately rose. Capital and emigration flowed into the State; and Illinois is now one of the most prosperous States in America. She has more miles of railway than any of the other States. Her broad prairies are one great grain-field, and are dotted about with hundreds of thousands of peaceful, happy homes. This is what honesty does.

The truth is, we have become too selfish. We think of ourselves far more than of others. The more devoted to pleasure, the less we think of our fellow-creatures. Selfish people are impervious to the needs of others. They exist in a sort of mailed armour, and no weapons, either of misery or want, can assail them. Their senses are only open to those who can minister to their gratifications. "There are men," says St. Chrysostom, "who seem to have come into the world only for pleasure, and that they might fatten this perishable body. ... At sight of their luxurious table the angels retire — God is offended — the demons rejoice — virtuous men are shocked — and even the domestics scorn and laugh.... The just men who have gone before left sumptuous feasts to tyrants, and to men enriched by crime, who were the scourges of the world."

We no longer know how to live upon little. A man must have luxury about him. And yet a man's life does not consist in the abundance of things he possesseth; he must live honestly, though poor. Retrenchment of the useless, the want even of the relatively necessary, is the high-road to Christian self-denial, as well as to antique strength of character. That of which our age stands most in need, is a man able to gratify every just desire, and yet to be contented with little. "A great heart in a little house," says Lacordaire, "is of all things here below, that which has ever touched me most. Happy the man who soweth the good and the true. The harvest will not fail him! "

Here is a fine specimen of honesty and truthfulness on the part of a poor German peasant. Bemardin de Saint Pierre has told the story in his Etudes de la Nature. He was serving as an engineer under the Count de Saint-Germain during his campaign in Hesse, in 1760. For the first time he became familiar with the horrors of war. Day by day he passed through sacked villages and devastated fields and farm3rards. Men, women, and children were flying from their cottages in tears. Armed men were everywhere destroying the fruits of their labour, regarding it as part of their glory. But in the midst of so many acts of cruelty, Saint-Pierre was consoled by a sublime trait of character displayed by a poor man whose cottage and farm lay in the way of the advancing army.

A captain of dragoons was ordered out with his troop to forage for provisions. They reached a poor cabin and knocked at the door. An old man with a white beard appeared. "Take me to a field," said the officer, "where I can obtain forage for my troops." "Immediately, sir," replied the old man. He put himself at their head, and ascended the valley. After about half an hour's march a fine field of barley appeared. "This will do admirably," said the officer. "No," said the old man; "wait a little, and all will be right" They went on again, until they reached another field of barley. The troops dismounted, mowed down the grain, and trussing it up in bundles, put them on their horses. "Friend," said the officer, "how is it that you have brought us so far? The first field of barley that we saw was quite as good as this." "That is quite true," said the peasant, "but it was not mine!

CHAPTER IV

MEN WHO CANNOT BE BOUGHT

Thou must be brave thyself,
If thou the truth would teach;
Live truly, and thy life shall be
A great and noble creed.

Tis a very good world we live in,
To lend, or to spend, or to give in;
But to beg, or to borrow, or get a man's own,
'Tis the very worst world that ever was known.
Bulwer Lytton

40

Good name in man and woman, dear my lord,
Is the immediate jewel of their souls:
Who steals my purse, steals trash: 'tis something, nothing;
'Twas mine, 'tis his, and has been slave to thousands;
But he that filches from me my good name,
Robs me of that which not enriches him.
And makes me poor indeed.

Shakespeare

L'honneur vaut mieux que l'argent.

French Provert

FIRST, there are men who can be bought. There are rogues innumerable, who are ready to sell their bodies and souls for money and for drink. Who has not heard of the elections which have been made void through bribery and corruption? This is not the way to enjoy liberty or to keep it The men who sell themselves are slaves; their buyers are dishonest and unprincipled. Freedom has its humbugs. "I'm standing on the soil of liberty," said an orator. "You ain't," replied a bootmaker in the audience. "You're standing in a pair of boots you never paid me for." The tendency of men is ever to go with the majority — to go with the huzzas. "Majority," said Schiller, "what does that mean? Sense has ever centred in the few. Votes should be weighed, not counted. That state must sooner or later go to ruin where numbers sway and ignorance decides."

When the secession from the Scotch Church took place, Norman Macleod said it was a great trial to the flesh to keep by the unpopular side, and to act out what conscience dictated as the line of duty. Scorn and hissing greeted him at every turn. "I saw a tomb to-day," he says in one of his letters, "in the chapel of Holyrood, with this inscription, 'Here lies an honest man! 'I only wish to live in such a way as to entitle me to the same éloge

The ignorant and careless are at the mercy of the unprincipled; and the ignorant are as yet greatly in the majority. When a French quack was taken before the Correctional Tribunal at Paris for obstructing the Pont Neuf, the magistrate said to him, "Sirrah! how is it you draw such crowds about you, and extract so much money from them in selling your 'infallible' rubbish?" "My lord," replied the quack, "how many people do you think cross the Pont Neuf in the hour?" "I don't know," said the judge. "Then I can tell you — about ten thousand; and how many of these do you think are wise? " "Oh, perhaps a hundred!" "It is too many," said the quack; "but I leave the hundred persons to you, and take the nine thousand and nine hundred for my customers! "

Men are bribed in all directions. They have no spirit of probity, self-respect, or manly dignity. If they had, they would spurn bribes in every form. Government servants are bribed to pass goods, fit or unfit for use. Hence soldiers' half-tanned shoes give way on a march; their shoddy coats become ragged; their tinned provisions are found rotten. Captain Nares had a sad account to give of the feeding of his sailors while in the Arctic

41

regions. All this is accomplished by bribery and corruption in the lower quarters of the civil service.

Much is done in the way of illicit commissions. A cheque finds its way to a certain official, and he passes the account. Thus many a man becomes rich upon a moderate salary. After a great act of corruption had been practised by the servant of a public company, a notice was placed over the office door to this effect: "The servants of the company are not allowed to take bribes." The cook gets a commission from the tradesman; the butler has a secret understanding with the wine merchant

"These illicit commissions," says the Times, "do much to poison business relations. But if the vice were ever to mount from the servants' hall or the market and invade any public office, there would be an end to efficiency or confidence in public men. It is all-important that the public service should be pure, and that no suspicion should rest on the name of any official in a post of confidence. It would be an evil day if it were generally suspected that civil servants took backsheesh or pots de vin."

An inventor suggested a method for registering the number of persons entering an omnibus, but the Secretary was unable to entertain it. "It is of no use to us," he said; "the machine which we want is one that will make our men honest, and that, I am afraid, we are not likely to meet with." We want honest men! is the cry everywhere. The police courts too often reveal the stealing and swindling of men in whom confidence has been placed; and the result is that they are dragged down from confidence to ruin. It is trustworthy character that is most wanted. Character is reliableness; convincing other men by your acts that you can be trusted.

Abroad it is the same. Russia, Egypt, and Spain are the worst In Russia the corruption of public servants, even of the highest grade, is most gross. You must buy your way by gold. Bribery in every conceivable form is practised, — from arrangements between furnishers and the of35cials who should control them, to the direct handing over of the goods, — is undeniably prevalent. The excuse is that the public servants are so badly paid. The Moscow and Petersburg Railway was constructed at great expense. Vast sums were paid to engineers and workmen, and stolen by overseers and directors. Prince Mentchikoff accompanied his Imperial Master in a jaunt through the capital, undertaken for the benefit of the Persian Ambassador, who was making a visit to the country. The Persian surveyed golden domes, granite pillars, glittering miles of shops, with true Oriental indifference. The Emperor at last bent towards his favourite and whispered with an air of vexation, "Can't we find anything that will astonish this fellow?" "Yes, your Majesty," replied the Prince; "show him the accounts of the Moscow and Petersburg Railway! "At Alexandria, in Egypt, the "leakage," as it is called, is enormous, unless bought off by gold. In Spain, every ship has to work its way into port after bribing the customs officers. The excuse is the same as in Russia; the civil servants of Spain cannot live except by taking bribes.

Even in republics men are apt and willing to be bribed Money gets over many difficulties; it solves many problems. In America, the cream of republics, bribery is conducted in a wholesale way. The simple salary of an official is not sufficient. Even the highest in office is bribed by presents of carriages and horses, and even by hard cash. The most farseeing and honest of American statesmen see that jobbery and corruption are fast undermining' the efficiency of the administration, and debasing the standard of public virtue.[17]

It has been the ' same all over the world. It does not matter what the form of government is called — whether a monarchy, an aristocracy, or a republic. It is not the form of government, but the men who administer it. Selfishly used, political power is a curse; intelligently and impartially used, it may be one of the greatest blessings to a community. If selfishness begins with the governing classes, woe to the country that is governed. The evil spreads downwards, and includes all classes, even the poorest The race of life becomes one for mere pelf and self. Principle is abandoned. Honesty is a forgotten virtue. Faith dies out; and society becomes a scramble for place and money.

Yet there are men who have refused to be bought, in all times and ages. Even the poorest, inspired by duty, have refused to sell themselves for money. Among the North American Indians a wish for wealth is considered unworthy of a brave man, — so that the chief is often the poorest of his tribe. The best benefactors of the race have been poor men, among the Israelites, among the Greeks, and among the Romans. Elisha was at the plough when called to be a prophet, and Cincinnatus was in his fields when called to lead the armies of Rome. Socrates and Epaminondas were amongst the poorest men in Greece. Such too, were the Galilean fishermen, the inspired founders of our faith.

Aristides was called "The Just" from his unbending integrity. His sense of justice was spotless, and his self-denial unimpeachable. He fought at Marathon, at Salamis, and commanded at the battle of Plataea. Though he had borne the highest offices in the state, he died poor. Nothing could buy him; nothing could induce him to swerve from his duty. It is said that the Athenians became more virtuous from contemplating his bright example. In the representation of one of the tragedies of Æschylus, a

---

[17] See North American Review for January 1871. Mr. Jacob D. Cox says that the degrading hunt for public place and public money extends all over the States. There is no backwoods hamlet so obscure that its moral atmosphere has escaped the contagion. When one of the conflicting parties in the State has overcome the other, there is almost a sweep of the places of pay and power, down to the pettiest clerkship. The war-cry is "To the victors belong the spoils ! ""We have to confess with shame," says Mr. Cox, "that its effect on our politics is the same as the cry of 'Beauty and booty' upon an army entering a captured city. We have become so familiarised with a disgraceful scramble to such an extent that we now wonder at our own apathy, and begin to realise the fact that the public conscience has become partially seared "(p. 89). During Mr. Johnson's administration "a condition of things existed which rivalled the most corrupt era that can be found in the history of any nation." Sycophancy, adulation, bribery, and all the rest of the loathsome catalogue of political vices, thicken as we descend, till we reach the "rough" doing the ballot-stuffing or the curbstone-fighting for his party, and making his gains by stealing the money he has received from some candidate to "treat the independent voters, who may be bought with a dram of whisky "(p. 92).

sentence was uttered in favour of moral goodness, on which the eyes of the audience turned involuntarily from the actor to Aristides.

Phocion, the Athenian general, a man of great bravery and foresight, was surnamed "The Good." Alexander the Great, when overrunning Greece, endeavoured to win him from his loyalty. He offered him riches, and the choice of four cities in Asia. The answer of Phocion bespoke the spotless character of the man. "If Alexander really esteems me," he said, "let him leave me my honesty."

Yet Demosthenes, the eloquent, could be bought When Harpalus, one of Alexander's chiefs, came to Athens, the orators had an eye upon his gold. Demosthenes was one of them. What is eloquence without honesty? On his visit to Harpalus, the chief perceived that Demosthenes was much pleased with one of the king's beautifully engraved cups. He desired him to take it in his hand that he might feel its weight "How much might it bring?" asked Demosthenes. "It will bring you twenty talents," replied Harpalus. That night the cup was sent to Demosthenes, with twenty talents in it. The present was not refused. The circumstance led to the disgrace of the orator, and he soon after poisoned himself.

Cicero, on the other hand, refused all presents from friends, as well as from the enemies of his country. Some time after his assassination, Caesar Augustus found his grandson with a book of Cicero's in his hands. The boy endeavoured to hide it, but Caesar took it from him. After having run over it, he returned it to the boy, saying, "My dear child, this was an eloquent man, and a lover of his country."

Bias, when asked why he did not, like others of his countrymen, load himself with part of his property when all were obliged to fly, said, "Your wonder is without reason; I am carrying all my treasures with me."

When Diocletian had quitted the imperial purple for some time, Maximilian invited him to reassume the reins of government Diocletian replied, "If I could show you the cabbages that I have planted with my own hands at Salona, and the fine melons that I have been ripening, and the delightful plantations I have made about my villa, I should no longer be urged to relinquish the enjoyment of happiness for the pursuit of power."

What he had worked for was his own, the fruit of his own labour and pains. He had imbibed the spirit of industry, which gives perseverance to the worker, enterprise to the warrior, and firmness to the statesman. Labour shuts up the first avenues to dishonesty; it opens a broader field for the display of every talent; and inspires with a new vigour the performance of every social and religious duty. Hence the Romans desired to call Diocletian back to his political duties.

Contentment is also better than luxury or power; indeed it is natural wealth. Mary, sister of Elizabeth, often wished that she had been born a milkmaid instead of a queen. She would have been saved the torture of unrequited love, and the degradation of power through the hands of her ministers. Many martyrs would have been saved from burning.

Brave and honest men do not work for gold. They work for love, for honour, for character. When Socrates suffered death rather than abandon his views of right morality; when Las Casas endeavoured to mitigate the

44

tortures of the poor Indians; they had no thought of money or country. They worked for the elevation of all that thought, and for the relief of all that suffered.

When Michael Angelo was commanded by the Pope to undertake the direction of the works of St. Peter's, he consented only upon condition that he should receive no salary, but that he should labour "for the love of God alone." "Keep your money," said Wiertz of Brussels, to a gentleman who wished to buy one of his pictures; "gold gives the death-blow to art." At the same time it must be confessed that Wiertz was a man of outrk character.

In political life, place and money are too much in request. The gift of office, when not fairly earned by public service, proves often the corruption of morals. It is the substitution of an inferior motive for a patriotic one; and wherever it prevails from considerations of personal favouritism, it degrades politics and debases character.

Andrew Marvell was a patriot of the old Roman build. He lived in troublous times. He was born at Hull at the beginning of the reign of Charles I. When a young man, he spent four years at Trinity College, Cambridge. He afterwards travelled through Europe. In Italy he met Milton, and continued his friend through life. On his return to England the civil war was raging. It does not appear that he took any part in the struggle, though he was always a defender and promoter of liberty. In 1660 he was elected member of Parliament for his native town, and during his membership he wrote to the mayor and his constituents by almost every post, telling them of the course of affairs in Parliament

Marvell did not sympathise with Milton's anti-monarchical tendencies. His biographer styles him "the friend of England, Liberty, and Magna Charta." He had no objections to a properly restricted monarchy, and therefore favoured the Restoration. The people longed for it, believing that the return of Charles II would prove the restoration of peace and loyalty. They were much mistaken. Marvell was appointed to accompany Lord Carlisle on an embassy to Russia, showing that he was not reckoned an enemy to the Court During his absence much evil had been done. The restored king was constantly in want of money. He took every method, by selling places and instituting monopolies, to supply his perpetual need. In one of Marvell's letters to his constituents he said, "The Court is at the highest pitch of want and luxury, and the people are full of discontent." In a trial of two Quakers, Penn and Mead, at the Old Bailey, the recorder, among the rest, commended the Spanish Inquisition, saying "it would never be well till we had something like it"

The king continued to raise money unscrupulously, by means of his courtiers and apostate patriots. He bought them up by bribes of thousands of pounds. But Marvell was not to be bought. His satires upon the Court and its parasites were published. They were read by all classes, from the king to the tradesman. The king determined to win him over. He was threatened, he was flattered, he was thwarted, he was caressed, he was beset with spies, he was waylaid by ruffians, and courted by beauties. But no Delilah could discover the secret of his strength. His integrity was proof alike against danger and against corruption. Against threats and bribes,

45

pride is the ally of principle. In a Court which held no man to be honest, and no woman chaste, this soft sorcery was cultivated to perfection; but Marvell, revering and respecting himself, was proof against its charms.

It has been said that Lord Treasurer Danby, thinking to buy over his old school-fellow, called upon Marvell in his garret. At parting, the Lord Treasurer slipped into his hand an order on the Treasury for £1000, and then went to his chariot. Marvell, looking at the paper, calls after the Treasurer, "My lord, I request another moment." They went up again to the garret, and Jack, the servant boy, was called. "Jack, child, what had I for dinner yesterday?" "Don't you remember, sir? you had the little shoulder of mutton that you ordered me to bring from a woman in the market" "Very right, child. What have I for dinner to-day?" "Don't you know, sir, that you bid me lay by the blade-bone to broil?" "'Tis so, very right child, go away." "My lord," said Marvell, turning to the Treasurer, "do you hear that? Andrew Marvell's dinner is provided; there's your piece of paper. I want it not. I knew the sort of kindness you intended. I live here to serve my constituents; the Ministry may seek men for their purpose; I am not one"

Marvell conducted himself nobly to the end He remained unimpeachable in his character. He was the true representative of his constituents. Though not poor, his mode of living was simple and frugal. In July 1678, he visited his constituents for the last time. Shortly after his return to London, without any previous illness or visible decay, he expired. Some say he died from poison. That may not be true. But certainly he died an honest man. He always preserved his purity. He ever defended the right. He was "beloved by good men; feared by bad; imitated by few; and scarce paralleled by any." These are the words on his tombstone at Hull.

Ben Jonson, like Marvell, was sturdy and plain-spoken. When Charles I. sent that brave poet a tardy and slight gratuity during his poverty and sickness, Ben sent back the money, with the message — "I suppose he sends me this because I live in an alley: tell him his soul lives in an alley."

Goldsmith also was a man who would not be bought He had known the depths of poverty. He had wandered over Europe, paying his way with his flute. He had slept in barns and under the open sky. He tried acting, ushering, doctoring. He starved amidst them all. Then he tried authorship, and became a gentleman. But he never quite escaped from the clutches of poverty. He described himself as "in a garret writing for bread, and expecting to be dunned for a milk score." One day Johnson received a message from Goldsmith, stating that he was in great distress. The Doctor went to see him, and found that his landlady had arrested him for his rent The only thing he had to dispose of was a packet of manuscript Johnson took it up, and found it to be the Vicar of Wakefield, Having ascertained its merit, Johnson took it to a bookseller and sold it for sixty pounds.[18]

---

[18] Goethe records what a blessing this book had been to him. When at the age of eighty-one, standing on the brink of the grave, he told a friend that in the decisive moment of mental development, the Vicar of Wakefield had formed his education, and that he had recently read, with unabated delight, the charming book again

Poor though he was then, and poor though he was at the end of his life — for he died in debt — Goldsmith could not be bought. He refused to do dirty political work. About £ 50,000 annually was then expended by Sir Robert Walpole in secret service money. Daily scribblers were suborned to write up the acts of the administration, and to write down those of their opponents. In the time of Lord North, "Junius "was in opposition. It was resolved to hire Goldsmith to baffle his terrible sarcasm. Dr. Scott, chaplain to Lord Sandwich, was deputed to negotiate with him. "I found him," says Dr. Scott, "in a miserable suite of chambers in the Temple. I told him my authority. I told how I was empowered to pay for his exertions; and, would you believe it? — he was so absurd as to say, 'I can earn as much as will supply my wants without writing for any party; the assistance you offer is therefore unnecessary to me;' and so I left him in his garret!"

Thus did poor and noble Goldsmith spurn the wages of unrighteousness! He preferred using his pen to write the famous tale of Goody Two Shoes for the amusement of children, rather than become the hack pamphleteer of political prostitutes.

Pulteney, the leader of the Opposition in the House of Commons, having in one of his speeches made a Latin quotation, was corrected by Sir Robert Walpole, who offered to wager a guinea on the inaccuracy of the lines. The bet was accepted, the classic was referred to, and Pulteney was found to be right. The minister threw a guinea across the table, and Pulteney, on taking it up, called the House to witness that this was the first guinea of the public money he had ever put into his pocket! The very coin thus lost and won is preserved in the British Museum, as "The Pulteney Guinea."

When Pitt, Earl of Chatham, was appointed Paymaster to the Forces, he refused to take one farthing beyond the salary which the law had annexed to his office. In times of peace, the paymaster was allowed to keep a large sum to his credit, amounting perhaps to several hundred thousand pounds; and he might appropriate the interest upon this sum to his own use. But Chatham refused all this advantage. He also declined the Vails or bribes offered to him by foreign princes in the pay of England, and which amounted to a large sum annually. His character was as honourable and disinterested as were his pecuniary transactions.

William Pitt, the great Commoner, was equally true. He considered money as dirt beneath his feet, compared with the public interest and public esteem. His hands were clean. While the contest between himself and the Opposition under Fox was raging, the Clerkship of the Rolls fell vacant. It was a sinecure place for life, with three thousand a year. Everybody knew that Pitt was poor, and it was thought that he would appoint himself. Nobody would have blamed him. It was usual to do so at that time. But he gave the appointment to Colonel Barr, a poor blind

from beginning to end, not a little affected by the lively recollection of how much he had been indebted to the author seventy years before. —Forster.

friend; and thus saved the pension which a previous administration had conferred upon him.

Everybody comprehended Pitt's disinterestedness. He was libelled, maligned, and abused. Though millions were passing through his hands, his bitterest enemies did not dare to accuse him of touching unlawful gain. When the richest people in the land were soliciting him for dukedoms, marquisates, and garters, he himself spurned them out of his way. He had almost a supreme contempt for money, and the consideration that money gives. Pitt was the magnanimous man so finely described by Aristotle in the ' Ethics,' who thought himself worthy of great things, being in truth worthy. Nothing did more to raise his character than his noble poverty.

It is related of Chamillard, the great French advocate, that he pleaded a case unsuccessfully, and all because an important document bad not been produced The judge's decision was reported to Parliament, and was confirmed. There was now no appeal The suitor called upon Chamillard, and deplored the loss of his fortune. He averred that it had occurred through Chamillard not having referred to an important document, the foundation of his case. Chamillard protested that he had not seen the document The client insisted that it had been handed to him with the other papers. At length Chamillard opened his bag, searched, and found the document. He found that the case would have been won, had it been produced and read; but there was no appeal. The advocate took his course on the instant. He told the suitor to call upon him next morning. He gathered together all the money that he could find, and on his client calling next day, he handed the whole over to him, although it involved the loss of his fortune. In this way did he maintain his respect for himsel£ He did his strict duty, though it cost him so much. He not only did this; he called upon the President of the Court, and begged him not to charge him again in any report to Parliament For he held himself a suspect after this great fault, although he had so nobly repaired it

Sir Arthur Wellesley (afterwards Duke of Wellington) was offered a large sum of money by the prime minister of the Court of Hyderabad, for the purpose of ascertaining what advantages had been reserved for his Prince after the battle of Assaye. Sir Arthur looked at him quietly for a few seconds and said, "It appears, then, that you are capable of keeping a secret?" "Yes, certainly." "Then so am I," said the English General. He refused the offer, and bowed the minister out The Rajah of Kittoor afterwards offered him, through his minister, a bribe of 10,000 pagodas for certain advantages. The bribe was indignantly refused, and the General said, "Inform the Rajah that I and all British officers consider such offers as insults, by whomsoever they are made."

His noble relative, the Marquis of Wellesley, in like manner, refused a present of £100,000 offered to him by the directors of the East India Company. Nothing could prevail upon him to accept it "It is not necessary," he said, "for me to allude to the independence of my character, and the proper dignity attaching to my office.... I think of nothing but our army. I should be much distressed to curtail the share of those brave soldiers." Sir Charles Napier exhibited the same self-denial while in India.

"Certainly," he said, "I could have got £30,000 since my coming to Scinde, but my hands do not want washing yet Our dear father's sword is unstained."

Sir James Outram was generous and unselfish to a degree. While a junior captain in India he was offered the command of the troops about to be assembled against the insurgents of Máhi Kánta. He declined the honour in favour of a friend very much his senior. He felt it his duty to point out that the appointment of so junior an officer might give umbrage in quarters where unanimity was necessary. The senior officer on the spot was almost the senior captain in the army. He said, "The qualifications of the officer are far superior to mine. I willingly stake my humble reputation on his conduct. Associated with him, as I presume I shall be, in the duty, while his will be the honour of success, mine will be the blame of defeat, in measures of which I am the proposer." But the commander-in-chief could not accept his suggestion. The offer was renewed and at last accepted.

When the Scinde prize-money was distributed amongst the officers and soldiers, Outram refused to accept for his own purposes the £ 3000 to which he was entitled as a major. He refused, he said, to accept a rupee of the booty resulting from the policy which he opposed. He distributed die whole amount in charitable objects. Among the other recipients were Dr. Duflfs Indian missionary schools. He also gave £800 to the Hill School Asylum at Kussowlee. Lady Lawrence afterwards wrote to him, "Your benefaction is not the less acceptable, because it comes in the form of allegiance to what we believe to be a righteous cause."

Advantage to himself was what Sir James Outram never thought of, and money was literally nothing to him, except when he could make it helpful to others. There never was a man more entirely simple and free from all self-consciousness. The more his life is studied in its details, the more it will be found how habitually he made a practice of esteeming others better than himself, of looking less at his own things and more at the things of others. His compassion, indeed, was boundless. It was this compassion, this faculty of seeing with other men's eyes, of thinking with other men's hearts — a faculty, the absence of which in our chief rulers brought us to our sorest straits in India — which made Outram so strenuous an opponent of injustice in all its forms.[19]

It is related of the great Lord Lawrence, that during the conduct of some important case for a young Indian Rajah, the prince endeavoured to place in his hands, under the table, a bag of rupees. "Young -man," said Lawrence, "you have offered to an Englishman the greatest insult which he could possibly receive. This time, in consideration of your youth, I excuse it. Let me warn you by this experience, never again to commit so gross an offence against an English gentleman."

It is by the valour and honesty of such men that the Empire of India has been maintained. They have toiled at their duty, often at the risk of their lives. At the time of the Indian Mutiny, many men, until then comparatively unknown, came rapidly to the front — such men as

---

[19] See Life of Outram by Sir F. J. Goldsmid.

49

Havelock, Neil, Nicholson, Outram, Clyde, Inglis, Edwardes, and Lawrence. The very name of Lawrence represented power in the North-West Provinces. The standard of duty of both brothers was of the highest. The first, John — Iron John, as he was called — and the second, Henry, inspired a loving and attached spirit to those who were about them. . It was declared of the former that his character alone was worth an army. Colonel Edwards said of both brothers — "They sketched a faith, and begot a school, which are both living things at this day."

At the time at which the Indian Mutiny broke out, Sir John was Chief Commissioner of the Punjaub. The country which he governed had just been conquered by the English. He governed his new province well and wisely. He trusted the people about him, and made them his friends. And then he did what is perhaps unexampled in history. He sent away the whole of the Punjaub native troops, to assist the English army at Delhi, leaving himself without any force to protect him. The result proved that he was right. The Shiks and Punjaubees proved faithful. Delhi was taken, and India was saved. All this depended on the personal character of John Lawrence. The words which his brother. Sir Henry, desired to be put upon his tomb, modestly describe his life and character — "Here lies Henry Lawrence, who tried to do his Duty!"

Men of science have displayed the same self-sacrifice. When Sir Humphry Davy, after great labour, invented his safety lamp for the purpose of mitigating the danger to colliers working in inflammable gas, he would not take out a patent for it, but made it over to the public. A friend said to him, "You might as well have secured this invention by a patent, and received your five or ten thousand a year for it" "No, my good friend," said Davy; "I never thought of such a thing: my sole object was to serve the cause of humanity. I have enough for all my views and .purposes. More wealth might distract my attention from my favourite pursuits. More wealth could not increase either my fame or my happiness. It might undoubtedly enable me to put four horses to my carriage; but what would it avail me to have it said that Sir Humphry drives his carriage and four?"

It was the same with his follower Faraday. He worked for science alone. He was as imaginative as he was scientific. Every new fact won by his intelligence resolved itself into a centre of greater mysteries. He was no materialist His philosophy, was at once a protest against scientific dogmatism and religious sectarianism. He was humble in his knowledge, and worked in the spirit of a child — wondering at the revelations of truth which dawned upon him. "That ozone, that oxygen," he said, "which makes up more than half the weight of the world, what a wonderful thing it is; and yet I think we are only at the beginning of a knowledge of its wonders."

Faraday was satisfied to be a comparatively poor man. He did not work for money. Had he done so he would have made a large fortune. He patented nothing, but made all his discoveries over to the public He nobly resisted the temptation of money-making — though in his case it was no temptation — but preferred to follow the path of pure science. He was emphatically a finder out of facts; and often they startled him. "These things," he said, "are unaccountable at present; they show us that, with all our knowledge, we know little as yet of that which may afterwards become known." The words remind us of one of the last sayings of Isaac Newton.

At a recent meeting of the Royal Institution, when Professor Tyndall presented Dr. Hoffman with the Faraday medal — the highest token of recognition which the Society had it in its power to bestow — he mentioned a touching example of Faraday's kindness. A young student at Edinburgh (in fact, Samuel Brown, afterwards M.D.), who was engaged in a bewildering study about matter and atoms, submitted his conjectures to the greatest chemist of the day. Overwhelmed as Faraday then was with work, he answered not with neglect or with cheap flattery. He wrote to the unknown youth as follows: — "I have no hesitation in advising you to experiment in support of your views, because, whether you confirm or confute them, good must come out of your experiments. With regard to the views themselves, I can say nothing of them except that they are useful in exciting the mind to inquiry. A very brief consideration of the progress of experimental philosophy will show you that it is a great disturber of preconceived theories. I have thought long and closely on the theories of attraction and of particles and atoms of matter, and the more I think, in association with experiments, the less distinct does my idea of an atom or a particle of matter become."

To turn to another subject — that of money-making. The fortunes of the house of Rothschild were based upon the honesty of their founder — Meyer Amschel or Anselm. He was born at Frankfort-on-the-Maine in 1743. His parents were Jews. What a frightful history might be written of the persecutions, tortures, and martyrdoms of the Jews in the Middle Ages, and even down to our own times.[20] At Frankfort, as well as in other towns and cities in Germany, the Jews were compelled to resort to their quarters at a certain hour in the evening, under penalty of death. The Judengasse at Frankfort was shut in by gates, which were locked at night. Napoleon blew them down with cannon, one of the best things he ever did; yet the persecutions of the Jews continued.

Young Anselm lost his parents at eleven, and had to fight his way through life alone. After a slight modicum of education — for Jews are always kind to each other — the boy had the good fortune to find a place as clerk to a small banker and money-changer at Hanover. He returned to Frankfort in 1772, and established himself as a broker and money-lender. Over his shop he hung the sign of the Red Shield — in German, Rothschild. He collected ancient and rare coins, and among the amateurs who frequented his shop, was the Landgrave William, afterwards Elector of Hesse.

When Napoleon overran Europe, William of Hesse was driven from

---

[20] The last persecutors of the Jews of whom we hear, are the Roumanians and Bulgarians. Having so far achieved their own liberty, they deny it to the Jews, who are still laden with suffering and sorrow. The Roumanians and Bulgarians scarcely deserve their freedom; they have achieved power, but not justice. Their injustice will return upon them. "Curses, like chickens, come home to roost."

his States, and left all the money he could gather together in the hands of Anselm, his hof-agent. It amounted to £ 250,000. How to take care of this money and make it grow in his hands, was Anselm's greatest object Money in those days was very dear; it returned twelve or even twenty per cent on good security. The war went on. Russia was invaded by Napoleon. His army was all but lost in the snow. The battle of Leipsic was fought, and Napoleon and his army were hurled across the Rhine. The Landgrave of Hesse then returned to his States. A few days after, the eldest son of Meyer Anselm presented himself at court, and handed over to the Landgrave the three millions of florins which his father had taken care of. The Landgrave was almost beside himself with joy. He looked upon the restored money as a windfall. In his exultation, he knighted the young Rothschild at once. "Such honesty," his highness exclaimed, "had never been known in the world." At the Congress of Vienna, where he went shortly after, he could talk of nothing else than the honesty of the Rothschilds. Anselm had a large family. They followed his example, and thus the Rothschilds became the largest money-lenders in the world.[21]

Of the late Lord Macaulay it may be said that he was a thoroughly incorruptible man. Among the men with whom he was brought up — Wilberforce, Henry Thornton, and Zachary Macaulay — he could hardly fail to become a patriotic and disinterested man. When he was only earning two hundred a year by his pen, the Rev. Sydney Smith, not given to overpraise, said of him, "I believe that Macaulay is incorruptible. You might lay ribbons, stars, garters, wealth, titles, before him in vain. He has an honest genuine love of his country, and the world could not bribe him to neglect her interests."[22]

Macaulay so arranged his affairs that their management was to him a pastime, instead of being a source of annoyance and anxiety. His economical maxims were the simplest; to treat official and literary gains as capital, and to pay all debts within the twenty-four hours. "I think," he said, that prompt payment is a moral duty; knowing, as I do, how painful it is to be deferred." "There is nothing," he said, "truer than Poor Richard's saw: "We are taxed twice as heavily by our pride, as by the State."' He early accustomed himself to a strict appropriation of his income, as the only sure ground on which to build a reputation for public and private integrity, and to maintain a dignified independence.

And yet he possessed but a slight competence. To Lord Lansdowne, who offered him a seat in the Council of India, he wrote as follows: — "Every day that I live, I become less and less desirous of great wealth. But every day makes me more sensible of the importance of a competence. Without a competence, it is not very easy for a public man to be honest; it

[21] The story is told at length by Frederick Martin in his Stories of Banks and Bankers.
[22] Sydney Smith once said that he was never afraid to open his letter bag. He was uprightly conscientious. He had robbed nobody. If he had lost money, as he did by the Pennsylvanian repudiation, the crime did not lie at his door, but at that of his creditors.

is almost impossible for him to be thought so. I am so situated that I can subsist only in two ways: by being in office, and by my pen.... The thought of becoming a bookseller's hack; of writing to relieve, not the fulness of the mind, but the emptiness of the pocket; of spurring a jaded fancy to reluctant exertion; of filling sheets with trash, merely that the sheets may be filled; of hearing from publishers and editors what Dryden bore from Thomson, and what, to my knowledge. Mackintosh bore from Lardner, is horrible to me. Yet thus it must be if I should quit office. Yet to hold office merely for the sake of emolument would be more horrible still.'

The result was that Macaulay obtained and filled an honourable office in India, and returned with a sufficient competence to be enabled to write his famous History of England.

CHAPTER V

COURAGE — ENDURANCE

Fear to do base unworthy things, is valour;
If they be done to us, to suffer them
Is valour too.

Ben Jonson

Give me no light, great Heaven, but such as turns
To energy of human fellowship;
No powers beyond the groviing heritage
That makes completer manhood.

George Eliot

Not alone when life flows still; do truth
And power emerge, but also when strange chance
Affects its current; in unused conjuncture.
When sickness breaks the body — hunger, watching,
Excess, or languor— oftenest death's approach—
Peril, deep joy, or woe.

Robert Browning

COURAGE is the quality which all men delight to honour. It is the energy which rises to all the emergencies of life. It is the perfect will, which no terrors can shake. It will enable one to die, if need be, in the performance of duty.

Who has a word to say in praise of cowardice? Does not the universal conscience condemn it? The coward is mean and unmanly. He has not the courage to stand by his opinions. He is ready to become a slave. "Half of our virtue," says Homer, "is torn away when a man becomes a slave;" and "the other half," added Dr. Arnold, "goes when he becomes a slave broken loose."

Yet it requires courage to deal with the coward. A foolish young man, who quarrelled with Sir Philip Sydney, and tried to provoke him to fight, went so far as to spit in his face. "Young man," said Sir Philip, "if I could as easily wipe your blood from my conscience as I can wipe this insult from my face, I would this moment take your life." This was noble courage. It is a lesson for every one; how to bear and how to forbear.

The courageous man is an example to the intrepid. His influence is magnetic. He creates an epidemic of nobleness. Men follow him, even to the death. It is not the men who succeed that are always worthy of estimation. The men who fail for a time, continue to exercise a potent influence on their race. The leader of the forlorn hope may fall in the breach, but his body furnishes the bridge over which the victors enter the citadel

The martyr may perish at the stake, but the truth for which he dies may gather new lustre from his sacrifice. The patriot may lay his head upon the block, and hasten the triumph of the cause for which he suffers. The memory of a great life does not perish with the life itself, but lives in other minds. The ardent and enthusiastic may seem to throw their lives away; but the enduring men continue the fight, and enter in and take possession of the ground on, which their predecessors sleep. Thus the triumph of a just cause may come late, but when it does come, it is due to the men who have failed as well as to the men who have eventually succeeded.

All the great work of the world has been accomplished by courage. Every blessing that we enjoy — personal security, individual liberty, and constitutional freedom — has been obtained through long apprenticeships of evil. The right of existing as a nation has only been accomplished through ages of wars and horrors. It required four centuries of martyrdom to establish Christianity, and a century of civil wars to introduce the Reformation.

It is the simple fidelity to truth that gives to martyrdom its eternal value. In the progress of freedom of thought, no matter what the truth adhered to is, all martyrs are our martyrs. They died that we might be free. Roman Catholics and Protestants, Christians and Pagans, orthodox and heretic, may share in this glorious heritage of the past "The angels of martyrdom and victory," says Mazzini, "are brothers: both extend their wings over the cradle of future life."

A story of the noble army of martyrs has come down to us from the beginning of the Christian era. It is that of Pancratius, or Pancras. He was born in Phrygia, a district visited by the Apostle Paul at the time when he confirmed the churches in Galatia. Pancratius was brought up to worship Jupiter, but his father having died, he was placed under the guardianship of his uncle Dionysius. The uncle removed to Rome in the year 305, that the orphan, heir to a vast fortune, might be near the Imperial Court Under the care and tuition of the aged and holy Marcellinus, Bishop of Rome, he was converted to Christianity. His uncle soon after died, and the youth, then only fourteen years old, was left with his wealth and his religion in a world without a friend.

Diocletian was then persecuting the Christians. It was reported to him that Pancratius had been converted. He was immediately ordered to attend at the palace of Diocletian. The Emperor threatened him with instant death unless he sacrificed to Jupiter. The boy replied that he was a Christian, and ready to die; "for Christ,' he said, "our Master, inspires the souls of His servants, even young as I am, with courage to suffer for His sake." The Emperor made no reply, but ordered him to be led out of the city, and put to death by the sword on the Aurelian Way. There he sealed his testimony with his blood. He lay until the light of early dawn, when a Christian Roman lady wrapped the body in fine linen, and bore it to a catacomb near by, where she covered it with fresh flowers, embalming it with her tears. His name is still remembered by the churches erected after his memory.[23]

The early Christians were torn to pieces by wild beasts in the Roman arenas, down to the end of the third century. They were "butchered to make a Roman holiday." Nothing gave the Roman people greater sport than the fights of the wild beasts, the tearing to pieces of the Christians, and the deadly combats of the gladiators. The same pleasures — so to speak — prevailed all over the Roman Empire. Wherever they settled, an amphitheatre was founded. Almost the only one in England is found at Richborough in Kent. At Treves, the capital of the Roman Empire north of the Alps, a great many Roman remains are found. Among others is an amphitheatre cut out of the rock, capable of accommodating thousands of spectators. In the year 306, Constantine entertained his subjects with an" exhibition of "Frankish sports." It consisted in exposing many thousand unarmed captive Franks to be torn to pieces by wild beasts. The animals were glutted with slaughter, and of their own accord desisted from their work of destruction. Those who survived were made to fight as gladiators against one another. But instead of doing this, they disappointed the ferocity of the spectators by voluntarily falling on each other's swords, instead of contending for life. In thesameyear, thousands of the Bructeri were barbarously sacrificed for the amusement of the people. The ruined amphitheatre, as well as the vaulted dens of the wild beasts, are still to be seen.

In France, many of the Roman amphitheatres still exist, though several of them have been used as quarries. Those at Nismes and Aries are the largest, the latter being so extensive that the Moors built four castles on the outer wall while defending the place against the Franks. The one at Verona is almost perfect, and is kept up from year to year. But the greatest

---

[23] It is said of Saint John Lateran at Rome, "This is the head and mother of all Christian churches, if you except that of St. Pancras, under Highgate, near London." The common seal of St. Pancras parish represents a youthful saint trampling upon heathen superstition. There are seven St. Pancras churches in England, and many others in Italy and France.

amphitheatre is the Coliseum at Rome, which was able to afford accommodation for about 87,000 spectators. Church tradition tells us that it was designed by Gaudentius, a Christian architect and martyr; and it is also said that many thousand captive Jews, brought by Titus from Jerusalem, were employed in its construction. At the dedication of the building by Titus, 5000 beasts were slaughtered in the arena. Only recently, the bones of wild beasts, lions and tigers, have been found in the vaults underneath the circus.

On the days of the great spectacles at the Coliseum, all Rome held holiday. Men, women, and children, assembled to see the bloody sports. The magistrates and senators, the functionaries of state, the nobles and the common people, even the Vestal Virgins, were there, presided over by the Emperor. The gladiators marched in front of the Emperor, crying, "Ave, Caesar! morituri te salutant" The wild beasts began the warfare, and the gladiators followed. The sports continued until night, when the spectators became drunk with carnage.

These sports continued until Rome was nominally Christian But at length, about the year 400, an old hermit, lamenting these bloody carnivals, determined to interfere, though at the cost of his poor body. What was his life compared with the commission of these horrible crimes? The very name of this martyr is unknown. Some say it was Alymachus, and others that it was Telemachus. No matter, his courage proved his worth. He had come from the far east. He knew nobody, and nobody knew him. The news went forth that there was to be a gladiatorial combat in the arena. All Rome flocked to it. He went in with the crowd, his heart intent upon his object. The gladiators entered the arena with sharp spears and swords. It was to be a fight to the death. As they approached, the old man sprang over the wall, and threw himself between the gladiators about to engage. He called upon them to cease from shedding innocent blood. Loud cries, shrieks, howls, arose on every side. "Back, back, old man! "No, he would not go back. The gladiators thrust him aside, and advanced to the attack. The old man still stood between the sharp swords, and forbade them to commit bloodshed. "Down with him!" was the general cry. The Prefect gave his consent. The gladiators cut him down, and advanced over his dead body.

His death was not in vain. The people began to think of what they had done. They had destroyed a holy man, who had given his life as a protest against their bloodthirstiness. They were shocked at their own cruelty. From the day on which the self-sacrificing old man was cut down, there were no more fights in the Coliseum. The hermits death was victory. The gladiatorial combats were abolished by Honorius in 402. Not long ago, the remains of this nameless man were carried in triumph round the arena, and afterwards deposited, with all religious honours, in the church of San Clemente, near at hand.

Rome fell from its ancient glory by means of corruption, profligacy, and cruelty. Immorality in high places never fails to exert a pernicious influence upon all classes of society. Profligacy of manners results in profligacy of principles. The baser influences of human nature obtain the ascendency, and crush out the moral vitality of character. Greece and Rome fell, because of the moral inferiority of their rulers, and the consequent corruption of the people. Rome, the ancient mistress of the world, fell before the onset of the savage tribes, which issued from the forests of central Europe. The rich were steeped in voluptuousness; the poor were wretched and dependent upon charity. They had no heart to defend their country. In fact, it was better that it should not exist

Then Christianity came, and revealed to men the true foundation of religion. St. Paul carried it to Rome, as adequate to regenerate the world. It first took root amongst the enlightened poor. And why? Because religion is the explanation of human destiny, the poetry of our earthly existence, and the consoling promise of a better futurity. It also embraced women. In Rome, the lives of wives were at the disposal of their husbands. They were merely slaves. Christianity restored them to justice. They had now, for the first time, hope. They secured the reverence and love of men. "all virtue lies in a woman," said an ancient knight; "they impart worthiness, and make men worthy."

Intemperance, profanity, and immorality were subdued by the power of religious motives working in the hearts of individual men and women. The desire to do evil was thus lessened or removed. Religion satisfied the noble wants of human nature. The day of rest was consecrated, and relieved the workman's toil. The Church convened its members to the solemnities, and under its splendid roofs the whole Christian population, without distinction of class, assembled to worship; for were they not all, in the presence of God, men and brethren? What a happy picture! Would that it had continued!

Alas! the old Adam had not been effaced. There is no Eden in nature. The priesthood became the instruments of oppression, the defenders of the interests of the few against the legitimate interests of all, and shared the fate of those whom they had supported. There were differences of opinion respecting religious dogmas. What the pagans had done to the early Christians, the Christians did to their opponents. The fires of persecution were relighted, and martyrs were burnt as before. Courage and endurance were again required for those who fought for the truth; and nobly did they suffer, nobly did they die.

Persecution began in Italy; it extended to Spain, France, and the Netherlands. Germany resisted it "God's design," said Luther, "is to have sons who eternally and perfectly are fearless, calm, and generous, who fear absolutely nothing, but triumph over and despise all things through confidence in His grace, and who mock at punishments and deaths; He hates all the cowards, who are confounded with the fear of everything, even with the sound of a rustling leaf."

"Strange," says Mr. F. W. Newman, "how religion, in any form, should have generated cruelty. The Inquisition, established after Christianity had supplanted paganism, was a system of deliberate cruelty. It was continued for centuries as a pious institution, and will ever be branded as infemous and execrable. Yet its pretensions were based on the name of a gentle and loving religion."

The priesthood of Spain, aided by the secular power, stamped out the Reformation by sheer physical force. In one night eight hundred Protestants were thrown into the prisons of Seville. They were everywhere seized and burnt. Fires blazed in the chief Spanish cities. A short time ago a drain was cut through a field, near Madrid, where the Protestants were burnt. The workmen laid open a deep layer of black shining dust, mixed with calcined bones and charcoal. It was the remains of those who had perished at the bidding of the Church.

And what did Spain gain by its terrible cruelty? Its wealth has left it; and the country is almost bankrupt. The people are uneducated and uncared for. Only one out of eight can read or write. They regard the priests as their natural enemies. The greater number are professed unbelievers. Even the priests are poor. "It is a strange thing to think of," says Pr. Lees, "that Spain was more prosperous under the Moors than she has been under Christian rulers. The government was more liberal, more tolerant, more cultured; her people were better educated; her land better cultivated. Since the Moors were driven away, Spain has almost continually retrograded."

Philip II of Spain was perhaps the greatest miscreant that ever sat upon a throne. He is only worthy of being compared to Nero and Caligula. In his edict of 1568, he sentenced every Protestant in the Netherlands to be put to death. The edict failed, because there were not means enough to carry out his diabolical decree. But his minister, Alva, did what he could. By the aid of his Council of Blood, and the sheriffs and executioners of the Most Holy Inquisition, he was sometimes able to put to death by torture eight hundred beings in a week. The first crime was Protestantism; the second was wealth. For the latter reason, Catholics as well as Protestants were plundered and destroyed. The possession of property made the proof of orthodoxy almost impossible. At the end of half a dozen years, Alva boasted of having strangled, drowned, burnt, or beheaded, more than eighteen thousand of his fellow-creatures. This was independent of the tens of thousands who had perished in sieges and battles during Alva's administration. His robberies, like his murders, were colossal.

But France was as bad as Spain. From the beginning of her adherence to Rome, she plundered, burnt, beheaded, or banished all who were opposed to the opinions of the great Roman Hierarch. The Albigenses were massacred or driven into the Pyrenees. The Vaudois, with the help of Savoy, were hanged and burnt all through the south-east of France, and the north-west of Italy. Persecution and burning went on throughout the whole of France. Half a dozen Lutheran counsellors were burnt at Paris to give pleasure to the grandees of Spain.

There were many noble exceptions to this mad riot of persecution. The Chancellor de l'Hôpital urged his coreligionists to adorn themselves with virtues and a good life, and to attack their adversaries with the arms of charity, prayer, and persuasion. "Let us put away," he said, "these diabolical words, the names of parties, of factions, and seditions; Lutherans, Huguenots, Papists; change them to the name of Christians." For this, the Chancellor was called an atheist

When Viscount Dorte, Governor of Bayonne, received an order from Charles IX for the massacre of the Protestants there, he replied that he had communicated his majesty's letter to the garrison and inhabitants of the town; but that he had been able to find among them only brave soldiers and good subjects, and not a single executioner.

Then came the massacres of Voissy and St. Bartholomew, which were repeated all over France. Present for ever, like a skeleton at a feast, was the massacre of St. Bartholomew in the thoughts of all the Protestants in Europa. That and the attempted invasion of England by the Spanish Armada of Philip II were the two great features in history of the latter half of the sixteenth century.

Nor was the Revocation of the Edict of Nantes by Louis XIV more merciful. By that decree, every Protestant was expelled from France under penalty of "conversion "or death. Protestant nobles, gentles, merchants, peasants, and artisans, refused to become hypocrites. They would not conform to what they did not believe. The nobles and proprietors abandoned their estates, renounced their titles, and gave up everything to their enemies. The merchants fled with the artisans, and sought other lands where they were free to worship God according to their conscience, and enjoy the fruits of their industry in peace.

It was not death they feared. The Duke de Maienne hit the secret of the Huguenot character, when he said, "Ces gens étaient de père en fils apprivoisés á la mort." They perished by thousands, by the axe, by the wheel, and by tortures inconceivable. They could not be conquered by death. They yielded up their lives as a sacrifice to duty. The noble stamp of life and conduct which we find in the great Huguenot leaders has never been reproduced in France. In fact, the nobility and breadth of soul, and the profound conviction of the French Protestants, generated this lofty type of character — the finest which the whole range of French history has to show. But history for the most part deals with the reigns of kings and queens. Victories and defeats are remembered; but the persecuted are forgotten.

Louis XIV. and all his armies could not prevail against the impenetrable rampart of conscience. His relentless policy maintained a perpetual St. Bartholomew in France for more than sixty years. And with what result? He was baffled and defeated. He left France ruined and laden with taxes. He destroyed commerce and agriculture by his banishment of the Huguenots and left France a prey to anarchy, which developed itself in the Revolution of 1789.[24] "The flight of the Huguenots," says Michelet, in his History of France "was a noble act of loyalty and sincerity. It was horror of falsehood. It was respect for thought. It is glorious for human

---

[24] " The prisons in the Pope's palace at Avignon," says Dr. Arnold, " were one of the most striking things I ever saw in my life. In the self-same dungeon, the roof was still black with the smoke of the Inquisition fires, in which men were tortured or burnt; and as you looked down a trap-door into an apartment below, the walls were still marked with the blood of the victims whom Jourdan Coup Tete threw down there into the ice-house below, in the famous massacre of 179 1. It was very awful to see such traces of two great opposite forms of human wickedness."

nature that so great a number of men and women should, for truth's sake, have sacrificed everything; passed from riches to poverty; risked life, family, and all, in the perilous enterprise of a flight so difficult. Some see in these people only obstinate sectaries: I see in them people of lofty ideas of honour who, over all the earth have proved themselves to have been the Elite of France. The stoical device which free-thinkers have popularised is precisely the idea which lies at the root of the Protestant emigration, braving death and the galleys to remain noble and true: Vitam impendere vero; Life sacrificed for the truth."[25]

Before this, the fires of persecution had extended to England and Scotland. Smithfield, in London, was often ablaze with the burning of Protestants and witches. But the Catholics have their book of martyrs as well as the Protestants. Forest, an Observant Friar, was burnt for denying the supremacy of Henry VIII Fire was used on both sides. In Queen Mary's time the executions for religion became ten times more frequent than before. John Rogers, vicar of St. Sepulchre's, was burnt at the stake, in sight of his church tower. John Bradford died embracing the stake and comforting his fellow-sufferer. John Philpot, archdeacon of Winchester, was burnt at the same time. It is not necessary to mention the names of Latimer, Cranmer, and Ridley. The great spirits of that time were not of the same temper as the men of to-day. We, who shrink at a scalded finger, wonder at the men who were not only burnt for their faith, but who gloried in it "Shall I disdain to suffer at this stake," said John Philpot, "seeing my Redeemer did not refuse to suffer a most vile death upon the cross for me?"

The persecution for conscience sake extended to the reign of Charles II. William Penn said, "There have been ruined since the late king's restoration about 15,000 families, and more than 5000 persons died under bonds for matters of mere conscience to God." Charles II, and after him James II, extended these persecutions to Scotland. In the old Catholic times, the only method of dealing with Protestants was fire. Cardinal Beaton burnt George Wishart before his castle of St. Andrews, and, looking out of the window, saw him shrivelled up with his own eyes. In the Protestant times of Charles and James, Protestants persecuted Protestants, because of their differences of opinion. The myrmidons of the Stewarts hunted the Pres-byterians, shot them, murdered them, and hanged them. The effect was to drive their special form of religion into their very hearts and souls. The boot and thumbscrews were horrible to endure, but the sufferers were brave and enduring.

"I treasure," says Robert Collyer of New York, "a small drawing by Millais. It is the figure of a woman bound fast to a pillar far within tide-mark. The sea is curling its waves about her feet. A ship is passing in full sail, but not heeding her or her doom. Birds of prey are hovering about

[25] Having already published two volumes on this subject — The Huguenots: their Settlements Churches, and Industries in England and Ireland; and The Huguenots in France, after the Revocation of the Edict of Nantes — the author considers it unnecessary to pursue this subject farther.

her; but she heeds not the birds, or the ship, or the sea. Her eyes look right on, and her feet stand firm, and you see that she is looking directly into heaven, and telling her soul how the sufferings of this present time are not worthy to be compared with the glory that shall be revealed. Under the picture is this legend, copied from the stone set up to her memory in an old Scottish kirkyard: —

"Murdered for owning Christ supreme
Head of His Church, and no more crime.
But for not owning Prelacy,
And not abjuring Presbyt'ry,
Within the sea, tied to a stake,
She suffered for Christ Jesus' sake.

"I treasure it because, when I look at it, it seems a type of a great host of women who watch and wait, tied fast to their fate, while the tide creeps up about them, but who rise as the waves rise, and on the crest of the last and the loftiest, are borne into the quiet haven, and hear the "Well-done.'"

"For what a length of years," says Sydney Smith, "was it attempted to compel the Scotch to change their religion. Horse, foot, and artillery, and armed Prebendaries, were sent out after the Presbyterian ministers and congregations. Much blood was shed, but, to the astonishment of the Prelatists, they could not introduce the Book of Common Prayer, nor prevent that metaphysical people from going to heaven their true way, instead of our true way. The true and the only remedy was applied. The Scotch were suffered to worship God after their own tiresome manner, without pain, penalty, and privation. No lightning descended from heaven; the country was not ruined; the world is not yet come to an end; the dignitaries who foretold all these consequences are utterly forgotten; and Scotland has ever since been an increasing source of strength to Great Britain"

Toleration is only a recent discovery. We have ceased to bum men; it is now necessary to persuade them. The age of martyrdom, like that of miracles, is past. We are not shot, or pinned to a stake, or broken alive on the wheel, as in bygone days; and yet we suffer by isolation, by misrepresentation, by ridicule, and by blame. Courage is as necessary as ever for those who would hold by the innate consciousness of the truth. It is even more difficult, in these days of indifferentism, to keep true to higher laws and purer instincts, than it was in the times of martyrdom. "Active persecution and fierce chastisements," says a wellknown writer, "are tonics to the nerves; but the mere weary conviction that no one cares, that no one notices, that there is no humanity that honours, and no Deity that pities, is more destructive of all higher effort than any conflict with tyranny or with barbarism."

But have we really abandoned our ideas as to the worthlessness of persecution? In these days printing and publishing are free; and men express their thoughts in the public press. What are we to think of this sentence, which recently appeared in a London newspaper? "Considering the end of man and the purposes of civil society, murder and robbery are light crimes, and the spread of epidemic disease of no consequence, in comparison with the crime which Luther and Calvin perpetrated when they revolted from the Church." The sentence would have been approved by the perpetrators of the Massacre of St. Bartholomew; and by all those who have burnt and beheaded the thousands of men who have held to their own religious belief. But it will not do now. Our forefathers have handed down to us the priceless heritage of a free state — won by the lives of some of the noblest men who ever lived; and it will be our own fault if we encourage this revolting appeal to intolerance on the part of those who differ from us. Even the Jesuits, like the Huguenots, have been banished from France; and they are free, like all persecuted people, to live under the protection of English laws. But they must have respect for these laws, and for the religious toleration of the country that protects them.

William Penn was of opinion that there was no greater mistake than to suppose that a country or a people were strengthened by all the people holding one opinion, whether upon religious doctrine or religious practice; and that a variety of opinions, of professions, and of practice, was a strength to a people and to a government, if all were alike tolerated. Individuality must be upheld; for without individuality there can be no liberty. Individuality is everywhere to be spared and respected, as the root of everything good. "Even despotism does not produce its worst effects," says John Stuart Mill, "so long as individuality exists under it; and whatever crushes individuality is despotism, by whatever name it may be called, and whether it professes to be enforcing the will of God or the injunctions of men."

Jeremy Taylor concludes his Apology for Christian toleration with an Eastern apologue. Abraham was sitting at his tent door, when an old man, stooping and leaning on his staff, appeared before him. Abraham invited him into his tent, set before him meat, and observing that he did not invoke a blessing, asked him why he did not worship the God of Heaven. "I worship the fire only, and acknowledge no other god." Abraham became angry, and drove the old man out of his tent. Then God called to Abraham, and asked him where the stranger was? "I thrust him away, because he did not worship Thee!" God answered him, "I have suffered him these hundred years, though he dishonoured me, and wouldest thou not endure him one single night?" Upon which, saith the story, Abraham fetched him back again, and gave him hospitable entertainment and wise instructioa

Even the great men who have laboured to advance the cause of science have endured the perils of martyrdom. In former times there was scarcely a great discovery in astronomy, in natural history, or in physical science, which was not denounced as leading to infidelity. Bruno was burnt alive at Rome for exposing the fashionable but false philosophy of his time. The followers of Copernicus were branded as misbelievers. After Lippersley of Middleburgh, in Holland, had invented the telescope, Galileo took up the idea, and constructed a telescope of his own, with which he ascended the tower of St. Mark, at Venice, to view the heavenly bodies. He directed it to the planets and fixed stars, which he observed with "incredible delight." He discovered the satellites and belts of Jupiter, the phases of Venus, and the spots on the sun. He faithfully recorded the revelations that came down to him direct from the skies. He proceeded with his observations, and discovered perhaps more during his lifetime than any future astronomer.

But all this was at variance with the received ideas of the time. The Inquisition undertook to regulate astronomical science. Galileo was called to Rome, and summoned before the Inquisitors to answer for the heretical doctrines he had published. He was compelled to renounce his opinions; he declared that he abandoned the doctrine of the earth's motion round the sun. The inquisitors inserted in the prohibited Index the works of Galileo, Kepler, and Copernicus. Galileo plucked up heart again, and published a new work, in the form of a dialogue, defending his doctrines. He was summoned before the Inquisition, and was compelled, on bended knees, to renounce and abjure his glorious discovery. Galileo wanted the courage of his opinions. But he was an old man of seventy when he denied his faith. Galileo would not have been persecuted, could he have been answered. Yet the truth lived, and men were set on the right track of observation for all ages to come.

Pascal said of his condemnation, "It is in vain that you (the Jesuits) have procured against Galileo a decree from Rome condemning his opinion of the earth's motion. Assuredly that will never prove it to be at rest; and if we have unerring observations proving that it turns round, not all mankind together can keep it from turning, nor themselves from turning with it." Truth may run for a long time underground, but it is sure to work its way to the surface at last; and in proportion to the obstacles it encounters, and the length of its struggle, are the extent and the certainty of its triumph.

The life of Kepler was as sad as that of Galileo. Originally a poor boy, he was admitted to the school at the monastery of Maulbroom, and eventually became a learned man. He accepted the astronomical chair at Gratz in Styria, and devoted himself to the study of the planets. He was afterwards appointed Imperial mathematician to the Emperor; though his salary was insufficient to maintain himself and his family. At Lints he was excommunicated by the Roman Catholics because of some opinions he had expressed respecting transubstantiation. "Judge," he says to Hoffman, ' how far I can assist you, in a place where the priest and school inspector have combined to brand me with the public stigma of heresy, because in every question I take that side which seems to me consonant with the will of God."

Kepler was then offered the professorship of mathematics at Bologna, but having the recantation and condemnation of Galileo before him, he declined the chair. "I might," he said, "notably increase my fortune; but, living a German among Germans, I am accustomed to a freedom of speech and manners, which, if persevered in at Bologna, would draw upon me, if not danger, at least notoriety, and might expose me to suspicion and party malice."

In 1619 Kepler discovered the celebrated law which will be ever

63

memorable in the history of science, "that the squares of the periodic times of the planets are to one another as the cubes of their distances." He recognised with transport the absolute truth of a principle which, for seventeen years, had been the object of his incessant labours. "The die is cast," he said; "the book is written, to be read either now or by posterity — I care not which. It may well wait a century for a reader, as God has waited six thousand years for an observer."

The next book Kepler published, The Epitome of the Copemican Astronomy , was condemned at Rome, and placed in the prohibited Index. In the meantime, his mind was distracted by a far greater trouble. His mother, seventy-nine years old, was thrown into prison, condemned to the torture, and was about to be burnt as a witch. Kepler immediately flew to her relief; and arrived at his Swabian home in time to save her from further punishment. But more troubles followed. The States of Styria ordered all the copies of his "Kalendar" for 1624 to be publicly burnt His library was sealed up by order of the Jesuits; and he was compelled to leave Lintz by the popular insurrection which then prevailed. He went to Sagan in Silesia, under the protection of Albert Wallenstein, Duke of Friedland; and he shortly after died there of disease of the brain, the result of too much study.

Even Columbus may be regarded in the light of a martyr. He sacrificed his life to the discovery of a new world. The poor woolcarder's son of Genoa had long to struggle unsuccessfully with the petty conditions necessary for the realisation of his idea. He dared to believe, on grounds sufficing to his reason, that which the world disbelieved, and scoffed and scorned at He believed that the earth was round, while the world believed that it was flat as a plate. He believed that the whole circle of the earth, outside the known world, could not be wholly occupied by sea; but that the probability was that continents of land might be contained within it. It was certainly a probability; but the noblest qualities of the soul are often brought forth by the strength of probabilities that appear slight to less daring spirits. In the eyes of his countrymen, few things were more improbable than that Columbus should survive the dangers of unknown seas and land on the shores of a new hemisphere.

Columbus was a practical as well as an intellectual hero. He went from one state to another, urging kings and emperors to undertake the first visiting of a world which his instructed spirit already discerned in the far-off seas. He first tried his own countrymen at Genoa, but found none ready to help him. He then went to Portugal, and submitted his project to John II., who laid it before his council. It was scouted as extravagant and chimerical Nevertheless, the king endeavoured to steal Columbus's idea. A fleet was sent forth in the direction indicated by the navigator, but, being frustrated by storms and winds, it returned to Lisbon after four days' voyaging,

Columbus returned to Genoa and again renewed his propositions to the Republic, but without success. Nothing discouraged him. The finding of the New World was the irrevocable object of his life. He went to Spain, and landed at the town of Palos, in Andalusia. He went by chance to a convent of Franciscans, knocked at the door, and asked for a little bread and water. The prior gratefully received the stranger, entertained him, and learned from him the story of his life. He encouraged him in his hopes, and furnished him with an admission to the Court of Spain, then at Cordova. King Ferdinand received him graciously, but before coming to a decision, he desired to lay the project before a council of his wisest men at Salamanca. Columbus, had to reply, not only to the scientific arguments laid before him, but to citations from the Bible. The Spanish clergy declared that the theory of an antipodes was hostile to the faith. The earth, they said, was an immense flat disc; and if there was a new earth beyond the ocean, then all men could not be descended from Adam. Columbus was dismissed as a fool

Still bent on his idea, he wrote to the King of England, then to the King of France, without effect. At last, in 1492, Columbus was introduced by Louis de Saint Angel to Queen Isabella of Spain. The friends who accompanied him pleaded his cause with so much force and conviction, that the queen acceded to their wishes, and promised to take charge of the proposed enterprise. A fleet of three small caravelles, only one of which was decked, was got ready; and Columbus sailed from the port of Palos on the 3d of August 1492. After his long fight against the ignorance of men, he had now to strive against the superstitions of seamen. He had a long and arduous struggle. The unknown seas, the perils of the deep, the fear lest hunger should befell them, the weary disappointment on the silent main, the repeated disappointment of their hope of seeing land, sometimes rose to mutiny, which Columbus, always full of hope, had the courage to suppress. At last, after seventy days' sail, land was discovered, and Columbus set foot on the island of San Salvador. Then Cuba and Hispaniola were discovered. They were taken possession of in the name of the King and Queen of Spain. At the latter island, a fort was built. A commandant and some men were left in it; and Columbus then returned to Spain to give an account of his discovery.

The enthusiasm with which he was received was immense; his fame was great, not only in Spain, but throughout the world. He did not remain long in Spain. He set out again for America, this time in command of fourteen caravelles and three large vessels, containing in all about 1200 men. A number of nobles took part in the expedition. On this occasion Guadaloupe and Jamaica were discovered; and San Pomingo and Cuba were explored. But the fabulous gold which the nobles expected was not forthcoming. Factions began, and ended in blood. Columbus vainly endeavoured to reanimate their enthusiasm. But they regarded him with disdain, and as the author of their misery.

Columbus returned to Spain a second time, but he was not received with the same plaudits as before. The Spanish sovereigns received him with interest, though not without a little coolness. He found that base and envious jealousy was springing up against him among the courtiers. Another expedition was however undertaken. Six large ships again carried Columbus and his followers to the New World. On this occasion, the main land of America was discovered, and other islands in the Caribbean Sea. In the meantime, the natives of San Domingo rebelled against the Spaniards, who treated them with great cruelty. The Spanish colonists also fell out among themselves, and waged incessant war against each other. Columbus, in great sorrow at these events, despatched messages to the King of Spain, desiring him to send out to San Domingo a magistrate and a judge.

At the instigation of some jealous and hostile members of the court, the king sent out Don Francisco de Bobadillo, furnished with absolute powers, and designated Governor of the New World. He was not a judge, but an executioner. The first thing he did after landing was to throw Columbus and his two brothers into prison. He commissioned Alonzo de Villego to convey the brothers to Spain. Columbus was laden with chains like a malefactor, and put on board ship. While on the way, Villego, compassionating the great navigator's lot, offered to relieve him of his irons. "No!" said Columbus; "I will preserve them as a memorial of the recompense due to my services." "These irons," said his son Fernand, "I have often seen suspended on the cabinet of my father; and he ordered that at his death they should be buried with him in his grave."

On the return of the ship to Spain, the king and the queen, ashamed of the conduct of Bobadillo, ordered that the prisoners should be set at liberty. Columbus was disgusted with his treatment. "The world," he said, "has delivered me to a thousand conflicts, and I have resisted them all unto this day; I could not defend myself, neither with arms nor with prudence. With what barbarism have they treated me throughout."

Yet his eager and mysteriously informed spirit was still brooding over the wide ocean. He obtained the means of making a fourth voyage, which, he thought, would eventually enrich Spain, a country which he had as yet so thanklessly served. This time he discovered the island of Guanaja. He coasted round Honduras, Nicaragua, and Panama. He landed at Veraguas, and found the rich mines of gold in these regions; he endeavoured to found a colony on the river Belen; but a tempest arising, his ships were blown hither and thither, and he was obliged to set sail for San Domingo to repair his ships. He was now growing old and worn out with fatigues and sufferings. He was sick and ill when his seamen mutinied, and threatened to take his life. He could not resist, for he had no one to help him. But suddenly the land came in sight, and he entered San Domingo in safety.

Shortly after, he set sail for Spain, It was his last voyage. He was now about seventy. After his "long wandering woe," he was glad to reach Spain at last. He hoped for some reward — at least for as much as would keep soul and body together. But his appeals were fruitless. He lived for a few months after his return, poor, lonely, and stricken with a mortal disease. Even towards his death he was a scarcely tolerated beggar. He had to complain that his frock had been taken and sold, that he had not a roof of his own, and lacked wherewithal to pay his tavern bill. It was then that, with failing breath, he uttered the words, sublime in their touching simplicity, "I, a native of Genoa, discovered in the distant West the continent and isles of India." He expired at Valladolid, on the 20th of May 1506, his last words being, "Lord, I deliver my soul into Thy hands." Thus died the great martyr of discovery. His defeat was victory. He struggled nobly, and died faithfully.

Some men are willing to throw themselves away in the pursuit of a great object The early martyrs, the early discoverers, the early inventors, the pioneers of civilisation — all who work for truth, for religion, for patriotism — are the forlorn hope of humanity. They live and labour and die without any hope of personal reward. It is enough for them to know their work, and by the exercise of moral power to do it. The man of energy and genius is guided by his apprehension of the widest and highest tendencies. He may be thwarted and discouraged Difficulties may surround him. But he is borne up by invincible courage; and if he dies, he leaves behind him a name which every man venerates. Death has fructified his life, and made it more fruitful to others. "When God permits His ministers to die for the gospel," said Brousson, "they preach louder from their graves than they did during their lives." "What we sow," said Jeremy Taylor, "in the minutes and spare portions of a few years, grows up to crowns and sceptres in a happy and glorious eternity."

Are not difficulty and suffering necessary to evoke the highest forms of character, energy, and genius? Effort and endurance, striving and submitting, energy and patience, enter into every destiny. There is a virtue in passive endurance which is often greater than the glory of success. It bears, it suffers, it endures, and still it hopes. It meets difficulties with a smile, and strives to stand erect beneath the heaviest burdens. Suffering, patiently and enduringly borne, is one of the noblest attributes of man. There is something so noble in the quality, as to lift it into the highest regions of heroism. It was a saying of Milton, "Who best can suffer, best can do."

It is a mistake to suppose that there is ever an age when there is not a demand for the heroic virtue, or that the martyr-ages, or the ages of death-struggle with t3Tanny, alone call for the practice of this virtue. To withstand the everyday course of a generation which has lost the sense of man's high destiny, and allowed pleasure to usurp the place of duty, may demand as much real heroism as to confront tyrant power, or to face the axe of the executioner.

Even in war itself, endurance is as high a virtue as courage; and now that war has become scientific, endurance has taken the higher position. The well-disciplined soldier must stand erect in the place that has been assigned to him. "Be steady, men! "is the order. He braves danger without moving, while bullets are dealing death around him. When he advances, he has still to endure. He must not fire until the word of command is given. And then the charge comes. But it is not merely in action that endurance is highest It is in retreat rendered necessary by defeat Viewed in this light, the retreat of Xenophon's Ten Thousand outshines the conquests of Alexander; and the retreat of Sir John Moore to Corrunna was as great as the victories of Wellington.

There are numerous men who have been martyred in defence of their country. There is an old story in France — indeed it is an old story everywhere. "It is a shame," said Clovis, looking on the rich fields across the Garonne; "that such territories should belong to villains who have a different creed from ours. Onward! let us take possession of their land! "

When Xerxes endeavoured to conquer Greece, Leonidas, with three hundred men, marched to the Pass of Thermopylae, to resist the immense Persian army. A fierce combat ensued; great numbers of the invaders were killed. Leonidas and the little band of heroes were destroyed, but Greece was saved.

Not less brave than Leonidas was Judas Maccabeus, "the hammerer." With his forlorn hope of eight hundred men he resisted the attack of twenty thousand Syrians, who were overrunning the Holy Land. Judas took his last stand at Eleasah. His followers would fain have persuaded him to retreat "God forbid," he answered, "that I should flee away before them. If our time be come, let us die manfully for our brethren; let us not stain our honour." The battle was heavy and fierce; Judas and his men fought valiantly, and were killed to the last man, with their faces to the foe. They did not die in vain. The Jews took heart; they beat back the invaders; the Temple was rebuilt; and Judea again became the most prosperous country in the East

The Romans also knew the value of heroism and devotion on behalf of their country. But let us come to more modem times. Little countries, of comparatively small populations, have contrived to maintain and preserve their liberties in spite of enormous difficulties. It is not the size of a country, but the character of its people, that gives it sterling value. We find men constantly calling for liberty, but who do nothing to deserve it. They remain inert, lazy, and selfish. There is a so-called patriotism that has no more dignity in it than the howling of wolves.

True patriotism is of another sort. It is based on honesty, truthfulness, generosity, self-sacrifice, and genuine love of freedom.

Look, for instance, at the little Republic of Switzerland, which has been hemmed in by tyrannical governments for hundreds of years. But the people are brave and frugal, honest and self- helping. They would have no master, but governed themselves. They elected their representatives, as at Apenzell, by show of hands in the public marketplaces. They proclaimed liberty of conscience; and Switzerland, like England, has always been the refuge of the persecuted for conscience sake.

It was not without severe struggles that Switzerland conquered its independence. The leaders of these brave men have often sacrificed themselves for the good of their country. Take, for instance, the example of Arnold von Winkelried. In 1481 the Austrians invaded Switzerland, and a comparatively small number of men determined to resist them. Near the little town of Sempach the Austrians were observed advancing in a solid compact body, presenting an unbroken line of spears. The Swiss met them, but their spears were shorter, and being much fewer in number, they were compelled to give way. Observing this, Arnold von Winkelried, seeing that all the efforts of the Swiss to break the ranks of their enemies had failed, exclaimed to his countrymen, "I will open a path to freedom! Protect, dear comrades, my wife and children! "He rushed forward, and, gathering in his arms as many spears as he could grasp, he buried them in his bosom. He fell, but a gap was made, and the Swiss rushed in, and achieved an exceeding great victory. Arnold von Winkelried died, but saved his country. The little mountain republic preserved its liberty. The battle took place on the 9th of July, and to this day the people of the country assemble to celebrate their deliverance from the Austrians, through the self-sacrifice of their leader.

But Swiss women can be as brave as Swiss men. Women pass through moral and physical danger with a courage that is equal to that of the bravest. They are pre-eminent in steady endurance; and they are sometimes equal to men in a becoming valour to meet the peril which is sudden and sharp. The saying is that the brave are the sons and daughters of the brave; simply because they are brought up by the brave and ate infected by their example.

In 1622, nearly two hundred years after the battle of Sempach, the Emperor of Austria desired to make himself master of the Grisons, in ordet to extinguish the Protestant religion and banish its ministers. His army first appeared in the valley of the Pratigau. The valley is shut in by high mountains. It is rich in pasturage, and is still famous for its large cattle. The men were high up on the hills, driving and watching their herds. Only the women remained; and so soon as they heard of the approach of the Austrians, between Klosters and Landquart, they took up their husbands* arms — pikes and scythes and pitchforks — and rushed out to meet them. There are passes in Switzerland where a few well-armed men or women can beat back a thousand. With the help of stones showered down from the hills upon the enemy, the women prevailed. The Austrians were driven back. Of course the men were as brave as the women. Not long after, the castle of Castel, opposite Fideris, was stormed and taken by the peasants, armed only with sticks! On account of the gallant defence of the women, it continues to be a standing rule in the valley, that the women go first to the Communion, and the men follow.

Such are the heroic men and women whom the Swiss venerate: — Tell, the dauntless cross-bowman, and Winkelried, the spearman. Though the former is probably traditional,[26] the latter is a man of history. The house in which he lived is still pointed out at Stanz, in Unterwalden; his coat of mail is still in the Rathhaus; and a statue is erected to him in the market-place, with the sheaf of spears in his arms.

Some five centuries ago, England suffered a grievous defeat in the North, which afterwards proved to be one of her greatest blessings. Scotland was poor, consisting principally of mountains and moors. It did not contain a fourth of the present population of London,[27] The people were widely scattered. The country lay close to England, and was always open to invasion. It was not, like Ireland, protected by a wide and deep sea-moat. Besides, it was not a united nation, nor were its people of the

---

[26] There are several Tells— a Danish Tell, a Finland Tell, and a Swiss Tell There is a Tell in the East It is probable that the story of Tell is an Indian myth.

[27] The population of Scotland at the time of the Union, in 1707, was only one million.

same race. On the north and west were the Celts or Highlanders; on the south and east were the descendants of the Saxons, Anglians, and Northmen. The Highland clans warred against each other. They gave no help to the Lowlanders in their wars for freedom. Robert Bruce was nearly killed by the Macdougals in his flight through Lorne.

Wallace preceded Bruce. The Lowland country was conquered by Edward I. All its strong places were in the hands of the English. Wallace endeavoured to rouse the spirit of patriotism throughout the western counties. Though a man of great personal prowess, he was not a great warrior. He was never able to raise a sufficient number of men to fight a pitched battle. He was defeated at Falkirk Indeed, he was a man who failed He was the forlorn hope of Scotland at that time. Yet his faith in the future of his country nourished the national spirit more than even the victories of his successor, Robert Bruce. At last Wallace was betrayed, and delivered over to the English. He was taken to London, and, on the eve of St. Bartholomew, 1305, he was dragged on a sledge from the Tower to Smithfield, where he was hanged, and quartered while still living. Thus died the martyr for freedom. He did not live in vain. He inspired his countrymen with the love of liberty; and the time came when they could follow his example with success.

Robert Bruce was the descendant of a Norman. He was half an Englishman and half a Scotchman; and, by his mother's side, he was a claimant to the Scottish crown. After many daring adventures and rude perils — borne up throughout by strong persevering conscience and an ardent love of liberty — Bruce was able to get together a patriotic army, to meet the English at Bannockbum in 1314. Before the battle began, the Scottish army knelt down in prayer. Edward II. was looking on. He turned to his favourite knight, and said, "Argentine, the rebels yield! They beg for mercy!" "They do, my liege," was the reply; "but not from you." The battle ended, not only in a victory, but in a rout.

The English ambassadors at the Papal Court induced John XXII to excommunicate Robert Bruce, and to lay his kingdom under an ecclesiastical ban. The interdict was met by a heroic Parliament held at Arbroath in 1320. Eight earls and twenty-one nobles appended their names to a letter from the Parliament to the Pope, which, for the principle it asserted, was worth any document in European history. It asked the Pope to require the English king to respect the independence of Scotland, and to mind his own affairs. "So long as a hundred of us are left alive," say the signatories, "we will never in any degree be subjected to the English. It is not for glory, riches, or honours that we fight, but for liberty alone, which no good man loses but with his life."[28]

Although numerous wars followed, and although attempts were made by the stronger nation to force new forms of religion upon the weaker nation, the result was always the same. The history of Scotland has been a perpetual protest against despotism. Its lesson is, — first, the power of individualism; and latterly, that of the rights of conscience.

---

[28] Professor Veitch's Border History and Poetry p. 277.

There was another great defeat which England sustained about the same time, which, though regarded as deplorable, yet turned out to be as great a blessing as that of Bannockburn. It was at the siege of Orleans, which. Dr. Arnold says, was "one of the turning points in the history of nations."[29] The English were overrunning France. They had won many battles; they had entered Paris, and were besieging Orleans. France was in a dismal condition. The principal nobles abandoned the king (Charles VII.), and each endeavoured to set up a petty sovereignty of his own. The towns gave themselves up without making any resistance. The taxes were levied by force, and even the king had scarcely the means to live upon, still less to maintain his army. The people lost faith in both king and nobles, and longed that God might work some means of deliverance for their country.

Strange! how small a circumstance may alter the destiny of a nation. It was a woman — a country girl, who spinned and knitted at home, and looked after the cattle out of doors — who came to the help of France. Joan of Arc was born at the village of Domrémy, in Lorraine. She was simple, virtuous, and religious. Being of a nervous temperament, in her exalted state she dreamt dreams, and heard solemn words spoken to her. She was told to "go to the help of the King of France," and was assured "that she would restore his kingdom to him." Captain Baudricourt, who was informed of her wishes, thought at first that she was mad. At last he was so touched by her earnestness, that he offered to furnish her with an equipment of armed men, and to conduct her to the king. She travelled through the 150 miles of country occupied by the English; and at length reached the king and court at Chinon in safety.

The king was only too glad to have any means of help, no matter from what quarter it came. The bishops and priests thought her a witch and inspired by the devil. Nevertheless the king sent her on to Orleans, and she reached the besieged city. The English were already beginning to be distressed. They had sat down before Orleans during the winter, and their forces were fast melting away. After the death of the Earl of Salisbury many of the men-at-arms whom he had enlisted separated from the camp. The Burgundians, who were in league with the English, were recalled by their duke. Only about 2000 or 3000 English troops remained, and these were distributed amongst a dozen bastilles, between which there was no connectioa "On reading," says Michelet, "the formidable list of captains

<hr>

29 The following are Dr. Arnold's words {Life and Letters by Dean Stanley} : — "The siege of Orleans is one of the turning points in the history of nations. Had the English dominion in France been established, no man can tell what might have been the consequence to England, which would probably have become an appendage to France. So little does the prosperity of the people depend upon success in war, that two of the greatest defeats we ever had have been two of our greatest blessings — Orleans and Bannockburn. It is curious, too, that in Edward IT.'s reign, the victory over the Irish at Athunree proved our curse, as our defeat by the Scots turned out a blessing. Had the Irish remained independent, they might afterwards have been united to us, as Scotland was; and had Scotland been reduced to subjection, it would have been another curse to us like Ireland."

who threw themselves into the city with their forces, the deliverance of Orleans does not seem so miraculous after all."

Joan d'Arc headed the attack upon the English in the bastilles. They were driven out, though in storming the last (the Toumelles) the Maid was wounded. But she was not satisfied with raising the siege of Orleans. The English must be driven out of the country. The army, under her direction, followed the enemy to Patay, where they were again defeated. Then followed, the crowning of Charles VII at Rheims, as she had predicted. "The originality of La Pucelle," says Michelet, "the secret of her success, was not her courage or her visions, but her good sense. By taking Charles VII straight to Rheims, and having him crowned, she gained over the English the decision of his coronation."

She had done and finished what she had intended to do j she now desired to return home to her parents, and to her flocks and herds. But the king refused his consent He had seen how Joan had brought back success to the ranks of the French army. He therefore desired her presence among the soldiers. From this time she had not the same confidence in herself; she felt irresolute and restless, and though she continued fighting, it was without any decisive results.

The English and Burgundians, having again coalesced, laid siege to Compiegne, on the river Oise. The citizens had already declared themselves in favour of Charles VII, and La Pucelle at once threw herself into the place. On the same day she headed a sortie, and had nearly surprised the besiegers, but she was driven back to the city gates, where she was surrounded by the French (Burgundians), dragged from her horse, and made prisoner. She was given by her countrymen to the English, who handed her over to the Inquisition at Rouen to be judged The Vicar presided, and was assisted by the Bishop of Beauvais, the Bishop of Lisieux, and other French priests. Estevet, one of the Canons of Beauvais, was appointed the promoter of the prosecution.

The sovereign, Charles VII, who owed his throne to the bravery of the young enthusiast, took no steps whatever for her deliverance. The Sorbonne, the great theological tribunal, was appealed to, and decided that "this girl was wholly the devil's," and ought to be treated accordingly. The French Burgundians did not protest against the hideous punishment she was about to receive. The usual process in those days was to burn all witches and sorcerers possessed by the devil; and Joan d'Arc was accordingly condemned to be burnt alive. Her martyrdom took place at Rouen, on the site now known as the Place de la Pucelle, not far from the Quai de Havre, where a statue has been erected to her memory.

"There have been martyrs," says Michelet; "history shows us numberless ones, more or less pure, more or less glorious. Pride has; had its martyrs, so have hate and the spirit of controversy. No age has been without martyrs militant, who, no doubt, died with a good grace when they could no longer kill . . . Such fancies are irrelevant to our subject. The sainted girl is not of them; she had a sign of her own — goodness, charity, sweetness of soul. She had the sweetness of the ancient martyrs, but with a difference. The first Christians remained pure only by shunning action, by sparing themselves the struggles and trials of the world. Joan was gentle in the roughest struggle; good amongst the bad; pacific in war itself; she bore into war the Spirit of God."[30]

The French people have not forgotten Joan d'Arc. Many statues have been erected to her memory. She has been an object of veneration to generation after generation of French soldiers. When a regiment marches through Domrèmy the soldiers always halt and present arms in honour of her birthplace. It is touching to hear of the custom having survived so long, and the memory of the maiden heroine being still kept green by the country she served so faithfully.

CHAPTER VI

ENDURANCE TO THE END — SAVONAROLA

Love masters agony; the soul that seemed
Forsaken feels her present God again,
And in her Father's arms
Contented dies away.

Keble

Better a death when work is done,
Than earth's most favoured birth.

George Macdonald

Tis not the whole of life to live,
Nor all of death to die.

Hymnal

Do you ask me in general what will be the end of the conflict? I answer, Victory. But if you ask me in particular, I answer, Death.

Savonarola

LET US go back to some of the great hero-martyrs of Italy, to Arnold of Brescia, Dante, and Savonarola. Shortly after the fall of the Roman Empire, the baser influences of human nature again obtained the ascendency. The Church could not prevail against them. Indeed the Church followed them. St. Bernard of Clairvaux stigmatised the vices of the Romans in these biting words: — "Who is ignorant of their vanity and

---

[30] Michelet's Histoire dc France liv. vii ch. 4.

73

arrogance? A nation nursed in sedition, untractable, and scorning to obey unless they are too feeble to resist. Dexterous in mischief, they have never learnt the science of doing good. Adulation and calumny, perfidy and treason, are the familiar acts of their policy."

Corruption and frivolity in high places never fail to exert a pernicious influence on the condition of society. They extend to the lower classes, when all become alike profligate. Italy was abandoned to luxury and frivolity by the higher classes, while poverty, misery, and vice pervaded the lower. The churchmen were no better than the multitude. "If you wish your son to be a wicked man, make him a priest," was a common saying. Thus a once brave and vigorous people were on the verge of moral destruction.

In the twelfth century Arnold of Brescia sounded the trumpet of Italian liberty. His position in the Church was of the lowest rank. He was an impassioned and eloquent preacher. He preached purity, love, righteousness. He also preached liberty. This was the most dangerous of all his teachings. Yet the people revered him as a patriot. There were not wanting enemies to report his sayings to the Pope. Innocent II condemned his views, and the magistrates of Brescia proceeded to execute his sentence. But Arnold, forewarned, fled over the Alps into Switzerland, where he found refuge at Zurich, the first of the Swiss Cantons.

Undismayed by fear, he crossed the Alps again, proceeded to Rome, and there erected his standard. He was protected by the nobles and the people, and for ten years his eloquence thundered over the Seven Hills. He exhorted the Romans to assert the inalienable rights of men and Christians, to restore the laws and magistrature of the republic, and to confine their shepherd to the spiritual government of his flock.

His rule continued during the lives of two Popes, but on the accession of Adrian IV., the only Englishman who ever ascended the throne of St. Peter, Arnold was opposed with vigour and power. The Pope cast an interdict over the whole people, and the banishment of the reformer was the price of their absolution. Arnold was apprehended and sentenced to death. He was burnt alive in the presence of a careless and ungrateful people, and his ashes were thrown into the Tiber, lest his followers should collect and worship the relics of their master.

Italy went on in its career of frivolity, dissipation, and vice. State warred against state, and Guelphs and Ghibellines wasted the country. In the thirteenth century Dante appeared, and again sounded the note of liberty. He believed in eternal justice. In virtue of the truth and love which dwelt in his own soul, he contrasted the life of Italy with the higher and nobler tendencies of humanity. The mad Italian world trembled in the light of time; between heaven above and hell beneath. He discerned eternal justice under the wild strivings of men. His whole soul rose to the height of the great argument, and he poured forth, in unequalled song, his vindication of the ways of God to man.

During the long centuries of Italian degradation and misery his burning words were as a watch-fire and a beacon to the true and faithful of his country. He was the herald of his nation's liberty — braving persecution, exile, and death for the love of it. In his De Monarchia he advocated, like Arnold of Brescia, the separation of the spiritual from the civil power, and held that the temporal government of the Pope was a usurpation. His De Monarchia was publicly burnt at Bologna, by order of the papal legate, and the book was placed upon the Roman Index. He was always the most national of the Italian poets, the most loved, the most read. He was banished from Florence in 1301. His house was given up to plunder, and he was sentenced, in his absence, to be burnt alive. During his banishment he wrote some of his noblest works. Men thought of him, reverenced him, and loved him. It was desired that his sentence of banishment should be repealed, and that he should return to Florence.

It was an ancient custom to pardon certain criminals in Florence on the festival of St. John — the apostle who "loved much." It was communicated to Dante that he would receive such a pardon on condition of his presenting himself as a criminal. When the proposal was made to him, he exclaimed, "What! is this the glorious revocation of an unjust sentence, by which Dante Alighieri is to be recalled to his country after suffering about three lustres of exile? Is this what patriotism is worth? Is this the recompense of my continued labour and study? ... If by this way only can I return to Florence, then Florence shall never again be entered by me. And what then? Shall I not see the sun and the stars wherever I may be, and ponder the sweet truth somewhere under heaven, without first giving myself up, naked in glory, and almost in ignominy, to the Florentine people? Bread has not yet failed me. No! no! I shall not return! " Dante accordingly refused the pardon thus offered. He remained in banishment for twenty years, and died at Ravenna in 1321.

About a century later, another herald of freedom appeared — a most faithful and courageous man, who ranks among the jewels of history, Girolamo Savonarola. He was born at Ferrara, in 1452. His parents, though poor, were noble. His father waited at court, the privilege being a patrimony of the family. His mother was a woman possessed of great force of character. It was at first intended that Girolamo should be educated as a physician, but his proclivities drew him in quite another direction.

Italy was still abandoned to its passions, its corruptions, and its vices. The rich tyrannised over the poor; and the poor were miserable, helpless, and abandoned. Girolamo had early imbibed religious ideas. He devoted himself to the study of the Bible, and to the writings of St. Thomas Aquinas. He found himself at war with the world, and was shocked by the profanations that existed around him. "There is no one," he said, "not even one remaining, who desires that which is good; we must learn from children and women of low estate, for in them only yet remains any shadow of innocence. The good are oppressed, and the people of Italy are become like the Egyptians who held God's people in servitude."

At last Girolamo determined to abandon the world of vice, and give himself up entirely to religion. In his twenty-third year he packed up his little things in a bundle, left his home without taking leave of his parents, and walked to Bologna. He went straight to the convent of San Dominico, and asked to be admitted to the order as a servant. He was at once received, and prepared to enter his noviciate.

He forthwith wrote to his father, informing him of the reasons why he had left home. "The motives," he said, "by which I have been led to enter into a religious life, are these — the great misery of the world; the iniquities of men; their adulteries and robberies their pride, idolatry, and fearful blasphemies. ... I could not endure the enormous wickedness of the blinded people of Italy; and the more so, because I saw everywhere virtue despised and vice honoured. A greater sorrow I could not have in this world; and I was thus led to utter a prayer to Jesus Christ that He would take me out of this sink of infamy. I had this short prayer continually on my lips, devoutly beseeching God to cause me to know the way wherein I should walk.... Nothing more remains for me to say, than to beseech you, as a man of strong mind, to comfort my mother, and I pray that you and she will give me your blessing."

The corruption of the Church at that time had become almost intolerable. The insatiable avarice of Paul 11.; the treachery and unscrupulousness of Sixtus IV the unmentionable crimes of Alexander VI (Borgia),[31] caused universal dismay among the good men throughout Italy. "Where," said Savonarola in his cell, "are the ancient doctors; the ancient saints j the learning, the love, the purity of past days? O God, that these soaring wings, that lead only to perdition, could be broken!"

At the same time, liberty had almost disappeared. The petty princes who tyrannised over the people showed neither the energy nor the sagacity of their fathers. Their only craving was for power without control Their conduct occasionally roused the resentment of their subjects. Thus, several of them were assassinated in the open day. Duke Galeazzo was assassinated in a church at Milan. The Duke Nicolas d'Este was killed at Ferrara. The Duke Giuliano de' Medici was assassinated in the cathedral at Florence, during the elevation of the Host.

In the midst of so much demoralisation, the life of Savonarola was formed The Superior of the Dominican convent at Bologna was not long in discovering the rare qualities of his mind. Instead of doing menial work, he was promoted to instruct the novices. Obedience was his duty, and he employed himself in his new office with a willing heart He was then raised from the office of teacher of the novices to that of preacher. At the age of thirty he was sent to preach at Ferrara, his birthplace. His sermons met with no attention there. He was only one of themselves. What could they hear from him that they did not know before? He received no honour in his own country. He preached also at Brescia, at Pavia, and at Genoa, where his eloquence was more appreciated.

After remaining for about seven years in the Dominican convent at Bologna, Savonarola was at last sent to Florence. The road took him through a new country. He had never travelled so far south before. He

<hr>

[31] The pontificate of Alexander VI is certainly the blackest page in the history of modem Rome. The general demoralisation of that period, of which abundant details are found in John Burchard's Diarium as well as in Panvinius, Muratori, Fabre's continuation of Fleury's Ecclesiastical History and other writers, Catholic as well as Protestant, appears in our time almost incredible. — English Cyclopedia.

went on foot, and had time enough to survey the beautiful scenery around him. He went steadily up the hill to Lugana, looking back towards Bologna and the landscape towards the north, which he was never again to see. He passed through the wild mountains, bleak and bare, to the summit at La Futa, about three thousand feet above the sea. He went by the valley of the Seive, and crossed the spur of the Apennines which divides the valley of the Seive from that of the Arno. And there lay the magnificent Florence beneath him — the scene of his brilliant career, of his courageous life, and also of his martyrdom.

On arriving at Florence, Savonarola went at once to the convent of St. Mark, where he was admitted as a brother. At that time Lorenzo the Great was in the zenith of his power. He had got rid of his enemies by exile, imprisonment, or death. He kept the people at his feet by his fêtes, dances, and tournaments. He was alike the favourite of the nobles and of the rabble. All the profligacy of his life seems to have been forgotten because he was the patron of letters and the fine arts. Villari says that in his time "the artists, men of letters, politicians, the gentry, and the common people, were alike corrupt in mind; without virtue, public or private; guided by no moral sentiment.

Religion was used either as a tool for governing, or as a low hypocrisy. There was no faith in civil affairs, in religion, in morals, or in philosophy. Even scepticism did not exist with any degree of earnestness. A cold indifference to principle reigned throughout"[32]

Savonarola was disgusted with all this. When he first preached at St. Lorenzo, he launched out against the corruptions of the times. He smote vice with whips of steel. He denounced gambling, lying, and cheating, quoting largely from the Bible. The audience were at first surprised, then disgusted, then indignant Who was this brown-clad monk who had come across the hills to denounce the corruptions of Florence? They sneered and laughed at him. In a city of beauty, he was anything but beautiful. He .was a man of middle stature, and of dark complexion. His features were coarse and sharp; his nose was large and aquiline; his mouth was wide, with full lips; and his chin was deep and square. Even at twenty-three, his forehead was furrowed with wrinkles. Was this a man to achieve influence or position in Florence?

When another learned monk preached, crowds flocked to hear him. He knew the people, and tickled their vices. He denounced nothing — not even the loss of piety or liberty. He was a friend of Lorenzo the Magnificent When Savonarola was taunted with the success of his rival, he answered, "Elegance of language must give way before simplicity in preaching sound doctrine." He felt convinced of his divine mission. He held it to be the highest duty of his life, and his only thought was how he should be best able to fulfil that duty.

At St. Mark's he resumed the instruction of the novices, and lectured occasionally in the cloister to a select number of indulgent hearers. He was urged to lecture from the pulpit He agreed, and preached an extraordinary

---

[32] Professor Villari, History of Girolamo Savonarola and his Times.

sermon on the I St. of August 1490. He was then thirty-eight. The following year, during Lent, he preached in the Duomo. The people crowded to his sermons. He roused in the excited multitude the fervour of his own feelings. He was no longer the insignificant man he had appeared at St. Lorenzo. He fulminated with all his might against the vices of the slumbering people; and endeavoured to rouse them from their lethargy. They hung upon his lips, and their enthusiasm for him increased from day to day.

All this caused the greatest displeasure to Lorenzo de Medici. He sent five of the principal citizens of Florence to represent to Savonarola the dangers that he was incurring, not only to himself but to his convent His reply was, "I am quite aware that you have not come here of your own accord, but have been sent by Lorenzo. Tell him to prepare to repent of his sins, for the Lord spares no one, and has no fear of the princes of the earth."

In the same year he was chosen Prior of St. Mark's. He preserved his integrity and independence. Notwithstanding Lorenzo's rich presents to the convent, Savonarola judged his character severely. He knew of the injuries which he had inflicted on public morality. He regarded him as not only the enemy but the destroyer of liberty; and that he was the chief obstacle to an amelioration of the habits of the people, and to their being restored to a Christian course of living. In his sermons he continued to denounce gambling, though it might be profitable to the State; he condemned the luxuries and extravagances of the rich, as demoralising to the people at large.

Savonarola always insisted on the necessity of good works, and consequently on human free will. "Our will," lie said, "is by its natiure essentially free; it is the personification of liberty." God is the best helper, but He loves to be helped. "Be earnest in prayer," said Savonarola; "but do not neglect human means. You must help yourself in all manner of ways, and then the Lord will be with you. Take courage, my brethren, and above all things, be united." And again he says, "By veracity we understand a certain habit by which a man, both in his actions and in his words, shows himself to be that which he really is, neither more nor less. This, although not a legal, is a moral duty; for it is a debt which every man, in honesty, owes to his neighbour, and the manifestation of truth is an essential part of justice."

At length Lorenzo the Magnificent retired from Florence to his Villa Corregi,[33] to die. He went in the early part of the month of April, when nature was at its freshest and brightest, — when the voice of the nightingale never is mute. The villa lies in the wide valley of the Arno, about three miles to the north-east of Florence. You see from its windows the Duomo and Campanile, and the spires of many churches, rising above the trees. Towards the north are the heights of Fiesole, and in the distance the soft outline of the Tuscan hills.

But all this beauty could not shut out disease and pain. Lorenzo was

---

[33] The villa has passed into private hands, and is now called MediaSloane.

on his deathbed. All remedies had been tried. Draughts of distilled precious stones produced no effect Nothing relieved the great man. Then he turned his thoughts to religion. His sins appeared to grow in magnitude as he approached death. The last offices of religion afforded him no relief. He had lost all faith in man; for every one had been obedient to his wishes. He did not believe in the sincerity of his own confessor. "No one ever ventured to utter a resolute no to me." Then he thought of Savonarola. That man had never yielded to his threats and flatteries. "I know no honest friar but him." He sent for Savonarola, to confess to him. When the friar was told of the alarming state of Lorenzo, he set out at once for Corregi.

Professor Villari thus tells the story of the last interview between Lorenzo and Savonarola. Pico della Mirandola had no sooner retired than Savonarola entered, and approached respectfully the bed of the dying Lorenzo, who said that there were three sins he wished to confess to him, and for which he asked absolution: the sacking of Volterra; the money taken from the Monte delle Fanciulla, which had caused so many deaths; and the blood shed after the conspiracy of the Pazzl While saying this he again became agitated, and Savonarola tried to calm him by frequently repeating, "God is good, God is merciful."

Lorenzo had scarcely left off speaking, when Savonarola said, "Three things are required of you."' "And what are they, father?" Savonarola's countenance became grave, and raising the fingers of his right hand, he thus began: "First, it is necessary that you should have a full and lively faith in the mercy of God." "That I have most fully! " "Secondly, it is necessary to restore that which you unjustly took away, or enjoin your sons to restore it for you." This requirement appeared to cause him surprise and grief; however, with an effort, he gave his consent by a nod of his head.

Savonarola then rose up, and while the dying prince shrank with terror in his bed, the confessor seemed to rise above himself when saying, "Lastly, you must restore liberty to the people of Florence." His countenance was solemn, his voice almost terrible; his eyes, as if to read the answer, remained fixed on those of Lorenzo, who, collecting all the strength that nature had left him, turned his back scornfully, without uttering a word. And thus Savonarola left him without giving him absolution; and Lorenzo, lacerated by remorse, soon after breathed his last

His son Piero succeeded him. He was in all respects worse than his father. He cared nothing for letters or the arts, but gave himself up to frivolity and dissipation. Savonarola went on preaching as before. His intensity increased, and his name spread far and wide. Through the influence of Piero, he was sent away from Florence for a time, and preached at Pisa, Genoa, and other towns. He again returned to Florence, He enforced the law of poverty in his convent, and desired that the monks should live by their own labour. He gave special encouragement to the study of the Holy Scriptures, and desired that he and his brethren should go forth to teach among the heathen. When troubles came upon him, he thought of leaving Florence, and giving himself up to missionary work.

But he remained. The people would not let him go. He continued to preach to crowded congregations in the Duomo. He was not only severe against the vices of the time, but against the prelates who neglected their duty. "You see them," he said, "wearing golden mitres, set with precious stones, on their heads, and with silver croziers, standing before the altar with copes of brocade, slowly intoning vespers and other masses with much ceremony, with an organ and singers, until you become much stupefied.... The first prelates certainly had not so many golden mitres, nor so many chalices; and they parted with those they had to relieve the necessities of the poor. Our prelates get their chalices by taking from the poor that which is their support. In the primitive Church there were wooden chalices and golden prelates; but now the Church has golden chalices and wooden prelates! "

Piero de' Medici, with a view to obtaining the sovereign power at Florence, had entered into an intimate alliance with the Pope and the King of Naples. But he suddenly deserted them when he knew that the French had invaded Italy. Ludovico, the Moor, usurped the government of Milan, and invited the French king, Charles VIII, to invade Italy and undertake the conquest of the Kingdom of Naples. A French army accordingly passed the frontier, and marched southward. They sacked the towns and cities which they took, and swept every obstacle away. Then it occurred to Piero to go to Charles VIII and make peace with him. Piero placed in his hands the important fortress of Sarzana, as well as the town of Pietra Santa and the cities of Pisa and Leghorn.

The people of Florence were exasperated at the meanness of their ruler. They refused him admittance to the palace of the magistrates. His personal safety was endangered, and he hastily withdrew to Venice. Florence was on the verge of a general revolt.

The followers of the Medici wanted a king; the mass of the people wanted a republic. The two parties were at daggers-drawn. Savonarola was the only man who had influence with the people. He brought them together in the Duomo, and there endeavoiured to pacify them. At the same time he called them to repentance, to unity, to charity, to faith. Thus the revolt that seemed impending was quelled.

An embassy of the principal citizens of Florence was chosen to wait upon the French king; of these, Savonarola was one. The ambassadors went in carriages; Savonarola went on foot — his usual method of travelling. The ambassadors had an interview with the king, and failed in their endeavours. On their way to Florence they met Savonarola on foot. He went alone to the French camp, and saw the king. He requested, almost demanded, that he should pay respect to the city of Florence, to its women, its citizens, and its liberty. It was in vain. The French army shortly after entered Florence without opposition. The troops proceeded to plunder the palace of the Medici, and to carry away the most precious specimens of art In this they were joined by the Florentines themselves, who openly carried off or purloined whatever they considered rare or valuable. Thus, in a single day, the rich accumulations of half a century were destroyed or dispersed.

When the French army marched southward, Florence was left without a ruler. The partisans of the Medici had disappeared as if by magic. The direction of the will of the people was left to Savonarola. With respect to the future government, he proposed to the council which he summoned, that the Venetian form should be introduced. That, he said, was the only one that had survived the general ruin, and had increased in firmness, power, and honour. A long discussion ensued upon the subject, until the government was temporarily settled. Thus, in a single year, the freedom of Florence was established.

Savonarola continued to preach. He urged the reform of the State, the reform of the Church, the reform of manners. He enforced upon the people the uses of freedom. "True liberty," he said, "that which alone is liberty, consists in a determination to lead a good life. What sort of liberty can that be which subjects us to be tyrannised over by our passions? Well, then, to come to the purpose of this dis-course, do you, Florentines, wish for liberty? Do you, citizens, wish to be free? Then, above all things, love God, love your neighbour, love one another, love the common weal. When you have this love and this unison among you, then you will have true liberty."

Among the things of practical value which the republic introduced, were, the reduction of taxation the improvement of justice; the abolition of usury by the institution of a Monte de Pieta. The Jewish money-lenders had been charging 32 for interest on small sums lent to working people. On the other hand, the Monte de Pieta was established as a public institution for giving on the most merciful terms temporary loans to the poor. It was to Savonarola's sole efforts that this institution was established. The republic also brought back the descendants of the banished Dante, who had by this time been reduced to the extremest poverty.

In the meantime, the appearance of the city had been entirely changed. The women gave up their rich ornaments and dressed with simplicity. Young men became modest and religious. During the hours of midday rest the tradesmen were seen in their shops studying the Bible, or reading some work of the Friar. The churches were well filled, and alms to the deserving were freely given. But the most wonderful thing of all was to find merchants and bankers refunding, from scruples of conscience, sums of money, amounting sometimes to thousands of florins, which they had unrighteously acquired. All this was accomplished through the personal influence of a single man.

After the Lent service of 1495 Savonarola was completely exhausted. He had lived on low fare. He kept his fasts faithfully. His bed was harder than any other; his cell was more poorly furnished; he abjured all comfort. If he was severe with others, he was still more so with himself. He became emaciated to an extraordinary degree; his strength was visibly exhausted; and his weakness was aggravated by an inward complaint. "Such, however," says Villari, "was the indomitable courage of the Friar, that the political struggles had scarcely ceased, ere he undertook a series of sermons on Job. His physical weakness increased his moral exaltation. His eyes darted fire; his whole frame shook. His delivery was more than usually impassioned, but at the same time more tender."

Burlamacchi says, "Savonarola had preached a very terrible and alarming sermon, which being written down verbally, was sent to the Pope.

81

The latter, being indignant, called a bishop of the same order, a very learned man, and said to him, "Answer this sermon, for I wish you to maintain the contest against this Friar." The Bishop answered, "Holy Father, I will do so, but I must have the means of answering him in order to overcome him." "What means?" said the Pope. "The Friar says that we ought not to have concubines, or to encourage simony. And what he says is true." The Pope replied, "What has he to do with it?" The Bishop answered, "Reward him, and make a friend of him; honour him with the red hat, that he may give up prophesying, and retract what he has said."

In 1495 Savonarola was threatened with assassination by the Arrabbiati, a Florentine club of conspirators in favour of the Medicis. They thought that by killing the Friar they would put an end to the republic. On this, a volunteer body of armed men surrounded him, and accompanied him from the Duomo to the convent of St. Mark's. The Pope, Borgia Alexander VI, sent a brief from Rome, suspending his preaching, and at the same time denouncing him as a disseminator of false doctrine. While he was silenced, the Arrabbiati prepared to revive the unbridled passions and the obscene amusements of the Carnival Savonarola endeavoured to stop this by the "Children's Reform." The children of his adherents formed themselves into a procession, and went through the streets of Florence, collecting money to be given to the friars of St. Martin's for the relief of the poor.

The Pope at length withdrew his order, and permitted Savonarola to preach as before. He offered to make Savonarola a cardinal, provided he would in future change the style of language used in his sermons. The offer was made to him, and refused. In his sermon, preached in the Duomo on the following morning, he said, ' I want no red hat nor mitre, great or small. I wish for nothing more than that which has been given to the saints — death. If I wished for dignity, you know full well that I should not now be wearing a tattered cloak. I am quite prepared to lay down my life for my duty."

Great troubles came upon the Republic. During the siege of Pisa the Florentines were reduced to great misery. The poor people were seen in the streets or by the roadsides dying of hunger. Then the plague broke out, and committed great ravages. It entered the convent of St. Mark's. Savonarola sent the timid and sick to the country, while he remained with his faithful followers. In the city about a hundred died daily. Savonarola was always ready to go to the plague-stricken houses, and perform the last holy offices for the dying. After about a month the plague abated, and conspiracies against the Republic began again.

Savonarola for the most part remained in his convent He was diligently engaged in writing his "Triumph of the Cross," and correcting the proofs as they came from the printer. In that treatise he shows that Christianity was founded on reason, love, and conscience. It was a complete answer to the Pope's briefs, and was adopted as a textbook in schools and by the congregation de propaganda fide. Notwithstanding this, the Pope passed sentence of excommunication on Savonarola in May 1497. Every one was prohibited from rendering him any assistance, or having any communication with him, as a person excommunicated and suspected of heresy. The excommunication was published with great solemnity in the cathedral in the following month. The clergy, the friars of many convents, the bishop, and the higher dignitaries, assembled there. The Pope's brief was read, after which the lights were extinguished, and all remained in silence and darkness.

Two days after, while the friars of St. Mark's were chanting their services, they were disturbed by persons outside shouting and throwing stones into the convent windows. The magistrates did not interfere, and matters became worse from day to day. Profligacy was again in the ascendant The churches were empty; the taverns were full all thoughts of patriotism and liberty were forgotten. These were the first-fruits of the excommunication of Savonarola by Borgia. Many attempts were made to have the excommunication recalled, but they all failed. The Pope threatened the city with an interdict, and with the confiscation of the property of the Florentine merchants settled at Rome. He ordered the Signory to send Savonarola to Rome. They answered that to banish the Friar from Florence would be to expose the city to the greatest perils. They again persuaded him to preach in the cathedral, and he did so. He preached his last sermon on the! 8th of March 1498.

Then followed a great change in public opinion. It went round suddenly, like a vane blown by the wind. Savonarola had worked for eight years in the city of Florence. He had warned the people to repent, to live at peace with each other, to struggle for liberty, to put aside profligacy and gambling, and worst of all — as regarded himself — he had urged them to proceed immediately, with the help of God, to a universal reform of the Church. He had been the most popular man in Florence; and now he was the most unpopular. The tide had suddenly turned. The followers of Savonarola had either disappeared, or concealed themselves, for now the whole of Florence seemed hostile to him.

The Franciscans challenged him to the ordeal of fire — one of the strange practices of the Middle Ages. Savonarola set his face against it, though his brother, Domenicho, was willing to accept it — for he had great faith in the Friar. Others were willing to join him; but Savonarola saw the utter weakness and foolishness of the proposed test, and he refused to enter the fire. The results soon followed. The convent of St. Mark's was attacked by the mob, led by the Compagnacci, who determined to set it on fire. Some of Savonarola's armed friends were there, who wished to defend the place; but he said to them, "Let me go, for this tempest has arisen on my account; let me give myself up to the enemy." The friars forbade him to deliver himself up.

The Signory then sent a body of troops to the Piazza. The mace-bearers ordered every man in the convent to lay down his arms, and declared that Savonarola was banished, and was required to quit the Florentine territory within twelve hours. The armed men in the convent proceeded to defend it, and many were killed on both sides. Savonarola continued in prayer. At last, seeing the destruction of life within and without, he called upon his brethren and friends to give up the defence and to follow him into the library, situated behind the convent

In the middle of that hall, under the simple vaults of Michelozzi, he placed the sacrament, collecting his brethren around him, and addressed them in his last and memorable words: — "My sons, in the presence of God, standing before the sacred host, and with my enemies already in the convent, I now confirm my doctrine. What I have said came to me firom God, and He is my witness in heaven that what I say is true. I little thought that the whole city could so soon have turned against me; but God's will be done! My last admonition to you is this. Let your arms be faith, patience, and prayer. I leave you with anguish and pain, to pass into the hands of my enemies. I know not whether they will take my life; but of this I am certain, that dead, I shall be able to do far more for you in heaven, than living I have ever had power to do on earth. Be comforted, embrace the cross, and by that you will find the haven of salvation."

The troops burst in, and Savonarola was taken prisoner. His hands were tied behind him, and he was led a prisoner to the Signory. The people were ferocious, and were with difficulty held from slaying him. Two of the brethren insisted on accompanying him. Arrived at the Signory, the three friars were shut up in then: respective cells. To Savonarola was assigned that called the Alberghettino — a small room in the tower of the Palazzo — the same in which Cosmo de' Medici had for some time been imprisoned.

Savonarola was immediately put to the torture. He was taken to the upper hall in the Bargello, before the magistrates; and after being interrogated, threatened, and insulted, they bound him to the hoisting rope. In this species of torture a rope was attached to a pulley fixed at the top of a high pole. The person to be tortured had his hands tied behind his back; the end of the rope was wound round his wrists; and in this position he was drawn up, and let down suddenly by the executioner. The arms, by being drawn up backwards, were made to describe a semicircle. The muscles were thus lacerated, and all the limbs quivered with agony. When persevered in for a time, the punishment was certain to produce delirium and death.

Savonarola, from his earliest life, was of a delicate and sensitive frame; and in consequence of his habitual abstinence, his long night watchings, his almost uninterrupted preaching, and his serious inward complaint, he had become so very weak and nervous that his life may be said to have been a constant state of suffering, and that it was only preserved by the force of his determined will all that occurred to him in his last days — his dangers, the insults he had received, his grief at finding himself forsaken by the people of Florence — had not a little added to his sensibility. In this condition he was subjected to this violent and cruel torture. He was drawn up by the rope, and suddenly let down many times. His mind soon began to wander, his answers became incoherent, and at last, as if despairing of himself, he cried out, in a voice enough to melt a heart of stone, "O Lord I take, O take, my life!"

At last the torture was discontinued. He was taken back, crushed and bleeding, to his prison. One can scarcely imagine his sufferings during the night. The day dawned, and towards midday his so-called trial was begun. His judges were all his enemies. He was interrogated, and he answered. A Florentine attorney, Ceccome, hearing the regrets among the Signory that they could find nothing against Savonarola, said, "Where no cause exists, we must invent one." An offer of four hundred ducats was made to him by the judges if he would make a false minute of the examinations, with alterations in the answers, so as to secure the condemnation of the Friar.

The torture proceeded from day to day, during the dark hours of Lent and the triumphant gladness of Easter. The examinations continued for a month. One day Savonarola was drawn up by the rope and let down violently on the ground fourteen times. He never failed in his courage. His body was quivering with pain, but his determination was undaunted. They applied live coals to the soles of his feet. But his soul never flinched He was again sent back to prison, where he remained a month.

The Pope's commissioners arrived on the 15th of May 1498. Savonarola was again subjected to examination for the third time. At the command of Cardinal Romolino, he was again stripped and tortured with savage cruelty. He became delirious, and made incoherent answers, which the attorney entirely altered. He made him say what the torturers wished him to say. And yet they entirely failed in their purpose. The minutes of the examination were never signed and never published.

The commissioners met on the 22d of May, and passed sentence of death on the three friars, with the assent of the Signory. The friars were at once told of the sentence. They were quite prepared for it Domenico received the announcement of his death as if it had been an invitation to a feast Savonarola was found on his knees, praying. When he heard the sentence, he still continued earnest in his prayers. Towards night he was offered his supper, but he refused it, saying that it was necessary to prepare his mind for death.

Soon after, a monk, Jacopo Niccolini, entered his cell. He was clothed in black, and his face was concealed under a black hood. He was a Battuto, the member of an association that voluntarily attends the last moments of condemned criminals. Niccolini asked Savonarola whether he could do anything that might be of service to him. "Yes," he replied; "entreat the Signory to allow me to have a short conversation with my two fellow-prisoners, to whom I wish to say a few words before dying." While Niccolini went on his mission, a Benedictine monk came to confess the prisoners, who, devoutly kneeling, fulfilled with much fervour that religious duty.

The three friars met once more. It was the first time they had seen each other after forty days of imprisonment and tortures. They had now no other thought than that of meeting death with courage. The two brethren fell on their knees at the feet of Savonarola, their superior, and devoutly received his blessing. The night was already far advanced when he returned to his cell. The benevolent Niccolini was there. As a sign of affection and gratitude, Savonarola laid himself down on the floor, and fell asleep in the monk's lap. He seemed to dream and to smile, such was the serenity of his mind. At break of day, he awoke and spoke to Niccolini. He tried to impress upon his mind the future calamities of Florence,

In the morning, the three friars met again, to receive the sacrament. Savonarola administered it with his own hands. They received it with joy and consolation. They were then summoned down to the Piazza. Three tribunals had been erected on the Ringhiera, where the Bishop of Vasona, the Pope's commissioner, and the Gonfaloniere, were placed. The scaffold extended into the square of the Palazzo Vecchio. At the end a beam was erected, firom which hung three halters and three chains. The three friars were to be put to death by the halters, and the chains were to be wound round their dead bodies, while the fire underneath consumed them.

The prisoners descended the stairs of the Palazzo. They were disrobed of their brown gowns, and left with their under tunics only. Their feet were bare and their hands were tied. They were first led before the Bishop of Vasona, who pronounced their degradation. The bishop took hold of Savonarola's arm, and said, "I separate thee from the Church militant and triumphant," when the friar corrected him, saying, 'Militant, not triumphant that is not yours to do! "They were then taken before the Pope's commissioner, who declared them to be schismatics and heretics. Lastly, they came before the Otto, who, in compliance with custom, put their sentence to the vote, which passed without a dissentient voice.

They were now ready for execution. The friars advanced with a firm step to the scaffold. A priest, named Nerotti, said to Savonarola, "In what state of mind do you endure this martyrdom?" to which he replied, "The Lord has suffered as much for me." These were the last words he spake. Friar Salvestro was executed first, then Friar Domenico; after which, Savonarola was directed to take the vacant place between them. He reached the upper part of the ladder, and looked round on the people, who had before hung upon his lips in the Duomo. What a change! The fickle mob were now screaming for his death. He submitted his neck to the rope, and was turned off by the hangman. His death was suddea. The chains were wrapped round the friars' bodies, and the fire below soon consumed them. Their ashes were carted off, and thrown over the Ponte Vecchio into the Arno. The execution took place on the 23d of May 1498, when Savonarola was only in his forty-fifth year.

Though Luther canonised him as the martyr of Protestantism, it was not because of this that he was put to death;[34] but because of his intense love of liberty. His aim was not to desert the Church, but to tighten the bonds of liberty and religion, restoring both to their true principles. It was for this that he bore his martyrdom; for this that he gave up his life for his God and for his country. When the reforms which he urged shall have advanced to the reality of facts, Christianity will reach its true and full development, and Italy may again stand at the head of a renovated civilisation.

---

[34] Indeed, Savonarola was more catholic than the Catholics themselves. One of the charges which he most frequently brought agamst the priests, was their want of belief in transubstantiation.

Florence is one of the most memorable of cities. It has been the dwelling-place of great thinkers, great poets, great artists — of Dante, Galileo, Leonardo da Vinci, Michael Angelo, Raphael,[35] Donatello, Lucca della Robbia, Machiavelli, and many more illustrious men. There are to be seen "the statue that enchants the world," the glorious works of the greatest painters in Italy, the observatory of Galileo, the birthplace of Dante, the dying-place of Lorenzo de' Medici, the home and tomb of Michael Angelo.

But perhaps the most interesting places in Florence are the Duomo, where Savonarola preached with such impassioned eloquence; the convent of St. Mark's, where he lived his life of poverty, piety, and study; and the Palazzo Signora, where he was delivered over to the hands of tyrants, and died the death of a martyr. At the convent of St. Mark's you see the little cell in which he lived, the Bible which he read and preached from in the pulpit — a little hand Bible, its margins covered with innumerable autograph notes, in a handwriting so small that it is almost impossible to read them without the aid of a microscope. All these are to be seen, together with his portrait, his manuscripts, his devotional emblems, and many other interesting memorials.

Italy has long since revoked the banishment of Dante from Florence, and she has rebuked it by erecting statues to his memory in all her great cities. Why should she not also do justice to Savonarola, the patriot and martyr, and erect a memorial of him, as an example to all time coming? The site is there — the square of the Palazzo Vecchio — where he so bravely gave up his life to the cause of religious liberty and of human freedom.

CHAPTER VII

THE SAILOR

England, bound in with the triumphant sea.
Whose rocky shore beats back the curious surge
Of watery Neptune.

Falconer

But oh! thou glorious and beautiful sea. There is health and joy and blessing in thee: Solemnly, sweetly, I hear thy voice, Bidding me weep and yet rejoice — Weep for the loved ones buried beneath, Rejoice in Him who has conquered death.

Captain Hare of the Eurydice

---

[35] Born in a dependency of Florence.

In the bow of the boat is the gift of another world. Without it, what prison would be so strong as that white and wailing sea? But the nails that fasten together the planks of the boat's bows are the rivets of the fellowship of the world. Their iron does more than draw lightning out of heaven; it leads love round the earth.

Ruskin

THE sea has nursed the most valorous of men. The dangers of a sea-going life educate men in courage; and not only in courage, but in a profound sense of duty. The life of a mariner is one of patience, activity, and watchfulness. It is full of care and responsibility. It is not like a life on shore, where a man, after his day's work is done, can go to bed and sleep without fear.

The sailor must be constantly on the watch, by night and by day. On a long voyage the pilot may sit quiet in his cabin when the winds are allayed and the waters are smooth. But he is vigilant and active when the storm rises and the sea grows tumultuous. The sails have to be reefed, or the ship has to be put about. It may be night. The sailor goes aloft to reef. He goes alone; it is at the risk of his life. He may be blown away by the fierceness of the wind; a sudden shock of the ship by the sharp stroke of the sea may shake him off; his fall is unheard in the storm and blackness of the night. But the ship goes on as before.

When the first man went to sea, in an open boat, and out of sight of land, he must have been appalled by his new conditions. Nothing about him — the sky above him, and the sea beneath him — only a plank between him and death. What a new sense of responsibility and courage that first seaman must have felt! Even to those on shore the sea is a great educator. Dr. Arnold said that nothing opens the character of an intelligent child so much as the first sight of the sea. Dr. Channing, when a boy, spent much of his time on the sea-shore at Newport. He afterwards said, "No spot on earth helped to form me more than that beach."

Some regard the sea as a great waste of waters. To one looking from a hill-top on the sea, it seems boundless. There is nothing but water, to the right and the left. In fair weather, the waves come in gently, to lick your feet upon the sand. Then it curls and curls, and comes in wildly, with its huge rolling waves, that dash into spray on the shore. At one time it is quiet and feline, at another it rages and howls like a panther. The sea remembers nothing. It crumbles the ship on the rugged rocks, and then slumbers into a dreamy haze. "There is sorrow on the sea," said Jeremiah;" it is never at rest" It drowns out humanity and time. It belongs to eternity. It mourns out its tone for ever and ever.

But the ocean has an intimate connection with the progress of humanity. How is it that England excels all other nations in her care for those at sea? It is because we are a nation of sailors; and it is because of that that we are a commercial people. From the fishermen round our coasts, who bring us our constant supply of fish, to the huge steamers that sail to America, China, India, and the Continental ports, to bring us our daily supplies of the comforts and necessaries of life, — we owe a great deal to our sailors. Perhaps we would never have been a great nation, or at all events a free and great nation, but for the sea that surrounds us.

The deep sea moat which lies between us and the Continent has rendered this country the refuge for the persecuted of all lands. Two hundred years ago, at the Revocation of the Edict of Nantes, we secured the best commercial men of France; and our present supremacy in commerce is in a great measure owing to the lessons of industry and manufacture which we learnt from the French Refugees. It is commerce that supports our navy. It is commerce that brings bread to our shores. Not only that; it is commerce that tends to civilise the world.

Sir Samuel Baker, in a lecture at Liverpool, declared that it was commerce alone with the nations of Africa which would prove the best missionary means of operation. The natives, who were men of common sense, would listen to what they knew would benefit their position. Nothing could benefit the savages so much as the introduction of commerce, which would tend to excite their energy in producing from their own soil what the soil was capable of producing; and to exchange their produce for different commodities, which were unknown at present, but when known, would become wants, and add to their requirements.[36]

It is to sailors that discovery of all the new countries belongs — from Columbus to Captain Cook. It is supposed that the Icelanders first discovered North America; but they made no settlements there. Columbus and Americanus were the first who made their discoveries known to the world. The Portuguese and the Dutch were among the greatest discoverers after Columbus. Fernando Magellan was the first to circumnavigate the world. He was only twenty years old when Columbus discovered America.

---

[36] On another occasion Sir Samuel Baker said : — " As travellers, we have a duty to perform — a duty which might be said to belong to England. It was not only that they penetrated into countries unknown, but that they returned with information which would be commercially valuable to this country. He had always noticed that, however great the trouble and pains a traveller might take, his explorations would be utterly valueless unless there was some natural product of the country he had traversed which would be commercially valuable, so that in his steps — which were the first steps — commercial enterprise would be sure to follow. They might well be proud of the part which England had taken in the last few centuries — at any rate since the reign of Elizabeth — in civilising the globe. The new world of America had been almost peopled by Englishmen, so had Australia; and it was curious to notice the enormous spread of English-speaking communities in various quarters of the universe. Those were the results more of commercial enterprise than the discoveries of travellers, and they afforded an augury of how, by degrees, countries hitherto barbarous might become civilised. The greatest travellers and discoverers were the Portuguese and the Dutch; but it was mainly, if not entirely, through commercial enterprise that the discoveries of travellers became permanently valuable to mankind; and he had returned to this country perfectly certain, after the little he had done, that if England took in hand the development of the resources of Central Africa, the day would come, and was not far distant, when countries hitherto inhabited only by savage tribes would by degrees be brought within the pale of civilisation; and that would be done simply by commerce."

His first voyage was to Africa and the Indies. His next was to South America. He voyaged along the coasts of Guinea, Brazil, and arrived in the bay of Rio de Janeiro. He went south and discovered the Straits of Magellan, from which he went into the Pacific

The Dutch were also great adventurers in discovery. They were the first, under Barentz, to encounter the dangers of the North Cape, when endeavouring to find a way to Cathay. Their only result was to discover the island of Nova Zembla. The Dutch navigators went south, and discovered Australia (New Holland), Van Diemen's Land, and the islands of the Malaysian Sea.

The discovery by Vasco de Gama of the route to India by the Cape of Good Hope, proved a great epoch in commercial history. It showed the nations of the west the sea-road to the remote East. The discovery is also claimed by the Dutch. They say that the brothers Houtman were the first to reach India by the Cape, and that there they laid the foundations of that great monopoly, the Dutch India Company, by which the little republic of Holland derived so much material power in ships, colonies, and commerce.

The English were not as yet a commercial people. Trade had travelled westward, but it had not reached England. This country produced only raw material. Even the English wool was sent abroad to Belgium, to be spun and woven into cloth. There were plenty of sailors in England, but they had no employment in navigating ships, because there was no commerce. They were, however, very pugnacious. When there was no foreign war on foot, they went out to sea to fight each other. The neighbouring seaports of Lowestoft and Yarmouth were often at war. They did not mind a little pirating at times. They ventured out to sea and took possession of the ships passing their ports.

It was not until the time of Elizabeth that England produced a race of great seamen. Everyone knows the history of Drake, Raleigh, Hawkins, and the early sea heroes. They sailed, as it were, blindfold, in their cockle-shells of ships, into unknown seas, — there to grope for the new countries which were at a future time to be the homes of their descendants. Spain and England were at war, and the English had many a hot fight with their enemies by sea and land A gallant host of seamen was thus formed and disciplined, of which England had every need, when Spain, the most powerful of European nations, bore down upon her with her Invincible Armada. That was one of the greatest struggles for country, religion, honour, and independence, which has occurred in history.

Sir Francis Drake is one of the sea-heroes who stands out most prominently in the annals of the time. Mr. Motley says of him that he was one of the great types of the sixteenth century. Drake was a thorough seaman. He was originally of humble condition. He was bound apprentice on board a small lugger, where he learnt the art of seamanship. When the skipper died, he bequeathed the lugger to his apprentice. After a period of coasting on the narrow seas, he risked his hard-earned savings in a voyage with Admiral Hawkins. He was captured by the Spaniards, and narrowly escaped with his life. His future expeditions against the Spaniards were eminently successful.

The King of Spain placed an embargo upon all English vessels, persons, and property in the ports of Spain. Drake went out to sea with six armed ships, and captured San Domingo, Carthagena, and St. Augustine. Philip II was now preparing the greatest armament that the combined navies of Spain and Portugal, of Naples and Sicily, of Genoa and Venice, could waft across the seas to crush the arch-heretic of England. Rome blessed the undertaking. Prophecies had been heard in divers languages that the year 1588 should be "the most fatal and ominous unto all estates;" and it was now discovered that England was to be the object of this great maritime enterprise. Yet England did not quail. The whole community became of one heart and mind. It knit together men of all parties — Protestants and Catholics alike. Shakespeare was alive at the time; he thus wrote of the daring attempt upon English liberty: —

> "Come the three comers of the world in arms,
> And we shall shock them: nought shall make us rue,
> If England to herself do rest but true."

Drake determined to deal a blow at the heart of the Spanish project He sailed from Plymouth with four Queen's ships and twenty-four furnished by the merchants of London. At the beginning of April 158 the English fleet entered the harbour of Cadiz and fell upon the Spanish ships destined for the invasion of England. Some of them were of the largest size then known. One was of 1500 tons, another of 1200, and several others of 1000 and 800 tons. Drake destroyed 10,000 tons of shipping with their contents. For two nights and a day he continued his work — scuttling, rifling, unloading, and burning the Spanish warships. Before he left, a hundred and fifty ships were burning and throwing a bright blaze upon the walls and forts of Cadiz.

On his return voyage to England, Drake captured and destroyed a hundred more vessels, appropriating part of the cargoes and taking the crews prisoners. He also captured a large Spanish carrack laden with a cargo of extraordinary value. This he also took with him to England. He confessed that he had done but little, and he gave the Government warning as to the enormous power and vast preparations of Spain. "There would," he said, "be forty thousand men under weigh ere long, well equipped and provisioned" and England could not be too energetic in its measures of resistance.

Everything was done by Philip to make his Armada invincible. He had spent nearly fifty thousand ducats on the fleet. The Pope lent him. a thousand ducats. Besides what he had spent, he had two millions of ducats in reserve. The Armada consisted of one hundred and thirty-six ships. They were by far the largest that had up to that time been constructed. They contained thirty thousand Spanish infantry and sailors, two thousand galley slaves for the purpose of rowing the ships when the wind failed, and two hundred and ninety monks, priests, and familiars of the Inquisition. Besides this large army, thirty thousand troops were in the Spanish Netherlands ready to embark, on a given signal, in aid of the troops of the

Armada. Such was the force which the English sailors had to combat Before the Armada sailed, the Pope, Sixtus V, fulminated his bull. He denounced Elizabeth as an illegitimate and usurper, and solemnly conferred her kingdom on Philip, with the title of Defender of the Christian faith, "to have and to hold as tributary and feudatory to Rome." Everything was now prepared for the subjugation of England, and the Invincible Armada set sail.

The first ships were sighted off the Lizard on the 29th of July 1588. They had long been looked for. The beaconfires blazed forth from the Lizard to Falmouth, Dodman Point, Gribbin Head, and Rame Head. When the news arrived at Plymouth that the enemy were in sight, Drake was playing a game of bowls with his comrades; but before the evening closed, sixty of the best English ships were warped out of Plymouth Harbour to meet the foe. They went down the English Channel. It was not until the next day that they saw the bulky Spanish ships through the drizzly haze. Another day elapsed, and then they met.

The English commanders were Drake, Hawkins, and Frobisher. They were thorough seamen, of tried endurance, skill, and valour. They had met danger in all its forms, and were now ready to endure everything for their country. Their influence was manifest on the first encounter. They obtained the weathergage, and cannonaded the enemy, escaping at will out of their range. The light English vessels, easily handled, sailed round and round the unwieldy galleons, pitching their shot into them as they passed. The Spaniards wished to engage in a general fight, but the English declined. They merely stuck to the enemy, and followed at their heels. The running fight continued along the coast, past Plymouth, from whence boats with reinforcements came out to join the English ships. When night came on the beacon fires blazed up, so that it might always be known where the battle raged. The Spaniards got into collision with each other, and one of their ships was blown up by a Fleming. One of their rear-guard vessels becoming disabled, Frobisher and Hawkins cannonaded her until night, but it was not till the following morning that she surrendered to the Revenge, commanded by Drake.

As the Armada, followed by the English fleet, went fighting along the coast of Devon and Dorset, the people on land looked on with intense anticipation. At every little port that they passed — at Dartmouth, Teignmouth, Lyme, and Weymouth — boats came out laden with men and provisions, and little ships darted out to sea, most of them merchantmen, to take part in the fray. The Armada reached the bay between Portland Bill and St. Alban's Head, when the wind shifted to the north-east, and gave the Spaniards the weathergage. The English made a tack seawards, and were soon after assualted by the Spaniards, who bore down upon them. Ship after ship was engaged, but the Spaniards were never able to close with or to board their ever-attacking, ever-flying adversaries. And so the roar of cannon ascended along the coast. One fight after another, but still nothing decisive.

The Armada passed the Isle of Wight on its way to the roads of Calais. The English, having received men and munitions from shore, following it slowly. They waited for a junction with Lord Henry Seymour and his squadron of sixteen ships, which lay between Dungeness and Folkestone. When the junction took place, the English fleet made for Calais, where the Great Spanish Armada was found drawn up in a half-moon shape, and riding at anchor. They were waiting for the thirty thousand armed veterans from the Netherlands. The greatest Spanish general, Alexander Farnese, was to lead the entire Spanish army in their triumphal march into the capital of England. But the Armada waited in vain. The combined Dutch and 2eland fleet closed all the ports of the Netherlands, so that not even a cockle-boat could escape.

Lord Howard, commander of the English fleet, called the commanders to a consultation. It was then determined to attack the Armada. It was dead at night. The sea was black, and thunder rolled in the distance. In a moment six blazing fire-ships were sent in amongst the Armada The Spaniards were seized with a panic. There was a yell throughout the fleet. Every cable was cut, and the ships began to drift. The larger ships became entangled with each other. Some were burnt by the flaming vessels. The largest and most splendid vessel of the Armada, the Capitana, was driven ashore, and .taken possession of by the French. When morning dawned, part of the Spanish fleet lay disabled, but the greater number had put to sea, and were observed making for the Netherland ports. The English lifted anchor and followed them. They came up with the Spanish fleet off Gravellines, and immediately attacked them. They broke through the vanguard, and attacked the Spanish flag- ships. They riddled them through and through, tore their sails and rigging to shreds, and forced them back upon the main body. Four of their ships ran foul of each other. The English continued the battle for six hours, always refusing the attempts of the Spaniards to lay themselves alongside. Three of the Spanish ships went down before the fight was over, and many others were drifting, helpless wrecks, towards the fatal sandbanks of Holland. Sixteen of the best Spanish ships had already been sacrificed, and from four to five thousand soldiers had been destroyed; yet not an English ship had been lost, and not more than a hundred Englishmen had been killed.

The wind was now blowing hard, and driving the ships on a lee shore, seeing which Medina Sidonia, the Captain-General of the Spanish Fleet, gave the order to retreat. The Invincible Armada then bore away towards the northwest, into the open sea. Lord Howard followed them with part of the English fleet; the remaining ships, being short of ammunition, made for the Thames. A tremendous gale set in. The wind from the south drove the Spanish galleons towards the cold, grim, hungry, northern seas. Howard pursued them as far as the Firth of Forth. It was unnecessary to go farther. The winds had his enemies in their power. The crippled ships went down one after another. They were scattered far and wide. Some were wrecked on the rock-girdled coast of Norway. They could not sail southward. The English Channel was blocked against them. They could only reach Spain round the western coasts of Scotland and Ireland. But the navigation was most dangerous. In trying to reach the Western Ocean many of the Spanish ships were wrecked on the Shetland and Orkney

Islands, or on the rocks in the dangerous tides of the Stronsa and Pentland Firths.[37]

And once into the west sea there were still the perils of the Hebrides, and the rocky islands of the west of Scotland, to be contended with. The season was now far advanced, and in storms the sea comes in from the west with tremendous power. The shores of Scotland and Ireland were found strewn with wrecks. Few of the Spaniards were left to tell the story; only the masses of driftwood found in heaps upon the beach told of the vessels destroyed This, however, is known, that thirty-eight Spanish ships, including Admiral Oquendo's great galleon, were wrecked on the Irish coast, when nearly every soul on board perished. The remainder of the Armada returned to Spain in a state of ruin. The ships were so damaged as to be rendered utterly worthless for future employment.[38]

Philip never repeated his enterprise of the Armada It was, however, necessary for him to keep up a large fleet to maintain his intercourse with his American possessions, as well as to guard his gold ships on their way home. As England and Holland continued at war with Spain, frequent sea-fights occurred between the fleets of the respective countries. The English and the Dutch looked out for the Spanish galleons, to wrest from them the gold with which Philip carried on the war against English and Dutch liberty.

Great deeds of valour were done by the sea heroes of England. Take the case of the last fight of Sir Richard Grenville, Vice-Admiral of the fleet in Queen Elizabeth's time. He was sent out to the Azores to intercept the Spanish La Plata fleet. Philip of Spain, being apprised of the adventure, despatched a powerful fleet, consisting of fifty-three ships, to frustrate the attempt, and to bring the gold ships into port. The fleets met — six English against fifty-three Spanish. The superiority of the latter was so great that five of the English ships, under Lord Howard, were compelled to give way* Sir Richard Grenville remained in the Revenge the old ship in which Sir Francis Drake had fought the Armada up the English Channel. He would not give way. He resisted the whole Spanish fleet.

He had only a hundred men with him, but they were each as brave as himself. For twelve hours the Spaniards poured their shot into the doomed ship. They boarded her fifteen times, and were repulsed with determined bravery. Sir Richard was twice wounded. He was carried below, and received another shot in the head, while the surgeon who was dressing him

---

[37] One of the wrecks is supposed to have taken place on Fair Island, a storm-beaten ledge of cliffs. Some of the crew must have been saved, for there is a tinge of Spanish blood among the islanders to this day.

[38] With respect to the Armada, it is possible that it might have succeeded, but for the gallant defence of the sailors. The fleet, then as now, is the first wall of defence. Queen Elizabeth had no standing army nor militia. She could only muster about 4000 volunteers. The Armada had been defeated, crippled, and driven to the north seas, before the Queen could meet her handful of volunteers at Tilbury. Had the English fleet not been able to prevent the soldiers of the Armada from landing, the prize of London might have been in their grasp. The safety of England, therefore, was entirely due to the seamen.

94

was killed by his side. In this helpless state he advised that the ship should be sunk rather than yield; but most of the crew opposed this, and the Revenge struck — the only ship yet taken by the Spaniards. But she was so terribly injured by the shot poured into her from all sides that she could not be kept afloat, and went down in two days.

The death of the hero was as noble as his life. "Here," he said, "I, Richard Grenville, die with a joyful and quiet mind, for that I have ended my life as a true soldier ought to do, fighting for his country, queen, religion, and honour; my soul willingly departing from the body, leaving behind the lasting fame of having behaved as every valiant soldier is in his duty bound to do." And so passed away the brave Sir Richard Grenville.

Power and commerce generally go together. When a country loses its commerce it loses its power. The one depends upon the other. The first great commercial state in modem times was that of Venice. We see the remains of it in the magnificent palaces along the Grand Canal, though the city is now in poverty. After the battle of Lepanto trade went still farther westward. Genoa then became the centre of commerce in the south, and the Hanse towns of Germany in the north Belgium, though small in extent, was one of the greatest producing countries in Europe, even while Holland had scarcely dragged itself together out of the slush of the Rhine.

But the terrorism of Alva, during the reign of Philip II, destroyed the commerce of Belgium. Spain, so long the tyrant of the New World — of Germany, of Italy, of the Netherlands — became the laughing-stock of Europe. Holland baffled her, and put her ships to flight Holland became the great emporium of commerce, while the trade of Spain steadily declined, until she became the impecunious country we now see her.

The commerce of England followed that of Holland. They were both nations of sailors, sprung from the same race. They inaugurated a new era in the history of the world. "Ships, colonies, and commerce," was their motto. They planted new lands, and spread their colonies over the world. France, Spain, Holland, and England, alike planted settlements in North America; but though the remnants of all survive, the English outnumber them all In Canada, North America, Australia, New Zealand, the Cape of Good Hope, the Isles of India, the English language is spoken; and in another century it will be the most widely spoken language throughout the world. All this arises from ships and sailors.

During the great Revolutionary war Napoleon shut all the ports of Europe against English ships. They were closed, from Naples in Italy, from Toulon in France, from Cadiz in Spain, round the coasts of Holland, Denmark, and Germany, to Danzig in the Baltic. Napoleon hated the English fleet. It followed him through the Mediterranean, and caught him at Aboukir. It destroyed his flat-bottomed boats at Bologne; it carried troops to Corunna, to Torres Vedras, to Belgium, to thwart him. Napoleon never forgave the English fleet.

Yet it made its power felt everywhere. It was led by many heroes, and most of all by Nelson. He was a man of extraordinary genius. He saw clearly and acted vigorously. He felt that it was his business and his duty to watch over the very existence of England. Men and women felt safe and tranquil while Nelson kept the sea. He was not merely an able and courageous seaman. The pure flame of patriotism burned ever in his heroic soul; and the sum of his religion might be expressed in the words of Homer

"The one best omen is to fight for fatherland."

His life was a romance. His weaknesses were as remarkable as his gifts and qualities. And yet he must remain one of the great heroic figures of the world. The very last words he spoke were these: — "I have done my duty: I praise God for it!"

Our sailors are our own men, formed by the traditions of a naval race, acting on the desire for commerce by its instincts, reacted on by commerce in its habits, and moulded into a special and peculiar type of the English people by their isolation. In all his gallery of portraits, Plutarch has nobody to show us, who makes us think of Drake, or Grenville, or Collingwood, or Nelson. Our sailors are our own peculiar men. Look at their character, as described by Lord Sandon, at Liverpool. He was addressing a number of boys training for merchant seamen. "What can be nobler," he said, "than to be a first-rate English sailor? And in what does the best type of character of the English sailor consist? I should say he is, above all things, to be true, to be brave, to be kind, to be considerate for the weak, to be determined to do his duty to his God and his country. The people who spend the happiest lives are those who think not first of themselves but of those around them, who do their duty and trust to God for the rest. That is the best receipt in life; that is the way in which the noblest English characters are formed."

The conditions laid down by the Queen for the prize given by her Majesty to the marine boys, are these: — *"Cheerful submission to superiors, self-respect and independence of character, kindness and protection to the weak, readiness to forgive offence, a desire to conciliate the differences of others, and, above all, fearless devotion to duty and unflinching truthfulness."* Such principles, if evoked and carried into action, would produce an almost perfect moral character in every condition of life.

The sailor is true to his ship. In the hour of danger, the captain is the last man to leave it. Whether it be peril by fire or storm, the captain first sees the women and children safe, then his passengers, then his men, lastly himself In such cases, courage, like virtue, is its own reward. It does not seek for applause, neither on sea nor land. "I have only done my duty," is the seaman's best praise. Danger proves the occasion for evincing the highest qualities. When many lives are at stake, honour requires every effort to save them. Although the courageous man may rate the danger at its full value, he does not dread it, but manfully faces it. He is ready to meet death and life with equal calmness.

One of the most remarkable cases of the captain of a king's ship remaining on board to the last, was that of Commander Riou. His ship, the Guardian, while in midocean, ran into an iceberg during a fog. Shipwreck appeared imminent. The pumps were worked without ceasing. Everything likely to lighten the ship was thrown overboard — guns, stores, and bombs.

After forty-eight hours of incessant working, without the hope of rescue, a cry arose for the "boats." Riou's servant asked him which boat he would go in, that he might take his place beside him. His answer was, "that he would stay with the ship, save her if he could and, if needs be, sink with her."

Before the boats left, with part of the crew, Riou wrote a letter to the Admiralty, informing them of the accident, praising the conduct of the officers and men, and taking leave of them, "as there seems no probability of my remaining many hours in this world." The boats left, and Riou remained with about half of the crew. Most of the boats were lost, but the ship survived. After eight weeks of heroic fortitude and skilful seamanship, the Guardian was kept afloat until she came into the track of the Dutch whalers, and was towed by them back into Table Bay. Captain Riou was afterwards killed while gallantly fighting his ship at the battle of Copenhagen.

Take another case — that of the captain of an ordinary merchant ship, inured to a sense of truthfulness and duty. We refer to the late Captain Knowles, whom Mr. Gladstone considers to be a "greater hero" than Napoleon, because his life was altogether untainted by selfishness. The greatest circumstance of his life was as follows: — The ship Northfleet, of which he was captain, bound from London to Hobart Town, with a number of emigrants on board, was anchored off Dungeness. It was eleven o'clock at night, and very dark. The ship's lights were burning as a warning for passing ships. In a moment the Spanish ship Murillo ran into her, and cleft a great hole in her bottom. She at once began to sink. The Spaniard backed out from amidships and steamed away, leaving over three hundred people to perish, without the slightest offer of assistance Captain Knowles ordered the pumps to be set to work, and sent up signals of distress. . There was great confusion among the passengers, and signs of distress among the women, when they saw the ship was sinking. The boats were let down, and the captain ordered that the women and children should at once be got into them. There was a rush of men towards the boats, and Knowles, with a revolver in hand, said he would shoot the first man who stood in the way. A man pushed forward. He was shot in the leg and disabled. The women and children now embarked. Two boats put away full of people. The ship was rapidly settling down, the waves were quivering about her, and then she sank. The heroic captain went down with his ship. His wife, newly married, was saved, together with eighty-five other persons.

> "He went by steady choice into the deep,
> Leaving his joyful Whole of love yet new,
> Because it was the thing he had to do:
> Thou trainest such, my country! shout and weep
> I Train such for ever, crown my faithful son."

When The London went down in the Bay of Biscay, about fourteen years ago, with two hundred and twenty persons, a great sensation was produced throughout the country. The ship was too heavily laden. The sea washed across her decks even in the mildest breeze. There was no load-line then. Mr. Plimsoll had not begun his warfare against the greedy shipowners. But the behaviour of the crew and passengers was splendid, with the exception of the Dutch portion of the crew, twenty-one in number, who refused to work. Gustavus V Brooke, the famous tragedian, was one of the most valorous men on board. He exerted his utmost strength to keep the ship afloat. He worked at the pumps night and day. . He went about the decks with bare feet, without a hat, and attired only in a red Crimean shirt and trousers. He went from one pump to another, working like death, and when last seen, about four hours before the steamer went down, he was leaning with great composure upon one of the half-doors of the companion. One of the rescued passengers who saw him, afterwards said, "He worked wonderfully; and, in fact, more bravely than any man on board that ship."

Mr. Plimsoll has told the story of how he came to espouse the cause of those friendless men, the merchant seamen. Once in stormy weather he had made a voyage from the Thames to Redcar, and had reached his destination in safety, thanks to being on board a passenger steamer submitted to Government inspection. But on the way they had passed three stranded wrecks, and had seen the masts of a sunken ship; and it turned out that the crews of three of those vessels had perished to a man. His wife was waiting for him, suffering from the terrible anxiety of the long watching and suspense, and then he bethought himself of the wives of those drowned men who might watch in vain for the husbands who would never come back to them. From that period he determined to devote himself, his time, and his money, to the exertions he has ever since been making to prevent those preventable shipwrecks which are caused by the cupidity of shipowners. Let who will step in to help him now, when seamen share in those safeguards for life which the law has provided for other classes of the community, Mr. Plimsoll must always have the credit of having not merely initiated the movement, but made it

Perhaps there is a more common bond of unity between the sailor captain and his crew, than there is between the land captain and his soldiers. The former are "in the same boat" They are more closely linked together. They know each other better. They are more devoted to each other. They are wonderfully ready to save each other's lives when the opportunity offers. As we write these lines, two striking cases come under our notice: —

While Her Majesty's ship The Invincible was steaming along, in February 1880, on her voyage from Alexandria to Aboukir Bay, the cry of "man overboard "rang through the ship. The life-buoys were let go. The engines were reversed, and the boats were let down in less time than can be described. Meanwhile, the man overboard was observed to seize hold of the leadline, which was out, and, in consequence, he was dragged under the water. He lost his hold, and floated astern, a mere lifeless mass.

The Hon. E. W. Freemantle, captain of the ship, who was on the bridge, saw that a moment's delay would be fatal to the drowning man. He sprang overboard just as he was — cap, coat, boots, and all. He was not a moment too soon for, after straining every nerve, when he reached the spot where the man had gone down, he found him already some distance under water. He dived and brought him up almost dead. Heavily-laden as the captain was, he felt much exhausted, and had some difficulty in keeping the man's head above water. Then Sub-Lieutenant Moore, and Cuningham the blacksmith's mate, jumped overboard to the assistance of both, and the boats arriving, the four men were hauled in, and all were taken safely on board. The rescued man was instantly removed to the sick-bay, where he was soon restored to consciousness; and the gallant rescuer, with a little rest, was soon all right again.

Not less brave and self-devoted was the conduct of Captain Moore and John M'Intosh, of the Annabella Clark in rescuing the burning crew of the French barque Meanie, in November 1878. The two ships were lying near each other in the river Adour, off Bayonne. The Melanie was laden with petroleum. Some of the petroleum took fire, the heat exploded the casks, and the ship was soon in a blaze. The burning petroleum ran through the scuppers into the sea, and the Melanie was soon surrounded by a broad belt of fire. Some of the crew jumped overboard, though others remained, fearing to face the double danger of fire and water.

The crew of the Annabella Clark heard the explosion, and saw the fire leaping high into the air. Notwithstanding the danger, two of the men determined to save the burning Frenchmea Captain Moore jumped into a boat, and John M'Intosh, the ship's carpenter, followed him. They went stroke for stroke through the sea of fire towards the Melanie, Their clothes were burnt; their hands and arms were burnt But they reached the ship, and considered themselves rewarded by saving the French crew and bringing them back in safety to the Annabella Clark, It was a most heroic act, exhibiting self-devotion and self-sacrifice in the highest form. It was not done for money; it was not done for glory; it was merely done for duty — doing for others as they would be done by themselves. But it seems hard that one of these men should have ruined himself for life by his noble act. John M'Intosh, the ship's carpenter, was so terribly burnt in his hands and arms that he was altogether unfitted for further work at his trade. He was carried home an invalid to Ardrossan, where he lives; and an invalid he remains to this day. It is true the captain and the ship's carpenter received the bronze medal of the first class from Her Majesty, a gold medal from the French Government, and the medal from Lloyds for saving life at sea. But a permanently disabled man cannot live upon medals. Is there no one to offer the means of subsistence to such a hero?

A case of a similar kind occurred in America; but, fortunately, the man died in his hour of victory, and did not need to appeal to the public for help. A steam vessel, running on Lake Erie, took fire. There were more than a hundred persons on board. The man at the wheel, John Maynard, stuck to his post His object was to run the ship ashore, to save the lives of the passengers. The fire spread along the vessel until it reached him. His clothes shrivelled into pieces. He was frightfully burnt, but he never left his charge. He stuck to the wheel. The ship was at last run ashore. The hundred persons were saved, but the helmsman died. He sacrificed himself while heroically saving the lives of others.

As great a victory as Waterloo may be gained by men on board a sinking or a burning ship. Who does not remember the grand behaviour of the sailors and soldiers on board the Birkenhead? Not less valiant was the conduct of the 54th Foot, on board the Sarah Sands in the Mid Atlantic The cry of "Fire "was sounded through the ship, and the men at once went to their posts. Every effort was made to reach the flames, but without avail. The most that could be done to save the vessel was to clear out the magazine in the afterhold. But while the men were at work, two barrels of gunpowder exploded, blowing away the port-quarter of the ship, and spreading the flames from the main rigging to the stem. The bulkhead, fortunately, withstood the shock, and enabled the crew to play the water with such effect on the burning mass as to prevent it spreading beyond midships. Rafts were prepared, and boats were launched with the utmost order. The women and children were placed there; while the soldiers mustered on deck with as much regularity as if on parade. They were told off' for special duties, principally for drowning the flames, which still threatened to consume the ship.

With indomitable pluck they fought the fire for two days, and beat it at last. But, by this time, the ship was half a. wreck. The wind rose, and the waves swelled, as if to engulph the brave crew and soldiers in the deep. But they stood to their posts. They passed hawsers under the ship's bottom to keep her together. They stopped up the yawning hole in the port-quarter with sails and blankets. The desperate fight for life continued without intermission, when at last the sea moderated a little, and permitted the vessel to be trimmed to the wind. After eight days' sail, under the unceasing directions of Captain Castle, the wreck reached the Mauritius without the loss of a single life.

When the tourist visits Norwich Cathedral, and asks what are the mouldering flags suspended in the chancel, the verger, with conscious pride, tells him that they are the colours of the 54th, the Sarah Sands men. Not a word is said about the military achievements of the corps, though they have been great. It is their valour at sea which is their chief honour. Let it remain so.

On another occasion, when a troop-ship was on fire, and two hundred and eighty men were doomed to perish, an unmarried officer, to whom the lot had given a right to a place in the boats, relinquished it in favour of another officer who had a wife and a family. The offer was accepted, and the single officer joined those who were in a few moments to be blown into eternity. Here was an instance of true heroism — a readiness to die for a brother-officer who was more responsible, and had more need of living for others than himself.

It is not the rough and stormy sea that is most perilous to the ship. It is the dangerous rock-bound shore. When a ship is well found, safely laden, and fully manned, she is as safe on the open sea as in a dry dock. It is only when she leaves the shore on departing, and reaches it on returning, that she runs the risk of shipwreck. Hence lighthouses are erected all round our coasts to speed the mariner on his homeward voyage. None can know the benefit of those lights save those who have neared their country's coast in a season of starless nights and wintry gale's; who have had experience of the navigator's struggle between hope deferred and the fear of unknown danger and sudden wreck. The first sight of the lights which guard the coast identified by their steady lustre, their colour, or their periodical occultation — while they mark the promontory or reef to be avoided, cheer the mariner's heart by pointing with confidence to the course which the ship is to pursue towards her destined port.

The building of a lighthouse is one of the heaviest dangers of the deep. The first lighthouses built along the south coast of England were of wood. Such were the lighthouse on the Smalls, and the first two lighthouses on the Eddystone. The Smalls is a little rock in the Bristol Channel, and was for a long time the cause of shipwrecks to vessels bound for the Avon or the Severn. The first attack on it was very bold. A gang of Cornish miners assembled at Solva on the mainland, about twenty miles from the rock. They set off for it in a cutter; their first object being to drive sockets into the stone, in which it was proposed that iron pillars should be soldered. The men landed from their cutter, and got a long iron rod worked into the rock, when the weather suddenly became stormy. The cutter had to sheer off, lest she should become wrecked. The men on the rock clung to the half-fastened rod; and a desperate struggle ensued between human fortitude and the lashing sea. They clung there all through the night into the morning, and all through the day into the night again, until the third day, when the storm abated and they were saved. They went to work again; rings and holding bars were let into the rock, to which the men could lash themselves when the sea rose. At last the wooden-legged barra-coon was erected on the Smalls. It stood there with its light as a warning to seamen for nearly a hundred years, until at length a strong granite tower was erected, which may be said, humanly speaking, to be done for ever.

Not less courage was displayed by Winstanley, Rudyerd, and Smeaton, in building the Eddystone lighthouse, far out at sea in front of Pl3rmouth Sound. The two first were destroyed. One was swept away by the tremendous storm of the 26th of November 1703; the other was destroyed by fire; for both were of wood. Then came Smeaton, who resolved that the lighthouse should be erected of stone and granite; though the Brethren of the Trinity upheld that "nothing but wood could possibly stand on the Eddystone." But Smeaton had his way, and a lighthouse of stone was eventually determined upon.

Smeaton went down to Plymouth, and went out to sea to observe the site of his proposed building. The waters were lashing with great violence over the crest of rocks, and he could not land. Three days later he succeeded in landing on the Eddystone. He could only find the iron sockets fixed by the two former builders. He made three more trials to reach the rock, but was driven back by the sea. His sixth attempt was successful, and he was able to effect a landing at low water. He then took all the accurate dimensions of the proposed lighthouse. It is not necessary to follow the engineer in the difficulties which he encountered, as these have already been told.[39] On one occasion Smeaton and his workmen nearly suffered

[39] See Lives of the Engineers vol. ii.

shipwreck. While returning to Plymouth, the wind rose higher and higher, until it blew a storm. The Neptune was steered for Fowey; and the ship had nearly got among the breakers. She was weared off, the waves breaking quite over her. In the morning the land was out of sight, and the ship was drifting down the Bay of Biscay. After being blown about at sea for four days, they at last made the Land's End, and eventually came to an anchor in Plymouth Sound.

Smeaton superintended the construction of the entire building. If there was any post of danger from which the men shrank back, he immediately stood forward and took the front place — the "post of honour "as he called it When he dislocated his thumb by falling among the rocks, he immediately determined to reduce the dislocation by himself, and giving it a violent pull, he snapped it into its place again, after which he proceeded to fix the centre stone of the building. The work proceeded steadily until its completion. Smeaton intended his work to be enduring and perpetual He stated that "in contemplating the use and benefit of such a structure as this, my ideas of what its duration and continued existence ought to be were not confined within the boundary of one Age or two, but extended themselves to look towards a possible perpetuity." Alas for human wishes! Though the Eddystone lighthouse has withstood the storms of a hundred and twenty years, it is about to be dismantled, and a new lighthouse is in course of erectioa Though it has stood as firm as a rock — yes, firmer than a rock, because it is the rock on which it is built that is being undermined by the lashings of the sea — it must necessarily give place to a new lighthouse; and all that will remain will be the mere remnant of Smeaton's building. Yet Smeaton did a great work. All the subsequent ocean lighthouses have been but modifications of that of Smeaton.

The foundation-stone of the new Eddystone Lighthouse was laid on the 19th of August 1879. ' Douglas succeeds to the honours and bravery of Smeaton. He is equally skilled, he is equally brave. He has encountered many dangers in the deep waters while laying the foundations of lighthouses. At the Bishop's Rock he was almost drowned by the mass of sea that tumbled in upon him. Like Smeaton, he never shrinks from danger. The men look upon him as their standing example. A few days before the foundation-stone of the new lighthouse at Eddystone was laid, the men continued at work even while the sea was lashing over them. When the tide rose they seemed to be washed off the face of the rock in a mass by the boiling surf. They scrambled off, wet to the skin, one over another, until all were safe on board.

The late James Walker, C.E., introduced the elder Mr. Douglas, who also was a great lighthouse builder, to the Duke of Wellington. "Here is a man," said Mr. Walker, "who has fought as many battles as your Grace, but he has never lost a single life." "I wish I could say the same," said the Duke. Indeed, bloody battles have been won, and campaigns conducted to a successful issue, with less of exposure to physical danger on the part of the commanderin-chief than is constantly encountered from day to day by the builders of lighthouses. The chief engineer always leads the way. He is the first to spring upon the rock, and the last to leave it By his own example he inspires with courage the humble workmen engaged in carrying out his plans, and who, like him, become accustomed to the special terrors of the scene.

One of the boldest undertakings of recent times was the erection of the Skerryvore Lighthouse about forty years ago. The Skerryvore Reef stands far out to sea, opposite the island of Tyree, on the west coast of Scotland. Many wrecks had occurred there, and the comminuted fragments of the slips were all that reached the shore. It was determined by the Northern Commission of Lights to erect a lighthouse on Skerryvore. Mr. Alan Stevenson received directions to commence a preliminary survey, which he was only able to complete in 1835. The work was begun three years later. It consisted in preparations for the temporary barrack. Little more than the pyramidal pedestals for this building could be finished before the workmen left the rock, and the whole was swept away next morning. During the next year the work began again. The foundation-pit of 42 feet was excavated, and in 1840 the barrack was reconstructed, and here the engineer and his party were contented to take up their quarters.

"Here," says the gallant chief, "during the first month, we suffered much from the flooding of our apartments with water. On one occasion we were fourteen days without communication with the shore and the steamer, and during the greater part of the time we saw nothing but white fields of foam as far as the eye could reach, and heard nothing but the whistling of the wind and the thunder of the waves, which was at times so loud as to make it impossible to hear any one speak. Such a scene, with the ruins of the former barrack not twenty yards from us, was calculated to inspire the most desponding anticipations; and I well remember the undefined sense of dread that flashed on my mind on being awakened one night by a heavy sea that struck the barrack, and made my cot swing inwards from the wall, and which was immediately followed by a cry of terror from the men in the apartment above me, most of whom, startled by the sound and the tremor, sprang from their berths to the floor, impressed with the idea that the whole fabric had been washed into the sea."

The storm abated, and the engineers, who were almost without food, had their stores replenished, and worked on as before. Then the heavy stones were landed and fixed in their proper places. After six years' labour the lighthouse was completed, and on the 1st of February 1844 the light was first exhibited to mariners on the western coast.

Lighthouses, however, are only a part of what is needed to help the mariner when approaching the coast in heavy storms. The sea swells and rages along the rocky coast, drowning the noise of all the parks of artillery that ever boomed forth the destruction of human beings. The lighthouse may point to the haven, but can the haven be entered? Let any one look at the Wreck Chart, published annually, and it will be found that the greatest number of wrecks occur along the east coast, along the track of the coal ships from Newcastle to London. The marks of wrecks are thickest along the north-east coast of England, especially in the neighbourhood of Tynemouth. It is not, therefore, surprising that the first lifeboat should have been invented by a native of that neighbourhood. The first person who conceived the design of an insubmergible and self-righting boat was Henry Greathead, of South Shields. Henry Lukin, of London, also fitted up an unimmergible boat for saving life at sea. The coast near Bamborough — off which the Fern Islands lie — being often the scene of shipwrecks, the Rev. Dr. Shairp, then at the castle, sent a coble to Mr. Lukin to be maide unimmergible. This was done, and the coble saved several lives in the first year of its use. Yet the lifeboat did not yet come into general use; the only one yet made was the coble at Bamborough.

In the year 1789 the Adventure of Newcastle was wrecked at the mouth of the Tyne. While the vessel lay stranded on the Herd Sand, at the entrance to the river, in the midst of tremendous breakers, her crew dropped off one by one from her rigging only 300 yards from the shore. This took place in the presence of thousands of spectators, not one of whom could venture to go to their assistance. No boat or coble of the ordinary construction could live amongst such breakers. Under the strong feeling excited by the disaster a committee was appointed, and a prize was offered for the best models of a lifeboat "calculated to brave the dangers of the sea, particularly of broken water." Two plans were selected by the committee, one by William Wouldhave, and the other by Henry Greathead. The Shields committee awarded Greathead the premium because of the form of keel of his model, but they took the hint from Wouldhave's model of making the boat more buoyant by means of cork. Now this is really the master invention of the lifeboat, and Wouldhave' was certainly entitled to a share in the prize. Wouldhave was first a painter, and afterwards clerk of St. Hilda's Church. A monument is erected to him in the burying-ground, headed by a model of his lifeboat; it is also hung on the pendant of the lamp in the chancel; and the model itself is preserved in the South Shields Free Library. On the monument it is claimed that he was the "inventor of that invaluable blessing to mankind, the lifeboat."

The lifeboat constructed by Greathead, including the cork adaptation of Wouldhave, was the means of saving nearly two hundred lives at the entrance to the Tyne. Another was ordered by the Duke of Northumberland, and endowed with an annuity for its preservation. The Duke also ordered another lifeboat for Oporto; and Mr. Dempster ordered one for St. Andrews, where it was the means of saving many lives. Before the end of 1803 Mr. Greathead had built no fewer than thirty-one lifeboats — five for Scotland, eight for foreign countries, and eighteen for England. The oldest of Greathead's lifeboats now in use was built in 1802. It is in the possession of the boatmen of Redcar — a place surrounded by dangerous rocks. Many a life it has saved, not only by the buoyancy of the boat, but by the braveness of the crew.[40]

---

[40] On seeing this fine old boat, the late Lord Stratford de Redcliffe composed some verses, which conclude as follows : —

"The voices of the rescued,
Their numbers may be read;
The tears of speechless feeling

The Lifeboat Society has now become a Royal and National Institution. Combined with the mortar apparatus of Captain Manby it saves the lives of hundreds of shipwrecked mariners year by year. The Institution has now a noble life-saving fleet of over 300 boats, manned by 25,000 brave men. During its existence it has saved more than 27,000 lives from the perils of shipwreck. Think of the happiness conferred on the wives and children of the rescued.

It would be impossible to give a detail of the valiant services rendered by the boatmen. Among the lifeboats of the National Institution, is the Van Kook, presented by the late K W. Cooke, R-A, It is so called because of his German descent. It was stationed at Deal in 1865. It has already saved 161 lives, and assisted to rescue seven vessels from destruction. While the aged artist was lying on his deathbed, the men of his lifeboat were doing their bravest work.

At one o'clock on Sunday, the 28th of December 1879, a gun from the South Sands Lightship, on the Goodwins, about seven miles from Deal, gave warning that a ship was engulphed among the breakers. It was blowing a whole gale from the south-west, and vessels, even in the comparative shelter of the Downs, were riding at both anchors. It was a wind, as some said, "to blow your teeth down your throat." As the congregations were streaming out of churches, their umbrellas were blown inside out, and they ran home as fast as they could. But the seamen were on the beach. The bell rang to man the lifeboat, and the boatmen gallantly answered to the summons. Fourteen men, with Robert Wilds, the coxswain, were the crew. With a mighty rush, they launched the lifeboat down the steep beach into the boiling surf. A prolonged cheer sent them on their perilous errand.

There were, in fact, three vessels on the Goodwin Sands. The crew of one of them took to their boats, and got into Margate, leaving their ship to be driven to pieces. Another schooner, supposed to be a Dane, disappeared, and was lost with all hands. The ship which was left was the Leda a German, carrying a cargo of petroleum from New York to Bremen. The crew of the lifeboat, on arriving at the Goodwins, saw the large ship enveloped by the breakers. It was stuck fast in the worst part of the Sands — the South Spit — where the waves, even in the mildest day, are continually tumbling. No matter! The ship must be reached. On approaching, it was found that the main and mizzen masts had been cut away, and that the men were clinging to the weather bulwarks, while sheets of solid water made a clean breach over them.

Our wives and children shed ;
The memories of mercy
In man's extremest need—
All, for the dear old lifeboat
Uniting seem to plead."

For those who would read about the gallantry of the lifeboat crews, and the number of lives they have saved yearly, see the Lifeboat Journal and The History of the Lifeboat and its Work.

The Van Kook fetched a little to the windward of the devoted ship, and dropping anchor, veered down upon her. If the cable parted, and the lifeboat struck the ship with full force, not a man could have been saved. But the lifeboat crew said, "We're bound to save them f and with all the coolness of the race, "daring all that men can do," they concentrated their energies upon getting their boat close enough to the wreck to throw their line. Though hustled and beaten by the tremendous seas that were breaking into and over them, so that the boat was full up to the thwarts, , the coxswain sang out, as he saw another wave approaching, "Look out, men" and they grasped the thwarts, and held on with both hands, breathless, for dear life. One sea hurled the boat against the ship, and stove in her fore air box; so that the safety of all made it necessary to sheer off.

Again they returned. The throw-line was at last got on board the barque, and the crew were got, by ones or twos, into the lifeboat The last man was saved, and the gallant coxswain called out, "Up foresail and cut the cable." This was done, and away went the lifeboat for home, with its goodly freight of thirty-four souls. One of the rescued crew had twice before been saved by the Van Kook, and encouraged his companions with a recital of his previous deliverances. And so at last, sodden through and through, the lifeboat landed the staggering and grateful Germans on the Deal Beach, where, despite the storm, crowds met them with wondering and grateful hearts. Edward W. Cooke lived long enough to hear the "Well done!" Seven days after, he died. But his good deed lives after him, and will serve as an example for others.

There are hundreds of similar deeds of bravery done yearly by the crews of the lifeboats surrounding our shores. When a ship, or even a fishing-coble, is seen labouring at sea, nothing will stop them. They launch their boat, and are driven back and again back by the pitiless storm. They try again, and at last, pulling their bravest, they get out to sea. Sometimes their boat is driven against the rocks; but she rights herself, and goes forward on her merciful mission. Not long ago the Redcar lifeboat went four" miles out to sea to rescue the crew of a fishing-coble. And they succeeded.

At Fraserburgh, in the same year, the lifeboat went out in a tremendous gale to rescue the crew of the schooner Augusta y which was wrecked on some rocks to the leeward of the harbour. After the crew were saved, the wreck went to pieces. The difficulty was not yet over. It was found that the utmost power of the oarsmen was insufficient to force the boat, against the gale, towards the mouth of the harbour. The anchor was let go, but did not bite. The lifeboat struck against the rocks, and the heavy seas rushed over her. The coxswain ordered the cable to be cut, trusting that the heavy sea would force so buoyant and light a boat far enough up upon the rocks to enable those on board to escape. The lifeboat, though reduced to the conditions of a wreck, carried the whole seventeen persons to hard firm rock; and from this the whole of the crews were saved.

One more touching instance of self-devotion. One stormy Sunday evening in March, as the people were coming out of church at Great Yarmouth, a signal gun was heard from a vessel on the Groby Sand. The ship had struck on the sand, and the waves were booming over her. The seamen were at once upon the beach, and prepared to launch a yawl. While they were waiting for a lull to run the boat through the surf, a young beachman fan up and jerked one of the yawl's crew from his post "No, no. Jack, not this time," he said; "you've been out three times already because I've got married. Fair's fair, — so now I'll take my spell again." The boat was launched, and was just clearing the surf, when a breaker lifted her up and flung her completely over. Three of the crew were drowned, and one of them was the newly married man who had refused to let his brother take his place. Without a moment's delay another yawl was got ready for launching; she was pushed out to sea, but it was too late. The ship on the Sand had gone to pieces, and all hands were lost.

CHAPTER VIII

THE SOLDIER

I am a man under authority, having soldiers under cometh and I say unto this man. Go, and he goeth; and to another, Come, and he cometh; and to my servant, Do this, and he doeth it.

The Centurion in St. Matthew

It is my destiny, rather it is my Duty. The highest of us is but a sentry at his post.

Whyte-Melville

The blood of man is well shed for our family, for our friends, for our God, for our country, for our kind; the rest is vanity, the rest is crime.

Burke

I came here to perform my Duty, and I neither do nor can enjoy satisfaction in anything excepting the performance of my duty to my own country.

Wellington in Portugal

THE life of a soldier is a life of duty. He must be obedient, disciplined, and always ready. When called out by the trumpet, he must come. When ordered to go forth on some perilous enterprise, he must go. There is no arguing; he must obey orders, even though it be to march into the cannon's mouth.

Obedience, submission, discipline, courage — these are among the characteristics which make a man; they are also those which make the true

107

soldier. There must be mutual trust and strict obedience, obedience to all who are over him. "Out of this fiery and uncouth material," says Ruskin, "it is only soldiers' discipline which can bring the full force or power. Men who, under other circumstances, would have shrunk into lethargy or dissipation are redeemed into noble life by a service which at once summons and directs their energies."

The soldier must be at his post, whether in victory or defeat. He must be constantly on the alert. If on guard at night, he must banish sleep. A moment's disregard might ruin the army over which he watches. The soldier must be always ready to give his life for the safety of his countrymen. To sleep at the advanced post is death.

The soldier must be prompt and active. He must always be ready. This was the motto of Lord Lawrence, "Be ready." The courage and activity of Henry IV made up for the scantiness of his resources. With 5000 men he withstood the Due de Mayenne, who was pursuing him with 25,000, and gained the battle of Argues in spite of the disparity of numbers. This extraordinary result was probably due in a great measure to the difference of personal character in the two generals. Mayenne was slow and indolent: of Henry it was said that he lost less time in bed than Mayenne lost at table; and that he wore out very little broadcloth, but a good deal of boot leather. A person was once extolling the skill and courage of Mayenne in Henr3r's presence. "You are right," said Henry; "he is a great captain, but I have always five hours' start of him." Henry got up at four in the morning, and Mayenne at about ten. This made all the difference between them.

Marshal Turenne was the soldiers' hero. He shared in all their hardships, and they entirely trusted him. In 1672, he was sent with his army into Germany, to make war upon the Elector of Brandenburg. It was the dead of winter, and the marches through the heavy roads were very trying and wearisome. Once, when the troops were wading through a heavy morass, some of the younger soldiers complained; but the older ones said, "Depend upon it, Turenne is more concerned than we are: at this moment he is thinking how to deliver us. He watches for us while we sleep. He is our father, and would not have made us go through such fatigue, unless he had some great end in view, which we cannot yet make out" These words were overheard by the Marshal, and he declared that nothing ever gave him more pleasure than the conversation. Turenne was quick to detect the merits of the commander against whom he was engaged. When in charge of the Royal forces during the wars of the Fronde, Condd was opposed to him, though he was reported to be absent when an engagement took place. But from the manner of the attack, Turenne at once knew that Condd had returned. "Yes," he said, "Conde is there!" He observed in the skilful movements of the enemy a master's hand.

After the Franco -Prussian war, a poet of Germany showered a volume of praise upon Von Moltke, in which he maintained that Hannibal and Alexander, Napoleon and Marlborough, were but poor military creatures compared with the illustrious head of the Prussian staff. Von Moltke acknowledged the volume of verses, and answered the poet's letter with much modesty. He told his panegyrist that truly great natures are best known by the test of adversity. "We have had great success," he said. "Let it be called chance, destiny, fortune, or the ways of Providence — men alone have not done it. Conquests so great are essentially the result of a state of things which we can neither create nor dominate. The excellent but unfortunate Pope Adrian had the following words engraved on his tomb — "How different is the action of even the best of men according to the times in which he lives! More than once the most capable has failed, owing to the invincible force of circumstances, while a less capable has been carried by it to triumph."

The soldier must have the courage of self-sacrifice. In the autumn of 1760 Louis XV sent an army into Germany. The Marquis de Castries despatched a force of 25,000 men towards Rheinberg. They took up a strong position at Klostercamp. On the night of the! 5th of October, a young officer, Chevalier D'Assis, was sent to reconnoitre, and advanced alone into a wood, at some little distance from his men. He suddenly found himself surrounded by a number of the enemies' soldiers. Their bayonets pricked his breast, while a voice whispered in his ear, "Make but the slightest noise, and you are a dead man I" In a moment he understood the situation. The enemy were advancing to surprise the French camp. He called out as loud as his voice could convey the words, "Here, Auvemgne! Here are the enemy! "The words decided his fate. He was at once cut down. But his death had saved the army. The surprise failed, and the enemy retreated.

It has been said that the fighting periods in all countries were those in which the arts of peace flourished most prosperously, and where literary genius shone forth with the greatest brilliancy.[41] This maybe doubted; but take the case of Greece. Socrates, Eschylus, Sophocles, and Xenophon, were all men who had fought their country's battles, and afterwards conferred honour upon her literature. It was the same in Rome, in the height of her glory. Imperial Caesar was the greatest of her warriors, and among the greatest of her writers. Even the poet Horace was a soldier in his youth, and entrusted by Brutus with the command of a legion.

It is surprising to find so large a number of illustrious men — poets, authors, and men of science — who have led a soldier's life, and fought by sea and land, at home and abroad. It may be that the obedience, drill, and discipline, which are the soul of the soldier's life, possess some potent and formative influence upon the character, and develop that power of disciplined concentration which is so essential to the formation of true genius.

Dante was present as a soldier at the battle of Campaldino, where he fought valiantly in the front line of the Guelph cavalry. It was because of this, and for other reasons, that he was afterwards banished from Florence. Peter the Hermit — the leader of the crusaders — was in early life a soldier, and served under the Count de Boulogne in his war against Flanders. He did not distinguish himself as a soldier, so he retired, married, and had several children. His wife dying, he retired to a convent, and afterwards

---

[41] Bruce, Classic and Historic Portraits, ii. 207.

became a hermit. He undertook a pilgrimage to Jerusalem, and on his return spread abroad the news of the miseries to which the pilgrims were subjected. He preached all over Europe, and led the first crusaders to the number of a hundred thousand men. Almost the whole of them were destroyed; though other crusades followed.

Among our own poets, Chaucer served as a soldier under Edward III in his invasion of France in 1379. He was made prisoner of war near the town of Retten, where he remained in captivity for some time. George Buchanan, when a young man, served as a private soldier in the Scottish army, and was present at the attack of the Castle of Wark in 1523. Ben Jonson served as a private soldier in the Low Countries. There, also, was Sir Philip Sydney, whose noble conduct while dying is one of the finest things recorded in history.[42] Algernon Sydney commanded a troop of horse in the Irish Rebellion. Davenant and Lovelace held commands under Charles I., while Withers was a major in the Parliamentary army. Bunyan was a private soldier in the service of the Commonwealth. Otway served as a comet of horse with the army in Flanders, while Farquhar held a commission in the Earl of Orrery's regiment.

Steele enlisted as a private in the Horse Guards, but his merit was soon discovered, and he was raised to the rank of ensign. He particularly distinguished himself at the siege of Namur, and afterwards at the siege of Venloo. Coleridge enlisted as a private in a dragoon regiment, but his commanding officer, instead of promoting him, helped him to his discharge. "I sometimes," said Coleridge to a friend, "compare my life with that of Steele (yet oh, how unlike!), from having myself, for a brief time, borne arms, and written 'private' after my name, or rather after another name, for being at a loss, when suddenly asked my name, I answered 'Cumberback,' and verily my habits were so little equestrian that my horse, I doubt not, was of that opinion."

Besides these, Sotheby was an officer in the 10th Dragoons, before he became the poet and translator of the Georgics of Virgil. William Cobbett rose from the ranks to become sergeant-major of foot before he became an author. F. R. Lee, R.A., served as an officer in the 56th Foot before he turned his attention to the art of landscape painting; and Sir Roderick Murchison was Captain of the Enniskilling Dragoons before he became one of the lights of modern geology.

---

[42] Sir Philip Sydney, while lying mortally wounded on the field of Zutphen, and being thirsty with excess of bleeding, called for some drink, which was presently brought him. As he was putting the bottle to his mouth, he saw a poor soldier carried along, casting his eyes up at the bottle. Sir Philip, perceiving this, took it from his head before he drank, and handed it to the poor man with these words, "Thy necessity is yet greater than mine." Sir Philip died a few days after at Arnheim. The self-sacrifice of a wounded Danish soldier was almost as great. He handed to a wounded Swede, who lay by him, his draught of beer from a wooden bottle, and asked him to drink from it. The reply was a pistol shot in the shoulder. "Now I will punish you," said the Dane; "I intended to have given you the whole bottle, now you shall only have half of it,"

In the noble age of Spanish literature, all her poets and great authors were soldiers and adventurers, who had fought at home and abroad, by sea and land. Lope de Vega was a soldier on board the Spanish Armada. He was one of the few that returned home to write his multitude of plays, and afterwards to become priest and familiar to the Inquisition. The great Cervantes was a soldier, and fought by sea and land. He distinguished himself by his bravery at the battle of Lepanto, where he received three arquebus wounds, two in the breast and one in the hand, which disabled him for life. But, as he himself afterwards said, "The lance never blunts the pen," and he lived to write his great Don Quixote.

Calderon, another Spanish soldier, became a dramatist and afterwards a priest. Mendoza de Santillana, a great Spanish soldier, was regarded as the most eloquent scholar at the court of Juan II; while Boscan, Montemayor, Garcillago, and Erscilla, were both eminent soldiers and great authors.[43]

There was a certain resemblance between Cervantes, the glory of Spain, and Camoens, the glory of Portugal. Both were soldiers and literary men. Cervantes lost his left hand in battle, and Camoens lost his right eye. Both became famous long after their bones had crumbled into dust. It is not known where Cervantes was born Madrid, Esquivias, Seville, and Lucena, contend for the honour of his birthplace. It does not matter. He died very poor, he was buried in a place which is now forgotten, and his remains are left unhonoured.

Not long ago the Portuguese celebrated the tricentenary of Camoens, their greatest poet. There were processions, bands, and flags, and general rejoicings in Lisbon. Yet 300 years before, Camoens died there of hunger, with scarcely a rag to cover him. How did this happen? Camoens was a valiant soldier and a noble poet. When employed at Ceuta with the troops, he displayed great bravery. In a naval action off Gibraltar he had the misfortune to lose an eye. But he received neither reward nor preferment. Shortly after his return to Lisbon, he embarked for India, beguiling the voyage by the composition of his Lusiad, From India he went to Macao, in China. Returning to Goa, he was wrecked at the mouth of the river Mecon. He made for the shore. In one hand he carried the manuscript of his poem, while he swam with the other. He lost all his worldly possessions. On his return to Lisbon the plague was raging. He was then very poor, as he always was. Two years after the Lusiad was published. It was received with great enthusiasm. The young king granted him a pension amounting to £, sterling. But Camoens fell into ill health, his pension was not paid, he was neglected by the court, and lived upon charity. His faithful servant was his only friend. He stole out at night to beg for bread. In 1580

---

[43] The last of the old Spanish infantry formed by Gonzalo de Cordova, were all cut off, standing fast to a man, at the battle of Rocroy, in 1643, not one man breaking his rank. The whole regiment was found lying dead in regular order. How different from the Spanish infantry during the Peninsular War I It was difficult to keep them in order. On one occasion the Duke of Wellington saw 10,000 of them run away. They ran until they were out of sight.

Camoens died in an hospital, and his body was removed to the church of Santa Anna, where it was buried.

"How miserable a thing it is," said Josefe Judis, the friar, on the fly-leaf of his Lusiad "to see so great a genius so ill rewarded! I saw him die in an hospital at Lisbon, without possessing a shroud to cover his remains, after having borne arms so victoriously in India, and having sailed 5500 leagues; a warning for those who weary themselves by studying night and day without profit, as the spider who spins his web to catch flies." This is the man whose ashes were done honour to at Lisbon on the loth of June 1880.

Ignatius Loyola was one of the soldiers of Spain, whose life has had as great an influence upon history as all the others combined. A severe wound in the leg, received at the siege of Pampeluna, confined him for a long time to his couch. The Lives of the Saints having fallen into his hands, he read it carefully, and from that time his mind awoke to a new life. He proceeded to the monastery of Monserrat, and remained there for a time. One night he went into the convent chapel to watch his arms, according to the ancient custom of chivalry, and dubbed himself the Virgin's Knight He issued forth as the founder of that militant order, the Company of Jesus, who, whatever may be said of them, renounce the habits of idle leisure and of pampered luxury.

One of the most remarkable of French soldiers was Rene Descartes. He was born in Touraine in 1596. He was educated by the Jesuits, who had a college in the neighbourhood of his father's house at La Flèche. He contracted a friendship with the eminent monk Marsenne, who determined Descartes' studies in mathematical and philosophical subjects. He did not venture to publish his first speculations. Being of noble condition, he engaged in the profession of arms. He first served as a volunteer with the French army in Holland, and then under the Duke of Bavaria. He was present at the battle of Prague in 1620, in which he conducted himself with great intrepidity. During his career as a soldier he occupied his' leisure hours in the pursuit of mathematics and philosophy. While at Breda with his regiment, he one day saw a group of people surrounding and reading a placard. It was written in Flemish, which he did not understand He therefore made inquiry as to its meaning. He found that it was a challenge to solve a difficult mathematical problem. The person who explained it to him was Beckmann, Principal of the college of Dort, who wondered that a young soldier should take such an interest in mathematics. Nevertheless, Descartes promised him a solution, which he sent to the Principal early next morning.

After the Bavarian campaign his regiment went into winter quarters at Neuberg on the Danube; and there, when only twenty-three years of age, Descartes conceived the bold idea of effecting a complete reform in modem philosophy. Leaving the army shortly after, he travelled through the greater part of Europe, visiting, in succession, Holland, France, Italy, and Switzerland. After completing his travels he resolved to devote his whole time to philosophical and mathematical inquiries, and, if possible, to renovate the whole circle of the sciences. He sold a portion of his patrimony in France — knowing the danger of living under the tyranny of the French kings — and retired to Holland. But even there his writings involved him in much controversy. The Church rose in arms against the heresy of his philosophy. He then accepted the invitation of Christina, Queen of Sweden, and retired to Stockholm to work and to die. He accomplished what he intended to do. He revolutionised philosophy, geometry, and optics.

There have been other French soldiers distinguished for their scientific career. Maupertuis carried on the study of mathematics, in which he afterwards became so distinguished, while acting as captain of dragoons. Malus, while serving with the army as an engineer, occupied his spare hours, at advanced posts, in the study of optics. Nièpce was acting as a lieutenant in the 1st French Dragoons when he began the study of chemistry, and more particularly the chemical action of light, which eventually led to the discovery of photography. M. Droz served for some years as a private soldier before entering upon the line of studies which ended in his being elected to the professorship of Moral and Political Science to the French Institute. Lamark, the naturalist, also served for many years as a soldier in the French army, and greatly distinguished himself, under Marshal Broglie, for his bravery. Having been wounded in battle, and suffering from ill-health, he was compelled to leave the army, after which he devoted himself to the study of the sciences in connection with which his name is so closely identified and so highly distinguished. His History of Invertebrate Animals is his best monument, being regarded as one of the most profound and complete works on natural history.

Of French literary men, De La Rochefoucauld, of the "Maxims," was in early life a soldier, and severely wounded both at the siege of Bordeaux and at the battle of St. Antoine, during the wars of the Fronde. Paul Louis Courier, author of the Simple Descours, served with the Republican army on the Rhine, and afterwards in Italy, as an officer of artillery. He mentions in his letters how great was his grief, when studying Greek, to find one day that his Homer had been pillaged, during his absence, by the Austrian hussars.

War has, in all ages, been accompanied by deeds of cruelty. Cities have been ravaged, countries have been made desolate, and lives innumerable have been lost, in the mad riot of conquest In the Middle Ages, chivalry was invented, to redress in some measure the horrors of war. In order to qualify a man for the duties of knighthood, he was subjected from boyhood to obedience and courtesy. He was instructed in the arts of managing a horse and lance; and in the society of ladies he was trained in gentleness, modesty, and grace. On his arrival at manhood he underwent the solemn installation of knighthood. Religion was associated with the institution. Hence the strict fast, the night vigil in the church, the baptism, the confession, and the sacrament. Thus a high standard of valour and true nobility was in many cases established.

The Chevalier Bayard has always been spoken of as the true and chivalrous knight, sans peur et sans reproche. Bayard was born in 1476, at the Chateau Bayard, in Dauphiny. He chose the profession of arms, and went through the usual training of the knight before entering the service of the king. It is unnecessary to follow his history, during which he conducted himself as a true knight His principal services were performed in Italy under Francis I; at Fornova, at Milan, at Genoa, at Padua, at Verona, at La Bastia, and at Brescia. At the siege of this latter place he led the attack. He leapt the rampart and received a terrible pike-thrust in his thigh, the spear-head remaining broken short off in his flesh. "The town is gained," he said, "but I shall never enter it I am wounded to the death." The Duke of Nemours, learning that the first fort was taken, but that Bayard was mortally wounded, felt as much grief as if he himself had received the blow. "Let us go, my men and comrades," he cried, "and avenge the death of the most accomplished knight that ever lived." Brescia was taken, and the Venetians were driven out.

While the French went about pillaging the town, Bayard was taken up from the dead and dying, and carried on a wooden gate to the nearest dwelling. The house belonged to a gentleman who had fled, leaving his wife and two young and beautiful daughters to the care of Providence. The lady herself opened the door, and received Bayard. Though supposed to be dying, he had strength enough left to order that the soldiers were not to be permitted to pillage the house, and he undertook to indemnify them for the loss of their plunder.

The lady had Bayard carried into a fair apartment, where she threw herself upon her knees before him, and said, "Noble lord, I offer you this house and all that it contains; all is yours by the laws of war. I only ask you for one favour, which is, that you will preserve the lives and honour of myself and my two daughters." Bayard, though scarcely able to speak, said, "I do not know whether I shall recover from this wound I have received, but as long as I live, neither you nor your daughters shall suffer any injury. I promise you all the respect and friendship in my power. But the most urgent need now is to procure me some help, and that quickly."

The lady, accompanied by one of the soldiers, went in search of a surgeon. As soon as he arrived, he examined the wound, which was large and deep, but happily, as he declared, not mortal. The Duke of Nemours also sent his surgeon, and what with the careful nursing and dressing of the wounds, Bayard was soon in the way of recovery. In the meantime he asked the lady where her husband was. "I don't know," she answered, weeping bitterly, "whether he is dead or alive, but I believe he has taken refuge in a convent" When they learnt the place of his retreat Bayard sent two archers and the maltre d'hôtel to bring him back to his home. He was then assured of his safety and protection, so long as the patient remained in his house.

When the surgeon assured him of his wound being healed, and that, with the help of his servant, he might easily heal the external scar by means of his ointment, Bayard rewarded the surgeon with his usual liberality, and resolved to join the army in two days. When the gentleman and lady of the house thought of the ransom they would have to give to Bayard for his protection, they collected together all that they had It consisted of 2500 golden ducats in a highly ornamented steel coffer. The lady entered Bayard's room, and threw herself on her knees. The good knight forced her to rise, and would not listen to her until she was seated near him.

"My lord," she said, "I shall thank God all my life that it pleased Him, in the midst of the sacking of our town, to lead such a generous knight to our house; and my husband and children shall always look upon you as our tutelar angel, and shall ever remember that it is to you we owe our lives and our honour.... We confess we are your prisoners; the house, with all it contains, is yours by right of conquest; but you have shown us such generosity and greatness of mind that I have come to beg you to have pity on us, and to be satisfied with the little present that I have the honour to offer you."

She presented the coffer, and showed Bayard its contents. "How much have you here?" he said. "My lord, there are only 2500 ducats; but if you are not satisfied, mention the sum you wish to have, and we will try to get it." Bayard, who thought nothing of gold or silver, immediately rejoined, "If you were to offer me 100,000 ducats, I should not value them so much as all the kindness you have shown me since I have been with you, and the company you have borne me, both yourself and your whole family."

The lady again threw herself on her knees, and, with tears in her eyes, begged him to accept her present. "I shall consider myself the most unhappy woman in the world if you refuse it." "As you wish it so much," replied Bayard, "I accept it; but I pray you send your daughters here that I may take leave of them." Bayard divided the ducats into three lots- — two of 1000 ducats each, and one of 500. When the young girls came, they threw themselves on their knees at his feet, but he made them get up and seat themselves.

"My lord," said the elder of them, "you see before you two young girls who owe their lives and honour to you. We are very sorry not to be able to show our thanks otherwise than by praying to God for you all our lives, and asking Him to reward you, both in this world and the next."

Bayard, affected almost to tears, thanked them for their help and charming society, for they had been his daily companions, and amused him by working in his room, and singing or playing to him on the lute. "You know," he said, "that soldiers are not ordinarily loaded with jewels to present to young ladies. But your mother has just compelled me to accept from her the 2500 ducats that you see there. I give you a thousand each to form part of your marriage portions; and as to the remaining 500, I intend them to be distributed amongst the poor convents which have suffered most from the pillage."

Thus the matter was settled, amidst the tears and thankfulness of the whole family; and when Bayard went away, he carried with him the joy and goodness and selfsacrifice of the true Christian knight.

About this time, Pope Julius offered to make Bayard Captain-general of the Church. To this proposal Bayard replied, that "he had but one Master- in heaven, which was God; and one master upon earth, which was the King of France, and that he would never serve any other."

After many battles and adventures, always conducted with loyalty and bravery, Bayard met his death-wound at Rebec, near Milan. Admiral Bonivet, a favourite of Francis I, had placed him in a most dangerous position — perhaps from jealousy. While on his post there, an arquebus was fired upon him by the Spaniards. The stone struck Bayard across the loins, and fractured his spine. When he felt the blow, he cried, "O God, I am slain." Then he kissed the cross hilt of his sword, using it as a crucifix.

His comrades wished to withdraw him from the fray. "No," he said; "I do not wish, in my last moments, to turn my back on the enemy for the first time in my life." He ordered himself to be carried under a tree. He had still strength left in him to call out "Charge I" "Let me die," he said, "with my face to the enemy." His followers were bathed in tears at his side. "It is God's will to take me to Himself. He has kept me in this world long enough, and showed me more goodness and favour than I deserved. ... I beg you all to leave me, for fear that you should be taken prisoners; and that would be another grief to me. I am dying; you cannot relieve me in any way."

Then the Spaniards approached to take him prisoner. The Marquis of Pescara said, "Would to God, Lord Bayard, that I might have given all the blood I could lose without dying, to have taken you prisoner in good health. Since I have held arms, I have never known your like." The marquis did the dying hero every courtesy and homage. But when the Constable of Bourbon advanced — the constable who had deserted his king and country to take service under the Spanish emperor — and said, "Ah! Bayard, how much I pity you!" — Bayard raised himself from his couch, and replied in a steady voice, "My lord, I thank you. I don't pity myself I die like an honest man. I die serving my king. You are the man to be pitied; for bearing arms against your prince, your country, and your oath." Shortly after, he expired

It was only after Bayard's death that Francis I. discovered the value of the knight he had lost Francis had entnisted the conduct of his army to his favourites, rather than to honest and noble men. "We have lost," said the king, too late, "a great man, whose name alone made his armies feared and honoured. Truly, he deserved more benefits and higher charges than those he had." After the battle of Pavia, in which Francis I. "lost all, save honour," he felt his loss much more severely. "If," said he, "the Knight Bayard, who was valiant and experienced, had been alive and near me, his presence would have been worth a hundred captains. Ah Knight Bayard! how I miss you. I should not be here if you were alive! " But the king's regrets were too late. Bayard was dead, and he himself a captive!

Bayard was manly, noble, and pure. He was spotless and fearless. He was just, generous, merciful, and truthful His courage always rose with the difficulties to be surmounted. He despised rich men, unless they were also good. He distributed all the money he received. He never refused to assist his neighbour, either by service or by money; and this he always did secretly and kindly. It was said of him that he endowed and married more than a hundred orphan girls, gentle and simple. Widows were always certain to obtain his help and consolation. He was most kind to those who served under him. He would remount one man at arms, give his clothes to another, and pay the debts of a third. He never left a lodging in a conquered country without paying for all that his men had taken. He was a sworn enemy to flatterers, and detested slander. His virtues appeared in childhood, and they were developed as he grew older. He was crowned with a renown which the remotest posterity will respect and admire.[44]

War in defence of one's country has always been regarded as honourable. War for conquest is for the most part regarded as dishonourable. Yet it is often defended, under the guise of spreading civilisation! In such cases, the vulture is the chief conqueror. Patriotism is a principle fraught with high impulses and noble thoughts. It springs from a disinterested love of country. Who does not sympathise with Arnold Von Winkelreid at Sempach, with Bruce at Bannockbum, and with Hofer at Innsbruck? Their deeds were noble; the very thought of their example has contributed to elevate the minds of their countrymen. They left behind them an idea of duty which can never be forgotten.

Nor is patriotism in any way incompatible with the exercise of a world-wide philanthropy. He whose heart is entwined by the ties of home and fatherland, is more susceptible of pure emotion, of warm sympathy, and of strenuous effort, than the man whose feelings centre in himself, and wastes his time in pleasure, frivolity, and indifference.

Every man should grasp the idea, that he is but a link in the chain of creation, and that, notwithstanding his love of country, he has the world open to him for the exercise of his deeds of devotion and charity.

Patriotism, nobility, and soldiership culminate in the life of Washington, the leader and deliverer of his country. He was one of the greatest men of the eighteenth century — not so much by his genius, as by his purity and trustworthiness. His English descent was a goodly heritage. He came from an Anglian stock settled in the county of Durham, from thence his ancestors emigrated to America, and settled in Virginia about the year 1657.

The character of George Washington was such, that at an early age he was appointed to positions of great trust and confidence. At the age of nineteen he was appointed one of the adjutants-general of Virginia, with the rank of major — nor did he ever deceive those who put trust in him. He was ever prompt, obedient, and dutiful. At the age of twenty-three he was appointed colonel, and commander-in-chief of all the forces raised in Virginia, for cooperation with the English troops in the defence of the Western Territory against the French. He was trained not only in success, but in failure, which evoked his indomitable spirit

The life of Washington has been so often written, that it is unnecessary to refer to it further than to point out the thorough conscientiousness, the self-sacrificing spirit, the purity of motive, with which he entered upon and carried out to completion the liberation and independence of his country. No man could be more pure, no man could be more self-denying. In victory he was self-controlled; in defeat he was

---

[44] It may be mentioned that the sword of Bayard is in the possession of Sir John P. Boileau, Bart. The shield given by the knight to Henry VIII., at the Field of the Cloth of Gold, is in the Guards' Chamber at Windsor Castle.

unshaken. Throughout, he was magnanimous and pure. In General Washington it is difficult to know which to admire the most — the nobility of his character, the ardour of his patriotism, or the purity of his conduct.

Towards the close of his address to the Governors of the several States, on resigning his position of Commander in-chief, he said; "I make it my constant prayer, that God would have you and the State over which you preside in His holy protection; that He would incline the hearts of the citizens to cultivate a spirit of subordination and obedience to government; to entertain a brotherly affection and love for one another, for their fellow-citizens of the United States at large, and particularly for their brethren who have served in the field; and finally, that He would most graciously be pleased to dispose us all to do justice, to love mercy, and to demean ourselves with that charity, humility, and pacific temper of mind, which were the characteristics of the Divine Author of our blessed religion; without a humble imitation of whose example in these things, we can never hope to be a happy nation." How simple, truthful, and beautiful are the words of Washington I

In speaking of the soldier's life, it would be impossible to conclude without referring to the Duke of Wellington. He was the Bayard of England. His first and his last word was Duty. It was the leading principle of his life. In public and in private, he was truth itself. As a public man, he had but one object in view, to benefit to the utmost of his ability and skill the service of his country. The desire of honour and power seems never to have moved him. He had no personal ambition. He was simply content to do his duty.

His first business was to understand his work as regimental officer, and he had not long assumed the command of a battalion, before it became the best disciplined in the service. Whatever he was commanded to do, he did energetically and punctually. He regarded time as a period in which something was to be done, and done seriously and actively. Another point in which he excelled was obedience. On his return from India, where he had commanded large armies, and administered the affairs of provinces equal in extent to many European kingdoms, he was appointed to the command of a brigade of infantry in Sussex. Not a word of complaint or murmur escaped him; and when taunted good-humouredly with the change of his condition, he said, "I have eaten the king's salt, and whatever he desires me to do, that becomes my duty."

The government of the empire was for him the king's government The throne was the fountain, not of honour only, but of all the rights and privileges which the people enjoyed. Yet the throne was as much hemmed in by law, and even by custom, as the humblest of the lieges. Like the best of the Cavaliers in the time of the first Charles, it was for the crown, as the greatest institution in the country, that he was prepared to risk everything.

Of his courage it is unnecessary to speak. In these days of artillery and infantry it is unnecessary for a General to expose himself to danger. He has to lead, not to fight — as Gough did, sword in hand, among the common soldiers at Chillianwalla. Nevertheless, as often as his presence on a point of danger, or at the head of a column of attack was necessary, he exposed himself gallantly. At the battle of Assaye he had two horses killed under him. On the Douro he was surrounded by a body of French horse, and made his way through them, sword in hand. At Salamanca he received a contusion on the thigh, and a ball through his hat "I found myself near him," says Napier, "on the evening of Salamanca, when the blaze of artillery and musketry flashing up as far as the eye could reach, made apparent all that he had gained. He was alone, the light of victory shone upon his forehead, his glance was quick and penetrating, but his voice was calm and even sweet"

The Duke's patience was extraordinary. When hemmed in by the army of Messina at Torres Vedras, in 1810, his own officers almost revolted against him. They were constantly claiming leave of absence, for the purpose of returning to England. "At this moment," he said, "we have seven general officers gone or going home; and excepting myself and General Campbell, there is not one in the country who came out with the army. The consequence of the absence of some of them has been, that, in the late operations, I have been obliged to be General of cavalry and of the advanced guard, and the leader of two or three columns, sometimes in the same day."

At home, the press took up the case against the Duke, and denounced him. "He did not venture to risk a battle I" Those wonderful men, the Lord Mayor and Common Council of the City of London, addressed the king, calling for an inquiry into the Duke's conduct. The House of Commons murmured. The Ministry wavered. Nevertheless, Wellington held on to his lines at Torres Vedras. He had only his English troops to support him, for the Portuguese did little or nothing. With regard to the charges made in the English press, he said, "I hope that the opinions of the people in Great Britain are not influenced by paragraphs in newspapers, and that those paragraphs do not convey the public opinion or sentiment on that subject. Therefore I (who have more reason than any other man to complain of libels of this description) never take the smallest notice of them, and have never authorised any contradiction to be given, or any statement to be made in answer to the innumerable falsehoods and the heaps of false reasoning which have been published respecting me and the orders which I have directed." As to the threat of the worshipful Lord Mayor and Common Council, he merely said, "They may do what they please; I shall not give up the game here, so long as it can be played."

The French had been baffled by the British troops behind the lines of Torres Vedras; and at length they began to retreat. The Duke followed them. They destroyed a great portion of their guns and ammunition, in order that their retreat might be less hindered. They plundered and murdered the peasantry at pleasure. Many of the country folks were found hanging by the sides of the road, for no other reason than that they had not been friendly to the French invaders. The French line of retreat was marked by the smoke rising from the villages to which they had set fire. The Duke overtook Massena's army at Fuentes d'Onoro, and inflicted upon them a sharp defeat. He next took Almedia, stormed Ciudad Rodrigo, stormed Badajoz, defeated Marmot at Salamanca, and immediately after entered Madrid. Strange to say, while the Spanish Brigadier Miranda had no fewer than forty-three aides-de-camp, Wellington, on his triumphal entry into Madrid, was accompanied by one officer only, Lord Fitzroy Somerset!

Wellington was most humane towards the people of the country through which he passed. The Spaniards feared their own troops more than the English. The Spaniards pillaged wherever they went, though this was forbidden to the English. Yet the latter were terribly hampered for money and means of transport When Wellington's troops were in pursuit of Massena, the soldiers took some wood to bum from the grounds of the Count Costello Melhor. With a generosity rare in the leaders of armies, the Duke paid out of his own purse the cost of the wood which his poor soldiers had taken. "A regard" he said, "to the interests of the army, added to a feeling of pity for the unfortunate inhabitants, ought to prevent the wanton destruction of forage, and of everything else."

While the Spanish soldiers in various ways, and particularly after Talavera, exhibited a hostile feeling to the English, the Duke required that "the peaceable inhabitants should be treated with the utmost possible kindness." When the Spanish troops entered France, they immediately began murdering and plundering the inhabitants. On discovering this, the Duke immediately ordered them back to Spain, and fought the battle of Orthez without them. "I am not base enough to allow pillage," he said to Don Freyre. "If you wish your men to plunder, you must name some other commander."

Wellington was ill supported at home. He had no power of honouring men for their deeds of bravery. While the French marshals had the power of stimulating their men by promotion, Wellington could not promote any officer for his gallantry. All the preferment was done by the Horse Guards at home; and men who had never quitted Britain were promoted over the heads of the heroes of the Peninsula I Lieutenant-Colonel Fletcher, who had entrenched the lines of Torres Vedras, directed the sieges of Ciudad Rodrigo, Badajoz, Burgos, and Salamanca, was a lieutenant-colonel three years later, when he was killed by the bursting of a shell in the trenches of San Sebastian. And the brave and indefatigable Lieutenant-Colonel Waters held in 181 5 the same rank at Waterloo which he had acquired in 1809 at the passage of the Douro. Yet Wellington was constantly reporting their valuable services in his despatches to the British Government.

His soldiers appreciated his unceasing efforts to better their condition; and they were touched with his anxiety to save their blood. They admired his impartiality, his truthfulness, his justice, and his disinterestedness. He inspired the officers, as well as the soldiers, with unbounded confidence. He forgave far more men than he punished. It was necessary to keep up the discipline of the army, but he always took the most favourable view of those in error. When an officer behaved ill before the enemy, instead of handing him over to a court-martial he begged that the resignation of the unfortunate man might be accepted. "I prefer," he said, "letting him retire rather than expose him to the world." On one occasion a sergeant deserted, taking with him the pay of the company. A

120

woman was at the bottom of it, and had fooled the man into committing the crime. He had before an excellent character. The Duke forgave him. He again became a non-commissioned officer; he was recommended for a commission, and afterwards became an excellent staff-officer in the Peninsular army.

Wellington treated his subordinates with extreme politeness. He possessed in a high degree the calmness, urbanity, and charm of manner, which spring either from high birth or from a natural elevation of character. In his orders he never commands, he only entreats and requests. In his conversations with his officers he entreated them not to use harsh language to their inferiors. "Expressions of this sort," he said, "are not necessary; they may wound, but they never convince."

Though in the midst of war, he had the greatest sympathy for his men. Napier states that he saw the Duke in a passion of tears when, after the assault of Badajoz, the report was made to him that upwards of 2000 men had fallen in that terrible night When Dr. Hume entered the Duke's chamber on the morning of the 18th of June to make his report of the killed and wounded at the battle of Waterloo, he found him in bed asleep, unshaved and unwashed as he had lain down at night. When awoke the Duke sat up in bed to hear the list read. It was a long list, and when the doctor looked up he saw Wellington with his hands convulsively clasped together, and the tears making long furrows on his battle-soiled cheeks.

Writing the same day to his friend Marshal Beresford, he said, "Our losses quite prostrate me, and I am quite indifferent to the advantages we have gained. I pray God that I may be saved from fighting any more such battles, for I am broken-hearted with the loss of so many old friends and comrades." To Lord Aberdeen he said, "The glory of a triumph like this is no consolation to me." And yet he had won a great battle, and the Allies were in the glow of victory! When riding over the field, and hearing the cries and groans of the wounded, the warrior gave vent to the lacerated feelings of the man in the memorable words, "I know nothing more terrible than a victory — except a defeat."

When afterwards addressing the House of Lords he said, "I am one of those who have probably passed more of their lives in war than most men, and principally, I may say, in civil wars, too; and I must say this, that if I could avoid by any sacrifice whatever even one month of civil war in the country to which I am attached I would sacrifice my life in order to do it."

The Duke was a most humane man. He protected the Spanish people against the cruelty of their own soldiers. He also protected his enemies. After the battle of Talavera the English came to blows with Cuesta's soldiers in order to prevent their killing or mutilating the wounded Frenchmen.

M. Chateaubriand has said, "We have too much respect for glory to withhold our admiration for Lord Wellington. Indeed we are touched, even to tears, when we see that great and venerated man promising, during our retreat in Portugal, two guineas for every French prisoner who should be brought in alive."

The whole of the Duke's career abounds in traits of this kind. In India he recovered and brought up the son of Doondiah, found lying among the wounded He interested himself in the recovery of General Franceshi, whom the Spaniards had left to die in a pestilential dungeon. He delivered young Mascarhenas, and many other victims of the cruelty of the Spanish Government. He protected with solicitude, against the fury of the Portuguese soldiers, the wounded French, and such of the enemy's soldiers as the fortune of war threw into his hands after the evacuation of Oporto. "By the laws of war," he said, "they are entitled to my protection, which I am determined to afford to them." He permitted the French surgeons to attend to the sick of Soult's army, and to pass to and from the Allied camp, with a safe-conduct

He possessed the same sense of honour in dealing with the enemy. When it was proposed to him in India to end the war with Doondiah Waugh by a stroke of the poniard, he rejected the offer with contempt And when there appeared a likelihood of a revolt of Soult's troops in Spain, and the J Duke was asked to support it, he gave the same steady refusal He considered it unworthy of himself and of the cause of which he was the champion, to obtain through a military revolt what ought to be the reward of ability and valour only.

When at Torres Vedras, the Prince of Essling was anxious to inspect the English lines. He advanced under one of the English batteries, and examined it with a glass resting upon a low garden wall. The English officers observed him, and although they might have overwhelmed the staff of the commander-in-chief by a general discharge of the guns, they only discharged a single shot in order to make him aware of his danger. The shot was discharged with such accuracy, that the wall was beaten down on which the Prince's glass rested. Massena understood the courteous notice. He saluted the battery, and remounting his horse, rode away.

It was the same with Wellington at Waterloo. While the Duke was watching the French formations, an officer of artillery rode up, and pointing to the place where Napoleon stood with his staff, observed, "that he could easily reach them, and had no doubt that he would be able to knock some of them over." "No, no," replied the Duke; "generals commanding armies in a great battle have something else to do than to shoot at each other."

After the fall of the empire, Wellington rejected with disdain the proposal to get rid of Napoleon by putting him to death. "Such an act," he said, "would disgrace us with posterity. It would be said of us, that we were not worthy to be the conquerors of Napoleon." To Sir Charles Stewart he wrote, "Blucher wishes to kill him; but I have told him that I will remonstrate, and shall insist upon his being disposed of by common concord. I have likewise said that, as a private friend, I advised him to have nothing to do with so vile a transaction; that he and I had acted too distinguished parts in these transactions to become executioners; and that I was determined that if the sovereigns wished to put him to death, they should appoint an executioner, which should not be me."

It was a strange return for his anxiety about the preservation of

Napoleon's life, that the latter should have bequeathed a legacy of 10,000 francs to the wretched creature who made an attempt to assassinate the Duke of Wellington!

The Duke was a man of truth, and he wished his subordinates to appear like himself. In 1809 he wrote to General Kellerman, "When English officers give their parole that they will not attempt to escape, you may depend upon it that they will keep their word. I assure you that I should not hesitate to arrest and send back immediately to you, any who should act otherwise.",

The Duke was a magnanimous man. Bribes could not buy him, nor threats annoy him. When a lower place was offered to him, he said, "Give me your orders, and you shall be obeyed." His obedience, rectitude, and fidelity were perfect. He thought nothing of himself, but of others. He was altogether devoid of envy. He never detracted from the fame of others in order to enhance his own. He was as careful of the reputation of his officers as he was of his own. When anything went wrong — as at Burgos — he took the entire fault upon himself. He bore up Graham, Hill, and Crawford, against the aspersions made upon them at home. He possessed that firmness of conviction and grandeur of soul which could afford to despise injustice and calumny. When complimented by the Municipality of Madrid, he took no credit for his own services, but observed that "the issues of war are in the hands of Providence."

But the greatest of all Wellington's characteristics was his abiding sense of Duty. It was the leading feature in his character — the one regal and commanding element that subordinated everything to itself. It was his constant desire and fixed determination faithfully to do whatever he saw to be his duty, — to do so because it was his duty. He lived for one thing — to do his duty as a soldier — to do it with all his might, to do it at all hazards, to do it in the best possible way, to the utmost of his ability, to the extent of his resources, and so as to secure ultimate success. It is instructive to observe what unity, simplicity, and strength, some one principle, clearly apprehended and consistently followed out, will impart to character.[45] Brialmont, at the close of his life, says that "he was the grandest, because the truest man, whom modern times have produced. He w the wisest and most loyal subject that ever served and supported the British throne."

Here is an instance of the way in which a solid nation has been made. When Prussia was under foot of Napoleon, when its government was a cipher, and Prussia a mere tributary of the French Empire, Von Stein came forward to rescue his country. In October 1807 Stein conceived the idea of emancipating it by conferring liberty upon the people. The essence of his plan was contained in these striking words — "What the state loses in extensive greatness it must make up by intensive strength." The true strength of the kingdom, he said, was not to be found in the aristocracy, but in the whole nation. "To lift up a people it is necessary to give liberty, independence, and property to its oppressed classes, and extend the protection of the law to all alike. Let us emancipate the peasant, for free

---

[45] See the Rev. Thomas Binney on "Wellington."

labour alone sustains a nation effectually. Restore to the peasant the possession of the land he tills, for the independent proprietor alone is brave in defending hearth and home. Free the citizen from monopoly and the tutelage of the bureaucracy, for freedom in workshop and town-hall has given to the ancient burgher of Germany the proud position he held. Teach the land-owning nobles that the legitimate rank of the aristocracy can be maintained only by disinterested service in county and State, but it is undermined by exemption from taxes and other unwarrantable privileges. The bureaucracy, instead of confining itself to pedantic book knowledge, and esteeming red tape and salary above everything else, should study the people, live with the people, and adapt its measures to the living realities of the times."

Such was the plan upon which Stein proceeded. Villanage was abolished by indemnifying the nobles. Class distinctions in the eye of the law were abolished. A municipal system was established. The youth of Prussia were gradually and yet universally trained to the use of arms. In the meantime Napoleon had heard of "one Stein,"[46] who was engaged in retrieving the reverses of Prussia; and in 1808 he was compelled to resign his office and take refuge in Austria. . But his plans were sedulously carried out by his successor. Count Von Hardenberg. Shortly after, the battle of Leipsic took place, when the armies of Napoleon were driven back towards France. Some of Stein's plans had not been carried out, and the national representation which he proposed was postponed until a fixture day. Still villanage was abolished, and the foundations of Prussia's future prosperity were laid. Stein died in 1831, leaving behind him the reputation of having been one of the firmest characters and the greatest statesmen that Prussia ever produced.

About three years ago, when a monument to Stein was unveiled at Berlin, Dr. Gneist, Professor of Law, called to remembrance the great things that the hero had done for Prussia. He said that he vindicated religion as the only true basis of moral life; that sensual pleasures, idleness, and the love of gain and riches can never be effectually counteracted except by patriotism and the love of one's neighbour; and that constitutional forms are a matter of comparative indifference so long as liberty exists. "The man to whom we are indebted for these teachings was not a man of words, but of deeds — deeds founded upon a character full of patriotism, energy, truth, and faith. Deeply imbued with the fear of God, and therefore free from all fear of man, aiming at great objects, and never hesitating to pursue them in the teeth of all difficulties, he frequently contented himself with laying down principles, leaving their execution and

---

[46] When Stein was about to leave Berlin for Breslau, the new French minister to the Prussian Court arrived, carrying with him the following decree : —
"I. Le nommè Stein, cherchant á exciter des troubles en Allemagne, est déclarée ennemi de la France et de la Confederation du Rhin.
"2. Les biens que ledit Stein possederait, soit en France soit dans le pays de la Confederation du Rhin, seront sequestres. Ledit Stein sera saisi de sa personne partout ou il pourra etre atteint par nos troupes ou celles de nos allies. Napoleon.
"Le 16th Dcembre 1808."

the cautious choice of ways and means to others. Full of noble indignation against fear and diffidence, selfishness, and false appearances; haughty, abrupt, and imperious where these qualities were required, he boldly warred against prejudice and obsolete customs. It was a merciful provision of Providence that this noble Stein, this precious stone and gem of our unity, was a rough diamond, preserving in his character the rigour and vigour indispensable in the reformer. Nor need we rejoice at having a monument to remind us of the departed statesman; all the institutions of modern Germany bear the impress of his mind. Neither do we wish to boast of this monument as a symbol of glory. The very idea of glory was utterly abhorrent to his pure soul, to all he wrote and did. No, as the inscription tells us in the most unpretending language, this is no monument of glory but of gratitude; no monument of victory but of thankfulness."

We who live now, have seen a nation grow up into vitality under our own eyes. Forty years ago the fortunes of Italy looked very dark to her warmest admirers. That capability for self-government, which, for a time, was the glory of the Italian republics, seemed to be extinct. It was thought that the people had lost their old political qualities. At the break-down of Napoleon, Italy was parcelled out among a set of petty absolutists, who governed the people with a rod of iron. It was not till 1848 that Charles Albert, King of Sardinia, came boldly forward and asserted the principles of constitutional government. In that year a great war of revolution spread over Europe. Barricades were erected in the streets of Paris, and Louis Philippe fled to England. At Berlin the troops and people fought in the streets, and the city was declared in a state of siege. A Polish insurrection broke out, which was subdued after a frightful slaughter. The city of Prague revolted against the Austrians. Messina was bombarded by the King of Naples. The Pope fled to Gaeta, and a Roman republic was set up. The people of Milan rose against the Austrians, and drove them out Venice followed, and a provisional government was formed under Daniel Manin.

Charles Albert went to the aid of the Milanese. The Austrians, in great force, drove him back towards Turin, defeated him at Novara, and resumed possession of the revolted provinces. The king abdicated in favour of his son Victor Emmanuel. When the young king accepted the crown, he pointed his sword to the Austrian camp, and said, "Per Dio, l'Italia sará!" It seemed at the time to be a vainglorious boast. Yet his prophecy was fulfilled. Marshal Radetzky proposed to him that he should abolish the constitutional charter granted to the people by his father, and follow the Austrian policy of repression and obscuration. The young king rejected the proposal, and declared that, sooner than subscribe to such conditions, he was ready to renounce not one crown only, but a thousand "The House of Savoy," he said, "knows the path of exile, but not the path of dishonour." Radetzky, though a conqueror, acknowledged the greatness of the young king. "This man," he said, "is a noble man; he will give us much to do."

The king was supported and upheld by able statesmen. In the days of sorrow that succeeded Novara, Cavour said, "Every day's existence is a gain." When the war with Russia took place, it seemed a bold thing on the part of the King of Sardinia to send fifteen thousand troops to the Crimea. When Cavour was told of the Sardinian infantry struggling with mud in the trenches, he exclaimed, "Never mind; it is out of that mud that Italy is to be made." Austria regarded with indignation the growing power of the king, and called upon .Sardinia to disarm, under threat of immediate hostilities. Victor Emmanuel issued a proclamation. "Austria," he said, "is increasing her troops on our frontier, and threatens to invade our territory, because here liberty reigns with order, because not might but concord and affection between the people and the sovereign here govern the state, because the groans of Italy here find an echo; and Austria dares to ask us, who are armed only in self-defence, to lay down our arms and submit to her clemency. That insulting demand has received the reply it deserved: I rejected it with contempt.... Soldiers, to arms!"

The Emperor Napoleon took part with the King of Sardinia his ally, and declared war against Austria. War commenced, and the Austrians were driven back at Montebello, Palestro, Magenta, Malignano, and Solferino. The treaty of Villafranca concluded the campaign; and Lombardy, Tuscany, Parma, Modena, and Bologna, were united Northern Italy. Then Garibaldi took the initiative, and to invaded Sicily. He won battle after battle, and entered Naples alone, as a first-class passenger in a railway train from the south. Never was a kingdom so conquered before. But the times were ripe, and the people were on the side of Italian unity. Venetia and Rome were the last to enter the national compact.

Italy was welded into one state. United, it became a new nation. It is now one of the great European powers. Italy has, within a few years, stepped forth into the theatre with a promise of future greatness. We regard this fact as one of the greatest moral conquests of the nineteenth century. Nations are not born in a day; but here is an instance of a nation preparing, through generations of struggles and vicissitudes, to assert its supreme right, and to claim its supreme privilege as a united people.

Let us not forget the horrors of war in our exemplification of the life of the soldier and the patriot. Europe is full of standing armies. Science has of late been devoted to the invention and manufacture of man-slaying machines — the steel rifled cannon, the Mini, the Catling, the Martini Henry gun, the torpedo, and other machines of war. Every nation stands watching each other, and on any slight provocation is ready to fight for revenge, for supremacy, or for conquest. It is the same in France, Germany, and Russia.

The last European war was in the East. The Russians bore down upon the Turks, and after much furious fighting, the Turks were driven within the walls of Constantinople. Let us look at a battlefield after the glories of a fight are over — the martial array, the charge, the intense excitement, the deeds of valour, and the glory after victory. In May 1879, Mr. Rose accompanied General Scobeloff on a visit to the Shipka Pass.[47] "Near the villages of Shipka," says Mr. Rose, "General Scobeloff came out of his tent, and being joined by the whole staff we commenced, under his direction, an

---

[47] "Senova and Shipka revisited." By W. Kinnaird Rose. Gentleman's Magazine.

inspection in detail of his positions. We had gone a few steps when we came upon a wooden cross erected under the shadow of four spreading beeches. The General at once uncovered, an example which all followed, and stood for a few minutes in silence. Turning away, the General said to me, 'That is the grave of a hero; and on the day of the battle I specially ordered that cross to be planted over his grave, so as to mark his last resting place. He was a mere boy of between fifteen and sixteen, of good family in Russia. During the war, fired by military ardour, and the righteousness of the cause for which the armies of Holy Russia were fighting, he escaped from school and home, and made his way to the seat of war. Turning up at Plevna, I accepted him as a volunteer, and he fought gallantly and well at the great assault and subsequent capture of Osman Pasha's stronghold. At Senova he led a company of the 32d regiment, and their duty it was to make the assault on the central redoubt. Carried away by his enthusiasm and utter disregard of danger, the brave boy speedily left his men a considerable way behind, and escaped the shower of bullets only to be bayoneted as he entered the redoubt. His was a brief but heroic life!" 'Such was heroism; and next for the result. "Crossing the stream, we entered the centre redoubt on the little peninsula, and what a sight was presented! All around the door of the redoubt were scattered broken cannisters, fragments of shell, rags of uniforms, as if the battle had only taken place a few days ago. But I was hardly prepared for the ghastly scene within. Several hundred men had been hastily buried there; but the rain and the snow had beaten aside the loose earth, wolves and dogs had done the rest, and all over the floor of the redoubt was scattered a vast milange of human bones. Vertebræ, arm and leg bones, commingled in the strangest fashion with skulls bleached by sun and rain. 'Mark how these lifeless mouthff grin without breath! Mark how they laugh and scorn at all you are, and yet they were what you are! ' I have experienced all the shuddering of a ride over a battlefield immediately after the event, when as yet the earth was covered thick with other clay — 'heaped and pent, rider and horse, friend and foe,' — but it did not possess half the ghastly horror of this scene sixteen months after war had ceased its tumults and alarms. General Scobeloff said to me as we gazed on this charnel house, 'And this is glory!' Yes, 'I responded,' after all, General,

> 'The drying up a single tear has more
> Of honest fame than shedding seas of gore.'

"You are right' he replied, 'and yet I am nothing but a soldier."

CHAPTER IX

HEROISM IN WELL-DOING

Main de femme, mais main de fer.

French Proverb

Chi non soffre, non vince.

Italian Proverb

He who tholes overcomes.

Scotch Proverb

The path of Duty in this world, is the road to Salvation in the next.

Tewish Sage

For none of us liveth to himself, and no man dieth to himself.

St. Paul

IN olden times, virtue and valour were synonymous. Valour, the old Roman valour, was worth, value. It was strength, force, available for noble purposes. He who best serves his fellow-creatures — who elevates them — who saves them — is the most valiant.

There is also an inward valour — of conscience, of honesty, of self-denial, of self-sacrifice, of daring to do the right in the face of the world's contumely. Its chief characteristic is great-heartedness. Endurance and energy are the dual soul of worth, the true valour.

The heroism whose theatre is the battle-field is not of the highest order. Amidst the clash of bayonets ' and the boom of cannon, men are incited to deeds of daring, and are ready to give their lives for the good of their country. All honour to them!

Women, whose province it seems to be to bear and forbear, are quite as capable of endurance as men. In the blood-stained stories of war, there is none, peiliaps, that more enlists our hearts, than that of the woman who put on male attire to follow her lover to the fight, stood by his side when he fell, and then braved death rather than be parted from his dead body. How many are there of these soldiers of the world, ever fighting the uphill battle of existence, ever striving for a position and never attaining one; ever decimated by the artillery of necessity; beaten back, discomfited, all but hopeless and despairing, and yet still returning to the charge!

The Christian hero is not incited by any such deeds of daring as the soldier hero. The arena on which he acts is not that of aggression or strife, but of suffering and selfsacrifice. No stars glitter on his breast, no banners wave over him. And when he falls, as he often does, in the performance of his duty, he receives no nation's laurels, no pompous mournings, but only the silent dropping of tears over his grave.

Man is not made for fame, or glory, or success; but for something higher and greater than the world can give. "God hath given to man," says Jeremy Taylor, "a short time here upon earth, and yet upon this short time eternity depends. We must remember that we have many enemies to conquer, many evils to prevent, much danger to run through, many difficulties to be mastered, many necessities to be served, and much good to da"

Self-sacrifice is the key-note of Christianity. The best men and women have never been self-seekers. They have given themselves to others, without regard to glory or fame. They have found their best reward in the self-consciousness of duty performed. And yet many pass away without hearing the "well-done "of those whom they have served. "Do unto others as ye would they should do unto you," is a command of infinite application. And yet it is not easy — at least for those who live in affluence or indifference — to carry out the obligation.

There is not an unnecessary thing in existence, could we but understand it; not one of our experiences of life but is full of significance, could we but see it Even misfortune is often the surest touchstone of human excellence. The most celebrated poet of Germany has said, "that he who has not eaten his bread in tears, who has not spent nights of pain weeping on his bed, does not yet know a heavenly power." When painful events occur, they are perhaps sent only to try and prove us. If we stand firm in our hour of trial, this firmness gives serenity to the mind, which always feels satisfaction in acting conformably to duty.

The opportunities of doing good come to all who work and will. The earnest spirit finds its way to the hearts of others. Patience and perseverance overcome all things. How many men, how many women too, volunteer to die without the applause of men. They give themselves up to visiting the poor; they nurse the sick, suffer for them, and take the infectious diseases of which they die. Many a life has thus been laid down because of duty and mercy. They had no reward except that of love. Sacrifice, borne not for self but for others, is always sacred.

Epimenides, a philosopher and poet of Crete,[48] was called to Athens in order to stay the plague. He went, and succeeded in arresting the pestilence, but refused any other reward beyond the goodwill of the Athenians in favour of the inhabitants of Gnossus, where he dwelt

In olden times the plague was a frightful disease. People fled before it They fled from each other. The plague -stricken were often left to die alone. Yet many noble and gentle men and women offered themselves up to stay the disease. About three centuries ago the plague broke out in the city of Milan. Cardinal Charles Borromeo, the archbishop, was then (1576) staying at Lodi He at once volunteered to go to the infected place. His clergy advised him to remain where he was; and to wait until the disease had exhausted itself. He answered, "No! A bishop, whose duty it is to give his life for his flock, cannot abandon them in their time of peril." "Yes," they replied, — "to stand by them is the higher course." "Well," he said, "is it not a bishop's duty to take the higher course? " And he went to Milan.

The plague lasted about four months. During that time the Cardinal personally visited the sick, in their homes, in the hospitals, and

---

[48] Supposed to be alluded to by St. Paul in his Epistle to Titus i. 12.

everywhere. He watched over them, gave them food and medicine, and administered to them the last rites when dying. The example which he set was followed by his clergy, who ministered to the people with as much self-devotion as himself. And it was not until the last man died, and the last man recovered, that the good Archbishop returned to his episcopal duties.

The Cardinal is entitled to consideration in another respect He was one of the first to institute a Sunday School for the education of the children of the poor. "The Sabbath was made for man, and not man for the Sabbath." Every good work could be done on that day, as well as on every other day. The Cardinal called about him the children from the streets into Milan Cathedral on Sunday afternoons, and taught them to read and write. They brought with them their copy-books and slates, on which to take down his instructions. His priests helped him, and the institution became popular. Three hundred years have passed, and Cardinal Borromeo's Sunday School is still continued In the spring of 1879 the writer of these words saw the children collecting in the Cathedral, with their slates and books, to receive their Sunday School instruction.

The Cardinal spent all his revenue in building schools and colleges, and in works of charity and mercy. Wickedness was rife in his day, and he did what he could to abate it. He began with his own class. He endeavoured to enforce a reform of the clergy, especially of the Monastic orders. He laboured to introduce better modes of life into the order of the Umilitati, who gave much cause for scandal by the licentiousness of their conduct They thought the Cardinal equally scandalous by teaching poor children to read in the great cathedral He was held to be a desecrator of the Sabbath, the sanctuary, and the priesthood.[49] His Sunday School was thought to be a "dangerous innovation." The Umilitati hired a man to shoot the Cardinal while at the altar. At the moment the choir was singing the verse, "Let not your heart be troubled, neither be ye afraid," the assassin fired point blank at the Cardinal with an arquebus. The bullet struck him on the back, but the silken and embroidered cope which he wore warded it off, and the bullet dropped to the ground. The Cardinal was brave and resolute. While all around him were in consternation, he himself continued silent in prayer.

To return to the plague. The disease repeatedly visited this country, at a time when the people were worse fed, and when the conditions of health were completely disregarded. It proved most fatal in London, where the streets were narrow, foul, ill ventilated, and badly supplied with water. Its

---

[49] "And to-day, "says an American author, "if any man tries to do Sunday School work in that broad and large way which embraces the whole life of the child, and which is the only practical and successful way of doing the work as Christ did it, he is met with denunciations. Let him, for instance, try to stem the tide of evil literature by giving good healthy secular books from his library, or let him try to conquer vagrancy by having an Employment Committee in his school, and immediately the protectors of the Sabbath, and the defenders of Scripture study, are aroused. For the Pharisees have never yet wanted a man to stand before the Lord in any generation. Brethren of the Holy Bones, will your obstructive race never be extinct?"

last appearance was in 1665; it carried off 100,000 persons, when the population of London was not one-sixth of what it is now. It extended from London into the country. Though most people fled from the disease, there were many instances of noble self-devotion. Bishop Morton of York was one of these. He thought nothing of himself, but only of his flock. A pest-house or hospital was erected for the accommodation of the poorest They were taken from their wretched homes, and carefully tended. Though it was difficult to find attendants, the Bishop was always there. Like a soldier, he stood by his post When food was wanted, he rode out to his farm in the country, and brought sacks of provisions on his horse for their use. He would not suffer his servants to run the risk which he himself ran; and not only saddled and unsaddled his horse, but had a private door made by which he could pass in and out without mixing with the people of the farm. Thus the plague was confined to York itself. The Bishop was a self-denying, generous, and thoroughly good man. When his revenues were increased, he expended all in charity, in hospitality, and in promoting every good work. His life was one entire act of sincere piety and Christian benevolence.

In London, Sydenham and most of the doctors fled; but some self-denying men remained. Among these was Dr. Hodges, who stuck to his post He continued in unremitting attendance upon the sick. He did not derive any advantage from his self-denying labours, except the approval of his own conscience. He fell into reduced circumstances, was confined in Ludgate prison for debt, and died there in 1688. He left the best account of the last visit of the plague.[50]

From London, as we have said, the disease extended to the country. In many remote country spots, places are pointed out in which, it is said, "they buried the plague." For instance, at the remote village of Eyam, in Derbyshire, a tailor received a box of clothes from London. While airing them at a fire he was seized with sickness, and died of plague on the fourth day. The disease spread. The inhabitants, only 350 in number, contemplated a general exodus; but this was prevented by the heroism of the rector, the Rev. William Mompesson. He urged upon the people that they would spread the disease far and wide, and they remained. He sent away his children, and wished to send away his delicate wife; but she remained by the side of her husband.

Mr. Mompesson determined to isolate the village, so that the plague should not extend into the surrounding districts. The Earl of Devonshire contributed all that was necessary — including food, medicine, and other necessaries. In order not to bring the people together in the church, he held the services in the open air. He chose a rock in the valley for his reading-desk, and the people arranged themselves on the green slope opposite, so that he was clearly heard.

---

[50] The best-known of these accounts is that which was written by Defoe, and published in 1722, being derived, to all appearance, from authentic journals and public and private records; but the best is Λοιμολία sive Pestis nupera apud Populum Londinensium grassantis Narratio Historica" by Dr. Hodges, which was published in 1672, and was translated into English by Dr. John Quincy in 1720.

The ravages of the plague continued for seven months. The congregation became less and less each time that it met. The rector and his wife were constantly among the sick, tending, nursing, and feeding them. At length the wife sickened with plague, and in her weak state she rapidly sank. She was buried; and the Rector said over her grave, as he had done over so many of his parishoners, "Blessed are the dead who die in the Lord: even so saith the Spirit; for they rest from their labours." The Rector was ready to die, but he lived on in hope. Four-fifths of the inhabitants died, and were interred in a heathy hill above the village. "I may truly say," he said in a letter, "that our town has become a Golgotha, a place of skulls.... There have been seventy-six families visited within my parish, out of which died 295 persons." Mr. Mompesson himself lived to a good old age. He was offered the Deanery of Lincoln, but he declined it He preferred to remain amongst his parishioners, and near the grave of his beloved wife. He died in 1708.

Strange to say, some fifty years later, when some labouring men were digging near the place where "the plague had been buried," they came upon some linen, no doubt connected with the graves of the dead; when they were immediately stricken by typhus fever. Three of the men died, but the contagion spread through the village, and seventy persons were carried off. The typhus seems to be the survival of the plague, and many are the towns of England where this terrible disease strikes off its thousands yearly.

The author remembers, while living at Leeds thirtythree years ago, an outbreak of typhus fever. It began in the poorest parts of the town, and spread to the richer quarters. In one yard twenty-eight persons had the fever in seven houses, three of which were without beds. It was the same in other yards and buildings. In one house, in which twelve had typhus, there was not a single bed. The House of Recovery and the Fever Hospital were completely full. A temporary wooden shed for an hospital was erected, and a mill was set apart for the reception of fever patients.

Dr. Hook, then Vicar of Leeds, and the Rev. G. Hills (afterwards Bishop of Columbia), visited these places daily. They administered every comfort and assistance in their power. The Catholic priests were most devoted. When the plague of typhus broke out, they went at once to minister to the poor. Into the densest pestilential abodes, where to breathe the poisoned air was death, they went fearlessly and piously. They were found at the bedsteads .of the dying and the newly dead. No dangers daunted their resolute hearts. They saw death before them, but they feared him not. They caught the pestilence, and one by one they sickened and died The Rev. Henry Walmsley, senior Catholic priest, first died. On the following day his junior died; he had been in Leeds only three weeks. Others pressed into the breach, as if a siege were to be won. They earnestly pleaded that they should be allowed to occupy the post of danger. The successor of Mr. Walmsley next fell a victim. Two others died, making five in all. A simple monument was erected to their memory, as men "who fell victims to fever in discharge of their sacred duties in 1847."

In addition to these, a curate of the parish church died from the same

132

cause. A gentleman well known for his efforts in the cause of temperance was carried off. Two of the town's surgeons were attacked, and one of them died. In all, 400 persons were smitten by the plague. Surgeons and medical men are always in contact with diseases, no matter how infectious. These men brave death in all its aspects, often without the slightest hope of reward. Wherever they are called they go, unshrinkingly doing their duty, sometimes even unthanked. They spend and are spent, labour and toil, till their strength fails and their heart sickens; and then the fever fastens on them and they are carried off. Heroes such as these pass silently through life, and fame never reaches them. The greatest heroes of all are men whom the world knows not of.

Surgeons have done their duty on the field as well as in the dwellings of the poor. They have gone out under fire, and brought back the wounded soldiers to be dressed and cared for. The French surgeon Larrey was quite a hero in this respect. During the retreat from Moscow he was seen performing an operation literally under the fire of the enemy. He had only a camp cloak to protect the patient. It was held over him in the manner of an awning to protect him during the falling snow. In another case which happened on the burning sands of Egypt, the dashing little surgeon showed a similar ardour. An engagement with the English had just occurred, and among the wounded was General Silly, whose knee was ground by a bullet. Larrey, perceiving that fatal results might ensue unless the limb was amputated at once, proposed amputation. The general consented to the operation, which was performed under the enemy's fire in the space of three minutes. But lo! the English cavalry were approaching. What was then to become of the French surgeon and his dear patient? "I had scarce time," said Larrey, "to place the wounded officer on my shoulders and to carry him rapidly away towards our army, which was in full retreat I spied a series of ditches, some of them planted with caper bushes, across which I passed, while the cavalry were obliged to go by a more circuitous route in that intersected country. Thus I had the happiness to reach the rearguard of our army before this corps of dragoons. At length I arrived with this honourably wounded officer at Alexandria, where I completed his cure."

Here is another hero. Doctor Salsdorf, Saxon surgeon to Prince Christian, had his leg shattered by a shell at the beginning of the battle of Wagram. While laid on the ground he saw, about fifteen paces from him, M. de Kerbourg, the aide-de-camp, who, struck by a bullet, had fallen and was vomiting blood. The surgeon saw that the officer must speedily die unless promptly helped. He summoned together all his power, dragged himself along the ground until he approached the officer, bled him, and saved his life. De Kerbourg could not embrace his benefactor. The wounded doctor was removed to Vienna, but he was so much exhausted that he only survived four days after the amputation of his leg.

On the advance of an army, it is usual to bring up the waggons in the rear for the accommodation of the wounded. When the men fall, they are carried back to the surgeon to be attended to. If the army is driven back, the surgeons and the wounded have to fly, or be taken prisoners. On the occasion of the battle of the Alma, the Russians fled, and the British and French followed. A large number of wounded men had been left. Several hundred Russians were brought to the eastern part of the field, where they were laid down in rows on a sheltered spot of ground near the river.

Happily there was a surgeon at headquarters, whose sense of honour and duty was supported by a strong will, by resistless energy, and by a soundness of judgment and command of temper rarely united with great activity. This was Dr. Thompson of the 44th Regiment Though the country was abandoned by the Russians, he succeeded in getting 400 lbs. of biscuit and the number of hands needed to sustain him in his undertaking. He immediately had the wounded fed, for they had had no sustenance during twenty-four hours. Then he attended to the dressing of their wounds. This occupied him from seven in the evening until half-past eleven at night

By this time the soldiers had left to carry the English wounded back to the ships at Eupatoria. And then Dr. Thompson and his servant, John M'Grath, remained among the Russian wounded. They remained there for three days and three nights alone, amidst the scorching sun by day and the steel-cold stars by night. At length the opportunity occurred for embarking the Russians and sending them to a Russian port under a flag of truce. "When at length," says Mr. Kinglake, "on the morning of the 26th, Captain Lushington of the Albion came up from the shore, and discovered his two fellow-countrymen at their dismal post of duty, he was filled with admiration at their fortitude, and with sympathy for what they had endured."[51]

In like manner, Dr. Kay, the surgeon of the hospital at Benares, during the Indian Mutiny, stood by his post at the risk of his life, for the enemy were advancing to destroy him as well as his suffering patients. Every one remembers the dreadful events at Cawnpore, where every one perished, to the last man, the last woman, and the last child. Yet the British held out to the end, under the withering fire of the mutinous Sepoys. "It is hard to believe," says Mr. Collier of New York, any man, as a rule, more empty of what we call religion than the common soldier. His whole life, poor fellow, makes it very hard for him to have any sense of it, and he has very little. But it has come out, since the great Sepoy Rebellion in India, that numbers of these men in the English army were offered the alternative of renouncing the Christian religion and embracing that of the rebels, or being murdered by all the horrible ways that the hate and rage of the heathen can invent It is believed that they died to a man, not one instance as yet has come to light of any common soldier giving way.... He was a man belonging to the Christian side, and the pincers could not tear that simple manliness out of his heart, or the fire burn it out.... And so there may be manliness where there is little grace, or if by grace you mean that gracious thing, a pure and holy life and a conscious religion."

And here let us mention the self-devotion of two noncommissioned officers of the 70th Regiment during the recent outbreak of cholera at Moultan. In the absence of women they nursed the sick and the dying,

---

[51] Kinglake's Crimea iii. 334.

They worked day and night in the cholera hospital Corporal Derbyshire at last broke down from sheer fatigue, but his place was supplied by others. The other non-commissioned officer, Corporal Hopper, volunteered for hospital duty at Topah, where he earned the gratitude of both the medical and military authorities. The surgeons were always at their task in both places, braving death at every moment. When the Commander-in-Chief visited Moultan, shortly after, he publicly thanked Derbyshire and Hopper in the midst of their admiring comrades.

But the same quality is sometimes displayed amidst the fire of shot and shell. At the siege of Cadiz by the French in 1812, men and women were killed in the streets, at the windows, and in the recesses of their houses. When a shell was thrown by the enemy, a single toll of the great bell was the signal for the inhabitants to be on their guard One day a solemn toll was heard in signal of a shell That very shell fell furiously on the bell and shivered it to atoms. The monk whose duty it was to sound it, went very coolly and tolled the other bell The good man had conquered the fear of death.

But a singular act of bravery on the part of a woman was displayed during the same siege. Matagorda was a small outlying fort without a ditch or bombproof. Within this fort 140 English troops were stationed, for the purpose of impeding the completion of the French works. A Spanish Seventy-four and an armed flotilla co-operated in the defence, but a hitherto masked battery opened upon the ships, and, after inundating them with hot shot, drove them for shelter to Cadiz harbour. Forty-eight guns and mortars of the largest size concentrated their fire upon the little fort. The feeble parapet at once vanished before the crashing flight of shot and shell, leaving only the naked rampart and the undaunted hearts of the garrison. For thirty hours this tempest lasted; and now occurs the anecdote of the woman of Matagorda.

A Serjeant's wife, named Retson, was in a casemate nursing a wounded man. The patient was thirsty and wanted something to drink. She called to a drummer boy, and asked him to go to the well and fetch a pail of water. The boy hesitated, because he knew that the well was raked by the shot and shell of the enemy. She snatched the bucket from his hand and went herself to the well. She braved the terrible cannonade, went down to the well, filled the bucket with water, and, though a shot cut the cord from her hand, she recovered it, went back with the water for her patient, and fulfilled her mission.

The shot fell upon the doomed fort thick and close. A staff* bearing the Spanish flag was cut down six times in an hour. At length Sir Thomas Graham (afterwards Lord Lynedoch), finding the defence impracticable, sent a detachment of boats to carry off' the survivors. A bastion was blown up under the direction of Major Lefebre. But he also fell, the last man who wetted with his blood the ruins thus abandoned. The boats were then filled, and the men returned to Cadiz. They were accompanied by the heroic woman of Matagorda.

Can any one believe that women can undertake to nurse soldiers in time of war? And yet it is done bravely and nobly. Nurses used to be taken from the same class as ordinary domestic servants. It was not until Miss Nightingale, by her noble devotion to the care of the sick and wounded, had made for herself an honoured place in history, that people began to realise that nursing was a thing to be learnt — that it required intelligence, willingness, and fitness, as well as charity, affection, and love. "It has been said and written scores of times," says Miss Nightingale, "that every woman makes a good nurse. I believe, on the contrary, that the elements of nursing are all but unknown."

But how came it that she devoted herself to the profession of nursing? Simply from a feeling of love and duty. She need never have devoted herself to so trying and disagreeable an occupation. She was an accomplished young lady, possessing abundant means. She was happy at home, a general favourite, and the centre of an admiring circle. She was blessed with everything that might have made social and domestic life precious. But she abjured all such considerations, and preferred to tread the one path that leads to suffering and sorrow. She had always a yearning affection for her kind. She taught in the schools, she visited the poor, and, when they were sick, she fed and nursed them. It was in a little corner of England that she lived and worked — Embley in Hampshire; but one can do as much good work in secret as in the light of day.

The gay world opened before her. She might have done what other young ladies do in town.[52] But her heart led her elsewhere. She took an interest in the suffering, the lost, and the downtrodden. She visited the hospitals, the gaols, and the reformatory institutions. While others were spending delightful holidays in Switzerland or Scotland, or by the seashore, she was engaged in a German nursing school or in a German hospital She began at the beginning. She learnt the use of the washing cloth, the scrubbing brush, and the duster; and she proceeded by degrees to learn the art of nursing. For three months she continued in daily and nightly attendance on the sick, and thus accumulated a considerable experience in the duties and labours of the hospital ward.

On Miss Nightingale's return to England, she continued her labours. The Hospital for Sick Governesses was about to fail for want of proper management, and she undertook its care. She denied herself the affection of her home, and the fresh breath of the country air, to devote herself to

---

[52] The Bishop of Manchester, preaching at Oswestry, read a letter from a young lady, giving him the following account of her day, and asking him whether there was any time in it for Christian work : — "We breakfast at ten. Breakfast occupies the best part of an hour, during which we read our letters and pick up Society news in the paper. After that we have to go and answer our letters, and my mother expects me to write her notes of invitation, or to reply to such. Then I have to go into the conservatory and feed the canaries and parrots, and cut off the dead leaves and faded flowers from the plants. Then it is time to dress for lunch, and at two o'clock we lunch. At three my mother likes me to go with her when she makes her calls, and we then come home to a five o'clock tea, when some friends drop in. After that we get ready to take our drive in the Park, and then we go home to dinner, and after dinner we go to the theatre or the opera, and then, when we get home, I am so dreadfully tired that I do not know what to do."

the dreary hospital in Harley Street, where she gave her help, time, and means to the nursing of her sick sisters. Though the institution was saved, her health began to fail under the heavy pressure, and she betook herself for a time to the health-giving breezes of Hampshire.

But a new cry arose for help. The Crimean War was raging. There was a great want of skilled nurses. The wounded soldiers were lying at the hospitals on the Bosphorus almost uncared for. She obeyed her noble impulses, and at once went to their help. She embarked in a ship bound for Scutari. It was at great risk — at the risk of life, hardships, dangers, and perils of all sorts. But who thinks of risk, when duty impels the brave spirit? Miss Nightingale undertook everything that was asked of her. She went into the midst of human suffering, nursed the wounded soldiers and sailors, organised the system of nursing, and undertook the control of the whole.

The wounded were inexpressibly relieved by the patient watching and care of the English lady. The soldiers blessed her as they saw her shadow falling over their pillows at night. They did not know her name, they merely called her "The Lady of the Lamp."

"He sleeps! Who o'er his placid slumber bends?
His foes are gone, and here he hath no friends.
Is it some seraph sent to grant him grace? No!
'Tis an earthly form with human face!"

The soldiers worshipped the maiden lady. They forbore from the expression of any rough language that might hurt her. When an operation was necessary, they bore the agony without flinching. They did all they could to follow her advice and example. She, on her part, took quite an affection for the common soldiers. She not only looked after their personal comfort, but corresponded with their friends in England, in Ireland, and in the far-away straths of Scotland She saved their money. She devoted an afternoon every week to receive and forward their savings to their friends at home. How thankful the soldiers were! And how thoughtful and careful she was of them!

"The simple courage," she says, "the enduring patience, the good sense, the strength to suffer in silence — what nation shows more of this in war than is shown by her commonest soldier? . . . Say what men will, there is something more truly Christian in the man who gives his time, his strength, his life if need be, for something not himself — whether it be his queen, his country, or his colours — than in all the asceticism, the fasts, the humiliations, the confessions, which have ever been made; and this spirit of giving one's life, without calling it a sacrifice, is found nowhere so truly as in England." Thus we have much to learn from the life and example even of the commonest soldier!

Miss Stanley followed Miss Nightingale to the Crimea. A second detachment of fifty nurses and ladies was confided to her charge. She took them to Constantinople, and she remained in Turkey for four months, assisting in the naval hospital at Therapeia, and afterwards in establishing the military hospital at Koulalee. When she saw the wounded soldiers brought from Inkerman, she wrote to a fnend at home, "I know not which sight is the most heartrending; to witness fine strong men worn down by exhaustion, and sinking under it, or others coming in fearfully wounded. The whole of yesterday was spent in sewing mattresses together, then in washing and assisting the surgeon to dress their wounds, and seeing the poor fellows made as comfortable as the circumstances would admit of, after five days' confinement on board ship, during which their wounds were not dressed. Out of the eleven wards committed to my charge, eleven men died in the night simply from exhaustion, which, humanly speaking, might have been stopped could I have laid my hands upon such nourishment as I know they ought to have had."

On Miss Stanle's return to England she devoted herself to befriending the soldiers' wives and widows. She purchased a house and garden in York Street, Westminster, where she founded a large industrial laundry. She obtained a contract from the Government for the supply of army clothing, and thus secured a large amount of employment for the forlorn women. Miss Stanley threw herself with great energy into the relief and nursing of the women of the London poor. She was only one where there ought to have been ten thousand, but the true woman finds and does the work that lies nearest her. She gave her life daily to the service of others. She was an embodiment of self-sacrifice. It did not matter whether she secured the approbation of others or not. To some, who wished to tread the steps she had trod, she said, "Never forget Dr. Arnold. I repeat his last entry in his journal to myself twice every day: 'Let me labour to do Gods will, yet not anxious that it should be done by me rather than by others, if God so wills it should be.'"

Good example always brings forth good fruits. Other ladies followed faithfully in the same steps. Among these may be mentioned Miss Florence Lees, who has not only nursed in the field, but taught to others the duties of scientific nursing. Strange, how the first impulse to do a good thing springs up in the heart. It was the loss of a dear brother in China that nerved her for the effort He had died in the naval hospital at Shanghai, and as she thought of him, tended by strangers' hands, she felt a great longing to do for others what others had done for him.

This happened when she was a girl. The late Bishop of Winchester was consulted. He said that it was too early to devote herself to such a mission. "Wait until your grief has passed away, wait till your mind has matured." But her mind was possessed by resolution and hope. Miss Nightingale was her heroine. She consulted her, and obtained from her the best advice and help as to her training. At last, after three years* waiting, she entered St. Thomas's Hospital, and began her training as a nurse. She afterwards went to King's College Hospital, and acquired valuable practical experience. To complete her knowledge of nursing she spent several years in Holland, Denmark, Germany, and France. At Kaiserworth, in Germany, she passed through the usual practical training of a nursing deaconess, and received a certificate as to her efficiency. Through the kindness of M. Hasson, the Director-General of civil hospitals in France, she obtained permission to work in the chief hospitals of Paris, under the charge of Roman Catholic sisters. She was associated as a "Sceur Postulante" with the Augustinians, the Dames of St. Thomas de Villaneuve, and the Soeurs de Charity of St. Vincent de Paul It was with great satisfaction to the Sisters, and with great happiness to herself, that she worked so harmoniously with them, notwithstanding their differences of religion and thought

The kindness of the Sisters to her, personally, was beyond words. She was indeed treated by them more as a sister and friend, than as one separated from them by creed, country, and secular life. In addition to the practical knowledge thus gained, she learnt from them many a lesson of quiet cheerfulness under difficulties, of hope and trust in an overruling Providence, even when all things seemed going wrong, and of firm self-denial and an utter giving up of themselves and all that they had to Him whose they were and whom they served. Here, too, she learnt what a virtue cheerfulness is for all those who would serve and nurse the sick

Miss Lees's last and most valuable training was obtained through the kind permission of General Lebœuf, then French Minister of War. Through his influence she was permitted to work in the French Military Hospitals, a training which was doubly valuable through the interest taken in her improvement by the late Michel Levy, the Director-General He had been what he termed a "comrade" of Miss Nightingale in the Crimea, and for her sake he made Miss Lees pass through a severer course of discipline and training than, he admitted, would have been possible for any French Sceur, or, as a general rule, for many Englishwomen. The practical experience, however, which she derived through the personal kindness of M. Michal Levy, at the Val-de-Grice, was so valuable, that in the course of her after life it was never forgotten.

Shortly after her return to England after this long probation in nursing, war was declared between France and Germany. The newspapers were full of the results of the first sanguinary battles. The conquering army swept on and left the wounded to die. They lay in the open air by thousands, untended and uncared for. The nurse's heart was roused by pity and by sympathy. She at once set out for the Continent, accompanied by three German ladies, but they were soon detached in different directions. She went across Belgium to Cologne, where she saw the wounded soldiers lying in rows along the station platform. Then to Coblentz and Treves, and then to Metz, which was her station. It was a rough journey when she left the steamer. In the midst of the confusion she had lost her baggage, but she was there herself, alone.

Marshal Bazaine had taken refuge in Metz, with a large body of French troops, and Prince Frederick was investing the city with an army of Germans and Bavarians. Miss Lees was appointed to an Hôpital at Marangue, in the rear of the investing army. She reached the place. It was only an old farm-steading. The barn was the hospital. It was a very comfortless place. The accommodation was miserable. The nurse slept on a bit of sacking filled with straw. There was little medicine and less food. The principal disease to be encountered was typhus fever, occasioned by the dampness of the trenches. The Lazaretto or Hospital accommodated twenty-two beds; and these were always full.

The nurse of a field -hospital has no light task before her. When the men came in fever-stricken, they had first to be cleaned. When they came from the trenches, their feet were so encrusted with dirt that it had to be scraped off before they could be washed. When cleansed, they were put into their beds, and had medicine administered to them. There was the washing out of the men's blackened mouths, the attention to their personal cleanliness, the wetting of their heads by night to keep down delirium, bathing their hands and faces, changing their couches to prevent bed sores, — and all this in the midst of the most depressing circumstances.

The men sometimes became furiously delirious. Miss Lees has herself told the story of her life in the Fever Hospital before Metz.[53] One night she was alone. She heard a noise in the room, upstairs. She went up and found a delirious soldier trying to force the door. The poor fellow wished to go home to his "liebe mutter." She called another patient to her help, and, telling him he would go home to-morrow, got him into his bed again. Another delirious soldier, downstairs, searched for a knife under his bed-fellow's pillow. Miss Lees got hold of the knife, which was really there, and hid it in some obscure place. But, when the surgeon came round, she entreated that she might not again be left alone in the hospital at night

The nurse worked there for many weeks. Many died, some were cured and invalided home, and a few returned to duty. At last Bazaine surrendered; his prisoners were sent into Germany, and the Red Prince and his troops marched on to the siege of Paris. Miss Lees had done her work at Metz, but her self-imposed task was not over. She was taken, partly on a locomotive engine, to Homburg, where she was put in charge of an hospital of wounded soldiers, under the superintendence of the Crown Princess of Prussia. The principal difficulty she had to encounter there was in securing proper ventilation. German doctors hate draughts. So soon as the nurse opened a window the doctors, in her absence, ordered it to be closed. She then appealed to the Crown Princess, and at length obtained the proper ventilation.

It is unnecessary to follow the history of Miss Lees. After her return from Germany, she prepared to make a voyage to Canada and the United States, to inspect the hospitals there. She accomplished her object in the winter of 1873, and saw everything that was to be seen at Halifax, Quebec, Montreal, Toronto, Cleveland, New York, Boston, Philadelphia, Washington, and Annapolis. Of late years, Miss Lees has become Directress of the Westminster Nursing Association, and still continues in her good work.

Many women, young and old, nobly devote themselves to work such as this. They go into the courts and alleys of our towns and cities, and nurse those who might lie and die but for their services. Neither their hands nor their minds are stained by performing the humblest and most repelling offices for their suffering fellow-creatures. Need we mention the

---

[53] Good Words 1873

work of Mrs. Walker among the poor girls in Poplar, Miss Octavia Hill in the West End Courts, Mrs. Vickars among the fallen women at Brighton, Miss Robinson among the soldiers at Portsmouth? It must be confessed that these are exceptional workers, and that the world is still crowded with the helpless, the fallen, the poor, and the destitute, without any help.

There is a great deal of heroism in common life that is never known. There is, perhaps, more heroism among the poor than among the rich. The former have greater sympathy with their neighbours. A street beggar said that he always got more coppers from the poor street girls than from anybody else. Virtue commands respect even in a beggar's garb.

"Men talk about heroes and the heroic element," says Mr. Binney; "there is abundance of room for the display of the latter in many positions of obscure city life, and many of the former have lived and worked nobly, though unknown. The noblest biographies have not always been written. There have been great, heroic men, who have toiled on in their daily duties, and suffered, and sacrificed, and kept their integrity; who served God, and helped their connections, and got on themselves; who have displayed, in all this, qualities of character, of mind, courage, goodness, that would have honoured a bishop, a general, or a judge."

We have lately had taken from us Mary Carpenter, a true sister of charity. In the course of her active life she devoted herself to the reclamation of the neglected poor. She founded and superintended a reformatory institution in Bristol, the success of which proved a revelation to the country at large. Armed with purity of purpose, she went into courts and alleys through which a policeman could scarcely walk. The horrors of the back slums were opened to her sight Nothing daunted, nothing disgusted her. She obtained the children for her Ragged Schools from these miserable quarters. She went to work with an intrepidity equal to that of John Howard himself. Her pen was always at work, keeping the subject continually before the public. At length she won a great victory, for the Government adopted her project, and established Reformatory and Industrial Schools which have done so much for the abandoned classes. There are thousands of men in our army and navy, and in all our industries, who have reason to bless the name of Mary Carpenter. Age did not stay her merciful work. In her sixtieth year she went out to India, to plant the seeds of her educational system in the eastern world. She paid in all four visits to India — the last being in 1876, when she was approaching her seventieth year. She lived to see the fruits of her labours springing up in all directions — in a generation of men and women, who, but for her, would have been left in the surroundings of vice and crime. What can be said of such women, and of their noble sisters in such self-den3dng labours, but that they constitute the honour and the hope of the human race?

The late Mrs. Chisholm adopted a new field of work. She devoted herself to helping young women to emigrate, and to watch over them until they were properly cared for. When about to start from Southampton with a large number of emigrants, she and her husband were entertained at a banquet, at which she gave an account of the manner in which she had been impelled to take up her labour. "The idea of life," she said, "being a task leading on, when well performed, to the inexpressible happiness of heaven, I learnt on the knee of Legh Richmond when a mere child. And I remember myself, after this, in my childish years, playing with boats of walnut shells, at removing the separated members of families across the sea to rejoin each other in a foreign country. And I also distinctly remember putting a Wesleyan preacher and a Roman Catholic priest in the same shell, as being part of my play. My notions on these points must have arisen from the practice of my mother of letting me stop in the room when neighbours called, some of whom were travellers, and men of thought, who talked of missions — missionaries then beginning to be a topic of conversation. These ideas continually haunted me as I grew up. And I had the advantage of a mother to whom I owe whatever energy of character I have; for it was her constant maxim to me, never to shed a tear, or allow a fear to turn me from my purpose."

As she grew up, she became attached to an officer in the Indian army. But before the betrothal she told him that she felt a commission had been given her from above, to devote all her energies to relieving human suffering, whenever the scene of his duties might lie abroad. He loved her all the more because of her maiden confession; he agreed to all that she proposed; and the handsome couple were married soon after. The husband feithfully adhered to the condition of his marriage; and not only so, but he helped his wife in her work. The time arrived when it was necessary to make arrangements for the interest of the emigrants who had been sent out in 1850; and Captain Chisholm immediately set sail for Australia at his own expense. Before going, the two halved their small income and separated.

Mrs. Chisholm afterwards went to India, and founded an Institution for the daughters of European soldiers, called a Female School of Industry, which still exists. In 1838 she and her husband visited Australia for change of air.

"There," she says, "I found some hundred single women, unprotected, unemployed, numbers more continuing to arrive in ships; and almost the whole falling into an immoral course of life, as a necessary result. I applied myself to the task of getting these poor creatures into safety, and decent situations as servants. I met with discouragement on all hands, but I persevered, and I succeeded in my object. The Governor, at length, allowed me to sleep in a small room with the girls at the Emigrant Barracks. It was, it is true, full of rats, as I found the first night I entered it; but these I poisoned, and stuck to my post. I was thus able to get a personal influence and control over the girls. I founded a college to get them engagements in the Bush, and I got some hundreds of girls into good places. In pursuing this object I at length found it necessary to take large parties of these unprotected girls into the Bush to procure places, and that I must accompany these parties myself. This I did for several years. The parties varied from loo to 150 each. So I worked on for many years in Australia. I advanced much money for the conveyance of emigrants; but so honestly was I repaid these advances, that all my losses did not amount, during this period, to £ 20. And, under God's blessing, I was the means of procuring engagements, and of settling no less than 1000 souls, in the aggregate, before I left — a vast proportion of whom, being young women, were saved from falling into a life of infamy. I shall never forget the warmth of my reception this day, and that of the health of my husband and children, whom I have bred up in the maxim — to trust to themselves, and work for themselves; and never, if they have any regard for their mother's memory, to look for Government patronage, or take Government pay.

Some may think that those are no true examples of heroism. More striking examples may be given — of men and women devoting themselves to rescue the lives of shipwrecked mariners at sea. A story comes to us from Western Australia, telling us of the brave deeds of a young gentlewoman — Grace Vernon Bussell. The steamer Georgette had stranded on the shore near Perth. A boat was got out with the women and children on board, but it was swamped by the surf, which was running very high. The poor creatures were all struggling in the water, clinging to the boat, and in imminent peril of their lives, when, on the top of a steep cliff, appeared a young lady on horseback.

Her first thought was how to save these drowning women and children. She galloped down the cliff — how, it is impossible to say — urged her horse into the surf, and, beyond the second line of the breakers, she reached the boat. She succeeded in bringing the women and children on shore. There was still a man left, and she plunged into the sea again, and rescued him. So fierce was the surf, that four hours were occupied in landing fifty persons. As soon as they were on shore, the heroic lady, drenched with the sea-foam, and half fainting with fatigue, galloped off to her home, twelve miles distant, to send help and relief to the rescued people on the sea-beach. Her sister now took up the work. She went back through the woods to the shore, taking with her a provision of tea, milk, sugar, and flour. Next day the rescued were brought to her house, and cared for until they were sufficiently recovered to depart on their solitary ways. It is melancholy to have to record that Mrs. Brookman, the heroine's sister, took cold in the midst of her exertions, and died of brain fever.

Not less brave was the conduct of a young woman in the Shetlands, who went to sea to save the lives of some fishermen, when no one else would volunteer to go. A violent storm had broken over the remote island of Unst, when the fishing fleet — the chief stay of the inhabitants — was at sea. One by one the boats reached the haven in safety; but the last boat was still out, and it was observed by those ashore that she was in great difficulties. She capsized, and the sailors were seen struggling in the water.

At this juncture, Helen Petrie, a slender lass, stepped forward and urged that an attempt to rescue them should be made at all hazards. The men said it was certain death to those who wished to put off in such a storm.

Nevertheless Helen Petrie was willing to brave death. She hastily stepped into a small boat. Her sister-in-law joined her; and her father, lame of one hand, went in to take charge of the rudder. Two of the crew of the fishing-boat had already disappeared, but two remained, clinging to the upturned keel of their craft. It was these the women went to save. After great exertions, they reached the wreck. Just as they approached it, one of the men was washed off, and he would certainly have been drowned, had not Helen caught him by his hair, and dragged him into the boat. The other man was also rescued, and the whole returned to the haven in safety. Helen Petrie afterwards earned her bread in obscurity as a domestic servant, until her death the other day reminded people who knew her story of her existence.[54] Heroines must, one would suppose, be abundant in a country where such a thing could happen.

And Grace Darling! Who can forget her — the heroic woman of the Longstone Lighthouse? The desolate Fern Islands lie off the north-east coast of Northumberland — a group of stem basaltic rocks, black and bare, with a dangerous sea roaring about them. In stormy weather they are inaccessible for days and weeks together. They have no other inhabitants but the gulls and puffins that scream about the rocks. But on the farthest point, the Longstone Rock, a lighthouse had been erected to warn off the ships passing between England and Scotland. Two old persons — z. man and his wife — and a young woman, their daughter, were the keepers of the lighthouse, on a wild night in September 1838.

The steamer Forfarshire was on its voyage from Hull to Dundee. The ship was in bad condition. The boilers were so defective that the fires had to be extinguished shortly after she left Hull. Nevertheless she toiled on until she reached St. Abb's Head, when a terrible storm drove her back. She drifted through the night before the wind, until, in the early morning, she struck with tremendous force on the Hawkers rocks. The ship broke her back, and snapped in two. Nine of the crew took possession of a boat, and drifted through the only outlet by which it could have escaped; they were picked up at sea, and taken into Shields. Most of the passengers and crew were swept into the sea and drowned. The fore part of the vessel remained stuck on the rock; it was occupied by nine persons, crying for help.

Their cries were heard by Grace Darling at the lighthouse, half a mile off. It was the last watch before extinguishing the light at sunrise, and Grace was keeping it Although the fog was still prevailing, and the sea was still boisterous, she saw the wrecked passengers clinging to the windlass in the fore part of the vessel She entreated her father to let down the boat, and go to sea to rescue the drowning people. William Darling declared that it would be rushing upon certain death. Yet he let down the boat, and Grace Darling was the first to enter it The old man followed. Why speak of danger? The chances of rescue, of self-preservation, were infinitesimal But God strengthened the woman's arm, as He had visited her heart; and away the two went, in dread and awe.

By dint of great care and vigilance the father succeeded in landing on the rock and making his way to the wreck, while Grace rowed off and on among the breakers, keeping her boat from being dashed to pieces. One by one, the nine survivors were placed in the boat and carried to the

---

[54] Standard June 28, 1879

lighthouse. There the mother was ready to receive them, to nurse them, to feed them, and to restore them to health and strength. They remained there for three days, until the storm abated, and they could be carried to the mainland.

The spirit of the nation was stirred by the heroic act. Gifts innumerable were sent to Grace Darling. Artists came from a distance to paint her portrait. Wordsworth wrote a poem about her. She was offered £20 a night to sit in a boat at the Adelphi Theatre during a shipwreck scene. But she would not leave her sea-girt rock. Why should she leave the lighthouse? What place so fitting to hold this queen? One who visited her speaks of her genuine simplicity, her quiet manner, her genuine goodness.

Three years after the rescue, symptoms of consumption appeared. In a few months she died, quietly, happily, religiously. Shortly before her death, says Mr. Phillips, she received a farewell visit from one of her own sex, who came in humble attire to bid her God-speed on her last journey. The good sister was the Duchess of Northumberland, and her coronet will shine the brighter for all time, because of that affectionate and womanly leave-taking. Joan of Arc has her monument Let Grace Of Northumbria have none. The deed is registered

> "in the rolls of Heaven, where it will live,
> A theme for angels when they celebrate
> The high-souled virtues which forgetful earth
> Has witnessed."

On the mainland of Northumberland, nearly opposite the Fern Islands, stands the Castle of Bamborough, on a high triangular rock. In olden times it was a strong defence against the incursions of the Scots, as well as an important fortress during the civil wars of England. Of late years it has been used as a refuge for shipwrecked mariners, chiefly through the instrumentality of Lord Crewe, Bishop of Durham, and Archdeacon Sharpe. Lord Crewe's noble appropriation of this castle has been productive of more good than any private benefaction in this country. Shipwrecks frequently occur along the coast, and every possible aid is given to the sufferers. Apartments are fitted up for thirty mariners. A constant patrol is kept every stormy night along the eight miles of coast, and if a ship appears in danger, the lifeboat is launched. During fogs bells are rung to keep off the vessels. When a ship is observed in distress, a gun is fired, and a second time if the vessel is stranded or wrecked on the rocks. At the same time a large flag is hoisted, so that the sufferers may know that their distress is observed from the shore. There are also signals to the Holy Islands fishermen, who can put off from the islands at times when no boat from the mainland can get over the breakers. Every help is given to those on land as well as at sea by this Samaritan Castle on the cliffs. "Thus, like a mighty guardian angel," says William Howitt, "stands aloft this noble castle, the watching spirit over those stormy and perilous seas, and this god-like charity lives, a glorious example of what good a man may continue to do upon earth for ages after he has quitted it. When any one sees at a distance the soaring turrets of this truly sacred fabric, majestic in its aspect as it is divine in its office, dispensing daily benefits over both land and sea, let him bless the memory of Lord Crewe, as thousands and tens of thousands, in the depths of poverty, and in the horrors of midnight darkness, have had occasion to do, and as they shall do when we like him sleep in the dust."

CHAPTER X

SYMPATHY

It is the secret sympathy,
The silver link, the silken tie,
Which heart to heart, and mind to mind,
In body and in soul can bind.

Sir W. Scott

I ask Thee for a thoughtful love.
Through constant watching wise.
A heart at leisure from itself,
To soothe and sympathise.

Miss Waring

Man is dear to man: the poorest poor
Long for some moments in a weary life,
When they can know and feel that they have been
Themselves the fathers and the dealers-out
Of some small blessings: have been kind to such
As needed kindness, for the single cause,
That we have all of us one human heart.

Wordsworth

SYMPATHY is one of the great secrets of life. It overcomes evil, and strengthens good. It disarms resistance, melts the hardest heart, and develops the better part of human nature. It is one of the great truths on which Christianity is based. "Love one another "contains a gospel sufficient to renovate the world.

It is related of St. John that when very old — so old that he could not walk and could scarcely speak — he was carried in the arms of his friends into an assembly of Christian children. He lifted himself up and said, "Little children, love one another." And again he said, "Love one another." When asked, "Have you nothing else to tell us?" he replied, "I say this again and again, because, if you do this, nothing more is needed."

The same truth applies universally. Sympathy is founded on love. It is but another word for disinterestedness and affection. We assume another's state of mind; we go out of ourself and inhabit another's personality. We sympathise with him; we help him; we relieve him. There can be no love without sympathy; there can be no friendship without sympathy. Like mercy, sympathy and benevolence are twice blessed, blessing both giver and receiver. While they bring forth an abundant fruit of happiness in the heart of the giver, they grow up into kindness and benevolence in the heart of the receiver.

"We often do more good," says Canon Farrar, "by our sympathy than by our labours, and render to the world a more lasting service by absence of jealousy and recognition of merit, than we could ever render by the straining efforts of personal ambition. ... A man may lose position, influence, wealth, and even health, and yet live on in comfort, if with resignation; but there is one thing without which life becomes a burden, — that is human sympathy."

It is true that kind actions are not always received with gratitude, but this ought never to turn aside the sympathetic helper. This is one of the difficulties to be overcome in our conflict with life. Even the most degraded is worthy of the mutual help which all men owe to each other. It should be remembered, as Bentham no less truly than profoundly remarked, that the happiness of the cruel man is as much an integral part of the whole human happiness as is that of the best and noblest of men. Then, again, a man cannot do good or evil to others without doing good or evil to himself.

Probably there is no influence so powerful as sympathy in awakening the affections of the human heart. There are few, even of the most rugged natures, whom it does not influence. It constrains much more than force can do. A kind word, or a kind look, will act upon those upon whom coercion has been tried in vain. While sympathy invites to love and obedience, harshness provokes aversion and resistance. The poet is right, who says that "power itself hath not one half the might of gentleness."

Sympathy, when allowed to take a wider range, assumes the larger form of public philanthropy. It influences man in the endeavour to elevate his fellow-creatures from a state of poverty and distress, to improve the condition of the masses of the people, to diffuse the results of civilisation far and wide among mankind, and to unite in the bonds of peace and brotherhood the parted families of the human race. And it is every man's duty, whose lot has been favoured in comparison with others, who enjoys advantages of wealth, or knowledge, or social influence, of which others are deprived, to devote at least a certain portion of his time and money to the promotion of the general well-being.

It is not great money power, or great intellectual power, that is necessary. The power of money is over-estimated. Paul and his disciples spread Christianity over half the Roman world, with little more money than is gained from a fashionable bazaar. The great social doctrines of Christianity are based on the idea of brotherhood. "Do unto others as ye would they should do unto you." Each is to assist the other; the strong the weak, the rich the poor, the learned the ignorant; and, to reverse the order those who have least are no less to assist those who have most all depends on higher degrees of power, for disciples do not make their teachers, nor the ignorant and helpless those who are to instruct and assist them.

Man can make of life what he will. He can give as much value to it, for himself and others, as he has power given him. When circumstances are not against him, he has entire control over his moral and spiritual nature. He can do much for himself,, and all that God gives must pass through man and his own exertions, as if it were his own peculiar work.

Though we may look to our understanding for amusement, it is to the affections only that we must trust for happiness. This implies a spirit of self-sacrifice, and our virtues, like our children, are endeared to us for what we suffer for them. "The secret of my mother's influence," says Mrs. Fletcher in her Autobiography, "was well expressed by her early friend, Dr. Kelvington of Ripon, and it may be called the key-note of her life. He says, in one of his letters to her at the age of seventeen, 'I have never known any one so tenderly and truly and universally beloved as you are, and I believe it arises from your capacity of loving."

The men most to be pitied are those who have no command over themselves, who have no feeling of duty to Others, who wander through life seeking their own pleasure, or who, even while performing good deeds, do so from mean motives, from regard to mental satisfaction, or from fear of the reproaches of conscience. Some of those who are vain of their fine feelings, love themselves dearly, but have little regard for the individuals about them. They are very polite to extraneous society; but follow them home and see how they conduct themselves towards their family. Very sad is the story told by the late Dean Ramsay, of a little boy who was told of heaven, and of the meeting of the departed there. "And will faather be there? " he asked. On being told that "of course he would be there," the child at once replied, "Then I'll no gang."

False sympathy is very common. Sharpe says that one of the most serious objections to pathetic works of fiction is, that they tend to create a habit of feeling pity or indignation, without actually relieving distress or resisting oppression. Thus Sterne could sympathise with a dead donkey, and leave his wife to starve. Montaigne speaks of a man as extraordinary, "qui ait des opinions supercelestes, sans avoir des moeurs souterraines." In Butler's profound discourses, these counterfeits of sterling benevolence are well detected and exposed.

"Goethe," says Professor Bain, "kept out of the way of suffering, because it pained and unhinged him; proving clearly that he had the greatest possible aptitude for taking in the miseries of his fellows, but positively declined the occasions when he might be called upon for that purpose."[55]

In the works of St. Augustine, Baxter, Jonathan Edwards, and Alexander Knox, the reader will find how large a place the religious affections held in their views of divine truth, as well as of human duty. The latter says, "Feeling will be best excited by sympathy; rather it cannot be

---

[55] Bain, On the Study of Character.

excited in any other way. Heart must act upon heart; the idea of a living person being essential to all intercourse of heart" True manliness can only exist when the good is sought for its own sake, either as a recognised law of pure duty, or from the feeling of the constraining beauty of virtue. This alone reacts upon the human character.

Men are regenerated, not so much by truth in the abstract, as by the divine inspiration that comes through human goodness and sympathy. That is the touch of Nature which "makes the whole world kin." The man who throws himself into the existence of another, and exerts his utmost efforts to help him in all ways — socially, morally, religiously — exerts a divine influence. He is enveloped in the strongest safeguard. He bids defiance to selfishness. He comes out of his trial humble yet noble. Canon Mozley has with a master hand shown that the principle of compassion and mutual help, that converts into a pleasure that which is of incalculable advantage to society — the alleviation of pain and misery — was a discovery of Christianity, a discovery like that of a new scientific principle.

The best and the noblest men are the most sympathetic. Bishop Wilberforce was distinguished by his power of sympathy. A friend was asked, "What is the secret of Wilberforce's success?" "In his power of sympathy," was the ready answer. He was large-hearted, generous, and liberal He went straight to the front, and threw himself heart and soul into every project which had good for its object He took the lead in every experiment which seemed to him worth trying. And success was the result

Sympathy is the capacity of feeling for the sufferings, the difficulties, and the discouragements of others. It was said of Norman Macleod that sympathy was the first and the last thing in his character. He found in humanity so much to interest him. The most commonplace man or woman yielded up some contribution of humanity. "When he came to see me," said a blacksmith, "he spoke as if he had been a smith himself, but he never went away without leaving Christ in my heart." Man is, above all, the central point of human action, so that what was in him and went forth from him, is alone important Man, during his life on earth, sympathising and active, is ever associated in his feelings with others; yet we tread alone the more important path which leads over the confines of the earthly state.

When about to enter on his Barony work in Glasgow, Norman Macleod said: — "We want living men! not their books or their money only, but themselves.... The pool and needy, the naked and outcast, the prodigal and brokenhearted, can see and feel, as they never did anything else in this world, the love which calmly shines in that eye, telling of inward light and peace possessed, and of a place of rest found and enjoyed by the weary heart. They can understand and appreciate the utter unselfishness — to them a thing hitherto hardly dreamt of — which prompted a visit from a home of comfort and refinement, to an unknown abode of squalor or disease, and which expresses itself in those kind words and tender greetings that accompany their ministrations." These words form the key to the general plan of his work in the Barony of Glasgow.

"I do think," he again said, "that a careful training of our people, to enable them to discharge their individual duties, such as steady labour, preservation of health, sobriety, kindness, prudence, chastity, their domestic duties as parents, their duties as members of society in courteous and truthful dealing, fulfilment of engagements, obedience combined with independence as workmen; their duties towards the State, whether with reference to their rulers or the administrators of law, along with information on the history and government of their country, — that upon such points as these their education has been greatly neglected, and requires to be extensively improved, and based upon and saturated with Christian principle."

Dr. Macleod's words might equally apply to London, the richest as well as the poorest city in the world. Few people know the East of London, with its seething mass of want, wickedness, and wretchedness. Some give their money to elevate the people, but few give their time or their brains. The late Edward Denison was an exception. He threw himself heart and soul into the work of reclaiming the East of London poor. He established penny banks among them, knowing that the first step to reclaim a man is to wrest his spare earnings from the gin-house, and make him provide for his family as well as for the future. He proceeded to erect schools, reading-rooms, and an iron church. To a certain extent he raised these people from misery to well-being. But what was he among so many? "What a monstrous thing it is," he said, "that in the richest country in the world, large masses of the population should be condemned, annually, to starvation and death. . . , The fact is, we have accepted the marvellous prosperity which has in the last twenty years been granted us, without reflecting on the conditions attached to it, and without nerving ourselves to the exertion and the sacrifice which their fulfilment demands." Mr. Denison could only make a beginning. He died before the fruits could be gathered in. But if there be any who are willing to follow in his footsteps, there is still the field of duty which he has marked out.

Hear the cry of Joseph de Maistre at the end of his life of strenuous and grievous travail: — "I know not what the life of a rogue may be — I have never been one — but the life of an honest man is abominable. How few are those whose passage upon this foolish planet has been marked by actions really good and useful. I bow myself to the earth before him of whom it can be said, 'Pertransivit benefaciendo' [He goes about doing good]; who has succeeded in instructing, consoling, relieving his fellow-creatures; who has made real sacrifices for the sake of doing good; those heroes of silent charity who hide themselves and expect nothing in this world. But what are the common run of men like? and how many are there in a thousand who can ask themselves without terror, 'What have I done in this world? wherein have I advanced the general work? and what is there left of me for good or for evil? '"

The last words which Judge Talfourd spoke were these: — "If I were to be asked what is the great want of English society so as to mingle class with class, I should say, in one word, The want is the want of sympathy." This is the main evil of our time. There is a widening chasm which divides the various classes of society. The rich shrink back from the poor, the poor shrink back from the rich. The one class withholds its sympathy and guidance, the other withholds its obedience and respect

Instead of the old principle that the world must be ruled by kind and earnest guardianship, in which the irregularities of fortune are in part made up by the spontaneous charity and affection of those who were better born; the rule now is, that self-interest, without regard to others, is the polar star of our earthly sphere, and that everything that stands in the way is to be trodden down beneath our hungry hoofs.

Sympathy seems to be dying out between employers and employed. In the great manufacturing towns the masters and workmen live apart from each other. They do not know each other. They have no sympathy with each other. If the men want higher wages, there is a strike; if the masters want lower wages, there is a lock-out. There is combination on both sides. Then a conference is proposed, sometimes with good results, sometimes with bad. Agitation goes on, and hard things are said. Sometimes the employer's house is set on fire and his carriages are burnt; the dragoons and infantry are called out, and there is a pause; but what an injury has been done to head and heart on both sides! ,

And what shall we say of domestic service? The want of sympathy has died out, at least in large cities. There is a constant change going on — one set of servants succeeds another. And yet the lives of families cannot be carried on upon the principles of mere barter— so much money, so much service. Servants, when they enter our homes, should be regarded, in one sense, as members of the family. It is now far otherwise; the servant, though her help is essential to our daily comfort, is regarded as but a hired person, doing her appointed work for so much current coin of the realm. She lives in the kitchen and sleeps in the attic. With the region between she has no concern, excepting as regards the work to be done there. No sympathy exists between the employer and the employed, no more than if they inhabited different countries, and spoke in different languages.

A lady writing to us about Annie Mackay, who lived with Robert Dick, her master, without fee or reward, but who would not receive poor rates after his death, says, "Her independent spirit is truly a worthy one, and is becoming sadly rare among our peasantry. It is a privilege to cherish it where it remains, for things roll on with such incessant and rapid change nowadays, that all old ideas are becoming overturned. Attachment such as she had for her master, dying with her and her generation, will, I fear, become an unknown sentiment in the one now growing up. I am often exasperated at hearing and reading reflections upon the lack of sympathy among masters towards their servants — as if we could stay the changed relations which railways, steamboats, and a little learning have effected on the feelings of servants towards us. They long for change, and cannot be satisfied without it,"

The want of sympathy pervades society. We do not know each other, or do not care for each other, as we ought to do. Selfishness strikes its roots very deep. In pursuit of pleasure or wealth we become hard and indifferent. Each person is eager to run his or her race, without regard to the feelings of others. We do not think of helping onwards those who have heavier burdens to bear than ourselves. Judge Talfourd's last words pointed out the mischief of such a condition. It makes men regardless of

151

fraud and crime. Not recognising the brotherhood of the race, they selfishly and keenly pursue their own interest over the bodies and souls, and over the lives and properties of others.

The idle and selfish man cares little for the rest of the world. He does nothing to help the forlorn or the destitute. "What are they to me?" he says; "let them look after themselves. Why should I help them? They have done nothing for me! They are suffering? There always will be suffering in the world. What can't be cured must be endured. It will be all the same a hundred years hence! "

"Don't care "can scarcely be roused by a voice from the dead. He is so much engrossed by his own pleasures, his own business, or his own idleness, that he will give no heed to the pressing claims of others. The discussions about poverty, ignorance, or suffering, annoy him. "Let them work," he says; "why should I keep them? Let them help themselves." The sloth is an energetic animal compared with "Don't care."

But "Don't care" is not let off so easily as he imagines. The man who does not care for others, who does not sympathise with and help others, is very often pursued with a just retribution. He doesn't care for the foul pestilential air breathed by the inhabitants of houses a few streets off; but the fever which has been bred there floats into his house, and snatches away those who are dearest to him. He doesn't care for the criminality, ignorance, and poverty massed there; but the burglar and the thief find him out in his seclusion. He doesn't care for pauperism; but he has to pay the heavy poor's-rate half-yearly. He doesn't care for politics; but there is an income tax, which is a war tax; and after all, he finds that "Don't care "is not such a cheap policy after all

"Don't care "was the man who was to blame for the well-known catastrophe: — " For want of a nail the shoe was lost, for want of a shoe the horse was lost, and for want of a horse the man was lost." Gallio was a "Don't care," of whom we are told that "he cared for none of these things." "Don't cares "like Gallio generally come to a bad end. .

The political economists say that the relationship of master and servant is simply a 'money bargain — so much service, so much wage. In the calculations of the economists, this is doubtless the contract which they are required to recognise. But the moralist, the philosopher, the statesman, the man, should acknowledge, in the positions of master and servant, a social tie, imposing upon the parties certain duties and affections growing out of their common sympathies as human beings, and the positions they respectively fill. There should be kindness on both sides, with the respect due to immortal beings. Without this sort of respect, which can only exist where the sense of the real dignity of man as a living soul has penetrated, not merely in the convictions but in the feelings, any amelioration of the condition of society is hopeless.

"Yes!" said Sydney Smith, "he is of the utilitarian school! The man is so hard that you might drive a broad-wheeled waggon over him, and it would produce no impression. If you were to bore holes in him with a gimlet, I am convinced sawdust would come out of him. That school treat mankind as if they were mere machines; the feelings or the heart never enter into their consideration."

Where has our faithfulness, loyalty, and disinterestedness gone? Fidelity seems to be a lost art. It is now a matter of money. Mutual respect has departed. "He that respects not is not respected," says Herbert. We have to go back to the old times for our guiding maxims. The workman respects not the master, and the master respects not the servant. For many years the workman in this country received higher wages than prevailed over the rest of Europe. That time has come to a close. Railways and steamboats tend to make the wages of all countries nearly equal. The time has come when all classes will have to begin a new course of life.

It is not so much literary culture that is wanted, as habits of reflection, thoughtfulness, and conduct. Wealth cannot purchase pleasures of the highest sort. It is the heart, taste, and judgment, which determine the happiness of man, and restore him to the highest form of being. Bums says: —

> "It's no in titles nor in rank;
> It's no in wealth like Lon'ou Bank,
> To purchase peace and rest;
> It's no in making muckle mair;
> It's no in books; it's no in lear,
> To make us truly blest:
> If Happiness hae not her seat
> And centre in the breast,
> We may be wise, or rich, or great,
> But never can be blest."

A man of great observation said that there are as many miseries beyond riches as there are on this side of them. The rich man has lost the spirit of encountering difficulties in his efforts to rise to the fortune which he has achieved. But what is he to do with what he has gained? If he has no other resource but the means of accumulating money, he is miserable. Like the rich tallow-chandler, his only pleasure is to go to his old shop "on melting days." He has not been educated to take pleasure in books, to look with interest on the progress of science, to enter into the many avenues which lead to the relief of distress. And yet he holds in his hand a wand of magic power, — he has money to relieve misery, and to supply the need of the famishing. He may silence the cry of hunger. He may make glad the heart of the widow and the orphan. But no! He cares more for the money which he has acquired than for the amelioration of the helpless and miserable.

The less we seek, the more strictly we live, and the more happy we are; for an unselfish life kills vices, extinguishes desires, strengthens the soul, and elevates the mind to higher things. "The fewer things a man wants," said Socrates, "the nearer he is to God." When Michael Angelo's servant, Urbino, lay on his deathbed, the aged sculptor watched over him night and day, notwithstanding his own infirmities. He thus writes of him to Vasari: "My friend, I shall write ill, but I must reply to your letter. Urbino, you know, is dead. That has been both a favour to me from God, and a subject of bitter grief — a favour, because he who in his life took care of me, has taught me in dying, not alone to die without regret, but to desire death. He lived with me for twenty -six years, always good, intelligent, and faithful. I had enriched him, and the moment when I thought to find in him a staff for my old age, he escapes, leaving me only the hope of seeing him again in heaven."

Dionysius, the Carthusian, addressed married persons thus: — "Act and speak to your servants as you would wish others to do to you if you were a servant. The master and mistress should show themselves towards all their servants loving, patient, humble, and pacific, while at the same time just. Never should they speak proudly or severely to them; but, if any fault should be committed in the family, they ought piously and patiently to bear it, or with charity to correct it, remembering how many faults are committed by servants, and yet how God has mercy on them."

It is not for ourselves alone that we work and strive. It is for others as well as for ourselves. There are moral laws, family ties, domestic affections, home government and guidance, which stand on a higher level and are based on nobler considerations than selfish pleasures or money payment We must beware how we allow our views to centre in ourselves. "No one," said Epictetus, "who is a lover of riches, or a lover of pleasure, or a lover of glory, can at the same time be a lover of mea" "To be a lover of men," said St. Anthony, "is, in fact, to live." Thus love is the universal principle of good. It is glorified in human intelligence. It is the only remedy for the woes of the human race. It is sweet in action — in learning, in philosophy, in manners, in legislation, in government.

The love of excellence is inseparable from a spirit of uncompromising detestation for all that is base and criminal Froissart describes Gaston de Foix as "one who was in everything so perfect that he cannot be praised too much; he loved that which ought to be beloved, and hated that which ought to be hated." St. Augustine says nearly the same thing: "Virtue is nothing but well-directed love, inducing us to love what we ought to love, and to hate what is worthy of hatred."

"What is temperance," said another divine, "but love which no pleasure seduceth? What is prudence, but love which no error enticeth? What is fortitude, but love which endureth adverse things with courage? What is justice but love which composeth by a certain charm the inequalities of this life?" The Stoics recognised this wonderful power. "Before the birth of love," said Socrates, "many fearful things took place through the empire of necessity; but when this god was born all things arose to men."

Thoughtfulness, kindness, and consideration for others, will always repay themselves. They will produce a grateful return on the part of the objects, and services will be performed with a willingness and alacrity which mere money could never secure. Sympathy is the true warmth and light of the home — which binds together mistresses and servants, as well as husband and wife, father, mother, and children; and the home cannot be truly happy where it is not present — knitting together the whole household in one bond of domestic affection and concord.

154

The late Sir Arthur Helps, in one of his wise essays, says, "You observe a man becoming day by day richer, or advancing in station, or increasing in professional reputation, and you set him down as a successful man in life. But if his home is an ill-regulated one, where no links of affection extend throughout the family, whose former domestics (and he has had more of them than he can well remember) look back upon their sojourn with him as one unblessed by kind words or deeds, I contend that that man has not been successful. Whatever good fortune he may have in the world, it is to be remembered that he has always left one important fortress untaken behind him. That man's [or woman's] life does not surely read well when benevolence has found no central home. It may have sent forth rays in various directions, but there should have been a warm focus of love — that home nest which is formed round a good man's heart"

In the charming picture of domestic peace given by an anonymous author of the fourteenth century, we find that youths of the noblest houses used to serve at table when their fathers entertained their friends.

Cardan, praising the Venetian patricians, particularly notices their gracious and liberal manners towards their servants. He recommends the utmost gentleness and humanity towards them. Of the noble warrior Vectius it was said, "He governs all who are subject to him less by authority than by reason. One would say he was rather the steward than the master of his house."

It is scarcely necessary to speak of the sympathy of the home. "The first society," said Cicero, "is in marriage, then in a family, and then in a state." The father ruling over his family is a monarch. But his power must be in sympathy with those he rules. All progress begins at home; and from that source, be it pure or tainted, issue the principles and maxims that govern society. The motive power of the parents is sympathy and love. "The noblest and fairest quality," observes Jean Paul Richter, "with which nature could and must furnish woman for the benefit of posterity, was love, the most ardent, yet without return, and for an object unlike herself. The child receives love, and kisses, and night watchings, but at first it only answers with rebuffs; and the weak creature which requires most pays least. But the mother gives unceasingly, yea, her love only becomes greater with the necessity and thanklessness of the recipient, and she feels the greatest for the most feeble, as the father for the strongest child."

On the father depends the government of the house, on the woman its management. Has the father learnt to rule the house by kindness and self-control? Has the woman learnt any of those arts by which home is made comfortable? If not, marriage becomes a fearful strife of words and acts. "Indeed," said Sir Arthur Helps, "I almost doubt whether the head of a family does not do more mischief if he is unsympathetic, than even if he were unjust." It was a beautiful sentiment of one whom her lord proposed to put away. "Give me then back," she said, "that which I brought to you." "Yes," he replied, "your fortune shall return to you." "I thought not of fortune," said the lady; "give me back my real wealth — give me back my beauty and my youth — give me back the virginity of soul — give me back the cheerful mind, and the heart that had never been disappointed."

155

For a man to be happy, he must have a soul-mate as well as a help -
meet. Both must be true, chaste, and sympathetic. Towards their children
they must be loving. There are many trials in family life; but with self-
control and self-sacrifice they may be overcome. "Patience," says
Tertullian, "ornaments the woman, and proves the man. It is loved in a
boy, it is praised in a youth. In every age it is beautiful" Don Antonio de
Guevarra, when instructing a gentleman of Valentia as to the duties of a
husband, tells him that if he wishes to reply to any word of an angry
person, neither the strength of Samson nor the wisdom of Solomon would
suffice to him. Therefore, patience and forbearance. An ounce of good
cheer is worth a ton of melancholy.

The life of a woman can never be seen in its outward form, much less
in its inner. But the best preparation for both is the careful preparation of
womanliness — her natural inheritance. The word is indefinable. It is seen
in the weakness, the need to lean upon, to trust, to confide, to reverence,
and to serve; as much as it is seen in the strength that enables her to
endure, to protect, to defend, and to support We find it in the plasticity
that gives such marvellous power of adaptation, as well as in the firmness
that yields only to duty; in the gentleness that wins, and in the self-
devotion that overcomes. The true wife takes a sympathy in her husband's
pursuits. She cheers him, encourages him, and helps him. She enjoys his
successes and his pleasures; and makes as little as possible over his
vexations. In his seventy- second year, Faraday, after a long and happy
marriage, wrote to his wife: — "I long to see you, dearest, and to talk over
things together, and call to mind all the kindnesses I have received. My
head is full, and' my heart also; but my recollection rapidly fails, even as
regards the friends that are in the room with me. You will have to resume
your old function of being a pillow to my mind, and a rest — a happy-
making wife."

No man was more sympathetic than Charles Lamb. There are few who
have not heard of the one awful event in his life. When only twenty-one,
his sister Mary, in a fit of frenzy, stabbed her mocher to the heart with a
carving-knife. Her brother, from that moment, resolved to sacrifice his life
to his "poor, dear, dearest sister," and voluntarily became her companion.
He gave up all thoughts of love and marriage. Under the strong influence
of duty, he renounced the only attachment he had ever formed. With an
income of scarcely;ioo a year, he trod the journey of life alone, fortified by
his attachment for his sister. Neither pleasure nor toil ever diverted him
from his purpose.

When released from the asylum, she devoted part of her time to the
composition of the Tales from Shakespeare and other works. Hazlitt
speaks of her as one of the most sensible women he ever knew, though she
had through life recurring fits of insanity, and even when well was
constantly on the brink of madness. When she felt a fit of insanity coming
on, Charles would take her under his arm to the Hoxton Asylum. It was
affecting to see the young brother and his elder sister walking together and
weeping together, on this painful errand. He carried the strait-jacket in his
hand, and delivered her up to the care of the asylum authorities. When she

had recovered her reason, she went home again to her brother, who joyfully received her — treating her with the utmost tenderness. "God loves her," he says; "may we two never love each other less." Their affection continued for forty years, without a cloud, except such as arose from the fluctuations of her health. Lamb did his duty nobly and manfully, and he reaped a fitting reward.

Sympathy for others often exhibits itself in the desire to save the lives of those who are in peril. We have already related many instances of this kind; but another remains to be mentioned. One day Lady Watson was walking along the sea-shore collecting shells for her museum. On looking up, she saw a solitary man on a ledge of rock surrounded by water. She knew not who he was; but he was in risk of losing his life, and she determined to save him. The tide was rising rapidly, and the waves were furiously rushing in upon the land. It appeared almost impossible to rescue the forlorn man from his perilous position. Nevertheless she appealed to the boatmen, and offered a high reward to those who would go to sea and save the man. At first they hesitated, but at length a boat started, and reached the rock just as the man's strength was exhausted. They got him on board, and bore him safely to land. What was the lady's astonishment to find in the rescued man her own husband, Sir William Watson 1

Even a word spoken in good season is remembered. The famous Dr. Sydenham remarked that everybody, some time or other, would be the better or the worse for having but spoken to a good or bad man. The curate of Olney, the friend of Cowper, was one of those persons to whom few people could speak without being the better for it. He said of himself, "he could live no longer than he could love."

"A woman's memory saved me from much temptation, wrote one who had lived a wild life in a wild land. Not one of my own people ever knew her; she was dead before I left home. But there were some things that might otherwise have been too much for me, that I was quite safe from, just because I had loved her. I never felt that I had in any way lost her love, and I could not go with it in my heart to places where I could never have taken her. When I felt a little lonely because I could not join those who had been my comrades, I just braced up my heart with the thought, 'for her sake.'"[56]

Here is a story which shows the utter want of sympathy. It was told in a sermon by Robert Collyer, pastor of the Unity Church of Chicago, now of New York. Mr. Collyer was born at Keighley in Yorkshire, but spent most of his early life at Ilkley, now a fashionable watering-place. He was apprenticed to Jackie Birch, a blacksmith. He married while a workman at the anvil. He became a lay preacher among the Methodists. Afterwards he went to America, and became a preacher there. His sermons are full of life, poetry, and eloquence, founded upon a large experience of human character.

"I remember," he says, "in one of our love feasts in the Methodist Church in England, thirty years ago and more, that a man got up and told

---

[56] Miss J. F. Mayo.

us how he had lost his wife by the fever, and then, one! one, all his children, and that he had felt as calm and serene through it as if nothing had happened; not suffering in the least, not feeling a pang of pain; fended and shielded, as he believed, by the Divine grace, and up to that moment when he was talking to us, without a grief in his heart.

"As soon as he had done, the wise and manful old preacher who was leading the meeting got up and said, 'Now, brother, go home, and into your closet, and down on your knees, and never get up again, if you can help it, until you are a new man. What you have told us is not a sign of grace; it is a sign of the hardest heart I ever encountered in a Christian man. Instead of you being a saint, you are hardly good enough to be a decent sinner. Religion never takes the humanity out of a man, it makes him more human; and if you were human at all, such troubles as you have had ought to have broken your heart I know it would mine, and I pretend to be no more of a saint than other people; so I warn you, never tell such a story at a love feast again.'"

Let us take from Mr. Collyer's "Sermons" another touching story, showing the power of sympathy in another and truer direction. "Away off, I believe in Edinburgh, two gentlemen were standing at the door of an hotel one very cold day, when a little boy, with a poor thin blue face, his feet bare and red with the cold, and with nothing to cover him but a bundle of rags, came and said, 'Please, sir, buy some matches.' 'No, I don't want any,' said the gentleman 'But they're only a penny a box,' the little fellow pleaded. * Yes; but you see I don't want a box.' 'Then I 'll gie ye two boxes for a penny,' the boy said at last 'And so, to get rid of him,' the gentleman, who tells the story in an English paper, says, 'I bought a box, but then I found I had no change, so I said, "I 'll buy a box to-morrow." "Oh, do buy them the nicht," the boy pleaded again; "I 'll rin and get ye the change; for I 'm very hungry." 'So I gave him the shilling, and he started away. I waited for him, but no boy came. Then I thought I had lost my shilling; but still there was that in the boy's face I trusted, and I did not like to think badly of him.

"'Well, late in the evening a servant came and said a little boy wanted to see me. When he was brought in, I found it was a smaller brother of the boy who got my shilling, but, if possible, still more ragged, and poor, and thin. He stood a moment diving into his rags, as if he were seeking something; and then said, "Are you the gentleman that bought the matches frae Sandie?" "Yes!" "Weel, then, here's fourpence oot o' yer shillin'. Sandie canna come. He's no weel. A cart ran ower him, and knocked him doon; and he lost his bonnet, and his matches, and your elevenpence; and both his legs are broken, and he's no weel at a', and the doctor says he'll dee. And that's a' he can gie ye the noo," putting fourpence down on the table; and then the poor child broke down into great sobs. So I fed the little man,' the gentleman goes on to say, 'and then I went with him to see Sandie.

"I found that the two little things lived with a wretched drunken stepmother; their own father and mother were both dead. I found poor Sandie lying on a bundle of shavings; he knew me as soon as I came in, and said, "I got the change, sir, and was coming back; and then the horse

158

knocked me down, and both my legs are broken. And Reuby, little Reuby! I am sure I am deein' I and who will take care o' ye, Reuby, when I am gane? What will ye do, Reuby?" Then I took the poor little sufferer's hand, and told him I would always take care of Reuby.

He understood me, and had just strength to look at me as if he would thank me; then the light went out of his blue eyes; and in a moment

> "'He lay within the light of God,
> Like a babe upon the breast;
> Where the wicked cease from troubling,
> And the weary are at rest.'"[57]

Sympathy glorifies humanity. Its synonym is love. It goes forth to meet the wants and necessities of the sorrow-stricken and oppressed. Wherever there is cruelty, or ignorance, or misery, sympathy stretches forth its hand to console and alleviate. The sight of grief, the sound of a groan, takes hold of the sympathetic mind, and will not let it go. Out of sympathy and justice, some of the greatest events of modern times have emanated. Need we mention the abolition of slavery in England, America, and France; the education of the untaught; the spread of Sunday Schools; the efforts for the spread of temperance; the levelling-up of the down-trodden classes, in which men and women of the best classes take so much interest?

There is room for the sympathetic help of all. He who loves God loves his neighbour — poor or rich — and cannot fail to be just, true, and merciful. "The just man," said Massillon, "is above the world, and superior to all events. All creatures are subject to him, and he subject unto God alone." To tend the sick, to visit the widow and fatherless in their afflictions, to set on foot or to help in the schemes of benevolence, in elevating the poor — all this needs diligence, mercifulness, and love.

"Say what you will," says Dr. Martineau, "of the failures and errors of Christian enthusiasm, no zeal which you might deem more rational has done half as much for suffering humanity. When it has missed its own ends, it has reached others to which no colder zeal would ever have addressed itself. But for the Church, where would have been the School in Christendom? But for the missionary army, baffled and beaten as it has often been, where would the advancing lines of civilisation have stood, which are everywhere reducing the barbarism of the world? But for the reverence felt for the souls of men, how long should we have had to wait for the various forms of pity and healing for the body? Christians may have attempted many foolish things; but who have effected more wise ones? They may have said too much of despising the world; but who have done more to render it habitable? " And again, "If once, among the poorest, the living springs of religion are touched, and a family becomes God-fearing, a transfonmation forthwith sets in; the rags disappear; the furniture returns;

---

[57] The Life that now is : and Nature and Life. Sermons by Robert Collyer, Pastor of Unity Church, Chicago.

the sickness abates; the children brighten; the quarrels cease; the hard times are tided over better than before; and sorrow, once dull and sullen, is alive with hope and trust."

"Even the poorest of the poor," says Wordsworth, "have been themselves the fathers and the dealers out of some small blessings." A cobbler began the ragged schools at Portsmouth. Of him Dr. Guthrie said, "John Pounds is an honour to humanity, and deserves the tallest monument ever raised within the shores of Britain." A printer at Gloucester began the English Sunday Schools, which deserve a monument even higher than that of John Pounds. A shoemaker at Newcastle began the Missions to India. A factory girl initiated the Foundry Boys' Religious Society at Glasgow.

The poor know so much better than the rich what poor people need. Great cities have nothing more sorrowful to show us than their old children, with their shrewd anxious faces and knotted brows, on which hard care is stamped. The home of the poor is very often no home. The rich and the poor live separate and apart. Many barriers intervene to prevent their social intercourse. The poor have no society beyond that of their own class. They have no means of escape from intercourse with the coarse and uneducated Very poor men's children only exist as so many rivals for food with their parents; and they are dragged up, to enter prematurely on the harsh realities of life. To the upper ranks, the poor are as the inhabitants of an unexplored country.

It is only the poor who really and truly feel for the poor. They alone know each other's sufferings; they alone know each other's need of sympathy and kindness. People may talk as they will of the charity of the rich, but this is as nothing compared with the charity of the poor. In seasons of privation, of sickness, of inclemency, of distress, the poor are each other's comforters and supporters, to an extent that, among better circles, is never dreamt of. Contented to toil on, from day to day, and from year to year, for a scanty pittance, they have yet wherewithal to spare when a brother is in want or in distress. Nor is there ever wanting some friendly hand to smooth the pillow, and do all those little kindly offices which make sickness and suffering tolerable. The women of the poorer classes are, in this respect, especially devoted and untiring. They make sacrifices, and run risks, and bear privations, and exercise patience and kindness, to a degree that the world never knows of, and would scarcely believe even if it did know.

Much has been written of late about Robert Raikes; so that our notice of him will be but short Sunday schools had existed before his time. We have already referred to Cardinal Borromeos school, which has been more than four hundred years in existence. There were Sunday schools in England at a much later date. It was William King, a woollen card-maker at Dursley, who first dropped the idea into Raikes's mind. He had established a Sunday school at Dursley, which failed for want of co-operation, though he never lost faith in his plan. When at Gloucester one Sunday, he called upon Raikes, and the two walked together by the Island — one of the lowest parts of the city. There the ragged children were occupied in various sports. "What a pity," said King, "that the Sabbath is so desecrated! " "But how," said Raikes, "is it to be altered?" "Sir, open a Sunday school, as I have done at Dursley, with the help of a faithful journeyman; but the multitude of business prevents my spending so much time in it as I could wish, as I feel that I want rest."

Raikes visited the Gloucester prison. He found a young man there condemned to death for housebreaking. "He had never," says Raikes, received the smallest instruction. He had never offered a prayer to his Creator." He knew God only as a name to swear by. He was utterly devoid of all sense of a future state. This interview made a great impression upon Raikes's mind. Very few of the young people about the city received any education whatever. As soon as they were able to do anything, they were put to work, and in their intervals of leisure, of which Sunday was the chief, the children were left altogether without restraint.

He then founded a Sunday school He had a sympathy for childhood, and won the love of the little ragamuffins, as he affectionately called them. He proposed to teach them to read and learn the Church Catechism, and to enforce order among the little heathens. In 1783 he proceeded to hire four schools, and agreed to give a shilling to each of the teachers of the neglected children. The curate of the parish was also invited to visit the schools on Sunday afternoons, and examine the progress made by the pupils. Raikes's schools possessed the most valuable elements of teaching — genuine love for children on the part of the teachers. Their little hearts were stirred by the love of those who ministered to them.

Nearly thirty years after the establishment of Raikes's first schools, there came to visit him in his retirement a young Quaker, named Joseph Lancaster, to whose energetic efforts was due the formation of the association afterwards known as "The British and Foreign School Society," for giving weekday instruction to the children of the poor. At that time the founder of Sunday schools was seventy-two years of age, and past active work, but he still took a lively interest in his much-loved institution. Many were Lancaster's inquiries respecting the origin of Sunday schools; and an interesting account has been preserved of one of Raikes's replies.

Leaning on the arm of his visitor, the old man led him through the thoroughfares of Gloucester to the spot in a back street where the first school was held. "Pause here," said the old man. Then, uncovering his head, and closing his eyes, he stood for a moment in silent prayer. Then turning towards his friend, while the tears rolled down his cheeks, he said, "This is the spot on which I stood when I saw the destitution of the children and the desecration of the Sabbath by the inhabitants of the city. As I asked, ' Can nothing be done?' a voice answered, 'Try.' I did try, and see what God has wrought I can never pass by this spot, where the word ' try ' came so powerfully into my mind, without lifting up my hands and heart to heaven in gratitude to God for having put such a thought into my heart."

Knowing that Raikes was for many years a constant visitor both at the city and county gaols, and had ample opportunities of ascertaining whether any of the three thousand children whose education he had superintended had come within its prison walls, Lancaster asked him directly whether such had ever been the case. Appealing to his memory, which even at that advanced age was strong and healthy, Raikes with confidence answered, "None."[58]

Mary Anne Clough, the factory girl of Glasgow, occupied a much humbler position in society than Robert Raikes. She was a mill-hand, while he was the editor of a newspaper. But she found the opportunity, as everybody can do, of helping to heal the wounds of humanity. It was not "culture "that inspired her, but tender womanly sympathy. She worked with her hands for her daily bread; but love, the great educator, lifted her up to a higher field of labour. It was only when her day's work was over, that her labours of love began. She saw a great many poor boys employed in the foundries, who seemed to have no one to care for them. They were utterly neglected, and were early initiated into the lessons of vice The girl had compassion on them. "I will try," she said, "if I can win them to God, and to doing what is good."

As soon as she had formed her resolution, she endeavoured to carry it into practice. She asked for, and obtained, the use of a room below the factory in which she worked. She opened it on a Sunday in June 1862. She soon drew a number of foundry boys about her, with ragged clothes and dirty faces — from the back courts where they were wont to spend their time in smoking or in coarse merriment She taught them to spell, to read, to be clean, to be good, to be religious. She loved these poor, wandering, neglected boys. She truly helped them in their time of need.

Nor were her efforts to bless and to save these boys confined to Sundays. They engaged all her spare time throughout the week. This noble girl, so soon as the day's work- was over, found out the homes of the boys — if homes they could be called. She knew them all, their sad histories, their dangers and hardships; and by her Christian principles, her winning ways, and overflowing kindness, she gained over them an influence which was productive of the happiest results. So distinguished, indeed, were they from others of the same class and calling — by their superior industry, their good conduct, and their freedom from profane language — that "Mary Anne's boys "became a proverb in the foundries.

"It makes one sad," says Dr. Guthrie, "to think how many Christians with tenfold more time, more money, more education, more influence, have not done a tithe of the good this girl did. If any might have justly pleaded the excuse, 'Am I my brother's keeper?' it was one who found it hard to keep herself, who, starting each morning to the sound of the factory bell, and hurrying along dark and silent streets, had gone through hours of work ere half the world was awake.... And many a night she went forth on her missions of mercy, to seek the lost and raise the fallen, and close with her own gentle hands the wounds of humanity."

For about three years Mary Anne Clough continued her noble labours, when at length she was compelled, by failing health, to resign them into the hands of others. But the seed which she had sown took root, and

---

[58] Robert Raikes : Journalist and Philanthropist, By Alfred Gregory, 1877.

ripened into a goodly crop. In 1865 Glasgow Foundry Boys.' Religious Society was formed in six years it had a roll of 14,000 boys and girls, superintended by a staff of about 1500 monitors, and more than 200 gentlemen. More than 300 gentlemen delivered addresses to the young people in various parts of the city. Everything was done for their social elevation. Their society formed a link between the Sunday school and the church. Religious and secular education was freely imparted. Temperance was the key-note of the institution. Penny banks and savings banks were established. Bands and choral societies proved another source of power. Every Saturday evening a musical entertainment was given Everything was done to withdraw the young people from the carelessness, ignorance, and wickedness of city life. With the exception of the superior secular teachers, all who work for the institution are volunteers — their labour is one of love.

In summer time the boys and girls, with their superintendents, take a holiday in the country. They generally go to the Duke of Argyll's park at Inveraray — his Grace being the Honorary President of the Society. It was on one of such occasions that we became acquainted with the noble work done by the Institution. Though it still preserves the name of the Foundry Boys' Society, its uses have been extended, until it has become a society for all classes of working boys and girls. The good which it has already done is inexpressible. Would that every city had an institution of a similar kind! As yet it has only been imitated in Scotland — in Greenock, Edinburgh, Dundee and Aberdeen. What of Manchester, Leeds, Bradford, and the densely-populated manufacturing towns of the north of England? Similar institutions in those places would prove of immense value.

CHAPTER XL

PHILANTHROPY

Sis amicus Dei, fide, spe, et opere.

Michael Scott

Sweet mercy is nobility's true badge.

Shakespeare

O brother, fainting on your road 1
Poor sister, whom the righteous shun,
There comes for you, ere life and strength be done,
An arm to bear your load.

The Ode of Life

Many groans arise from dying men, which we hear not. Many cries

are uttered by widows and fatherless children, which reach not our ears.
Many cheeks are wet with tears, and faces sad with unutterable grief,
which we see not. Cruel tyranny is encouraged. The hands of robbers are
strengthened, and thousands are kept in helpless slavery, who never
injured us.

John Woolman (Quaker), 1775

MEN are very slow to give up their faith in physical force, as necessary for the guidance, correction, and discipline of others. Force is a very palpable thing, and dispenses with all inquiry into causes and effects. It is the short way of settling matters, without any weighing of arguments. It is the summary logic of the barbarians, among whom the best man is he who strikes the heaviest blow or takes the surest aim.

Even civilised nations have been very slow to abandon their faith in force. Until very recent times, men of honour, who chanced to fall out, settled their quarrels by the duel; and governments, almost without exception, resort to arms to settle their quarrels as to territory or international arrangements. Indeed, we have been so trained and educated into a belief in the efficacy of force, — war has become so identified in history with honour, glory, and all sorts of high-sounding names, — that we can scarcely imagine it possible that the framework of society could be held together, were the practice of force discarded, and that of love, benevolence, and justice, substituted in its place.

And yet doubts are widely entertained as to the efficacy of the policy of force. It is suspected that force begets more resistance than it is worth, and that if men are put down by violent methods, a spirit of rebellion is created, which breaks out from time to time in violent deeds, in hatred, in vice, and in crime. Such, indeed, has been the issue of the policy of force in all countries and in all times. The history of the world is, to a great extent, the history of the failure of physical force.

Are we growing wiser? Do we begin to see that if we would make men better and happier, we must resort to a greater and more beneficent force — the force of gentleness? Such methods of treating human beings have never in any case produced resistance or rebellion; have never made them worse, but in all cases made them better. Love is a constraining power; it elevates and civilises all who come under its influence. It indicates faith in man, and without faith in man's better nature no methods of treatment will avail in improving him. Kindness draws out the better part of every nature — disarming resistance, dissipating angry passions, and melting the hardest heart. It overcomes evil, and strengthens good. Extend the principle to nations, and it still applies. It has already banished feuds between clans, between provinces; let it have free play, and war between nations will also cease. Though the idea may seem Utopian now, future generations will come to regard war as a crime too horrible to be perpetrated.

"Love," says Emerson, "would put a new face on this weary old world, in which we dwell as pagans and enemies too long; and it would warm the heart to see how fast the vain diplomacy of statesmen, the impotence of armies and navies, and lines of defence, would be superseded by this unarmed child. Love will creep where it cannot go; will accomplish that, by imperceptible methods — being its own fulcrum, lever, and power — which force could never achieve. Have you not seen in the woods, in a late autumn morning, a poor fungus or mushroom; a plant without any solidity, nay, that seemed nothing but a soft mush or jelly, by its constant, bold, and inconceivably gentle pushing, manage to break its way up through the frosty ground, and actually to lift a hard crust on its head? This is the symbol of the power of kindness. The virtue of this principle in human society, in application to great interests, is obsolete and forgotten. Once or twice in history it has been tried, in illustrious instances, with signal success. This great, overgrown, dead Christendom of ours still keeps alive, at least, the name of a lover of mankind. But one day all men will be lovers, and every calamity will be dissolved in the universal sunshine.'*

The principle of force has, in past times, been dismally employed in the treatment of lunatics, lepers, galley slaves, and criminals. Lunatics were chained and put in cages like wild beasts. The lepers were banished from the towns, and made to live in some remote quarter, away from human beings — though themselves human.[59] The galley slaves were made to tug at the oar until they expired in misery. Criminals were crowded together without regard to age or sex, until the prisons of Europe became the very sink of iniquity. Some four hundred years ago criminals were given over to be vivisected alive by the surgeons of Florence and Pisa. Their place has now been taken by dumb brutes.

St. Vincent de Paul was a philanthropist of the highest order. He was the son of a farmer in Languedoc. His father educated him for the ministry, selling the oxen from the plough to provide for his college expenses. A small legacy was left him by a friend at Marseilles, and he went thither by

---

[59] The following touching passage was written by the late poet Heine — the last words he ever wrote for publication : — "In the year 1480, says the Limburg Chronicle, everybody was piping and singing lays more lovely and delightful than any which had ever yet been known in German lands, and all people, young and old, the women especially, went quite mad about them, so that their melody was heard from morning to night Only, the Chronicle adds, the author of these songs was a young clerk, afflicted with leprosy, who lived alone in a desolate place hidden from all the world. You doubtless know, dear reader, what a fearful malady this leprosy was in the Middle Ages, and how the poor wretches who fell under this incurable sickness were banished from all society, and allowed to come near no human being. Like living corpses they wandered forth, closely wrapped from head to foot, their hood drawn over their face, and carrying in their hand a rattle called the Lazarus rattle, with which they gave notice of their approach, that every one might get betimes out of their way. This poor clerk, then, whose fame as a poet and singer the Limburg Chronicle extols, was just such a leper, and he sat desolate in the dreary waste of his misery, while all Germany, joyous and tuneful, sang and piped his lays. . . . Ofttimes in my sombre visions of the night I think I see before me the poor clerk of the Limburg Chronicle, my brother in Apollo, and his sad suffering eyes stare strangely at me from under his hood; but at the same moment he seems to vanish, and dying away in the distance, like the echo of a dream, I hear the jarring creak of the Lazarus rattle."

sea to receive it. He returned home by sea, and the ship by which he sailed was captured, after a sharp engagement, by three African corsairs. During the fight Vincent was severely wounded by an arrow. The crew and passengers were put in chains, Vincent among them. He was taken to Tunis and made a galley slave. Being unfit for sea work, and constantly sick, he was sold to a Moorish physician At the end of a year his master died, and he was sold again to a farmer, who was a native of Nice. Vincent reconverted his master to Christianity, and they resolved to escape together. They put to sea in a small bark, and landed at Aigues Mortes, in the south of France.

Shortly after, St. Vincent de Paul entered a brotherhood at Rome, whose office it was to wait on the sick in hospitals. He next removed to Paris, where he carried on the same work. He then became a tutor in the family of the Count de Joigni, who was Inspector of the Galères or Hulks. There the young priest saw terrible sights — men chained to the oar, and toiling like African slaves. He devoted himself to their help with such effect, that Louis XIII., hearing of his doings, made him Almoner-General to the Galleys. On one occasion he actually changed places with a miserable outcast The prisoner went free, while Vincent wore his chain, and did the convict's work. He lived on convict fare, and lived in convict society. He was soon sought out and released; but the hurts he had received from the convict's chain lasted all his life. He was replaced in his position; and worked on in holy ardour. He won many of the convicts back to penitence; and by his strong representations improved both the prisons and the galleys.

The rest of his life is well known. He returned to Paris and established the order of Sisters of Mercy, thus giving a noble scope for the charity and benevolence of women. These Sisters of Mercy have been the prime workers in every charitable task in France and elsewhere — nursing the sick, teaching the young, and attending deserted children — ever foremost in every good work. Remembering his captivity, he devoted himself to raising money for redeeming the African captives. He was thus the means of ransoming no less than twelve hundred slaves. The deeds of the corsairs were finally put an end to by the combined fleets of France and England, in 18 16, when the old den of pirates was razed at Algiers.

We hear of the dungeons and chains in the castles of chivalry; but what tales of misery and of cruelty are unfolded before the legal tribunals of the modems! Search the annals of the poor in our great cities, and how often will you have to say with Jeremy Taylor, "This is an uncharitableness next to the cruelties of savages, and an infinite distance from the mercies of Jesus! "

The benevolent spirit of John Howard was first directed to the reform of prisons by a personal adventure of a seemingly accidental nature. He was on a voyage to Portugal at a time when Lisbon was an object of painful interest — still smoking in ruins from the effects of the memorable earthquake. He had not proceeded far on his voyage when the packet in which he had embarked was captured by a French privateer. He was treated with great cruelty. He was allowed no food or water for forty-eight hours; and after landing at Brest, he was imprisoned in the castle with the rest of the captives. They were cast into a filthy dungeon, and were kept for a considerable time longer without food. At length a joint of mutton was flung into the den, which the unhappy men were forced to tear in pieces, and gnaw like wild beasts. The prisoners experienced the same cruel treatment for a week, and were compelled to lie on the floor of the horrible dungeon, with nothing but straw to shelter them from the noxious and pestilential damps of the place,

Howard was at last set at liberty, and returned to England; but he gave himself no rest until he had succeeded in liberating many of his fellow-prisoners. He then opened a correspondence with English prisoners in other gaols and fortresses on the Continent; and found that sufferings as bad, or even greater than his own, were the common lot of the captives.

Shortly after, his attention was called to the state of English prisons, in the course of his duties as High Sheriff of the county of Bedford. This office is usually an honorary one, leading merely to a little pomp and vain show. But with Howard it was different. To be appointed to an office was with him to incur the obligation to fulfil its duties. He sat in court and listened attentively to the proceedings. When the trials were over, he visited the prison in which the criminals were confined There he became acquainted with the shameful and brutal treatment of malefactors. The sight that met his eyes in prison revealed to him the nature of his future life-mission.

The prisons of England, as well as of other countries, were then in a frightful state. The prisoners were neither separated nor classified. The comparatively innocent and the abominably guilty were herded together; so that common gaols became the hotbeds of crime. The hungry man who stole a loaf of bread found himself in contact with the burglar or the murderer. The debtor and the forger — the petty thief and the cut- throat — the dishonest girl and the prostitute — were all mixed up together. Swearing, cursing, and blaspheming pervaded the gaol Religious worship was unknown. The place was made over to Beelzebub. The devil was king.

Howard thus simply tells his impressions as to the treatment of prisoners: — "Some who by the verdict of juries were declared not guilty — some on whom the grand jury did not find such an appearance of guilt as subjected them to a trial — and some whose prosecutors did not appear against them — after having been confined for months, were dragged back to gaol, and locked up again until they should pay sundry fees to the gaoler, the clerk of assize, and such like." He also remarked that the "hard-hearted creditors." who sometimes threatened their debtors that they should rot in gaol, had indeed a very truthful significance; for that in gaol men really did rot — literally sinking and festering from filth and malaria. Howard estimated that, numerous as were the lives sacrificed on the gallows, quite as many fell victims to cold and damp, disease and hunger.

The gaolers' salaries were not paid by the public, but by the discharged innocents. Howard pleaded with the Justices of the Peace, that a salary should be paid to the gaoler. He was asked for a precedent He said he should find one. He mounted his horse, and rode throughout the country for the precedent. He visited county gaols far and near. He did not find a precedent for the payment of a salary to the gaoler, but he found an amount of wretchedness and misery prevailing amongst the prisoners, which determined him to devote himself to the reformation of the gaols of England and of the world.

At Gloucester he found the castle in the most horrible condition. The castle had become the gaol. It had a common court for all the prisoners, male and female. The debtors' ward had no windows. The night room for men felons was close and dark, A fever had prevailed in the gaol, which carried off' many of the prisoners. The keeper had no salary. The debtors had no allowance of food. In the episcopal city of Ely the accommodation was no better. To prevent the prisoners' escape they were chained on their backs to the floor. Several bars of iron were placed over them, and an iron collar covered with spikes was fastened round their necks. At Norwich the cells were built underground, and the prisoners were given an allowance of straw, which cost a guinea a year. The gaoler not only had no salary, but he paid £ 40 a year to the under-sheriff for his situation! He made his income by extortion.

Howard went on from place to place, inspired by his noble mission. The idea of ameliorating the condition of prisoners engrossed his whole thoughts, and possessed him like a passion. No toil, nor danger, nor bodily suffering could turn him from the great object of his life. He went from one end of England to the other, in order to drag forth to the light the disgusting mysteries of the British prison-houses. In many cases he gave freedom to such as were confined for some petty debt, and to many others who were utterly guiltless of crime. Upon the conclusion of his survey, the House of Commons resolved itself into a committee, in order to ascertain the actual state of the case. He appeared before it, laden with his notes. In the course of the inquiry, a member, surprised at the extent and minuteness of his information, inquired at whose expense he had travelled. Howard was almost choked before he could reply.

The thanks of the Legislature were given him at the close of his evidence. They followed in the track which he had pointed out Bills were passed in 1774 — the year after he had begun his work — abolishing aU fees, providing salaries for the gaolers, and ordering all prisoners to be discharged immediately upon acquittal It was also directed that all gaols should be cleansed, whitewashed, and ventilated; that infirmaries should be erected for the healing and maintenance of prisoners; and that proper gaols should be built Howard was confined to his bed while the bills passed; but so soon as he had recovered from the illness and fatigue to which his self-imposed labours had subjected him, he rose again, and revisited the gaols, for the purpose of ascertaining that the Acts were duly carried out.

Having exhausted England, Howard proceeded into Scotland and Ireland, and inspected the gaols in those countries. He found them equally horrible, and published the results of his inquiries with equal success. Then he proceeded to the Continent, to inquire into the prison accommodation there. At Paris the gates of the Bastille were closed against

168

him; but as respects the other French prisons, though they were bad enough, they were far superior to those of England. When it was ascertained that Howard was making inquiries about the Bastille, an order was issued for his imprisonment, but he escaped in time. He revenged himself by publishing an account of the State prison, translated from a work recently published, which he obtained after great difficulty and trouble.

Howard travelled onwards to Belgium, Holland, and Germany. He made notes everywhere, and obtained a large amount of information — the result of enormous labour. After returning to England, to see that the work of prison reform had taken root, he proceeded to Switzerland, on the same errand of love. He there found the science of prison discipline revealed. The prisoners were made to work, not only for their own benefit, but to diminish the taxes levied for the maintenance of prisons.

After three years of indefatigable work, during which he travelled more than thirteen thousand miles, Howard published his great work on the "The State of Prisons," It was received with great sensation. He was again examined by the House of Commons as to the further measures required for the reformation of prisoners. He recommended houses of correction. He had observed one at Amsterdam, which he thought might be taken as a model

He again proceeded thither to ascertain its method of working. From Holland he went to Prussia; crossed Silesia, through the opposing ranks of the armies of Austria and Prussia. He spent some time at Vienna, and proceeded to Italy. At Rome, he applied for admission to the dungeons of the Inquisition, But, as at the Bastille in France, the gates of the Inquisition were closed against him. All others were opened. He returned home through France, having travelled four thousand six hundred miles , during this tour. Wherever he went, he was received with joy. The blessings of the imprisoned followed him. He distributed charity with an open hand. But he did more. He opened the eyes of the thoughtful and the charitable of all countries to the importance of prison reform.

He never rested. He again visited the prisons in Great Britain, travelling nearly seven thousand miles. He found that his previous efforts had done some good. The flagrant abuses which he had before observed had been removed; and the gaols were cleaner, healthier, and more orderly. He made another foreign tour to amplify his knowledge. He had visited the gaols of the southern countries of Europe. He now resolved to visit those of Russia. He entered Petersburg alone and on foot. The police discovered him, and he was invited to visit the Empress Catherine at Court. He respectfully informed her Majesty that he had come to Russia to visit the dungeons of the captives and the abodes of the wretched, not the palaces and courts of kings and queens.

Armed with power, he went to see the infliction of the knout A man and woman were brought out The man received sixty strokes, and the woman twenty-five. "I saw the woman,'" says Howard, "in a very weak condition some days after, but could not find the man any more," Determined to ascertain what had become of him, Howard visited the executioner. "Can yon," he said, "inflict the knout so as to occasion death in a very short time?" "Yes!" "In how short a time?" "In a day or two." "Have you ever so inflicted it?"' "I have!" "Have you lately?" "Yes! the last man who was punished by my hand with the knout died of the punishment." "In what manner do you thus render it mortal?" "By one or two strokes on the sides, which carry off" large pieces of flesh." "Do you receive orders thus to inflict the punishment?" "I do! " Thus the boast of Russia, that capital punishments had been abolished throughout the empire, was effectually exposed.

He wrote from Moscow, that 'no less than seventy thousand recruits for the army and navy have died in the Russian hospitals during a single year." Now, Howard was an accurate man, incapable of saying anything but the truth; and therefore, this horrible fact cannot but heighten our detestation both of war and of despotism. From Russia he travelled home by way of Poland, Prussia, Hanover, and the Austrian Netherlands. In 1783 he travelled for the same purpose through Spain and Portugal. He published the results of his travels in a second appendix to his great work.

Twelve years had now passed since Howard had given himself up to the absorbing pursuit of his life. He had travelled upwards of forty-two thousand miles in visiting the gaols of the chief towns and cities of Europe; and he had expended upwards of; 30,000 in relieving the prisoners, the sick, and the friendless. He had not, however, finished his work He determined to visit the countries where the plague prevailed, in order, if possible, to discover a remedy for this frightful disease. His object was to go, in the first place, to Marseilles, through France.

In November 1785 he set out for Paris. The French, remembering his pamphlet on the Bastille, prohibited him from appearing on the soil of France. He disguised himself, and entered Paris. During the same night in which he arrived, he was roused from his bed by the police. A lucky thought enabled him to dispose of them for a few minutes, during which he rose, dressed himself, escaped from the house, and was forthwith on his way to Marseilles. He there obtained admission to the Lazaretto, and obtained the information which he required.

He sailed for Smyrna, where the plague was raging. From thence, the resolute philanthropist sailed to the Adriatic by an infected vessel, in order that he might be subjected to the strictest quarantine. He took the fever, and lay in quarantine for forty days — suffering fearfully, without help, alone in his misery. At length he recovered, and made his way home to England. He visited his country estate, provided for the poor of the neighbourhood, and parted from his humble friends as a father from his children.

He had one more journey to make. It was his last. His intention was to extend his inquiries on the subject of the plague. In 1789 he proceeded through Holland, Germany, and Russia, intending to go to Turkey, Egypt, and the States of Barbary. But he was only able to travel as far as Kherson, in Russian Tartary. There, as usual, he visited the prisoners, and caught the gaol fever. Alone, amidst strangers, he sickened and died in his sixty-fourth year. To one who was by his bedside he marked a spot in a churchyard in Dauphiny, where he wished to be buried. "Lay me quietly in the earth, place a sundial over my grave, and let me be forgotten."

But the noble Howard will not be forgotten so long as the memory of man lasts. He was the benefactor of the most miserable of men. He thought nothing of himself, but only of those who without him would have been friendless and unhelped. In his own time he achieved a remarkable degree of success. But his influence did not die with him, for it has continued to influence not only the legislation of England, but of all civilised nations, down to the present time.

Burke thus described him: — "He visited all Europe to dive into the depths of dungeons; to plunge into the infection of hospitals; to survey the mansions of sorrow and pain; to take the gauge and dimensions of misery, depression, and contempt; to remember the forgotten; to attend the neglected; to visit the forsaken; to compare and collect the distresses of all men in all countries. His plan is original, and it is as full of genius as it is of humanity. It is a voyage of discovery, a circumnavigation of charity; and already the benefit of his labour is felt more or less in every country."

From the time of Howard the treatment of prisoners has been greatly improved. At first it was only benevolent persons who aimed at their improvement, such as Sarah Martin, Mrs. Fry, and other kindred spirits. Sydney Smith mentions that on one occasion he requested permission to accompany Mrs. Fry to Newgate. He was so moved by the sight, that he wept like a child. Referring to the subject afterwards, in a sermon, he said—" There is a spectacle which this town now exhibits, that I will venture to call the most solemn, the most Christian, the most affecting which any human being ever witnessed. To see that holy woman in the midst of the wretched prisoners; to see them all calling earnestly upon God, soothed by her voice, animated by her look, clinging to the hem of her garment, and worshipping her as the only being who has ever loved them, or taught them, or noticed them, or spoken to them of God! This is the sight that breaks down the pageant of the world; which tells them that the short hour of life is passing away, and that we must prepare by some good deeds to meet God that it is time to give, to pray, to comfort; to go, like this blessed woman, and do the work of our heavenly. Saviour, Jesus, among the guilty, among the broken-hearted and the sick, and to labour in the deepest and the darkest wretchedness of life."

Mrs. Fry succeeded, by her persevering efforts, in effecting a complete reformation in the state of the prison, and in the conduct of the female prisoners; insomuch that the grand jury, in their report made to the Old Bailey, after their visit to Newgate in 1818, state, "that if the principles which govern her regulations were adopted towards the males as well as the females, it would be the means of converting a prison into a school of reform; and instead of sending criminals back into the world hardened in vice and depravity, they would be repentant, and probably become useful members of society,"

Mrs. Tatnall also, a woman less known than Mrs. Fry, devoted herself to the reformation and improvement of the prisoners in Warwick gaol, of which her husband was governor. Many a criminal was brought back by

171

her from the ways of vice to those of virtue and industry. Boys and girls, being younger in iniquity, were the especial subjects of her care. She was almost invariably successful in her efforts to restore them to society.

But individual help could do but little in improving or reclaiming the mass of prisoners. It was only by the help of the Legislature that so large a question could be treated. One of the chief objects of legislation is to prevent crime by removing the inducements to commit it; and the main object of prison discipline is to reform the moral condition of the criminal, and to lead him back to the bosom of the society against which he has sinned. This, as a matter of justice, is due to the criminal, who is too often made so by the circumstances in which he has been brought up, by his want of training, and by the unequal laws which society has enacted.

Before, society took its revenge upon criminals, and treated them like wild beasts; now, a milder treatment is adopted, with a view to their reclamation. The governors of the Sing Sing Penitentiary, in the State of New York, led the way in the reformatory treatment of criminals. Their attention was directed to the subject by the reports of Mr. Edmonds. He said that "he had no faith whatever in the system of violence which had so long prevailed in the world, — the system of tormenting criminals into what was called good order, and of never appealing to anything better than the base sentiment of fear. He had seen enough in his own experience to convince him that, degraded as they were, they had still hearts that could be touched by kindness, consciences that might be aroused by appeals to reason, and aspirations for a better course of life, which needed only the cheering voice of sympathy and hope, to be strengthened into permanent reformation." A new system of criminal treatment was, accordingly, in conformity with Mr. Edmonds's recommendations, commenced at Sing Sing prison, and was soon attended by the happiest effects. The rule now was, to punish as sparingly as possible, and to encourage where there was any desire for improvement. Many criminals, formerly regarded as irreclaimable, were thus restored to society as useful and profitable citizens, and but a very small proportion of these were found to relapse into their former habits.

The system was found especially successful in the case of women. One of the matrons addressed them in the chapel on the duty of self-government, and the necessity of a reformation of character if they wished to escape from misery, either in this world or the next "The effect of this little experiment," says the matron, in an after statement, "has been manifest in the more quiet and gentle movements of the prisoners, in their softened and subdued tones of voice, and in their ready and cheerful obedience. It has deepened my conviction that, however degraded by sin, or hardened by outrage or wrong, while reason maintains its empire over the mind, there is no heart so callous or obdurate that the voice of sympathy and kindness may not reach it, or so debased as to give no responses to the tone of Christian love."

Captain Pillsbury, governor of Westbury prison, in Connecticut, was also remarkably successful in his treatment and reclamation of criminals by humane methods. He possessed a moral courage which approached almost to the sublime. Previous to his appointment, the usual harsh mode of treatment was enforced, with the usual hardening and debasing effects upon the prisoners, producing in them a "deep-rooted and settled malignity," Crime was increasing in enormity, and the prison was every year running the State into deeper debt. Captain Pillsbury completely altered the mode of treatment; he directed his efforts to the reformation of the prisoners by means of kind treatment. He encouraged them in a course of good conduct j he cheered them on in their return to virtue. He at once liberated the worst convicts from the degradation of irons, and told them he would trust them! The policy was magical in its effects. The men gave him their confidence; they manifested the greatest respect for his rule; order and regularity prevailed in the prison; and the institution soon began to pay for itself by its own labour.

His treatment of one of the prisoners was remarkable. The man was of herculean proportions, a prison-breaker, the terror of the country, and had plunged deeper and deeper into crime for seventeen years. Captain Pillsbury told him when he came that he hoped he would not repeat the attempts at escape which he had made elsewhere. "I will make you as comfortable as I possibly can, and shall be anxious to be your friend; and I hope you will not get me into any difficulty on your account There is a cell intended for solitary confinement, but we never use it; and I should be very sorry ever to turn the key upon anybody in it. You may range the place as freely as I do, if you will trust me as I shall trust you." The man was sulky, and for weeks showed only very gradual symptoms of softening under Captain Pillsbury's influence. At length information was given him that the man intended to break out of prison. The captain called him, and taxed him with it; the man preserved a gloomy silence. He was told that it was now necessary that he should be locked up in the solitary cell. The captain, who was a small, slight man, went before, and the giant followed. When they had reached the narrowest part of the passage the governor turned round with his lamp, and looked in the criminal's face. "Now," said he, "I ask you whether you have treated me as I deserve? I have done everything I could think of to make you comfortable; I have trusted you, and you have never given me the least confidence in return, and have even planned to get me into difficulty. Is this kind? And yet I cannot bear to lock you up. If I had the least sign that you cared for me "The man burst into tears. "Sir," said he, "I have been a very devil these seventeen years; but you treat me like a man." "Come, let us go back," said the captain. The convict had the free range of the prison as before. From this hour he began to open his heart to the captain, and cheerfully fulfilled his whole term of imprisonment; confiding to his friend, as they arose, all impulses to violate his trust, and all facilities for doing so which he imagined he saw.

Captain Pillsbury is the gentleman who, on being told that a desperate prisoner had sworn to murder him, speedily sent for him to shave him, allowing no one to be present. He eyed the man, pointed to the razor, and desired him to shave him. The prisoner's hand trembled, but he went through it very well. When he had done, the captain said, "I have been told you meant to murder me, but I thought I might trust you." "God bless you, sir! " replied the regenerated man. Such is the power of faith in man.[60]

Major Goodell, governor of the State prison at Auburn, New York, and Mr. Isaac T. Hopper, another prison inspector, were equally successful in the treatment and reclamation of criminals. Of fifty individuals whom this last-named admirable man succeeded in reclaiming, only two relapsed into bad habits — a fact which speaks volumes in favour of the power of gentleness.[61]

One of the greatest difficulties that a criminal has to encounter, is in getting employment after fulfilling his term of imprisonment He is willing to work, and determined to be honest. But the policeman knows his whereabouts, and gives information against him. He is immediately turned off, and forced back upon his old habits. Thus it becomes almost impossible for a quondam prisoner to return to honesty. Thomas Wright, the philanthropist of Manchester, distinguished himself as the true friend of forlorn prisoners. He was a man of no position in society. He possessed no wealth, excepting only a rich and loving heart.

Though he was imperfectly educated, he received strong religious impressions in early life from his mother. At length the time came when he was loosened from her apronstrings, and had to face the world, with its labours, its pleasures, and its vices. He very soon got mixed up with the wickedest men and boys in Manchester. That lasted for some time; but at length his mind and conscience revolted against the blasphemy of his companions. The lessons imbibed from his mother's lips came to his help. He made the acquaintance of a religious young man, and began regularly to attend a place of worship.

At fifteen he was apprenticed to an iron -founder at Manchester. His wage at first was five shillings a week. Being a steady, sober, diligent fellow, he gradually worked his way up, until, at twenty-three, he became

---

[60] Western Travel by Miss Martineau.

[61] Notwithstanding the humane treatment of criminals in some of the State prisons of the Union, William Tulloch, in a letter to the Times of the 3d of February 1880, complains of the treatment of juvenile criminals in some of the States. "For example," he says, "in a recent Philadelphia newspaper there is an account of a visit to the convict establishment of the State of Georgia, where, amid the most objectionable conditions of mutual corruption, scores of convicts are worked in association in a coal-mine. They are wretchedly lodged, guarded by bloodhounds, and kept in chains. Among them the visitor observed a boy of fifteen years of age, who had already endured five years of this slavery since he was ten years old, at which tender age a Judge sentenced him to forty years' imprisonment for a burglary! From the journal in which this appears, and from the evident character of the writer, there is reason to fear that it is too true, for there are in America innumerable prison abuses almost as bad, which are fully verified by official statements. A Judge who could pass such a sentence on so young a child one would like to see himself incarcerated, though not under the easy conditions in which I once witnessed an American Judge in a Pennsylvania State prison. He was committed for two years for taking bribes; but his apartments were furnished with every luxury, and it was rather surprising that an offence locally regarded as laudably 'smart ' should, even on this occasion, be thus reached by the law."

foreman of the moulders, at a weekly salary of £ 3108. This was his highest income, but the good that he afterwards did was altogether independent of his money wages.

His attention was early awakened to the criminal classes, the most hopeless of objects. The convict, when let loose from gaol, can very rarely get employment in his old place. New masters will not employ him without a character, which he cannot give. Imprisonment has probably made him worse. It has brought him in contact with more vicious persons than himself. He is thus thrown back upon his former associates, and begins his criminal career as before.

One day a man called at the foundry, and obtained employment as a labourer. He was a steady, careful, and industrious workman. But it oozed out that the man was a discharged convict Thomas Wright was asked whether he was cognisant of the fact. He was not, but he promised to ascertain. In the course of the day Wright incidentally asked the man "where he had worked last?" "I've been abroad," was the man's reply. At last, after some further pressing inquiries, the poor man, with tears running down his cheeks, admitted that he was a returned convict, that he was desirous of not relapsing into his old ways, and that he hoped, by perseverance, to wipe out his evil character.

Mr. Wright believed the man. He was convinced that he was sincere in his intentions. He acquainted the employers with his history, and offered to place £ 20 in their hands as a guarantee for his future good conduct. The promise was then given that the convict should be retained; but on the following morning the man was missing, the order for his dismissal having, through inadvertence, not been countermanded. A messenger was at once sent to the man's lodging to bring him back to work. But the man had already left his lodging, taking with him a bundle containing all his worldly belongings.

Having ascertained that the man had set out in the direction of Bury, Mr. Wright immediately followed him on foot. He found the fugitive sitting by the roadside, a few miles from Manchester, heart-broken, wretched, and despairing. Wright lifted him up, shook him by the hand, told him that he was retained in his employment, and that everything now depended upon himself, whether he would maintain his character as a respectable workman. They returned together to Manchester, they entered the shop together, and the future conduct of the man amply and nobly justified the guarantee into which the foreman had entered.

This circumstance greatly affected Mr. Wright himself. He saw how much could be done by sympathy and human affection to rescue these poor criminals from the depths of misery into which they had fallen. He felt that they should not abandon all hope of recovery, and that it behoved every Christian man to give them a helping hand towards reentering industrial life. This subject became the great idea of his soul. It was his mission, and he endeavoured to fulfil it. He was as yet without a helper. But he had strong faith, and he persevered until he succeeded.

Mr. Wright lived near the Salford prison, and desired to have access to the prisoners. For a long time he failed in his application. At last one of the young men in the foundry, whose father was a turnkey in the gaol, obtained for him an introduction to the governor. He was then permitted to attend the Sunday afternoon services. He was not permitted, as yet, to see the prisoners individually. But he had the patience to wait.

At length, one Sunday afternoon, the chaplain stopped Mr. Wright on leaving the prison chapel, and asked him if he could procure a situation for a prisoner whose term of office had nearly expired, and who desired to have the chance of proving the reformation of his character. "Yes," said Wright; "I will do my best, I will endeavour to find a situation." He succeeded, and work was found for the discharged prisoner.

The governor now gave him a freer run of the gaol. He allowed him to visit the prisoners personally. Wright advised and counselled them. He strengthened their determination to amend. He conveyed messages home to their families, and made himself their friend and benefactor in many ways. He made it a practice to meet the prisoners on their discharge. He took them to their homes, and helped them, out of his scanty means, to subsist, and then he endeavoured to find employment for them.

He was in most cases successful Employers of labour came to believe in Thomas Wright They knew him to be a good and benevolent man, and that he would not counsel them wrongly. He took the employers into his confidence, and they usually employed the released felons. Where they had doubts, he guaranteed their fidelity by deposits of his own money — gathered together out of his foreman's wages of seventy shillings a week.

He went on quietly and unostentatiously in this way — preferring that no notice should be taken of his name, lest it might interfere with the good that he was doing; until he had succeeded in a few years in finding employment for nearly three hundred discharged prisoners! He even succeeded — the worst task of all — in reclaiming women from drunkenness. He would sometimes go miles into the country, to plead with husbands, even on his knees, to take back the wife who was no longer drunken, but was penitent and longing for home.

A remarkable case is mentioned by one of his friends.[62] A man who had been undergoing penal servitude at Portland was discharged, and repaired to Manchester with a ticket of leave and a letter from the chaplain to Thomas Wright Employment was found for him as a scavenger. Mr. Wright had him promoted to be a mender of roads; and here also his conduct was approved. He obtained admission for him to the late Canon Stowell's Sunday and week-day night schools, in both of which he became a teacher. He showed so much capacity for learning that Canon Stowell felt a great interest in him. The Canon was made acquainted with his antecedents. Nevertheless he made arrangements for "reading "with him, and in due time the Portland convict was ordained a clergyman

In another case a young man, engaged in a position of trust in a warehouse, had fallen into bad company, and embezzled his employer's money. The theft was discovered, and he was about to be prosecuted. The young man's father besought the mediation of Thomas Wright He

---

[62] The author of Lives that Speak.

immediately went to the employer, and succeeded in eliciting a promise not to prosecute, but to give the youth another trial "Give him another chance," was often Thomas Wright's urgent advice. The young man was taken on again. His behaviour was most satisfactory. He gave himself more to business pursuits than before. He was at length taken in as a partner, and eventually became the head of the firm. He never ceased to bless the name of Thomas Wright

After he had been thus working on for years, his voluntary labours at length obtained official recognition. Captain Williams mentioned him in his annual reports on the state of prisons. He says, "To show the extent to which this humble and unassisted good man has carried his benevolence, and the success with which it has been crowned, it is but necessary to state that out of ninety-six criminals befriended by him, and re-established in life, only four have returned to a prison. It is delightful to witness the implicit confidence and reliance reposed in him by the guilty and wretched, and which seem to be wholly induced by his simple, unassuming, and truly fatherly way of doing good."

There were many cases in which Mr. Wright could not get employment for the released prisoners. In such cases he either lent them money of his own, or raised a private subscription among his friends, to enable them to emigrate. In this way he assisted 941 discharged prisoners and convicts to go abroad, and to begin life under new circumstances and separated from their old companionships. In many cases the discharged prisoners themselves helped him in his philanthropic labours. They got employment for their friends, or they helped to raise subscriptions to enable others to emigrate. Thus charity begot charity.

One of these forlorn emigrants, who had been sent to North America, wrote to Mr. Wright in 1864, addressing him as "My dear adopted father." He enclosed £ 2 as a contribution to the London Male Reformatory. The emigrant, who was now a prosperous man, said, "To your never to-be-forgotten fatherly aid I owe my present success. You were indeed my best, my kindest, and my sole advising friend on this earth. You rescued me from a life of vice by your own unaided help. When all others had turned their faces from me as a miscreant and a vagabond, you, like the prodigal's father of old, welcomed me back to the paths of virtue and integrity of life, consoling my youthful heart with the hope of brighter days yet in store, and blending your fatherly counsel with a still purer hope beyond the grave. God bless you, dear father! God bless you for all your kindness! Tears of kind remembrances fall from my cheeks as I think upon all your noble efforts for your poor fellow-men."

In the meantime, Mr. Wright was working daily at the foundry — working from five o'clock in the morning until six o'clock at night; and sometimes to a still later hour. All his evening leisure and most of his Sundays were devoted to his self-imposed services; either in the gaol, the penitentiary, the ragged Sunday schools, or at the homes of the unfortunate and the criminal. He was now sixty-three years old, and his health was beginning to fail He had saved, nothing. All his surplus earnings had been devoted to the relief and emigration of discharged prisoners. He frequently reduced himself to the lowest means of subsistence — always considering that while he had the means, he would not be justified in withholding them from those who were in distress.

The Government of the day, recognising the value of his services, offered Mr. Wright the post of travelling inspector of prisons, at the salary of £ 800 per annum. Here, it would seem, was a method by which he could lay by a little money, and at the same time extend the sphere of his operations. But he unhesitatingly refused the offer. He said that it would limit his power of doing good, as he felt convinced that if he once became a Government official, he would soon cease to be regarded as The Prisoner's Friend.

Accordingly, the attempt was made by the people of Manchester to raise a sum for the purchase of an annuity equal to the amount of his weekly wages — a mere tithe of the amount which his exertions had saved to the State. A sum of £ 100 was allotted from the Royal Bounty Fund in aid of the subscription. The Manchester people did the rest They raised a sum which provided Mr. Wright with an annuity of £ 182, the exact amount which he had before earned by his daily toil

In connection with the testimonial, an admirable picture of "The Good Samaritan" was presented by Mr. G. F. Watt, R. A., to the Manchester Corporation, "as an expression of the artist's admiration of, and respect for, the noble philanthropist, Thomas Wright" The picture was placed in a prominent position in the Manchester Town Hall It is a testimony at once to the kindness and generosity of the artist, and to the nobility of the character whom his painting represented.

Mr. Wright still continued in his works of mercy. He went from town to town, like Howard, visiting the gaols of the country. He inspected the Field Lane Night Refuge, the Redhill Industrial Schools, the hulks and convict establishments at Millbank, Pentonville, Portland, Portsmouth, and Parkhurst. He worked hard in the establishment of Ragged Schools. He wished to train the poor boys to earn an honest livelihood, and thus to prevent their becoming criminals. He regarded ignorance and bad example as the fruitful parents of all evil; and he did what he could to eradicate them by secular and religious instruction. He urged upon Mr. Cobden, who was then engaged in advocating a system of National Education, that it should be made compulsory, as the primary means of diminishing crime and pauperism. Besides his Ragged Schools, he instituted Reformatory Schools, Penny Banks, and the Shoeblack Brigade. Wherever a good work was to be done, his hand and help were never wanting. He loved to have every moment occupied. His motto was — "Work, work, whilst it is called to-day; for the night cometh,"

Thus he went on to the end. When he had arrived at eighty-five years of age, his health rapidly failed. Yet he was always ready to receive those who wished to see him — especially poor persons, discharged prisoners, or returned convicts. His life gradually faded away. The twenty-third psalm was continually on his lips, and at the end of each day's illness he felt himself "a day's march nearer home." He had fought the good fight, and was about to finish his course. He passed peacefully and calmly to his rest on the 14th of April 1875. This was surely a "life worth living."

Wright reformed criminals by trusting them. Trust is confidence. By trusting men you bring out the good that is in them. Their heart responds to the touch. Except in the worst cases, where young people have been carelessly and dishonestly brought up, the trust will be reciprocated. Always think the best of a man. "To think the worst," said Lord Bolingbroke, "is the sure mark of a mean spirit and a base soul." You may be deceived, it is true. But better be deceived than unjust.

Not long since the mass of the English people were shut out from all public places. The principal buildings were closed on week-days, except to those who could obtain "orders," or who were willing to pay an admission fee to the beadles and showmen of the curiosities. The British Museum was closed the National Gallery was closed; St. Paul's Cathedral and Westminster Abbey were closed; Windsor Castle, the Tower, the Houses of Parliament, and all other public buildings, and collections of curiosities, and works of art, were closed, except to the few. It seems to have been believed that if the common people were admitted to these places, they would forthwith whittle the wood, chip the stone, and smash and destroy these venerable buildings.

The late Joseph Hume was, we believe, the first public man who devoted himself to alter this deplorable state of things; and the first of our public collections which he succeeded in getting thrown open to the public was the British Museum. It was not without great opposition that he thus far accomplished his purpose. There was the old cry that the collection would be irretrievably injured, damaged, chipped, spoiled, and perhaps some of its valuable contents stolen. Besides, it was such an innovation! Nevertheless the British Museum, thanks to Mr. Hume's dogged pertinacity, was ordered to be thrown open to the public, and, as a matter of course, "the Deluge" was predicted. Previously to the throwing open of the Museum parties of only five or six at a time were admitted, and they were shown round by one of the officials — a sort of policeman in plain clothes — who was expected to be on his guard against the iconoclasts, and ready to pounce upon any Goth who, as a matter of course, was only waiting his opportunity of destroying the valuables placed within his reach.

Well! the fiat of Parliament went forth that the British Museum should be opened to butchers, bakers, common soldiers, sempstresses, milliners, and the commonest of common servants. And what said my Lord Stanley (the late Earl of Derby) after the irruption of the barbarian Goths had taken place? He came down to the House of Commons (of which he was then a member, as well as a Commissioner of the British Museum) on the very day after the irruption He rose up in his place, and, in an emphatic voice declared, "was alarmed and afraid but I can now state that 31,500 persons passed through the British Museum yesterday (May day), and there was not the value of sixpence injured!" Thus "the Deluge" did not happen, and it was found that the people at large might be admitted freely to inspect their own national collection of antiquities and works of art, without causing the general overturn of society. The secret was easy to find out; the people had merely been trusted.

Mr. Hume persevered in his good work. He perpetually dinned it into the ears of public men, that they should trust the people more, that they should open to them the public collections in which they could find amusement, refinement, and education; and, by dint of constant reiteration from year to year, he succeeded in getting thrown open to the public the Tower, Hampton Court, Westminster Abbey, and St. Paul's. The movement gradually spread, and now parks are set apart for the enjoyment and amusement of the people, not only in London, but in most of the large manufacturing towns and cities.

Even at the time of the great Exhibition of 1851 it was a subject for grave discussion in Parliament, whether London should not be surrounded by troops in order to keep the people quiet. The advice was overruled, and the Crystal Palace was not surrounded by troops. What was the result? Hardly a pennyworth belonging to the collection was stolen, not an article was wantonly injured. Colonel Rowan, one of the heads of the Metropolitan Police, was asked a question on the subject before a Committee of the House of Commons, and he answered that it was attributable to "the good conduct of the people;" and he added, that much of the recent improvement had originated in the facility, which had of late years been afforded, in admitting the people to public places — in short, by trusting them.

This is the true way of staving off "the Deluge." Admit the people freely to inspect works of art, which are eminently illustrative of God's gift to maa Let them be allowed to contemplate forms of beauty — full of grace, devotion, and virtue — commemorative of some genuine feeling, some sublime thought, or some noble deed in history, and the gazer is unconsciously elevated, humanised, refined, and civilised. Our picture-galleries might thus be made instrumental in promoting national education of the best kind, by elevating and purifying the taste, and at the same time instructing the mind. The mere fact of trusting the people, and allowing them free access to such places, is an education of the moral character. Trust a man — show that you are ready to place confidence in him as a man-exhibit by your conduct towards him that you believe, so to speak, in his honour, and you will do far more to win the heart of that man, and to draw forth the better feelings of his nature, than by all the exhibitions of law and authority. You disarm a man's evil nature when you prove by your acts and demeanour that you have confidence in his better nature. Thus it is that evil can be overcome by good

Indeed, we need but to trust men more to bring out the good that is in them. Trust them with privileges, and, by practice, they will learn the right use of them. The only ciure for the evils of newly-acquired fireedom, is fireedom. Accustom the prisoner who has come out of his cell to the light, and he will soon be able to bear the brightest rays of the sun. To humanise men, they must be familiarised with humanising influences. To make men good citizens, they must be allowed to exercise the rights and functions of citizens. Before a man can swim, he must first have gone into the water; before a man can ride, he must first have mounted a horse; and before he can be an intelligent citizen, he must first have been admitted to the duties of citizenship.

180

CHAPTER XII

HEROISM IN MISSIONS

Patience is the exercise
Of saints, the trial of their fortitude;
Making them each his own deliverer,
And victor over all
That tyranny or fortune can inflict.

Milton

For still we hope That in a world of larger scope. What here is
faithfully begun Will be completed, not undone.

A. H. Clough

But all through life I see a cross
Where sons of God yield up their breath:
There is no gain except by loss,
There b no life except by death,
There is no vision but by faith,
Nor glory but by bearing shame,
Nor justice but by taking blame;
And that Eternal Passion saith,
Be emptied of glory and right and name.

Olrig Grange

IT is related of the Duke of Wellington that when a certain chaplain asked him whether he thought it worth while to preach the gospel to the Hindoos, the man of discipline asked, "What are your marching orders?" The chaplain replied, "Go ye into all the world, and preach the gospel to every creature." "Then follow your orders," said the Duke; "your only duty is to obey."

Though an unwelcome, an unpopular, and a perilous duty, there have been found men in all ages who have followed the directions of their Saviour. Christ preached to the Jews and the Gentiles. St. Paul was the first missionary apostle. He founded churches in the East, at Corinth, at Ephesus, at Thessalonica, and elsewhere, and left his bones at Rome, where he had gone to preach the gospel

The career of a missionary is the most dutiful and heroic of all He carries his life in his hand. He braves danger and death. He lives amongst savages, sometimes amongst cannibals. Money could not buy the devotion with which he encounters peril and misery. He is only upheld by the mission of mercy with which he is charged. What are called "advanced thinkers "have nothing to offer us for the self-imposed work of missionaries, at home and abroad. Mere negation teaches nothing. It may pull down, but it cannot build up. It may shake the pillars of our faith and leave nothing to hold by, nothing to sanctify, to elevate, or to strengthen our natures.

But savage human nature is "vile." "How can they be vile to us," said Bishop Selwyn, "who have been taught by God not to call any man common or unclean? I quarrel not with the current phrases of 'poor heathen,' and 'the perishing savages.' Far poorer and more ready to perish may be those men of Christian countries who have received so much and can account for so little. Poorest of all may we be ourselves, who, as stewards and ministers of the grace of God, are found so unfaithful in our stewardship. To go among the heathen as an equal and a brother is far more profitable than to risk that subtle kind of self-righteousness which creeps into the mission work akin to the thanking God that we are not as other men are."

How much are we indebted to St. Augustine, the first missionary into England, for our liberty, our integrity, our learning, and even our missionary enterprise! At the end of the sixth century, Augustine, or Austin, was consecrated l Pope Gregory, and entitled beforehand Bishop of England. He proceeded on his mission, and, after passing through France, he landed at Thanet, accompanied by a number of monks. He was received by Ethelbert, King of Kent, at Canterbury. The king had married a Christian wife, and, partly through her influence, he became baptized, and was afterwards admitted to the Church. The missionary labours of Augustine extended throughout the country, until, at his death in 605, the greater part of England acknowledged the See of Rome.

But the north of England remained pagan. Edwin, chief of the country north of the Humber, became engaged to a Christian princess, sister of Edbald, King of Kent. The bride proceeded northwards, accompanied by a priest of Roman birth, named Paulinus. After some years Edwin became a Christian, though the Eldermen and Thanes remained pagan. A meeting of the Wittenagemote was called to consider the new doctrines. Edwin laid before the assembly his motives for the change in his belief, and, addressing each of them in turn, he asked what they thought of the matter. The story is told by Bede in his History, and is exceedingly touching.

The first who replied was the chief of the priests. He declared that the old gods Thor, Odin, and Freia,[63] had no power, and he desired to worship them no more. The chief of the warriors then rose and spoke in these terms: —

"Thou mayest recollect, O king, a thing which sometimes happens in the days of winter, when thou art seated at table with thy Eldermen and Thanes, when a good fire is blazing, when it is warm in thy hall, but rains, snows, and storms without. Then comes a little bird, and darts across the hall, flying in at one door and out at the other. The instant of this transit is sweet to him, for then he feels neither rain nor hurricane. But that instant is short; the bird is gone in the twinkling of an eye, and from winter he passes forth to the winter again. Such, to me, seems the life of man on this earth; such its momentary course compared with the length of time that

---

[63] Hence Thursday, Wednesday, and Friday.

precedes and follows it. That eternity is dark and comfortless to us, tormenting us by the impossibility of comprehending it. If then, this new doctrine can teach us anything certain respecting it, it is fit that we should follow it"

The old warrior's speech settled the question. It was put to the vote, and the assembly solemnly renounced the worship of their ancient gods. But when Paulinus, the missionary, proposed that they should destroy the images of their gods, there was not one among them who felt sufficiently firm in his convictions to brave the dangers of such a profanation. But the high priest mounted a horse, and girt with a sword, and brandishing a lance, he galloped towards the temple, and, in sight of all the people, he struck the walls and images with his lance, and finally destroyed them. A wooden building was then erected, in which Edwin and a great number of his followers were baptized. Paulinus then travelled throughout the countries of Deïria and Bernicia, baptizing in the waters of the Swale and the Ure all who were willing to obey the decree of the Assembly of the Sages.

In the seventh century the light of Christianity was spread through the benighted regions of Europe by the aid of the missionaries Andomar, Amand, and Columba, in Gaul; Paulinus, Wilfred, and Cuthbert, in England; and Kilcan, Rudpert, and subsequently Boniface, in Germany. When Boniface landed in Britain, he came with the gospel in the one hand and a carpenter's rule in the other. I He had the true spirit of work in him. When he after wards went to Germany, he carried with him the art of building.

Anschar, with one companion, went in 826 to the confines of the Danish kingdom, where, inspired by his success, he instituted seminaries for future missionaries. Evangelisers went to Hungary and Poland in the tenth century, where they established themselves in the diocese of Cracow. They laboured under the greatest difficulties; though difficulties were the obstacles which they were bound to conquer. Without any fear of death, they devoted themselves to the help of those who were stricken by the plague. Besides christianising, they raised money to redeem captives from the Ottoman Empire. Who could resist such loving missionary enterprise?

In the tenth and eleventh centuries, there were missions of workmen and architects, all connected with "the Church. These were the men who erected the splendid cathedrals of this and other countries. They put their spirit into their work; , they put religion into their work Their architecture had life, and truth, and love, and joy in it. It was chiselled music. How different from the shoddy work of to-day, when modern buildings crumble into rubbish, while the old cathedrals stand in their magnificence, a delight to all beholders.

It is said that China had Nestorian missionaries as early as the seventh century, and French missionaries as early as the twelfth century. Protestant missionaries were only sent to China in 1807. Asia and Africa are merely skirted with a line of missionary pickets. In Africa, the heroic age of missions has just begun to dawn. But how much land remains to be possessed!

St. Francis Xavier, the Apostle to the Indies, was a lesson to all. He went to Goa in a Portuguese ship in 1542, to preach the gospel to the benighted. He was a man of noble lineage, and might have lived a life of pleasure and luxury like others. But he forsook everything, and chose to live a life of sacrifice, devotion, and well-doing. Sounding his hand-bell in Goa, he implored the people to send him their children to be instructed. He went from thence to Cape Comorin, to Travancore, to Malacca, to Japan. He tried to get into China, but failed; at last he died of fever in the island of Sanchean, where he received his crown of martyrdom.

Nor can we forget Las Casas, who was, in like manner, the Apostle of the West Indies. "At a period," says Sir Arthur Helps, "when brute force was universally appealed to in all matters, but especially in those that pertained to religion, he contended before Juntas and Royal Councils that missionary enterprise is a thing that should stand independent of all military support; that a missionary should go forth with his life in his hand, relying only on the protection that God will vouchsafe him, and depending neither upon civil nor military assistance. In fact, his works would, even in the present day, form the best manual extant for missionaries."

Las Casas accompanied his father in an expedition under Columbus to the West Indies in 1498. He then saw America for the first time. He returned to Spain, and made a second voyage to Hispaniola. He was there ordained priest. In the performance of his new functions he was found eloquent, acute, truthful, bold, self-sacrificing, pious. He went from place to place with the Spaniards, and endeavoured to gain the confidence of the Indians. He prevented many disorders and much cruelty; for the Spaniards were far more savage than the Indiana After being witness to several massacres, Las Casas determined to return to Spain and intercede for the poor people. He obtained an interview with King Ferdinand, and informed him of the wrongs and sufferings of the Indians, and of how they died without a knowledge of the faith. But Ferdinand was now an old and failing man, whose death was near at hand, and nothing came of his representation.

Ferdinand died shortly after, when Las Casas endeavoured to interest Cardinal Ximenes, the Regent, in the sufferings and miseries of the Indians. The Cardinal promised that the evils should be abated. He appointed three Jeronimite fathers to accompany Las Casas to the West Indies. On their arrival at San Domingo the fathers took the part of the governor and judges, on which Las Casas again returned to Spain to appeal against them; but on his arrival he found the Cardinal at the point of death. The king (Charles V.) was only sixteen years old, and the affairs of Spain were managed by his Chancellor. When Las Casas had made a good beginning with the Chancellor, this man, like the Cardinal, died also; and thus death seemed always to interfere between the missionary and the fulfilment of his projects. The Bishop of Burgos regained his ascendency, and Las Casas went "into the abysses," as he expresses it. The Jeronimite fathers were, however, recalled. But the missionary was able to obtain no further help, and he went out to the Indies as before. He endeavoured to found a colony at Cumani, where he made friends of the Indians, and endeavoured to preserve them from the cruelty of the Spaniards. But he was always thwarted, and his attempt at colonisation was suspended. He had no one to help him, and the work which he contemplated could not be done alone.

Las Casas then embraced a monastic life. He remained for eight years in the Dominican monastery at Hispaniola, during which time he led a life of extreme seclusion He afterwards devoted himself to missionary work. He went on a mission to Peru, accompanied by two of his brethren. They returned to Mexico, and instructed the Indians in the Christian faith. While at Nicaragua Las Casas organised a formidable opposition to the governor, whom he prevented from undertaking one of those expeditions into the interior which were always so injurious to the natives. The most outrageous atrocities took place on those occasions. It has been known that on an occasion when 4000 Indians accompanied an expedition to carry burdens, only six of them returned alive. Las Casas himself describes how, when an Indian was sick with weariness and hunger, and unable to proceed, as a quick way of getting the chain free from the Indian, his head was cut off, and he was thus disengaged from the gang with which he travelled. "Imagine," he says, "what the others must have felt."

Las Casas and his associates now resolved to make their way into Tuzulutan for the purpose of christianising the natives. That district was a terror to the Spaniards. They called it "The Land of War." They had been thrice beaten back by the inhabitants. But the missionaries were inspired with the courage of faith, and determined to invade the land, though at the peril of their lives. The first thing they did was to translate into verse, in the Quiche language, the great doctrines of the Church. Their next thought was how to introduce their poem to the notice of the Indians. They called to their aid four Indian merchants who were in the habit of going with merchandise several times a year into the district These four men were taught to repeat the couplets perfectly. The couplets were also set to music, that they might be accompanied by Indian instruments. Las Casas also furnished the merchants with small wares to please the aborigines, such as scissors, knives, looking-glasses, and bells.

The merchants were well received by the Cacique. In the evening, when the chiefs were assembled, the merchants called for an instrument of music, and began to recite the verses with an accompaniment The effect produced was great For several days after, the sermons in song were repeated. The Cacique inquired where these verses came from, and wished to know what was the origin and meaning of these things. The merchants replied that they came from the Padres. "And who are the Padres? " Then the merchants explained, and the Cacique proceeded to invite these extraordinary men to his country. This is how Las Casas and his companions obtained access to "The Land of War."

It is unnecessary to pursue the subject farther. The Cacique embraced the Christian faith. He pulled down and burnt his idols. He preached to his subjects, who followed his example. Las Casas and Pedra de Angulo built a church at Rabinal. There they preached and taught the people, teaching not only spiritual things but manual arts, and instructing their flocks in the elementary processes of washing and dressing. The example spread to Coban, a neighbouring territory; and thus every success gained by these brave monks was a step toward continued exertion.

Las Casas again returned to Spain in 1539. He was detained there because of his knowledge of Indian affairs. He proceeded to write his work, entitled The Destruction of the Indies which has been very widely read. He was offered the bishopric of Cusco (in New Toledo), but he refused it He was again offered the bishopric of Chiapa, in New Mexico, and his superiors pressed it upon him as a matter of conscience. At last he submitted himself to the will of his superiors. He again set sail for the New World, and was installed at Ciudad Real, the capital of the province. The episcopal dignity made no change in his ways and manners. His dress was that of a simple monk, often torn and patched. Everything in his household was of the simplest character. He refused absolution to those who bought and held slaves contrary to the provisions contained in the new laws. He met with great difficulties in his endeavours to put down slavery. His life was attempted. He was called "the Devil of a bishop;" "that Antichrist for a bishop." He heeded not, but went on his way, rejoicing when he had put down an evil He finally returned to Spain in 1547 when he resigned the bishopric

Las Casas was a man of indomitable courage. He crossed the ocean between Europe and America twelve times. He made his way into Germany four times, to see the Emperor. He led a most energetic life; and he must have had a vigorous constitution, for he did not meet death until he was ninety-two years old. He died at Madrid, after a short illness, in July 1566.

What Las Casas deplored three centuries ago, we have to deplore now — that missionaries are either preceded or followed by horse, foot, and artillery, and that the heathen are killed before they can be converted. Love of conquest is at the root of all this mischief. From 1800 to 1850 not less than £ 14,500,000 was devoted by the British people to Christian missions, certainly a noble monument of the faith, energy, and devotedness of the British churches. But, during the same time, we had expended on war and the materials of war not less than £ 200,000,000 sterling. This is a still greater monument to our belief in war and the materials of warfare.

Missionaries entered the south of Africa and made their way to the north amidst difficulties innumerable. They lived among the natives, and gaye their minds and hearts and souls to them, endeavouring to bring them to a belief in the loving doctrines of Christianity. Men of education, accustomed to the comforts and conveniences of civilised life, endured privations of the most severe kind, which were all the harder to bear as they fell upon their wives and children. No motives of gain could support them in such a position. When Dr. Moffat crossed the Orange River in 1820, as a missionary to the Bechuana tribes, his salary was £ 18:7s, for himself, and £ 5:5s, for his wife and family.

When Moffat went amongst these tribes he did not know their language, and he had none to teach him. Unmindful of their abominations, and fearless of their ferocity, he lived entirely amongst the natives. He walked, he slept, he wandered, he hunted, he rested, he ate, he drank with them, till he thoroughly mastered their language, and then he began to preach to them the gospel. He laboured on amidst difficulties and afflictions of all kinds, occasionally attended by threats of murder, without any apparent tokens of success. At length they believed in him and in the healing words he taught. The once naked, filthy savages became clothed and cleanly. Idleness gave place to industry. They built houses and cultivated gardens. Provisions for the wants of the mind kept pace with those of the body; they reared schools for the young, and chapels for the old. And thus the work of education and religion rapidly advanced.

Moffat was followed by Livingstone, his son-in-law, who gave his life to the same work. Livingstone opened up the heart of Africa, and trod the lands of savage tribes where the foot of the white man had never trod before. He travelled thousands of miles amongst savage beasts, and still more savage men, and was often delivered from danger almost by the "skin of his teeth;" but he never doubted in the success of the gospel, even amongst the degraded He did not live to see the outbreak of war in South Africa, and to hear of the thousands of men who were slain in resisting the attempt to annex their territories.

Men, even savage men, judge each other by their deeds, not by their words. Professing Christians, like vendors of bad coinage, often expose genuine religion to suspicion. "In true kindness of heart," said Dr. Guthrie, "sweetness of temper, open-handed generosity, the common charities of life, many mere men of the world lose nothing by comparison with such professors; and how are you to keep the world from saying, 'Ah! your man of religion is no better than others; nay he is sometimes worse'? With what frightful prominence does this stand out in the never-to-be forgotten answer of an Indian Chief to the missionary who urged him to become a Christian. The plumed and painted savage drew himself up in the consciousness of superior rectitude, and with indignation quivering on his lip and flashing in his eye, he replied — ' Christian lie! Christian cheat! Christian steal, drink, murder I Christian has robbed me of my lands, and slain my tribe! 'Adding, as he haughtily turned away — 'The Devil, Christian! I will be no Christian! 'May such reflections teach us to be careful how we make a religious profession! And having made the profession, cost what it may, by the grace of God let us live up to it, and act it out"

Let us turn to another quarter of the globe — the islands of Polynesia, where many missionaries have done heroic work. Take, for instance, the case of John Williams, known as "the Martyr of Erromanga." His life is a romance. There was nothing peculiar about his boyhood.

He was put apprentice to a London ironmonger, and from the counter he proceeded to the workshop. He had the mechanical instinct, and executed ironwork that required peculiar delicacy and skill. In his youth he became connected with irreligious companions, who threatened to exert a fatal influence upon his character. They were avowed unbelievers and Tom Painers. But better influences prevailed; and at length Williams joined a Mutual Improvement Society, and then became an active Sunday school teacher.

Missionary operations in heathen lands were then exciting much interest, and, after much deliberation, he offered his services to the London Missionary Society. They were accepted, and in 1810 he left his master before the termination of his apprenticeship. He was only twenty years old. During the short period allowed him for literary and theological studies he contrived to visit manufactories and workshops, in order to improve his knowledge of mechanics, and thus to introduce the arts of peace, as well as religious instruction, to the people amongst whom he was to labour.

Captain Cook discovered a large number of islands in the Pacific Ocean, inhabited by savages, some of whom were comparatively innocent, and others dreadfully cruel, but all idolaters. These islands were selected by the London Missionary Society, at the instance of Dr. Haweis, father of the South Sea Missions, as the scene of their earliest labours. For many years the missionary pioneers laboured with very little success; but in course of time the natives gradually embraced Christianity, and in some islands the rites of idolatry were entirely abandoned.

The missionaries were constantly calling for more helpers. The London Missionary Society, recognising the necessity, sent John Williams, notwithstanding his comparatively small amount of preliminary study. But he was young, ardent, and earnest. Before starting on his voyage, Williams married Miss Mary Chauner, who proved an invaluable coadjutor in his future labours. Within six months after quitting his apprenticeship he embarked for Sydney with some other young missionaries. From thence they went to Eimeo, one of the Society Islands. Mr. Williams, besides helping the missionaries, proceeded to perfect himself in the Tahitian language. During this time he made the ironwork for a small vessel, which the missionaries were building for Pomare, King of Tahiti

Mr. Williams was shortly after removed to Huahine, and afterwards to Raiatea. The latter is the largest and most central island of the Society group. Here his labours were attended with great success. Without neglecting the primary objects of his mission, he endeavoured to improve the moral and physical condition of the people. The natives were very debased and inveterately idle. Promiscuous intercourse was common. When Williams had obtained some influence over them, he induced them to adopt legal marriage.

He next induced them to build habitations for themselves. He himself proceeded to build a comfortable house in the English style, as a model for the natives to follow. It was divided into several apartments, with wooden floors and framed walls, plastered with coral lime. The rooms were provided with tables, chairs, sofas, bedsteads, carpets, and hangings. Almost everything was done with his own hands.

The natives, being an imitative people, shortly followed his example. With the missionary's assistance they built houses for themselves, and were thus taught the decencies and comforts of civilised life. He also instructed them in boat-building; and, with a view to the future commerce of the island, he induced them to plant tobacco and the sugarcane, so as to prepare both articles for the market. The rollers required for the sugar-mill were turned in a lathe formed by Williams's own hand.

Having thus fairly started the natives in industrial operations, he next desired to find sufficient markets for their produce. He wished to extend his peaceful conquest throughout the other islands of the group. He believed that nothing was more likely to improve the civil and religious condition of the islanders than by establishing commercial relations between them. For this purpose a ship was required, for small boats could not answer the purpose.

Full of his idea, and eager to carry it out, he proceeded to Sydney in 1822, and bought a schooner of eighty tons, called The Endeavour. Sir Thomas Brisbane, governor of New South Wales, presented him with several cows, calves, and sheep, for propagation in the islands. In carrying out this enterprise Williams took the entire responsibility upon himself. It was held that his business was to preach and not to trade; but he believed that when the importance of the undertaking was considered, the Society in London would continue to give him their support.

He returned to Raiatea in safety, and, in 1823, he sailed for the Harvey Islands in order to discover the island of Raratonga. This splendid island escaped the untiring researches of Captain Cook. It was only from some traditions and legendary tales among the islanders that Williams knew of its existence. After a long search for the missing island Williams returned to Raiatea. At length, after some interval, he set out again. After sailing about for many days, buffeted by contrary winds, and after his provisions had become nearly exhausted, the captain came to him and said, 'We must give up the search, sir, or we shall all be starved" A native was again sent to the topmast to look ahead It was the fifth time he had ascended He cried out that Raratonga was in sight!

"When we were within half an hour of relinquishing the object of our search," says Mr. Williams, "the clouds which enveloped its towering heights having been chased away by the heat of the ascending sun, he relieved us from our anxiety by shouting, 'Here, here is the land we have been seeking!' The transition of feeling was so instantaneous and so great, that although a number of years have intervened I have not forgotten the sensations which that announcement occasioned. The brightened countenances, the joyous expressions, and the lively congratulations of all on board, showed that they shared in the same emotions; nor did we fail to raise our voices in grateful acknowledgment to Him who had graciously ' led us by a right way"[64]

The missionary and his companions (natives of the neighbouring islands) were favourably received on landing. The teachers at once stated the object of their mission. It was to instruct them in the knowledge of the true God. The king was willing to be instructed, and his people with him. Afler remaining in the island for some time, he left one of the native teachers there, and the Endeavour returned to Raiatea. He was prepared to

[64] A Narrative of Missionary Enterprise in the South Sea Islands, By the Rev. John Williams. 1841.

bring the whole of the Navigator and other islands under his care. He was ready to set out on another expedition, when intelligence reached him from London that the missionary society disapproved of his proceedings, being jealous lest anything of a worldly character should become mixed up with his mission. At the same time, the merchants of New South Wales obtained an enactment of fiscal regulations from the Governor, which had the effect of greatly impeding the development of trade from the South Sea Islands. Williams was thus compelled to part with the Endeavour. He filled the vessel with the most marketable produce that he could collect, and sent it ,to Sydney, with orders for the sale of both ship and cargo.

Williams continued stationed at Raiatea, but visited Raratonga from time to time. In 1827 he accompanied Mr. and Mrs. Pitman, who were about to settle there as missionaries. They found that the old idols had been mostly destroyed, and that the moral and religious tone of the people had greatly improved. It was now Mr. Williams's duty to translate portions of the Bible into the popular dialect, the books heretofore known to the missionaries being in the Tahitian language. He accordingly reduced the Raratongan dialect to a written form and a grammatical system. At his instance also a church was built. The design and arrangement were after his plans, and the chiefs and natives helped him so cheerfully and willingly that the building was finished in two months. It was completed without a single nail or any iron work whatever. The chapel furnished accommodation for about three thousand persons.

In the course of executing the work a curious circumstance occurred. One morning Mr. Williams came without his square. He took up a chip of wood, and with a piece of charcoal wrote upon it a message to his wife, desiring her to send the square by the bearer. He called a chief, and asked him to take the chip to Mrs. Williams. He took it, and asked, "What am I to say?" "You have nothing to say; the chip will say all I wish." The chief went away, thinking himself a fool. On giving it to Mrs. Williams, she read it and threw it away; then she brought the square and gave it to the chief. He caught up the chip, and ran along shouting, "See the wisdom of these English people! They can make chips talk! "He tied a string to the chip and hung it round his neck. For some days he was seen sunounded by a crowd, who listened with intense interest to the wonders which the chip had performed.

No ship appearing at the island, by which Mr. Williams might return to his station at Raiatea, he proceeded to make the most of his time. He built schools, wherein he taught the people to read. They were, however, very slow learners compared with their sprightly brethren in the Society Islands. The language at first taught was Tahitian, but it was like a foreign language to them. It was not until he had translated the Gospel of St. John and the Epistle of Galatians into Raratongan that the people began to learn in their own dialect; and after that they made rapid progress.

A conspiracy was formed by some wild dissolute young men to murder Williams and his colleague, and throw their bodies into the sea, while passing from Raratonga to the neighbouring island of Tahaa. Fortunately the conspiracy was discovered. The chiefs held a meeting, and determined to put the four ringleaders to death. Williams interfered, and implored the chiefs to spare their lives. In the course of conversation the chiefs inquired what would the English people do under such circumstances. They were told that in England there were established laws and judges, by whom all offenders of every kind were tried and punished. "Why can we not have the same?" the chiefs asked.

It was accordingly determined to establish a code of laws, as the basis of public justice. Mr. Williams and Mr. Threlkeld prepared it in plain and perspicuous language. At the same time, they included the greatest barrier to oppression — trial by jury. In the meantime, a judge had been nominated, pro tempore before whom the criminals were tried. They were banished for four years to an uninhabited island

After waiting for months and months at Raratonga, and seeing no vessel passing within sight, Williams determined upon adopting a most extraordinary course — that of building a ship with his own hands. He was much in want of tools, and had none used for shipbuilding. His first step was to make a pair of smith's bellows. There were four goats on the island, one of which was giving milk; the other three were sacrificed, and with their skins, he succeeded, after three or four days' labour, in making a pair of smith's bellows. But instead of blowing the fire, they drew it in. The bellows soon came to grief. During the night the rats set to work, and devoured every particle of the goats' skins, so that next morning there was nothing left but the bare boards. Still bent upon accomplishing his object, it struck Williams that, as a pump threw water, it 'must, if completed on the same principle, of necessity throw wind. After many difficulties, he at length constructed a machine which answered the purpose.

With this wind-pump he did all his iron-work, using a perforated stone as a fire iron, a large stone as an anvil, and a pair of carpenter's pincers as his tongs. For coals he used charcoal, made from the cocoanut and other trees. As he had no saw, he split the trees with wedges, and then the natives adzed them down with small stone hatchets. When he wanted a twisted plank, he bent a piece of bamboo to the required shape, or sent into the woods for a crooked tree, and by splitting this, he obtained two planks suited for his purpose. Having but little iron he bored large augur holes through the timbers, and through the outer and inner planks of the vessel, and drove in wooden trenails, by which the whole fabric was held firmly together.

Cocoanut husk was used for oakum. The bark of the hibiscus was used for ropes and cordage, for which purpose a rope machine was constructed The mats on which the natives slept were used as sails; and they were quilted together to resist the wind. A lathe was constructed, and the aito or ironwood was turned for the sheaves of blocks. The anchor was of wood, and a cask full of stones was also used. The vessel was of between seventy and eighty tons burden. After about fifteen weeks' labour, the Messenger of Peace was launched. The rudder was then attached. This important work occasioned much difficulty. Having no iron sufficiently large for pintles, these were made from a piece of a pickaxe, a cooper's adze, and a large hoe.

With these promiscuous pieces of ironwork, the rudder was mounted, and the wonderful ship was ready to sail.

Thinking it might be dangerous to run for Raiatea in the Tahitian islands, which was about 800 miles distant, it was determined, in the first place, to sail for Aitutake, which was only about 170 miles distant Makea, the king of Raratonga, accompanied the expedition. The vessel was found seaworthy. The voyage to Aitutake was accomplished without any more serious casualty than the breaking of the foremast, through the inexperience of the native crew; and yet the ship encountered a strong wind and a heavy sea. Fortunately, Mr. Williams had a compass and quadrant; and these enabled him to make the voyage without much difficulty. Nothing appeared to strike the king so much as to be told in what direction the land was first to be seen. His inquiries were unceasing, as to how it was possible we could speak with so much precision as to that which we could not see. One of his expressions was, "Never again will I call those men warriors who fight on the shore; the English only, who battle with the winds and waves of the ocean, are worthy of that name."

The Messenger of Peace remained at Aitutake for eight or ten days, and shipped a return cargo. It consisted principally of pigs, cocoanuts, and cats! The native pigs of Raratonga were very diminutive and difficult to be reared; and seventy of a superior breed were now imported. The reason why Cats formed part of the cargo is easy to be explained. Rats abounded in Raratonga. They were like one of the ten plagues of Egypt. They ran over the table among the eatables. They snatched away pieces of meat and bread. They sat on the chairs. They slept in the beds. "When kneeling at family prayers,'" says Mr. Williams, "they would run over us in all directions."

> "Great rats, small rats, lean rats, brawny rats,
> Brown rats, black rats, gray rats, tawny rats,
> Grave old plodders, gay young friskers,
> Fathers, mothers, uncles, cousins,
> Cocking tails and pricking whiskers.
> Families by tens and dozens,
> Brothers, sisters, husbands, wives."

In fact, the rats ate up half the food of Raratonga. They ate up Mr. Williams's bellows. They ate up Mrs. Pitman's shoes. And when other food failed them, they became cannibals, and ate up their infant rats. The Cats were therefore a welcome addition to the population of Raratonga. They soon made a clearance of the rats, helped by the newly imported pigs, which became very voracious, and helped to dear the island of the intolerable nuisance.

Mr. Williams was not contented to settle down in his mission at Raiatea. Everything was going well there. But there were more islands to conquer, and he determined to conquer them. He was full of life, full of vigour, full of courage. There were several groups of islands to the westward, which had never been visited by the Missionary — the Hapai, and Samoan or Navigator's groups. He made a round among them in the Messenger of Peace, and accomplished the same objects as he had done elsewhere. He destroyed idolatry, and established the worship of the true God.

"Christianity," said Mr. Williams, "triumphed not by human authority, but by its own moral power — by the light which it shed abroad, and by the benevolent spirit it had disseminated; for kindness is the key to the human hearty whether it be that of savage or civilised man. When they were treated with kindness, the multitude immediately embraced the truth j for they naturally attributed this mighty transformation on these formerly sanguinary chieftains to the benign influence of the gospel upon their minds." "There are two little words in our language which I always admired, Try and Trust. You know not what you can or cannot effect until you try; and if you make your trials in the exercise of trust in God, mountains of imaginary difficulties will vanish as you approach them, and facilities will be afforded which you never anticipated! "

At length Mr. Williams resolved to revisit England. Having sent the Messenger of Peace to Tahiti to be sold, he took passage in a homeward-bound whaler for London, which he reached in June 1834. He laid his manuscript of the Raratongan New Testament before the British and Foreign Bible Society. It was ordered to be printed. He also wrote an account of the most important circumstances connected with his extraordinary missionary career.[65] The appearance of the Narrative excited the deepest interest. He spoke at numerous meetings in all parts of the country. He made the friendship of many of the dignitaries of the Established Church, of men eminent for their scientific attainments, and of many of the nobility. Donations were made to him in aid of the general object of the mission. The Corporation of the City of London unanimously voted a sum of £ 5 00 towards its support. In all, £ 4000 were subscribed. With this, the missionary ship Camden was purchased; and on the nth of April 1838, she sailed from Gravesend with Mr. and Mrs. Williams on board, and sixteen other missionaries and missionaries' wives, who were to be left at their respective stations.

The Camden reached the South Sea islands in safety. After making a round of the Society and other Islands in which missionaries had already been established, Mr. Williams proceeded to visit the islands farther westward, where nothing had as yet been done for the instruction of the savages. The expedition was proceeding satisfactorily, when the Camden at length reached Erromanga in the New Hebrides group. A party from the ship landed at Dillon's Bay. It seems that the natives had been irritated by the barbarous treatment they had received from the crew of a vessel that had previously visited the island. In revenge, they attacked the missionaries who had just landed. Mr. Williams and his friend Mr. Harris were killed and eaten.

---

[65] A Narrative of Missionary Enterprises in the South Sea Islands; with remarks upon the Natural History of the Islands, Origin, Languages. Traditions and Usages of the Inhabitants. By the Rev. John Williams, of the London Missionary Society.

Thus perished, in the forty-fourth year of his age, one of the noblest and most self-denying of men. With him duty consisted in doing good. He scattered broadcast the seeds of Christianity and civilisation. He was a man of unswerving perseverance. Nothing deterred him from doing works of mercy; and yet he could wait patiently. He knew that the time would come when the seeds he had sown would spring up and flourish. His works lived after him. Even the cannibals of Erromanga at length abolished idolatry, and received the truths of Christianity with gladness.

Other noble workers followed the example of Williams. The Rev. George A. Selwyn was consecrated first Bishop of New Zealand in 1841. He at once proceeded to perform the duties of his mission.[66] After seven years of unremitting work on the mainland of his diocese, the Bishop deemed that, in fulfilment of the charge committed to him by the English Primate, the time had come for attempting the evangelisation of the five groups of islands between New Zealand and the Equator, to which the name of Melanesia had been given; and for the next twelve years this missionary work occupied much of his time. At first, opinions were divided as to the prudence and expediency of the enterprise, which sober people might be pardoned for thinking too romantic to be practical.

To the remonstrances of his friends as to the personal danger it involved, he replied with the axiom, "that where a trader will go for gain, there the missionary ought to go for the merchandise of souls j "and to his father he wrote, "It is the duty of a missionary to go to the extreme point of boldness, short of an exposure to known and certain danger. In those islands something must be risked if anything is to be done."

The risk was certainly considerable, especially as he would never permit a weapon of any kind on board his little vessel; and on one occasion, at Malicolo in the New Hebrides, it seems that nothing but "his perfect presence of mind and dignified bearing (to borrow Captain Erskine's words) saved him and his party from the fate which a few years before had befallen Williams at Erromanga, and a few years later befell Patteson at Nukapu."

To an objection of another kind, that he would be neglecting his diocese proper, and have too many irons in the fire, he opposed his persuasion that he could undertake the personal inspection and supervision of the whole of Melanesia, not only without injury, but with the greatest possible benefit to his own work in New Zealand. His heart was in those distant islands, yearning over their dark inhabitants with* a brother's love; and he felt as if God, by leading him in His Providence to

---

[66] Sydney Smith, in his bantering way, said in one of his letters : "The advice I sent to the Bishop of New Zealand, when he prepared to receive the cannibal chiefs there, was to say to them, ' I deeply regret, sirs, to have nothing on my own table suited to your tastes, but you will find plenty of cold curate and roasted clergyman on the sideboard;' and if, in spite of this prudent provision, his visitors should end their repast by eating him likewise, why, I could only add, "I sincerely hoped he would disagree with them.' In this last sentiment he must cordially have agreed with me 5 and, upon the whole, he must have considered it a useful hint, and would take it kindly." — A Memoir of the Rev, Sydney Smithy i 386.

become such a thorough sailor, had "marked his path upon the mountain wave, his home upon the deep."

The Rev. John Coleridge Patteson went out to the help of Bishop Selwyn. This was another noble and self-denying man. He might have obtained honourable promotion at home, but he preferred giving himself up to the missionary cause. He went out to New Zealand in 1855. He was appointed to missionarise the natives of a group of islands which had rarely been visited since their discovery by Captain Cook. The reputation of cannibalism hung about them. They formed a third group round the north-eastern curve of Australia, and consisted of the New Hebrides, Banks Islands, Solomon Isles, and the islands of Santa Cruz. The inhabitants were called Melanesians or Black Islanders from having much of the negro in their composition and complexion.

After remaining for some time at New Zealand, learning the native languages, and learning navigation for the purpose of managing the Southern Cross, the missionaries' schooner, Mr. Patteson set sail for Norfolk Island, accompanied by the Bishop. Then to Aaiteum, occupied by the Scotch Presbyterian Mission. They then passed Erromanga, where Williams was killed — a wooded island, beautiful beyond description. Then to Fat, where the Samoan teachers had been murdered. The ship passed the splendid island of Espiritu Santo — with its mountainchain about 4000 feet high. The ship next touched at Remael Island, when the Bishop and his fellow priest swam ashore, and made friends with the natives, who were Maoris. Several boys were taken from the island, to be educated as teachers at St. John's College, New Zealand.

The ship next touched at Mara, in the Solomon Islands; where it was found that, though Maori-speaking, the sailors had given them a knowledge of the worst and most abominable parts of the English language. The next group sighted was the large island of Santa Cruz. The natives came off in their canoes with yams and taro; but the numbers were so great that no quiet work could be done. They sailed quite round the island, and saw the fiery appearance of the great volcano. They went on to Nukapu — now full of melancholy memory, as Bishop Patteson met his death there. The natives came off in canoes, and brought bread-fruit and cocoa-nuts. After a much longer cruise— to Tubua, to Vanicora, and to the Banks group of Islands, — the Southern Cross returned to New Zealand.

This, then, was the missionary field in which Mr. Patteson was to work. In writing home, he said, "Don't believe in the ferocity of the islanders. When their passions are excited, they do commit fearful deeds, and they are almost universally cannibals — that is, after a battle there will always be a cannibal feast, not otherwise. But treat them well and prudently, and I apprehend that there is little danger in visiting them — meaning by visiting, merely landing on the beach a first time, going perhaps to a native village the next time, sleeping on shore the third, spending ten days the fourth, and so on."

He described his fundamental method of teaching the natives. He held fast to the fact of man having been created in the image of God. While preaching at Sydney, he said, "This love, once generated in the heart of man, must needs pass on to his brethren.... Love is the animating principle of all In every star of the sky, in the sparkling glittering waves of the sea, in every flower of the field, in every creature of God, most of all in every living soul of man, it adores and blesses the beauty and love of the great Creator and Preserver of all."

"My dear father," he says, "writes in great anxiety about the Denison case. Oh dear! what a cause of thankfulness it is to be out of the din of controversy, and to find thousands longing for crumbs which are shaking about so roughly in these angry disputes. It isn't High or Low or Broad Church, or any other special name, but the longing desire to forget all distinctions, and to return to a simpler state of things, that seems naturally to result from the very sight of these heathen people."

Patteson went on his visits to the Melanesian Islands, hoping everything and fearing nothing. He was made much of by the men and by the women. When the women were present, he knew he was safe. He did everything by trusting the people. He went to Futuma, wading ankle-deep to the beach. Then to Erromanga. Then to Fat Isle, where the people were said to be amongst the rudest in those seas. They were cannibals, and had killed the whole crew of the Royal Sovereign when it was wrecked upon the island; they had eaten nine men at once, and sent the other nine as presents to their friends.

In! 86! John Coleridge Patteson was consecrated Missionary Bishop of the Melanesian Islands. He went on with his work as before. He was often in danger of death. He went among the natives alone and unarmed. They might have finished him off at once with a poisoned arrow. Yet he was always cheerful and zealous. "Thank God!" he says, "I can fall back upon many solid points of comfort — chiefest of all. He sees and knows it perfectly. He sees the islanders too, and loves them, how infinitely more than I can. He is, I trust, sending me to them. He will bless honest endeavours to do His will amongst them. The light is breaking forth in Melanesia; and I take great comfort for this thought, and remember that it does not matter whether it is in my time; only I must work on."

Again he says, when speaking of the men who were to be sent out to help him: "A man who takes the sentimental view of coral islands and cocoa-nuts is worse than useless; a man possessed with the idea that he is making a sacrifice will never do; and a man who thinks any kind of work 'beneath a gentleman' will simply be in the way, and be rather uncomfortable at seeing the Bishop doing what he thinks degrading to himself. And if the right fellow is moved by God's grace to come out, what a welcome we will give him, and how happy he will soon be in a work, the abundant blessings of which none can know as we know them."

It was not for money that these ordained clergymen left England. It was only for a hundred pounds a year, afterwards increased to a hundred and fifty pounds. But they taught the natives everything — habits of economy, attention, punctuality, tidiness, and such like. How much character comes out of these homely virtues. The Bishop established schools and colleges wherever he went. He got the Island boys to accompany him on his voyages, in order that he might understand their language, and they his. At Santa Cruz, in 1864, the Bishop and his party were shot at One, Pearce, received the long shaft of an arrow in his chest; and Edwin Nobbs received an arrow in his left eye. An oarsman, Young, was shot through the left wrist The Bishop took out the arrows — the one in the chest after a long operation. Fisher Young died of tetanus. When dying, he said to the Bishop, "Kiss me; I am very glad that I was doing my duty." Nobbs died of the same disease. Pearce, though his wound had been the most severe, recovered.

He next visited Norfolk Island, Pitcairn Island, the New Hebrides Islands, the Fiji Islands, the Solomon Islands, the Tahitian Islands — everywhere doing good, and enlisting new members of the Church. He had the New Testament printed for them in their own language, and abstracts of the books of the Old Testament. When at Norfolk Island one Christmas Day, he was awoke by a party of some twenty Melanesians, headed by Mr. Bice, singing Christmas carols at his bedroom door. "How delightful it was says he; "I had gone to bed with the Book of Praise by my side, and Mr. Keble's hymn in my mind; and now the Mota versions, already familiar to us, of the Angels' song, and of 'the Light to lighten the Gentiles,' sung too by one of our heathen scholars, took up, as it were, the strain. Their voices sounded so fresh and clear in the still midnight, the perfectly clear sky, the calm moon, and the warm genial climate I lay awake long afterwards, thinking of the blessed change wrought on their minds, thinking of my happy happy lot, of how utterly undeserved it was and is, and losing myself in God's wonderful goodness, and mercy, and love."

We must hasten on to his last voyage to the Santa Cruz archipelago. The kidnapping vessels from Queensland were haunting the islands for the purpose of forcibly taking away the natives to work at their plantations. Some of the islands were nearly depopulated. Five men had been taken from Nukapa by the Queensland men. As the Bishop's vessel approached the island, they saw four canoes hovering about the coral reef. The Bishop, feeling a regard for these poor people, ordered the boat to be lowered. He entered it with four other men. On approaching the canoes, the Bishop entered one of them, in which there were two chiefs, who had formerly been friendly to him. The canoe made for the shore, on which the men in the ship's boat saw the Bishop landed, and then lost sight of him.

The boat remained with the other canoes. A native suddenly started up from a canoe, and shot off one of his yard-long arrows at the men in the boat Others did the same. The boat was pulled back rapidly, until it was out of range; but not before three out of the four men had been struck. But what had become of the Bishop? He had been murdered on shore. Two canoes were observed approaching; one full of natives, the other apparently empty. The natives went back in their canoe, the other, with a heap in the middle, drifted onwards. The boat from the ship met it, and the sailor, looking at the canoe, said, "Those are the Bishop's shoes." The canoe was brought alongside, and the body was taken up, rolled in a native mat. When the mat was taken away, there was the Bishop, with the placid smile upon his face. There was a palm-leaf fastened over the breast, and when the mat was opened, there were five wounds, and no more.

"The strange mysterious beauty," says Miss Yonge, "of these circumstances, almost makes one feel as if this were the legend of a martyr of the Primitive Church." There were none of those who loved and revered him, who did not feel that such was the death he always looked for, and that he was always willing to give his life for doing his duty. It was certain that he was killed from revenge. Five men had been stolen from Nukapa by the wretched Queensland freebooters; and this was the result!

The sweet calm smile of the Bishop's face preached peace to the mourners who lost his guiding spirit, but they could not look on it long. On the next morning, the body of John Coleridge Patteson was committed to the waters of the Pacific. He went to his rest, dying, as he had lived, in his Master's service. His end was peace.

Not many years after, in 1875, the island of Santa Cruz was visited by Commodore Goodenough, of Her Majest's ship Pearl He was anxious to see the scene of the Bishop's death; though he was warned against doing so, on account of the treacherous character of the natives. Nevertheless he landed on the island. The people appeared at first to be friendly. He landed again, but their behaviour appeared so suspicious, that he ordered his men at once to the boats.

In a letter — the last he everwrote — he describes the scene. "I saw a native to the left fitting an arrow to a string, and in an instant, just as I was thinking it must be a sham menace, thud came the arrow into my left side. I shouted, 'To the boats! pulled the arrow out, and leaped down the beach, hearing a flight of arrows whiz past me. On reaching the boats the surgeon came at once and dressed the wound, burning it well with caustic." Five days after, he adds, "I am exceedingly well; my only trouble is a pain in my back, which prevents me sleeping. I don't feel" Here the words cease. He could not end the letter.

He was seized with tetanus, and all hopes of his living were relinquished. He received the intelligence of his dangerous state with the perfect calm of a man whose whole life had been one long preparation for death. He caused himself to be carried on deck, and while his men gathered around him in speechless grief, he spoke to them lovingly and tenderly, and besought them to follow in his footsteps. He passed away to his rest peacefully and quietly, and his body was committed to the deep. Thus perished a man whom England could but ill spare. He was a noble specimen of a true sailor and a Christian gentleman.

We have not space to mention the heroic deeds of other Christian missionaries — of the Jesuits in Japan, China, and North and South America; of the Moravians in Greenland, the United States, and Africa; of John Elliot, the first missionary among the American Indians, and of David Brainerd, and Jonathan Edwards,[67] who followed him; of Martyn,

---

[67] When President Edwards was driven from his church at Northampton, Connecticut, because of his attempt to reform the morals of his congregation, he went on a mission to the Indians at Stockbridge, to preach to them the gospel. He remained among them for six years, greatly helped by his wife; and during that time he composed his profoundest and most valuable works. The reason of his

Heber, Carey, and Marshman, in India; of the Judson family in Burmah; of Charles Frederick Mackenzie, the martyr-missionary of the Zambesi; and of Samuel Marsden, the patriarch of Australian Christianity.[68]

All honour to you, noble Christian heroes, known and unknown; to all who give their time and their labour to spread abroad the knowledge of that which alleviates, comforts, and saves; to those who give their lives for the faith j and to all who help the poor, the struggling, and the uncivilised, to reach to higher blessings than those of this very transitory life!

CHAPTER XIIL

KINDNESS TO ANIMALS

He who feels contempt
For any living thing, hath faculties
Which he has never used.

Wordsworth

The wanton troopers riding by,
Have shot my fawn, and it will dye.
Ungentle men! they cannot thrive,
Who killed thee. Thou ne'er didst alive
Them any harm: alas I nor could
Thy death yet do them any good.

Marvell

There is in every animal's eye a dim image and gleam of humanity, a flash of strange light through which their life looks out and up to our great mystery of command over them, and claiming the fellowship of the creature, if not of the soul.

RUSKIN

---

dismission was as follows : — Some young persons of his flock had procured some obscene publications, and propagated them for the infection of others. Edwards called the leading members of his charge together, and told them of these doings. He mentioned the names of the persons who were implicated. It appeared that almost all the families in the town had some relation or other concerned in the matter. The heads of the congregation set their pastor at defiance with the greatest insolence and contempt; and he was eventually dismissed by a majority of two hundred against twenty. Such was the cause of his missionary life among the Indians.

[68] An admirable account of these missionaries is to be found in Miss Yonge's Pioneers and Founders.

WHAT an enormous amount of cruelty is perpetrated upon dumb animals, — upon birds, upon beasts, upon horses, upon all that lives. The Roman gladiators have passed away, but the Spanish bull-fights remain. As the Roman ladies delighted to see the gladiators bleed and die in the public amphitheatre, so the Spanish ladies clap their hands in exultation at spectacles from which English warriors sicken and turn away. "It must be owned," said Caballero, "and we own it with sorrow, that in Spain there is very little compassion shown to animals among the men and women; and among the lower classes, there is none at all."

But we are not clean-handed. Not long ago, bullbaiting was one of our public sports; cock-fighting and badger-drawing were common until our own time. The sports were patronised by rich and poor. In 1822, Richard Martin, of Galway, the friend of animals, succeeded in obtaining the enactment of a law, which invested animals with rights under the social contract; yet two of the judges, in a case brought before them, declared that bulls were not entitled to the benefit of the Act

In 1829 a bill to suppress bull-baiting was rejected by the House of Commons, by a majority of 73 to 28. But public' opinion grew, until bull-baiting became only a poor man's sport It was not until 1835 that an Act was passed, putting an end to bull-baiting. The Society for the Suppression of Cruelty to Animals was founded upon Martin's law. Animals were placed under legal protection, though some were unhappily excluded. There are yet many survivals of cruelty.

For instance, birds were excluded. One need only go to Hurlingham on a ladies' day, to see the cruelty with which pigeons are treated. The poor things are let out of their trap, and are shot down for a bet, dyeing the ladies' dresses with their blood. There is as much clapping of hands as at a Spanish bull-fight. The pricked bird, the bird with a broken leg, contrives to fly out of the field, and falls into some covert place, and there dies after a long agony. Is this the lesson of humanity that English women would teach to their sons and daughters?

The fashion for birds' wings in ladies dresses has been a woeful time for birds. They have been shot down in all countries to supply "gentle woman's" passion for birds' wings. The Spectator mentions a marriage in which eleven bridesmaids wore dresses trimmed with swan's down and robins. What a slaughter of birds for that one wedding! The robins should have been draped in blood. But ladies will permit the slaughter, rather than be out of fashion.

But bird-slaughter as a trade has now reached proportions which threaten the extinction of some of the most beautiful of God's creatures. Humming-birds, kingfishers, larks, nightingales, are all shot down. One London dealer in birds received a single consignment of 32,000 dead hummingbirds, 80,000 aquatic birds, and 800,000 pairs of wings I

Some years ago an Act was passed by Parliament, "for the protection of wild birds during the breeding season;" and an Act was afterwards passed "for the preservation of wild-fowl" But these Acts have had little effect. The wild-fowl are still killed for the pleasure of women. One of the last things out is the every-day ladies' hat, "trimmed with glossy wild duck." If they cannot get their adornment at home, the comers of the earth are ransacked for them. India is a great field for kingfishers, whose wings are of the most beautiful colour. They are shot down for the English market[69]

Englishmen are exposing themselves to the contempt of the Norwegians for their wholesale slaughter of birds and game, carried on by the lower class of English tourists. The Christiania Punch says of our countrymen: "Long has the time gone by, since England dared to take part in politics: since then, she has faithfully slept. [Perhaps referring to Lord John Russell's policy with regard to Denmark.] The whole of God's summer, every English lout comes hither to plague us, fishing, shooting, and destroying; thus, all our game will soon be annihilated."

In consequence of the swarm of English tourists, the Storthing has passed a law, prohibiting any foreigner from carrying a gun or fishing-rod without a license. It is quite enough to enjoy the splendid scenery of Norway, without destroying its wild-fowl and game. The law will at all events put an end to the wholesale destruction.

The capture of larks in this country is enormous. At Lakenheath, in Suffolk, 2000 dozen of larks were taken in three days, and sent to London to be made into lark pies — that delicacy of the gourmand. Indeed, lark pies have become very popular, and every means are taken to capture the birds in large quantities, both at home and abroad.

Let us tell how a good man undertook to save the larks and defeat the gourmands. It occurred in the neighbourhood of Aberdeen only a few years ago. Towards the middle of March a heavy snow-storm set in. The country was white as far as the eye could reach. The inland birds were driven down by the stress of weather, by cold, and by hunger, to the sea-coast. They were seen fluttering about with that peculiar motion of the wings characteristic of the lark over the earth, before lighting upon it The fields by the sea-shore were almost black with larks.

A number of people went out to snare, and gin, and lime, and shoot them. The number caught was immense. The season being late, the birds had paired. They were all husbands and wives. Poor things! They were driven by hard times to seek their fortune or their fate together. The good

---

[69] A "Lover of Nature "writes to a Lahore paper from Khairpur: "A couple of evenings ago I was strolling along the banks of a large lake here, when I came upon two men with peculiarly-shaped baskets. To my inquiries as to what they were and what they were doing, they replied that they were bird-catchers from Madras. What kind of birds? Kingfishers; and in their basket they showed me 200 kingfishers' feathers, for which they said they would receive Rs.40 on their return to Madras. They said this was their yearly occupation, and all the year through there were bands of them spread throughout the country, and that the plumages were sent to England. As they were on their road south, I asked if they went to Guzerat. They said no, they were prevented from carring on their occupation there. Good Guzeratis! I hope their example is followed in other parts of British India, or if it be not, that it soon will be. For it is plain that if this wanton destruction of the beautiful bird goes on for very long, we shall have cause to lament the total disappearance of one of the handsomest of the wild feathered tribe."

man we speak of found a Rough offering a lark for sale, and at his feet he saw a whole cageful of birds. It was a perfect Black Hole of Calcutta. They were struggling and pushing each other in their frantic efforts to escape. The sight of this was too much for the good man's feelings. He bought the whole lot, and sent them to his warehouse for better accommodation. He then went to the Secretary for the Prevention of Cruelty to Animals to see if nothing could be done to put a stop to the infamous traffic, but found to his sorrow that, while many of our favourite birds had been protected by the Wild Fowls Preservation Act of 1876, the lark had strangely been omitted.

He therefore took upon himself the preservation of the larks. He told the persons who were engaged in destroying them to bring them alive, and he would buy the birds at the same price which they were receiving from the game-dealers in town. They agreed to his offer, for they knew that in the one case the birds would have been killed and eaten, whereas, in the other, they would be taken care of and set free. The number of larks brought to him was so great — over a thousand — that, besides the larks in cages in his warehouse, he obtained the use of a large room in the country for their accommodation. The noise of their singing in the morning became almost deafening, and crowds of birds gathered over the house to listen to the musical throng.

The great storm passed away. The snow disappeared, and the green grass and dark earth became visible once more. Then came the delivery of the captives. The windows of the room were thrown open, and out they streamed, chattering and singing, and winging their way in every direction. Then the cages of larks were brought from the warehouse to a sweet spot outside the city. The doors were opened, and the benefactor stood to one side to see the escape of his friends. It was curious to watch them. Some would dart out, soar aloft, and burst into song,

> "Pouring their full heart
> In profuse strains of unpremeditated art;"

Others would flutter on the surface of the ground and disappear in the adjoining woods. One may imagine, but can scarcely express, the joy felt by our northern friend in his little act of well-doing. The larks settled down and built their nests in the neighbourhood. They reared their young there; and from that time the city has been surrounded by the music of the skylark.

> "Higher still, and higher
> From the earth thou springest,
> Like a cloud of fire;
> The blue deep thou wingest,
> And singing still dost soar, and soaring ever singest."

The great Leonardo da Vinci — a man great in his kindness to birds and animals — great as an architect, a military engineer, a philosopher, and an artist — was accustomed to buy birds in cages for the purpose of restoring them to liberty. A picture has been painted of this noble artist doing his deed of mercy, with the released birds fluttering round their deliverer, and the empty cages at his feet. The picture is to be seen at the gallery of the Louvre in Paris.

The old hermits had a great love for animals. They were their only companions. The birds used to flutter about them; and even the wild animals took shelter with them. They seemed to feel that no harm would be done to them. Even birds know and feel their danger when a man appears amongst them with a gun. Crows rise from picking up the grubs along the ploughman's furrow, and immediately disappear; though the crows by feeding themselves were furthering the next year's harvest

St. Francis had a notion that all living things were his brothers and sisters, and he carried his idea beyond the confines of poetry into literal fact. He even preached to the birds. He used to speak to all created things as if they had intelligence; and he loved to recognise in their various properties some trace of the divine perfection. "If your heart be right," said another ancient sage, "then every creature is a mirror of life, and a book of holy doctrine."

A very different state of feelings prevails at the Bass Rock in the Firth of Forth. The solan goose has made it the favourite haunt of bird-killers. Yachts and steamers sail round the rock, and for hours keep up an incessant and deadly fusilade. The birds, young and old, fall in scores, and, whether wounded or dead, are left to their fate. The wounded, with broken legs or bleeding wings, toss about the restless ocean, mutilated waifs, and die in tortures impossible to describe. And yet inhuman beings call this "sport."

Birds are more human than some men. They help each other when in difficulty. When Edward of Banff shot a tern, he was amazed to see two of the unwounded terns take up their brother, bear him aloft on their wings, and take him out to sea. Edward might have shot down many of the terns, but "he willingly allowed them to perform an act of mercy, and to exhibit an instance of affection which man himself need not be ashamed to imitate."

The "battue" has for the most part been introduced into this country from Germany. Whole droves of partridges, pheasants, hares, and such like, are driven by keepers from miles about, and brought into some sheltered spot, where they are shot down in hundreds. This is also called "sport." "I venture to hope," said the Archbishop of York, "that the time is not far off when it will be a matter of curious history that English gentlemen once used to publish it abroad with satisfaction that they and their friends had in a couple of days killed 2000 head of game that had been driven together into a wood for certain death. Then, again, the trapped bird, released without a chance, wounded again and again, and picked up fluttering and suffering, is made a pastime for strong men, and when women make a holiday over such a sport, it shows that they are without love or pity. It reflects a shadow, and becomes a painful study indeed."

Is this the Chivalry to which England has sunk? Is this craving for inhumanity and cruelty the highest idea of manhood? Sir Charles Napier gave up sporting because he could not bear to hurt dumb creatures; and yet he won the battle of Meeanee. He was courageous, and yet he was not cruel. He could not bear the sport that feeds upon the sobs and dying shrieks of harmless creatures. When General Outram — the Bayard of India — was seeking health in Egypt with his wife, a friend of his, knowing that they had no meat for dinner, shot a bird Outram, sportsman though he was, said sadly, "I have made a vow never to shoot a bird." He would not eat the bird when cooked; his friend gave it to an old peasant woman, and "we dined as we could."

Albertus of Siena is represented in old miniatures as caressing a hare, for he often preserved them when pursued by the hunters. He is represented moralising over the spectacle, like melancholy Jacques weeping and commenting upon the sobbing deer. "One man," says St. Chrysostom, "keeps dogs to catch brute animals, himself sinking into brutality; another keeps oxen and asses to transport stores, but neglects men wasting with hunger; and spends gold without limit to make men of marble, but neglects real men, who are becoming like stones through their evil state."

A French novelist somewhere says of the Englishman, "Let us go out and kill something!" This is his idea of the Englishman's practice. But he forgets his own countrymen. We have still kept our birds, though many have been destroyed by cold and hunger during these later winters; and many more by shooting and battues. Still our birds are the glory of the land — Gloria in excelsis! But in France, the fields are mute. There is no music from the skies. The larks have been netted and eaten. The birds of gay plumage have been shot, and their wings put in ladies' bonnets. All over the country, sparrows, finches, robins, and nightingales have disappeared. All are killed and eaten.[70]

But now comes the punishment The trees are eaten bare; the vine is destroyed by phylloxerae; the leaves of the shrubs are devoured by caterpillars. They are seen hanging in bunches from the trees. The birds have been killed that destroyed the grubs and the phylloxerae. Hence destruction is spreading over France. The crops are eaten up at the roots, and the vine is in some districts entirely fruitless. Thus inhumanity, like curses, comes home to roost. Waterton has calculated that a single pair of

---

[70] For the matter of birds, France is a dark and silent land. The eye searches in vain, the ear listens in vain, for Nature there sits lamenting her children that are not Whatever may be said for Republican institutions and peasant proprietary, they can claim no partnership with Nature, who clings rather to her old friends, feudalism and aristocracy. If there were reported anywhere in France as great a number of birds of gay plumage and thrilling song as may be seen and heard almost anywhere a few miles from the metropolis, populations would turn out in fancy costumes, carrying guns and large bags, followed by nondescript dogs, and ready to watch whole days for the chance of a victim within easy range. — The Times,

sparrows destroy as many grubs in one day as would have eaten up half an acre of young corn in a week.

We are glad to see that some steps have been taken in France for the protection of birds and animals, under the fostering help of the Minister of Public Instruction. The boys — for it is always the young that imitate cruelty — are taught kindness and humanity to dumb animals, as well as to everything that is dependent upon human care. This is the new order of chivalry in France, and it will doubtless prove of great service. There are already five hundred juvenile societies for the care and protection of animals. In America there has been a similar movement; and two thousand boys are already enrolled in the juvenile branch of the Society for the Protection of Animals at Philadelphia. Kindness to speechless animals is inculcated, and the twofold duty of reverence and compassion is strongly enjoined.

How much time is spent in cramming children with useless knowledge, and how little is spent in teaching them useful humanity. They are taught literature from books, which does nothing to make them better or more humane. They are not taught gentleness, kindness, or urbanity. Their head is taught, but not their heart But it might be difficult to find teachers who could evoke the better feelings of the inner nature. Physical force is at hand, and is more generally resorted to. It is a direct and palpable thing. It can be felt. Its immediate effects are sometimes apparent; but its ultimate effects are concealed in the heart These are generally under-estimated, because obscure and remote.

When Euffordius of Cologne heard a great cry issuing from a schoolhouse which he was passing, he opened the door, entered, and rushed up like a lion, raising his staff against the teacher and his assistant, and delivered the boy from their hands. "What are you doing, tyrant?" he said, "You are placed here to teach, not to kill scholars!"

The cruelty done to children by some parents, as well as by teachers, is indescribable. Children are held to be of the same mental nature, of the same temperament, of the same adaptability to learn, as their parents and teachers. Yet the boy who cannot learn his lessons as quickly as another is thrashed; or he is degraded in some way. Grown people forget the intense misery to which children are thus exposed. The child's horizon is so limited, that he sees no remedy to his woes; and his sorrow absorbs h whole little being.

"Fathers, provoke not your children to wrath, lest they be discouraged." If the life of a child be embittered, the result is shyness and secret aversion. Even a child feels itself wronged, and a sense of bitterness is implanted in its heart. We can never think without pity of the parent who lost a promising son by death, and was haunted through life by his parental severity. "My boy," he said to a friend, "used to think me cruel, and he had too much reason to do so 3 but he did not know how I loved him at the bottom of my heart and now it is too late!"

We often think, when we hear of parents beating their children, that they should rather be inflicting the punishment upon themselves. They have been the means of bringing into being the inheritors of their own moral nature. The child does not make his own temper; nor has any control, while a child, over its direction. If the parents have conferred an irritable temper on the child, it is a duty on their part to exercise self-control, forbearance, and patience, so that the influence of daily life may, in the course of time, correct and modify the defects of its birth.

But "the child's Will must be broken! "There is no greater fallacy than this. Will forms the foundation of character. Without strength of will, there will be no strength of purpose. What is necessary, is not to break the child's will, but to educate it in proper directions and this is not to be done through the agency of force or fear. A thousand instances might be cited in proof of this statement

When the parent or teacher relies chiefly upon pain for controlling the child's will, the child insensibly associates duty and obedience with fear and terror. And when you have thus associated command over the will of others with pain, you have done all that you could to lay the foundations of a bad character — a bad son, a bad husband, a bad father, a bad neighbour, and a bad citizen.[71] Parents may not think of this when they are beating into their children their own faults; but it is true nevertheless. There is no doubt that the command over the wills of others by pain, leads by degrees to all the several stages of irritation, injustice, cruelty, oppression, and tyranny.

When a boy at the Blue-coat school hanged himself not long ago, rather than submit to the hardships of the school, another "old Blue-coat boy "came forward and described the punishments practised in that richly endowed establishment "The punishments," he says, "were simply brutal in their severity, and were often meted out with but scanty justice."[72] There is a farther point to be mentioned. The tyranny of teachers to their scholars

---

[71] "Every first thing," says Richter, "continues for ever with the child; the first colour, the first music, the first flower, paint the foreground of his life. . . . The first inner or outer object of love, injustice, or such like, throws a shadow immeasurably far along his after years."

[72]The Rev. Andrew A. W. Drew, M.A., made an appeal to the public on the subject, in a letter to the Times, "Fortunately," he says, " I was never flogged myself, but as long as I live I shall never forget a scene that I witnessed in the case of another boy, who had been flogged. He was a small and delicate lad, by name Blount, and he slept in the bed next to me. A big boy had compelled Blount to go and bring him some lumps of sugar out of the monitor's sugar-basin. The big boy ate the sugar himself, and the small boy had none of it. The facts of the case became known to the monitor, who reported it to the Steward, who flogged Blount as a thief, and did not punish the big boy. That night poor little Blount could not sleep, and at last he begged me to help him. I accordingly took his shirt off, and found his back, from the shoulders down to the waist, one mass of lacerated flesh, the blood sticking to the shirt so as to cause agony in getting it off I then, with my finger and thumb, pulled out of his back at least a dozen pieces of birch-rod, which had penetrated deep into the flesh. The boy's back looked more like a piece of raw meat than anything else. . . . Compare this, sir, with a modem garroter's flogging at the Old Bailey, where, as the newspapers tell us 'the man's back was slightly reddened, but no blood drawn,' and let your readers say what they think of a Christ's Hospital flogging."

implants in them a tyranny towards others. Blows teach them cruelty to the objects which are in their power. As their sense of pain has been disregarded, so do they acquire a disregard for the pains of others. They come to take a pleasure in inflicting pain upon school-fellows under their own age, and upon dumb, sentient creatures.

There is an enormous amount of cruelty practised upon animals, originating, we believe, in the physical punishment which has been received in the family or in the school You see it in a lot of boys beating a poor ass upon a common — or in drowning a cat — or in tying a pan to a dog's tail — or in spinning a cockchafer, or in sundry other boyish diversions. Parents and teachers ought carefully to teach children to have a tender respect for everything that possesses life, and to abstain from the infliction of all unnecessary pain; and they cannot do this more effectually than by abstaining from the infliction of all unnecessary suffering upon them.

We have mentioned donkeys. This animal is by no means unkind. It carries heavy loads with dogged surefootedness. In Switzerland you see the donkeys heavily laden with wood, walking along the brink of precipices, and duly coming home with their load. The donkey is the poor man's daily helper. People say it is obstinate. But that arises from the ill-treatment which it receives. We have known affectionate donkeys — most willing and persevering workers.

The expression "dumb animals" is perhaps fallacious. Animals seem to have the means of communicating with each other, though not in spoken words. They whimper, or mutter, or cry. They communicate with each other by arbitrary signs. They know even the language of man. They come when they are called. Dogs, horses, elephants, and other animals, obey the human voice.

The dog is, of all animals, the most trusted. The dog possesses love, obedience, discipline, conscience, and even reason. Lord Brougham has told a story of a shepherd who lost his collie at a fair. The dog searched about in all directions, and at last scented the footsteps of his master. He followed the scent along a certain road, until he came to a point at which three roads diverged. He scented the first road, then the second, and then, without scenting the third, he galloped into it. The dog's reasoning seemed to be this: my master has not gone into this, the first road; he has not gone into this, the second road he must therefore have gone into this, the third road. Q.E.D.

Then about conscience. A dog rushed out of his kennel one night in the dark, and bit an old woman. She shrieked, and the dog quitted his grip in an instant. It was the old woman who had fed him! What distress the dog was in! If he could have spoken, he would have said, "I have bitten my best friend — the one who fed me and showed me every kindness. What a brute I have been! "The dog was thoroughly ashamed of his ingratitude. He would not come out of his kennel for three days, not even for food. At last the old woman made it up with the dog, and he overwhelmed her with expressions of love, and gratitude.

Then how affectionate the dog is! Everybody knows the story of the faithful dog Bobby. The dog attended his master's funeral at the Greyfriars' Churchyard, Edinburgh. There was no stone to mark the place, but for four years Bobby watched over the little mound. He never forgot the spot in which his master was buried. In summer or winter — in rain or in snow — Bobby was there. Though driven from the grave by whipping, he always returned. He loved his master better than himself. He became skin and bone — a tattered hunger-stricken dog.

At last the facts were brought to light by the Revenue officers, who wished to levy a tax upon the dog. But there was no one to claim him. His master lay below. Some gave him food, some wished to claim him, but he would not leave the grave. His was a love utterly unselfish. After four years' watching and waiting, the affectionate dog died. And then a monument was erected in the street outside the gate of Greyfriars' Churchyard, to perpetuate the memory of the faithful and self-sacrificing Bobby. What a lesson of gratitude and love for human beings 1

Captain Hall relates an incident of Sir Walter Scott's boyhood, which had a powerful influence upon his after life. One day, a dog coming towards him, he took up a stone and threw it He broke the dog's leg. The poor dog had strength enough left to crawl up to him and lick his feet. This incident, he said, had given him the bitterest remorse. He could never forget it; because he was a thoroughly tender-hearted man. He had always his pets about him. He had a fund of kindness for every created being. He wrote his novels with his dogs about him — Maida, Nimrod, and Bran. Maida was his favourite. It died during his lifetime, and he had a sculptured monument of it set up before his door. In his novel of Woodstock he commemorated the elaborate and affectionate portraiture of old Maida under the name of Bevis.

Wonderful are the fidelity and attachments of dogs. Have we not the famous Bedgellert of Wales? the St. Bernards who have saved so many lives from the snow of the Alps? the famous dogs Rab and Nipper, so wonderfully described by Dr. John Brown? the dog of Montargis, who vainly defended his master, Aubri de Montdidier, when set upon by his deadly foe Macaire, and afterwards led to the discovery of the murderer? and the Duke of Richmond's dog, commemorated by Vandyke, whose sagacity and courage saved his master from assassination?

Sir Walter Scott, in his journal, relates the story of a dog that saved its master from being burnt alive. "Lord R. Kerr," he says, "told us he had a letter from Lord Forbes (son of Earl Granard, Ireland), that he was asleep in his house at Castle Forbes, when awakened by a sense of suffocation, which deprived him of the power of stirring a limb, yet left him the consciousness that the house was on fire. At this moment, and while his apartment was in flames, his large dog jumped on the bed, seized his shirt, and dragged him to the staircase, where the fresh air restored his powers of resistance and of escape." This is very different from most cases of preservation by the canine race, when the animal generally jumps into the water, in which element he has force and skill. That of fire is as hostile to him as to mankind

And lastly, there are the dogs of Pompeu and Herculaneum. The cast of the former is taken from the ash cavity in which he was discovered. He died of suffocation and agony. But, like the sentinel, he never left his post. The Herculaneum dog Delta has left behind him a wonderful record of valour. In the disinterment of the buried city, his skeleton was found stretched over that of a boy of about twelve years old, most probably clasping his charge to prevent his being suffocated or burnt The boy perished as well as the faithful Delta; but a collar remains to tell of the noble courage of the dog. It relates that he had three times saved the life of his master — from the sea, from robbers, and from wolves.

It will thus be seen that the moral and intellectual tendencies of man are foreshadowed in a remarkable degree in the animal mind; that they are capable of love, fidelity, gratitude, sense of duty, conscientiousness, friendship, and the highest self-sacrifice. Hartley, in his Observations on Man says of the dog, that we seem to be in the place of God to him; to be His vicegerents, and empowered to receive homage from them in His name; and he adds, that we are obliged, by the same tenure, to be their guardians and benefactors.

Darwin says, "We see some distant approach to this state of mind in the deep love of a dog for his master, associated with self- submission, some fear, and perhaps other feelings. The behaviour of a dog when returning to his master after an absence, and as I may add, of a monkey to his beloved keeper, is widely different from that towards his fellows. In the latter case, the transports of joy appear to be somewhat less, and the sense of equality is shown in every action."[73] Thus, says Nicholson, many animals are wiser and better than many men, and some entire races of men.

Here, for instance, is a case in which the brute was much better than the man. A certain dog belonged to a farmer in Cumberland. The man made a bet that his dog would drive a flock of sheep from Cumberland to Liverpool, a distance of more than a hundred miles, without help or supervision. Considering the tortuous road, the groups of animals and conveyances to be met on the road, and the length of the journey, the dog's chances seemed hopeless. Nevertheless, in the course of a few days, the dog reached Liverpool with all his flock. The dog had done his duty, but he was famished. After delivering up his charge, he fell down dead on the street of Liverpool — a victim to his master's brutality.

Every one will remember the story of Androcles and the Lion. Androcles had hid himself in a cave when he saw a lion approaching. He feared that he should be devoured. But the lion was limping, and appeared to be in great pain. Androcles approached with courage, took up the lion's paw, and took out a large splinter of wood which had caused the flesh to fester. The lion was most grateful, and fawned upon him. Afterwards, when Androcles was taken prisoner and sent to Rome to be delivered up to the wild beasts, a lion was let loose to devour him. It was the same lion that Androcles had relieved in his agony. The animal remembered with gratitude his deliverer, and, instead of devouring him, went up and fawned

---

[73] Descent of Man i. 68.

upon him. Appian declares that he witnessed with his own eyes the scene between Androcles and the lion in the Roman circus.

Has an animal any rights? No legal rights, certainly, except those provided by law. But it has the right to live and to enjoy. Justice, says John Lawrence, in which are included mercy and compassion, obviously refers, to sense and feeling; and justice in any form may be applied to it "The question," says Jeremy Bentham, "is not. Can they reason? nor, Can they speak; but. Can they suffer? This is the gist of the whole question. The conscience of the most civilised people tells them to treat animals kindly, to consult their happiness as well as that of the people about them."

Sir Arthur Helps quotes a passage from Voltaire, in which we find him speaking in defence of the rights of animals.

"Is it possible any one should say or affirm in writing that beasts are machines, void of knowledge and sense, have a sameness in all their operations, neither learning nor perfecting anything? How! This bird which makes a semicircular nest when he fixes it against a wall, which, when in an angle, shapes it like a quadrant, and circular when he builds it in a tree; is this having a sameness in its operations? Does this hound, after three months' teaching, know no more than when you took him in hand? Your bullfinch, does he repeat a tune at first hearing? or rather, is it not some time before you can bring him to it? is he not often found out, and does he not improve by practice?

"Is it from my speaking, that you allow me sense, memory, or ideas? Well, I am silent; but you see me come home very melancholy, and with eager anxiety look for a paper, open the bureau where I remember to have put it, take it up, and read it with apparent joy. You hence infer that I have felt pain and pleasure, and think, I have memory and knowledge.

"Make the like reference concerning this dog, which, having lost his master, searches for him in all the streets with cries of sorrow, and comes home agitated and restless; he goes up stairs, down stairs, roves from room to room, till at length he finds his beloved master in his closet, and betokens his gladness by his soft whispers, his gesticulations, and his caresses.

"This dog, so very superior to man in his affection, is seized by some barbarian virtuosos, who nail him down to a table, and dissect him while living, the better to show you the mezeraic veins. All the same organs of sensation which are in yourselves, you perceive in him. Now, anatomists, what say you? Answer me. Has nature created all the springs of feeling in this animal, that it may not feel? Has he nerves to be without pleasure or pain? For shame! charge not nature with such weakness or inconsistency.

"But the scholastic doctors ask what the soul of beasts is? That is a question I do not understand.... Who formed all these properties? Who has implanted all these faculties? He who causes the grass of the field to grow, and the earth to gravitate towards the sun,"

Strange how a dumb animal can wind itself round the human heart Ebenezer Elliot, the Com Law Rhymer, said, "If 'twere not for my cat and dog, I think I scarce could live." Even a cat may attach a person to his home. Once, a little boy left school, and did not know what to do with himself. He became unquiet. He longed to run away. He wished to see the world and the things it contained. But he had a great affection for the old Tabby. He thought it might be drowned or given away; so he remained at home. It was well that he did so, as all things turned up right for him in the end.

Thoreau, of Concord, Massachusetts, was like the old hermits in his love for animals. He took to the woods, near Walden Pond, in 1845. He began to build a house, to the surprise of the racoons and squirrels. But the animals soon began to know that he meant them no harm. He would lie down on a fallen tree, or on the edge of a rock, and remain quite immovable. The squirrel, or racoon, or woodchuck, would come closer and closer upon him, and even touch him. The news went through the woods that there was a man amongst them who would not kill them. There arose a beautiful sympathy between the man and the birds and animals. They came at his call. Even the snakes would wind round his legs. On talking a squirrel from a tree, the little creature would refuse to leave him, and hide its head in Thoreau's waistcoat. Even the fish in the river knew him. They would let him lift them up from the water in entire confidence that he would do them no harm. He had built his house over a wood-mouse's nest; and at length, the wood-mouse, at first terrified, came and picked up the crumbs at his feet. Then it would run over his shoes and over his clothes. At last, the wood- mouse became so tame, that it ran up his clothes, and along his sleeves, while he was sitting at his bench, and round and round the paper which held his dinner. When he took up a bit of cheese, the wood-mouse came and nibbled it, sitting in his hand, and when it was finished, it cleaned its face and paws like a fly, and walked away. We have never heard of such a communion between man and animals, except in the case of the hermits, so plentifully recorded by Kenelm Digby, in his Mores Catholia.

When Theodore Parker took up a stone to throw at a tortoise in a pond, he felt himself restrained by something within him. He went home and asked his mother what that something was? She told him that this something was what was commonly called Conscience, but she preferred to call it the voice of God within him. "This," said Parker, "was the turning point in my life;" and this was his mode of accepting the truth of the divinity of the Eternal Spirit that speaks to our own spirits.

"There is nothing," says the Rev. J. S. Wood, "in the will of man half so powerful in educating the lower animals as thoughtful kindness. Inflexible decision, combined with gentleness and sympathy, are irresistible weapons in the hands of man; and I do not believe that there is any animal which cannot be subdued if the right man undertakes the task.

"By the mixture of firmness and kindness, that raging wild beast of a horse 'Cruiser,' was in three hours rendered gentle and subservient, obeying the least sign of his conqueror, and allowing himself to be freely handled without displaying the least resentment.

"I once saw Mr. Rarey operate on a splendid little black -Arab horse that flew like a tiger at him, kicking, biting, and screaming at once, now attacking him with his jaws, now with his heels.... Within half an hour,

Rarey and the horse were lying together on the ground, Rarey's head resting on one of the hind hoofs, and the other hoof being laid on his temple He had impressed upon the animal's memory that no harm was intended; and so the horse, instead of feeling fear and anger, conceived an affection for the man, who inflicted no pain, and yet showed that he must be obeyed."[74]

A great deal of cruelty to birds and animals exists everywhere, partly from want of thought In Italy it quite sickens one. Birds are used for the amusement of children. A string is tied to a bird's leg. When the bird tries to fly, it is pulled down by the string. When its powers of flight are exhausted, it is generally plucked alive, and dismembered. The children do not understand that a beast or a bird can be a fellow-creature. When expostulated with, they answer, "Non è Cristiano" — It is not a Christian.

At Naples you see the active little horses galloping about, carrying whole loads of passengers behind them. The harness cuts into their flanks until they are quite red. As you pass along the roads, you see the horses lying useless. They are waiting for their wounds to heal, and then they are set to work again. One morning, an open car was seen coming down the Strada de Roma, heavily overladen. It contained men and women coming to the market, with their vegetable produce. A priest was in the midst of them. The horse was galloping as usual. The street was wet; the horse missed its foot and fell. There was a shriek, and a general scattering of the passengers over the horse's back, — women, cabbages, men, oranges, and priest. It was but a wonder of the moment. The horse was pulled up; the car was filled with the baskets; the women, the men, and the priest, clambered in. The horse was flogged, and away it went galloping down the street.

There is no slavery in England! But look at the 'bus and cab and cart horses, and you will find that slavery exists for horses. It was said by James Howell, Clerk of the Council, as long ago as 1642, that England is called "The hell of horses, and not without cause." Cabs are driven by worn-out animals, and one or more of their feet are full of pain. You see how one of them gently lifts up its fore foot, and gently lets it down again. Perhaps the road along which it is driven is full of big stones, along which it has to crawl. Ask the cart-horse how it is treated. It is doomed through a long life of labour to be kicked and flogged, to strain and stagger under its burdens, to bear heat and cold and hunger without resistance. At last he is consigned to the knacker's yard.

To mitigate the torture of heavy laden horses, climbing and often slipping on the steep streets leading from the Thames near London Bridge, a kind lady came out daily with her servant, and strewed the roads with gravel. We have often seen her in the midst of the traffic, under the very noses of the horses, strewing gravel along the paths; she continued this work for many years. When she died, she did not forget the poor horses. She left a considerable sum in the hands of trustees, to be applied "for ever "to the distribution of gravel in steep and slippery London roadways. Her

---

[74] Wood's Man and Beasts i 296-7

name should not be forgotten. She was Miss Lisetta Rest; and had filled the place of organist at the Church of Allhallows, Barking, Tower Street, for forty-three years.

Ask the carriage horse, galled with its detestable bearing-rein, drawing the proud beauty along the Row, its mouth covered with foam and sometimes with blood; and what would it say? That men and women were alike its merciless tyrants. And yet such ladies go to anti-vivisection meetings to protest against cruelty to animals![75]

Man has enslaved the horse, the ass, the camel, the reindeer, and other animals. They do his bidding; they bear his burdens; they* lose a life of freedom in one of pain and labour. They groan and wince under the lash, the curb, and the chain. At one steeple-chase at Liverpool no less than five horses had to be killed after the race. Three had their backs broken, and two had their legs snapped.

"I sometimes think," said Sir Arthur Helps, "that it was a misfortune for the world that the horse was ever subjugated. The horse is the animal that has been the worst treated by man; and his subjugation has not been altogether a gain to mankind. The oppressions he has aided in were, from the earliest ages, excessive. He it is to whom we owe much of the rapine of ' the dark ages.' And I have a great notion that he has been the main instrument of the bloodiest warfare. I wish men had their own cannon to drag up-hill. I doubt whether they would not rebel at that. And a commander obliged to be on foot throughout the campaign would very soon get tired of war."[76]

In the book of Job, written some 3400 years ago, we have a description of the war-horse. "Hast thou given the horse strength? Hast thou clothed his neck with thunder? ... The glory of his nostrils is terrible. He paweth in the valley, and rejoiceth in his strength; he goeth on to meet the armed men; he mocketh at fear, and is not affrighted, neither tumeth he back from the sword; he smelleth the battle from afar off ... the thunder of the captains and the shouting."

---

[75] The following letter is from the Times April 28, 1880 : — "Sir — In the cause of helpless suffering I appeal to you for a little space in your columns to protest against the cruelty practised daily on carriage horses — generally those of the most valuable kind. Besides the tight bearing-rein, bits are now in use which cause positive torture. A well-appointed landau, drawn by a magnificent pair of grays, passed me yesterday in Bond Street; the bearing-rein was frightfully tightened, and the mouth of the "off" horse was foaming with blood. Is it possible, I thought, that the young couple, the occupants of the carriage, can know of all this suffering? To those who, like myself, love horses and study their comfort, these sights are heartrending. We are close observers of horses, and can see at a glance if they are at ease. Alas! nothing escapes us, and the afternoon's drive is almost daily embittered by sights such as I have described — either the mouth full of blood, or the tongue swollen and nearly black from the pressure of the bit, the head braced up to an unnatural position, with other signs of distress. I would ask, is all this miserable suffering inflicted by ignorance, or heedlessness, or merciless cruelty? Let me entreat those who are the owners of horses to have mercy on them; they are among the noblest of God's creatures, and the most devoted and faithful servants of man."

[76] Animals and their Masters p. 20.

213

Virgil, in his Third Georgic, written many centuries later, again speaks of the war horse: —

> "The fiery courser, when he hears from far
> The sprightly trumpets and the shouts of war,
> Pricks up his ears, and, trembling with delight.
> Shifts place, and paws, and hopes the promised fight."

The war-horses in the frieze of the Parthenon at Athens, now placed in the British Museum as the Elgin Marbles, show the Greeks' pride in these noble animals. They are triumphantly pawing and galloping on, as if to a fight. At at a later period we know that Mexico and Peru were conquered principally through the aid of the horse. The natives looked upon the horse-mounted warrior as a god. They flew before his charges, and were destroyed by thousands. And yet these countries had attained to a high degree of civilisation without the use of the horse. The Spaniards, when they devastated the country, found thousands of houses well built, with gardens attached to them. "I doubt," says Sir Arthur Helps, "whether there was a single Mexican so ill lodged as millions of our poor countrymen are." Thus the question often recurs. Are we really making any progress in civilisation? Are we better than the Greeks, or the Romans, or the Mexicans were, in the times of their greatest enlightenment?

CHAPTER XIV

HUMANITY TO HORSES EDWARD FORDHAM FLOWER

He was the soul of goodness,
And all our praises of him are like streams
Drawn from a spring, that still rise full, and leave
The part remaining greatest.

Shakespeare

He prayeth well, who loveth well,
Both man, and bird, and beast; He prayeth best, who lovest best.
All things, both great and small; For the dear God who loveth us.
He made and loveth all.

Coleridge

The gentleness of chivalry, properly so called, depends on the recognition of the order and awe of lower and loftier animal life.... There

214

is, perhaps, in all the Iliad, nothing more deep in significance — there is nothing in all literature more perfect in human tenderness and honour for the mystery of inferior life — than the verses that describe the sorrow of the divine horses at the death of Patroclus, and the comfort given them by the greatest of the gods.

Ruskin

HOW much do we owe to the horse! He is the source of joy and pleasure to many. In his youth and beauty he is the pet of his owner. Men, women, and boys love the horse; his trot, his canter, or gallop, show him at his best. The horse carries us long and faithfully; he draws our burdens; he relieves man of a great load of labour. But the time comes when he is degraded and made a slave.

The cart-horse is kicked and beaten, and compelled to draw heavier weights than he is fit to carry; the carriage horse is gagged with brutal bits until he draws his burden with torture. The cab-horse is exposed to constant labour, often in the worst weather. He works till he can scarcely stand. His feet become diseased by dragging his freight over rough stones, or by standing in sloppy pools. If he does not fall down and die, he is condemned to the knacker's yard, and there he ends his life of labour and torture.

In the south of France the horse is put an end to in a different way. The Courtier du Centre says that the speculators of Bordeaux are trying to make their fortunes out of that disgusting object, the leech. They have made artificial swamps on the banks of the Garonne, and filled the swamps with leeches. Into these swamps all the old and worn-out horses of the province are sent. The leeches fasten on them instantly by thousands. An eye-witness describes in terms of horrible vividness the vain struggles of the animals, drawn downward into the mud, bleeding at every pore, striving in frantic terror to shake off the leeches which hang on their eyes, their lips, their nostrils, all their most sensitive parts, and at last, exhausted by loss of blood, sucked down into the noxious slime, they are seen no more. From eighteen to twenty thousand horses are annually sacrificed in this manner at Bordeaux.

France must be "the hell of horses" as well as England. But let us look at home. It is not every one, who, like the Duke of Wellington, allows the charger that bore him in his last victory to live out his life in peace and plenty. Horses are for the most part tortured while they live, and thrown away when they become useless. Miss Braddon speaks of the "high-mettled horses champing their bits in that eloquent martyrdom, by which fashion contrives to make the life of a three hundred guinea pair of carriage-horses a good deal worse than that of a costermonger's donkey." A lady wrote recently to Truths describing the tortures which she had seen inflicted on a pair of horses standing in Regent Street.

"I observed," she said, "an open barouche and a pair of horses standing at the side of the street. So tightly were the bearing-reins fastened back, that it was impossible for the poor brutes to close their mouths, and their distress was so painful to behold that I went and tried in vain to get the coachman to loosen the reins a little. All! could get from the man was: "They are used to it; missus likes 'em to be like that' The off-side horse seemed to suffer the most In vain the poor brute tried to get relief; the look of misery in its eyes will haunt me for many a long day."

The man who has done more to abate the misery of carriage-horses than any other, is Edward Fordham Flower. He may almost be called "The Missionary of Horses." He has devoted his time, his money, and his labour, to suppressing the cruelty of gag bearing-reins. He has taken up the work with his usual determination. He has written pamphlets, and addressed meetings in all parts of the country. There was no uncertain tone in his language. At a public meeting called by the Baroness Burdett Coutts, he compared that cruel instrument, the gag bearing-rein, to the soldier's stock of former days; and he maintained that those who used it — though as a rule they were not cabmen, but private' ladies and gentlemen — should be sent to gaol! Mr. Flower has a room in his house called the "Chamber of Torture," in which the dreadful bits are arranged in a row, as a protest against the cruelty of man to animals. Mr. Flower has also been a consistent and thorough advocate of the abolition of slavery of men as well as of horses, as the following narrative will show; though we fear we cannot give it in the vivid manner in which he relates the story of his past life.

Mr. Flower was born at Hertford in 1805. He was the youngest of a family of five. His father, who was a man of property, bought the estate of Harden Hill, about three and a half miles from Hertford. The family went to live there in 1808. Young Edward had a great fancy for animals. When five years old he began to ride. He had a small Shetland pony called "Little Moses." He rode to the post-office daily for the letters. The pony became his greatest friend. They were like playfellows together.

At six he got a pony. His uncle, Edward King Fordham, bought him a beautiful present — a saddle, bridle, and whip. One day he was out with his father, and flogged the pony because he shied at something on the road. His father saw it, and called him back. "Now, Ned, why did you flog that pony?" "Because it shied." "Well, don't you see that there was a deep hole into which you were leading him?" His father took from his hand the whip, and laid it across his shoulders. "Do you like that?" "No," said the boy, "I detest it." "Well then, Ned, never flog a pony unless it is absolutely necessary."

Shortly after, an accident befell him. He went one day to the new threshing machine to see how it worked. He put his fingers among the cogs. He was caught, and his arm would have been drawn in, but for a labourer who stopped the machine and drew his arm out. As it was, he lost about half of one of his fingers. He was then laid up sick for a time. He could not read, he could not write. Though Hertford was only about three miles off, he did not go to school. He disliked learning, and his father did not wish to force him to go to school.

While at Harden his father had often to go from his country seat to London; and while on the journey with his son, he would call upon him to "jump out and unhook the bearing-reins." This, he afterwards said, gave him the first idea of bits and bearing-reins upon the pleasant going of a horse.

216

The farms at Marden Hill and West End — consisting of about a thousand acres— did not answer very well. Mr. Flower had been unfortunate in introducing merino sheep. They could not breed nor thrive there. Besides, the condition of agriculture was much depressed in England after the conclusion of the French war. George, the eldest son, had been sent out to the United States to descry the glories of the land. He sent home a letter to his father, saying it was the richest and most prosperous country in the world. "Come out here," he said, "and you will have no cause to regret it."

Mr. Flower sold his English property in 1817, and prepared, with all his family, to emigrate to the United States. Young Flower was then twelve years old. His father hired two ships at Liverpool to contain his belongings. Besides his family, he took out about a hundred men and women, including labourers, blacksmiths ploughsmiths, a shepherd and a coachman, as well as several domestic servants. The cargo included two cows, a dozen sheep, some English pigs, six couples of hounds, and two Scotch staghounds. The ships sailed from Liverpool to America in March 1818.

One of the ships (the Anna Maria) went to New York, and the other to Philadelphia. At New York the family went on shore to see the wonders of the great western city. As young Flower and his father were going along Broadway they met William Cobbett coming along the street in his shirt - sleeves. Mr. Flower being a well-known political character in his own country, they recognised each other, and had some conversation as to the state of affairs in England and America.

The Anna Maria went round from New York to Philadelphia to join its sister ship. All the labourers, the servants, and the cattle, were disembarked. Philadelphia was then a nice clean Quartier town — not large in population, nor very much separated from the unclaimed land to the west About fifty miles from Philadelphia no roads had yet been made. The Philadelphians had not yet borrowed the money to make the roads and canals, which they afterwards repudiated. Shortly after landing, Mr. Flower proceeded to make up his convoy, for the purpose of travelling westward to the large tract of land, amounting to about 20,000 acres, which his eldest son had purchased in Wabash, Illinois. He hired three waggons, each drawn by six horses, and three waggons with a pair of horses for the servants.

The whole convoy started from Philadelphia in May 1818. As the weather was very fine, the travelling must have been delightful. The country was only half settled. The uncleared primeval forest was avoided, and the cavalcade of waggons clung along the beaten track. As there were no inns nor resting-places along the road, the emigrants slept in the waggons at night, watched by their powerful dogs. Occasionally they passed a village, the beginning of some future town or city. They kept up their stock of food and bread by buying from the settlers. Gettysburg was one of these. Though quiet and peaceful then, it was afterwards the scene of one of the bloodiest battles in modem times. The convoy went on to Chambersburg, where it crossed the Alleghany Mountains. The ascent of the hills was very steep, and the waggons went on, with many a stoppage to give the horses rest. They could only travel at the rate of ten or twelve miles a day.

After this difficulty had been surmounted, they went on to Pittsburg, where they came in sight of the river Ohio There were no steamboats on the river at that time; accordingly, Mr. Flower determined to float his cargo down the Ohio, to the place of his destination He had three large arks or rafts constructed, on which he embarked the men, the waggons, the horses, sheep, cows, hounds, and everything. The rafts went down the river slowly, passing villages and towns along the bank, until they reached Cincinnati, then a small town, though now a large city. After stopping there for a time, the rafts went on again, along the south coast of Indiana, to Louisville. The Flowers stayed for some time at Lexington Mr. Henry Clay lived there at that time. Mr. Flower made his acquaintance. Mr. Clay, in his kindly manner, offered to take charge of the cows and their calves, for better feeding on shore, until Mr. Flower could return for them.

It was now that the Flowers began to understand slavery. The river Ohio ran between the Free States' and the Slave States. On the one hand was Kentucky, .and on the other, Indiana and Illinois. The slaves often crossed the river to seek freedom, and were followed by the kidnappers, who took them back again to slavery.

One morning Mr. Flower heard a terrible screaming going on in the cellar underneath. He at once rose from his chair, rushed down to the cellar, peeped through the door, and found the master flogging a young negro girl. He burst open the door, stood between the girl and her master, and dared him to strike another blow. The girl was rescued for the time. The master threatened to prosecute Mr. Flower. But he refrained, and his guest left unharmed.

The convoy again proceeded over land to find out the estate on which the emigrants were to settle. It was situated west of the Wabash, in Edward County, Illinois. On their way they passed the settlement of Harmony, founded by George Rapp and his German followers. It consisted of a number of log-houses, with a church, a school, a grist mill, and some workshops. The place was afterwards purchased by Robert Owen, and the Rappites removed to Economy, near Pittsburg.[77]

---

[77] It has been said of the Rappites, that the mystical tendency of the members in their religious seclusion, and their millennarian expectation of a speedy advent of Christ, were in strange contrast with their practical good sense and thrifty habits of life. They are not Spiritualists, like the Shakers. Father Rapp taught them to be practical Christians, and inculcated the "duties of humility, simplicity of living, self-sacrifice, love to neighbours, regular and persevering industry, prayer and selfexamination." As they held community of goods, in imitation of the early Christians, to be one of their articles of faith, every one was bound to work with his own hands. "As each labours for all," said one of them to NordhofF, a German traveller, "and as the interest of one is the interest of all, there is no occasion for selfishness, and no room for waste. We were brought up to be economical; to waste is to sin. We live simply, and each has enough, all that he can eat and wear, and no man can do more than that." They are fond of flowers and music, painting and

218

The convoy went up the east side of the Wabash to the ferry. The country was then entirely without population. The ferry-man was the only person they saw. They had to wait for him for some time, but at last he arrived. Business was not pressing in those parts. They succeeded in crossing the ferry. It took a long time for the whole convoy of persons, beasts, and waggons to pass oven. After a rest they made their way northwards through the prairies. Beautiful were the prairies! They lay in long swelling far-reaching mounds, covered with grass and lovely wild flowers. A silvery haze lay over them, and stretched away into the measureless distance. At night, the fireflies came out in infinite numbers, and floated away into the darkness. The grass on the prairies was so high as to cover a man and his horse. The convoy now went entirely by the compass, for there was no other means to guide them, except the constellations of the heavens. There was "George's Wain" to lead them to the north.

After about a thousand miles of travelling by road, and track, and rafts, they were at last reaching their home in the Far West. There was nothing to the west of them, save the prairies and the desert, with occasional Indians, trappers, and squatters. They made for Piankishaw, formerly an Indian settlement, from which the Shawnees had just departed. It was difficult to found a home in that far-off district. But they set to work with a will. The labourers and blacksmiths sawed down the highest trees in a neighbouring forest, and by dint of daily labour, they set up a log hut for the family and servants, — the family in the meanwhile sleeping in the waggons. Then the men built loghuts for themselves. At last a settlement was made. But death comes everywhere. Young Flower was the first to dig a grave in the country. It was to contain the first dead — the child of his eldest brother.

But what were they to do for food for the living? The season was too far advanced to plough the land. It was now July. After eating up the provisions they had, they began to feel extremely hungry. Occasionally a deer was killed, and that sufficed for a time; but there were more than a hundred persons to be fed, and that was not enough. It was only occasionaly that a deer was brought home with rejoicing. "What shall he have that killed the deer?"

At length the colony became so starved that they had to find food elsewhere. Young Flower set out with some men to Shawney Town for provisions. The place was a long way off. It took the men two days to reach it, though it was only sixty miles off. They gave their horses rest at night, while about them they heard the howling of wolves. Their brave dogs protected them. At Shawney Town they were so fortunate as to obtain flour, meal, and several hams, with which they set off at once for home. The horses had to swim the Little Wabash going and returning. There was the greatest difficulty in getting the food across without wetting it. When

---

sculpture. Father Rapp's house contained a number of pictures of great value, and they had a library; still, the traveller was told, "the Bible is the chief book read among us.'

219

they got safely to land they lit a great fire, dried their clothes, and warmed themselves and the horses, and laid themselves down to sleep. In the early morning they mounted and galloped home with the food. One may imagine the joyfulness with which they were received.

Thus the colony struggled on. After the family had lived for some time in the log hat, the site of a house was marked out, and Park House was built. Young Edward went over to Lexington to bring his mother to the new house. She had been living there while the colony was in its greatest straits. And now she found a happy family to gather round her. In the meantime new settlements had been made in the district. There was Warrington, logbuilt; and the town of Albion was begun — now the capital of Edward's County.

When Edward was fourteen and a half years old, his father began to think of his education. A schoolmaster had settled in a log hut at Warrington. "Now, Ned," said his father, "you have been very sharp and clever, and we must do something for you. You must go to the schoolmaster, and there get some knowledge and education." The school was a good way off. To shorten the way, the scholar went through a bog when the weather was fine. It was the resort of wild turkeys. Of course the scholar took his gun and dog with him. On his way to school he brought down a splendid turkey, and took it to the schoolmaster. The schoolmaster was elated at the idea of dining on a turkey, and Ned became a great favourite.

Next day he said he would like to present the schoolmaster with a deer. The schoolmaster went out hunting with him, and hunted constantly. Deer, and turkeys, and game flowed into the schoolmaster's house. He thought there was nothing like it. But Edward's education went on very badly. In fact, he hated learning, and liked hunting much better. One day, at home, he was catechised about the multiplication table. He began to answer: "Twice two's three; twice four's five; twice five's eight" "Stop," said his mother; "that's all nonsense. Go back to the schoolmaster."

But the schoolmaster went out hunting with him as before. Ned never settled down to schooling. His father tried him in arithmetic as before. He was no better. "Twice two's six; twice three's eight," and so on. He had been six months at school, and this was the result. At last his father took him away to look after the cattle at home. And this was the only learning he received in America.

Edward still continued to hunt the deer, which was, of course, one of the necessaries for food. One day he went out hunting with some friends on foot After long walking, his dog at last struck the trail of a deer. He took the scent, and ran forward, but stopped until his master came up. He had left his friends far behind. After a long trail through the woods the dog pointed, and he shot the deer. It was now late, and he was twenty-five miles from home. He cooed to his friends, but none of them were within reach of his voice. They were on their way homewards. Desirous of possessing his deer, he sat himself down at the foot of a tree, with his dog beside him, and fell fast asleep. He was awakened suddenly by the howling of wolves. They had scented the prey, and were on their way to devour it.

He fired his rifle at them again and again to drive them away; but he still heard them whirring about him, and howling from time to time. The night was as dark as a pocket. At length, as the morning light streamed through the forest branches, he got up and went his way home. When he reached it he was dreadfully hungry, for he had been thirty hours without food.

When the Flowers first went to Illinois there were many bears about — black bears, grisly bears, and such like. "One morning," says Mr. Flower, "when I was riding through a field of maize, to cut down trees in the neighbouring wood, I saw a great big fat bear rise up. He went through a swamp to escape us. There were four men with me and my dogs. Three of the men went with me to attack the bear. The dogs went first. The bear grasped the dogs, hugged them, and killed them. Then we went at him with our axes, and after a heavy fight we killed him, brought him home, and ate him. He was a great help to our provender during the winter."

One evening at dusk, while Edward was on horseback, with his rifle slung behind him, his dog began to bark at something approaching. He was then near the Prairie, with a small forest close at hand. He looked up, and thought he observed a large beast coming on. On approaching nearer, he found that it was a man on horseback. "Are you an Englishman?" the man cried. "Yes, I am!" "Where are you going?" "Well, I am just going home. Come with me, and receive our hospitality." Indeed, any stranger was welcome in these lonely plains in the forest or the prairie. They were all treated with the usual kindness and hospitality.

After a large outlay of capital, the face of the country became greatly changed. Corn was raised and cattle bred, but not without immense labour of various kinds — not the least of which was protecting the crops and live stock from the attacks of wild animals. Edward Fordham took an active part in all this work, and it was doubtless this early training — and not the Warrington schoolmaster — that helped to form his remarkably energetic character, and taught him not to shrink from any undertaking because it is difficult, nor from any obstruction that might be overcome by energy and labour.

The fact is that the elder Mr. Flower had made a mistake in purchasing so large a property, before it became surrounded by a consuming population. The country was still unpeopled. It took about twenty years before the emigrants came as far westward as the Wabash. Albion was five hundred miles in advance of the settlers. The consequence was that Mr. Flower had the greatest difficulty in selling his stock. Yet the emigrants were coming nearer, and many of them came to settle near Albion. Many of the free negroes who had bought their liberty, lived in the town, and it became a thriving place. A few of the English emigrants failed, and were forced to return home again. Among these was Mr. Hookham (now librarian in Bond Street, London), who emigrated with his wife, and tried to settle. One day young Flower called upon them, and found them killing a fowl. The lady fainted when she saw the blood. They gave up their settlement and returned to England.

Another difficulty the Flowers had to encounter was with the slaves, bond and free. It will be remembered that the river Ohio separated the

221

Free State of Illinois from the Slave State of Kentucky. There were many slaves, who, in the hands of kind owners, were allowed to buy their liberty. Those in the western parts of Kentucky crossed the river, and for the most part settled in the rising town of Albion. But there were also multitudes of slaves in the hands of their owners across the river, who were treated with barbarous cruelty. Husbands, wives, and children, were separated from each other, and sold indiscriminately in all parts of the Slave States. Many of the slaves, men and women, escaped from their masters, crossed the rivers, and concealed themselves in swamps and forests, to enjoy liberty. Many swam the Ohio, and took refuge at Albion. Others went northwards until they reached the free country of Canada.

The slave-owners tracked their slaves with bloodhounds, and often brought them back to their work, and increased their floggings. And now a regular set of kidnappers crossed the Ohio, and endeavoured to capture the negroes, both slave and free, in order to take them down the Mississippi and sell them at New Orleans. One of the slave negroes was hired by Mr. Flower. He was a fine large negro — an excellent man, and a faithful servant Mr. Flower said to him one day, "You must surely be a slave; or have you bought your liberty?" "No, massa," said the slave; "but my owner flogs me so, and treats me so badly, that I was forced to escape from him." Not long after, the master, with his gang, followed him, and found him working on Mr. Flower's farm. He immediately seized the man, handcuffed him, and dragged him away.

But the slave again fled from his master, and took refuge with Mr. Flower. He was exhausted and half-starved. "The master's just behind me," he said Young Flower put the man into a well, and put a board over it. He threw in bread from time to time. The master, who followed his property, searched all about, and could not find the slave. Young Flower dragged the man out of his pit, loaded him with bread, and told him to fly for his life. He at once set out northwards towards Canada. But before the man could cross the river, his pursuers had placed themselves on his track. They caught him, handcuffed him, and delivered him over to "justice"! He told his master that he would never be a slave, that he would not return with him, even at the cost of his life. So, when the constable came up and apprehended him for being a runaway slave, he took out a pistol which he had concealed about his person, and shot him dead. The runaway slave was immediately hanged.

There were scores of cases such as these. Mr. Flower was inexpressibly shamed by such deeds occurring in a so-called free country. He began to think of leaving the country; but he had invested so much capital in settling and opening up the district, that for a time he forbore. The kidnappers continued to increase. They came in gangs, hunting about the country for negroes. The slave-dealers determined, if they could, to get Flower out of the State. But he would not go without a hard fight. The magistrates were then a very queer lot One day, when Mr. Flower went to Mr. De Pugh, the nearest magistrate, to get some documents signed, he found De Pugh sitting up stark naked in his bed. "Now," he sard, "I think I must get some of my little jackets on." Accordingly, he got up and signed

222

the documents. Mr. Flower made the acquaintance of another magistrate, Mr. Moses Michel, who afterwards proved of some use to him, as the following account will show: —

"I was now eighteen or nineteen years old," says Mr. Edward Flower. "I was coming home with another person, very tired and weary, having been out walking all day. As we neared home, we came to a spot in the forest where we heard a great altercation going on amongst the bushes. I heard the words, 'I will never leave hold of these reins as long as I live.' It .was the voice of my father! I immediately rushed in with my companion, and found my father holding the reins of a horse, on the back of which was strapped one of our free negroes. 'If you don't let go,' said one of the kidnappers, 'I'll shoot you in an instant.' I immediately went at him, and cut him down with my axe. My companion went at the other, and nearly cut off his arm. My father was saved, and the kidnappers immediately fled through the wood.

"We immediately got a warrant for their apprehension from Moses Michel, the magistrate. We supposed that the kidnappers had come across the Wabash at a particular place. We determined to capture them. I undertook to head our party, and the magistrate accompanied us. We started late at night, and got to the Wabash just before the break of morning. We went to the ferry, and found that the kidnappers had not passed. We then returned, and tied up the horses to the trees, and advanced about half a mile forward, to the track along which the kidnappers would come. After waiting for some time, we heard the traffickers approaching on horseback. We heard them by their tramp over the decayed leaves and broken branches. They came nearer, and were now in sight. The magistrate ordered us to cover every man with his rifle. We were all ready. Every man of the approaching gang was covered; the rifles were at full cock.

"The magistrate advanced forward. 'Men,' he said, 'surrender! Every man of you is covered! I have a warrant for the apprehension of every one of you.' The men stopped to take counsel 'No, no!' said the magistrate, 'surrender immediately. If you move, you are shot. Now, all of you unclothe, and come here to be bound.' At last they laid down their arms, they unclothed, they came forward one by one, and were bound.

"There were eight of them in all. They were about to be carried back twenty miles to Albion to be tried. But as we were on our way, the magistrate said to me, 'I think we have got too many on hand: there are two good sort of fellows whom you may let off with a word of counsel.' They were unbound, and allowed to go. Two more men were sounded, and they promised never again to take part in such an enterprise. They were also let off. The prisoners were now reduced to four — those who had been most inveterate in their attempts to capture the free negro. The four were tried, sentenced, and condemned to two years' imprisonment with hard labour in the penitentiary of Vandalia." Thus the entire system of kidnapping was broken up along the Ohio, and by the powerful efforts of Mr. Flower and the English colony, Illinois was prevented from becoming a Slave State.

Meanwhile, the kidnappers thirsted for young Flower's blood; and a gang was got up for the purpose of assassinating him. He had been the most active and energetic person in the colony to put down kidnapping and now he or his relations were to suffer for it. It happened that Jack Ellis, the backwoodsman, became acquainted with their doings. Jack had been young Flower's trainer, and accompanied him in his deer-stalkings through the woods and prairies. He had thus acquired a fondness for his young master. Somehow he got entangled with the kidnappers; and then he knew of their intention to assassinate Edward. He had before been shot at while sitting round the fireside. One night a bullet came smashing through the window, and broke the looking-glass behind his head. The whole family sprang up, rushed to the door; but the kidnappers had escaped.

The war grew hotter. One night Jack Ellis came to Edward's sister, and told her as a secret that the kidnappers were determined at all hazards to have her brother's life. "My advice is," said he, "that Ned should leave the country at once that is, if he would avoid being murdered." Jack's advice was taken. The elder Mr. Flower roused Edward from his bed early next morning, and they set out at once for England But now comes the tragedy. Two nights after, when it was not known that they had started, some six kidnappers called at the house, and asked for young Mr. Flower. It was pitch dark, and the men could not be recognized. A young fellow, Richard, Edward Flower's cousin, and very like him, went to the door. The men at once laid hold of him, cut him down with their axes, and left him dead on the spot. Poor Richard was very much regretted; but his murderers were never discovered.

When Edward left his home he ordered "Little Penn," his favourite dog, to be shut up. The dog was always with him, slept with him and hunted with him. The dog would not be separated from his master. He somehow got out, followed his master's track down to the boat, and got on board. He was sent out, and put into the arms of Flower's brother. When the boat left the pier, the dog sprang out of his brother's arms, and leapt into the Ohio. Of course the dog could not be waited for. The boat went on, and the last thing that Flower saw was the little dog swimming up the Ohio, until he became a mere speck in the distance.

Edward and his father embarked for England in a little brig of 150 tons. They were the only passengers. They landed at Liverpool in 1824. Nearly seven years had passed since they had left the same port, and everything was greatly changed. Edward had grown from a boy of thirteen to a well-grown man of nearly twenty. He was still dressed in the clothes of a backwoodsman — a coon cap with the tail hanging down his back, a hunting-shirt with fringes, corduroy trousers, black leggings, moccasin shoes, and a dark greatcoat over all. He was soon dressed up in civilised clothing.

Shortly after, the two made their way to Barford, in Warwickshire. After staying there for some time, they went to visit Benjamin Flower, editor of a Cambridge newspaper, His daughters were Eliza and Sarah Flower. The latter was the author of the beautiful hymn, sung in all churches, "Nearer, my God, to thee." A few months later Edward went to New Lanark, in Scotland, to meet Robert Owen, who was then regarded as a great philanthropist. On his return to London to join his father, he told him that it was his intention to remain in England to get some education. His father was surprised, but the son remained firm to his purpose. He did not tell his secret; but it was love that constrained him to remain in England. His father agreed to give him £ 2000 of American stock, out of the income of which he might contrive to live; and if not, there was his home in America, to which he might return any day.

After seeing his father off from Liverpool, he returned to New Lanark with Robert Dale Owen. There he received his first literary education, though the practical education which he received in the backwoods proved much more useful to him in life. He lived for a fortnight in Robert Owen's house, and afterwards in lodgings. One day, when he was walking out, he met a gentleman, who asked him the way to New Lanark. He answered, "I will take you to it; I live there myself." The two got into conversation, and became very friendly. It proved that the gentleman was Dr. Andrew Combe, of Edinburgh, who was on his way to see for himself the wondrous things done in the education of factory boys and girls at New Lanark. Dr. Combe dined with the young backwoodsman, when the latter freely communicated his history and his intentions to "get education." "Well," said the Doctor, "get Murray's Grammar, and take to reading directly. Read the best books, and think about them. You will find no difficulty."

Flower remained for six months at his studies at New Lanark. He worked so close at his books that he lost his health. There was indeed a great difference between sitting on a chair in a small room, occupying his brain with learning and writing words, and roaming about the prairies of the far west, drinking in the delightful breezes of the unpolluted skies. At last he left New Lanark, and travelled from Edinburgh to London on foot, through towns and cities, which were always a wonder to him. He lived with Dr. Kelly, of Trinity Square, London, as a pupil, for six months; and with him he perfected himself in arithmetic, algebra, and other branches of superior education.

He was now twenty-one, and ready for business. He went to Birmingham, and was engaged as clerk to a corn merchant on commission, at £ 100 a year. He was found so useful that, in two years, his salary was raised to £ 400. He then got married to a noble and affectionate wife; and after that, his way through life was pleasant. He settled at Stratford-upon-Avon, where he became one of the greatest brewers of the country. He was Mayor of the town for four years, and justice of the peace for the county of War-wick. Everywhere he was honoured and respected His home was the home of hospitality. Above all, he loved his American friends, and in summer time his house was full of them. He organised and carried out the Shakespearian Tercentenary of 1864 in his own gallant manner.

In that year he had a stroke of paralysis, and retired from business. But he had a wonderful amount of strength and pluck in him. In 1865 he had another attack, and lost the use of one side of his body. Yet in 1868 he stood as a candidate for the House of Commons for North Warwickshire.

He was defeated, but not cast down. He tried for Coventry in 1872, but was again defeated. He had another stroke in 1869, and lost the use of the English language. He had to begin again with nouns, adjectives, adverbs, and so on.

He went to Rome, and his health improved. Then he went to Pau in the south of France. In all places he saw the cruelty inflicted upon horses, mules, and donkeys. He almost cried over them. When he came to live in London in 1873, he set himself to work to cure the mischief that was being done to horses — especially by the use of bits and bearing-reins. He bought a black horse. It had previously been curbed, bitted, and tortured. He cured the horse at once by taking off the instruments of torture. He wrote a letter to the Times and, through the instrumentality of the late Sir Arthur Helps, it was inserted. It was at his instance that Sir Arthur composed his work upon Animals and their Masters, He went to a meeting of the Society for the Prevention of Cruelty to Animals, and found a dozen carriages at the door with the horses gagged up by bits and bearing-reins, standing there for hours together. He went to the Committee, but they would not hear him. The chairman ordered him out of the room.

He went on his way, nevertheless. He was not to be gagged. He wrote letters to all the daily papers, which were inserted. He thus roused public opinion on the subject. He next published his pamphlet on Bits and Bearing Reins, and scattered it broadcast throughout the country. It was followed by Horses and Harness, a sequel to the first pamphlet; and that, too, was largely circulated, Mr. Flower gives the following description of the harnessing of the horses of a fashionable "turn-out:" — A tight bearing-rein is used to pull the horses' heads up, a fixed martingale to pull them down, close blinkers to prevent them seeing their way, cruppers which are obliged to be tight to hold the bearing-reins in their places, so that the heads and tails of the animals are tied tight together. To obtain a little ease by shortening its back when standing still, the horse extends its fore legs beyond their natural position, while the hinder ones are proportionably thrown back, causing inflammation and navicular lameness. The tight bearing-rein, by holding the head in an unnatural and fixed position, strains the windpipe and respiratory organs, inducing roaring and other maladies. The front part of the bridle is frequently too short, thereby hurting the lower part of the ears; also the winker strap, which, .when tight, besides drawing the winkers too close, pulls forward the top of the bridle so as to press upon and hurt the back of the ears; and when the horse shows signs of uneasiness by throwing up its head, he is punished by more and tighter Straps, the coachman seldom troubling himself to find out and remedy the cause of the irritation.

"Fashion is strong — stronger, I fear, than humanity — but still I have hopes. Fashion no longer orders horses to be cropped, docked, and nicked; therefore these new forms of distortion and cruelty may give way. If a few leaders of fashion would join with men and women of common sense and lovers of humanity, we should soon wipe out this blot upon our civilisation. I am happy to have been allowed to raise my feeble voice in the cause; and I heartily thank all those (and they are many) who have come forward to help and encourage me. I shall persevere, and, though I am old, I do not despair of living long enough to have it engraved upon my tombstone: 'He was one of those men who caused the bearing-rein to be abolished.'"

Mr. Flower appeals to the ladies, as if ladies were the most cruel of all in their treatment of dumb animals. "Ladies," he says, "are accused of liking to see horses with their heads stuck up in the air and their legs prancing. Surely it is because they do not know how much more graceful it is to see a handsome, well-fed horse in its free and natural attitudes. Do, ladies, look at your horses' mouths. Do not mind what your coachmen say about the necessity of the barbarous atrocity of gag bearing-reins, and sharp bits, and the irritating use of the whip. Make yourselves acquainted with the delicate organs of the animals to whom you owe so much of your comfort and pleasure, and they will well repay you for any consideration and kindness."

The result of Mr. Flower's labours up to the present time has been, that about thirty per cent of the torture inflicted by bearing-reins has been done away with by humane gentlemen. It only remains to enlist kind ladies to do away with the rest of the cruelty. "It is ignorance, prejudice, fashion and, in too many cases, wilful cruelty, that has to be contended with. I am happy to have made many converts, and I hope to be able to go on talking, writing with the aid of my wife, probably boring my friends and the public, till the sight, now every day to be seen, of horses foaming, fretting, prancing, maddened with pain from their curbs, gags, and whips, is banished from this so-called civilised country. Go into the Park or fashionable streets: just look at the gagged-up horses, either standing or in motion, and you will see that my picture of ' Torture ' is no exaggeration; and the fair occupants of the carriages sit smilingly unconscious of the pain they are causing; the coachman careless of it, perhaps rejoicing that he has the power to tyrannise over the unhappy victims of his ignorance, bad temper, or conceit."

Lord Leigh wrote to Mr. Flower a short time ago, "I congratulate you on your success, and I trust the day is not far distant, when a horse with a bearing-rein on him will be as rare an object as a soldier in armour; and should that happy day arrive, you may have the satisfaction of feeling that you have done as great a service to the poor horses as Wilberforce did in his day to the poor slaves."

Mr. Flower was not content with helping the carriage-horses. He next came to the help of the cart-horses. In his seventy-fifth year, after his golden wedding had passed, he wrote, with the help of his wife. The Stones of London very different from Ruskin's Stones of Venice, He prefaced his work with a portrait of Macadam, the great improver of roads. But the principles of Macadam had long been forgotten. The roads in London were found covered with large stones; and his heart would have bled to see the effect of his system, as carried out by ignorant vestries in league with corrupt contractors. In Macadam's time, the stones had to pass through a two-inch ring, and were to be of not more than six ounces in weight. The stones were to be broken so as to unite by their own angles into a firm, compact, and impenetrable body. But the stones have now became so large, that many of them are as big as the size of a man's fist How can the poor cart-horses drag their heavy loads over stones so impracticable? This set Mr. Flower's mind to work; and hence his pamphlet He invaded the vestry boards, and poured out his complaints. Wisdom herself cries out in the streets, but no vestryman regardeth her. Let us hope that Mr. Flower's voice will not call out longer in vain!

Altogether, we regard Mr. Flower as a true lover of his fellow-creatures — not only of men, but of animals. During the war between North and South in America, he went all over this country, lecturing upon the liberation of African slaves. He remained true to the instincts which he had imbibed in Illinois. When his father died in America, while the civil war was raging, an American journalist said of him, "In the eventful strife which accompanied the daring attempt in 1823 to legalise slavery in Illinois, no one enlisted with a truer heroism than he. We, of the present day, and amidst the dire commotion of civil war, can but poorly comprehend the ferocity and the gloomy portents of that struggle. So nearly balanced were the contending parties of the State, that the vote of the English colony, ever true to the instincts of freedom, turned the scale; a handful of sturdy Britons being the forlorn hope to stay the triumph of wrong and oppression, whose success might have sealed for ever the doom of republican and constitutional liberty in America."

Let this not be forgotten, when the engraving on Edward Fordham Flower's tombstone comes to be written. May he yet see an end put to the tortures inflicted upon horses, which he has so gallantly contended against during his lifetime.

CHAPTER XV

RESPONSIBILITY

So when a good man dies.
For years beyond his ken, The light he leaves behind him lies
Upon the paths of men.

Longfellow

For his chaste muse employed her heaven-taught lyre.
None but the noblest passions to inspire.
Not one immoral, one corrupted thought,
One line which, dying, he would wish to blot.

Lord Littleton on Thomson

Learn as if you were to live for ever; live as if you were to die to-morrow.

Ansalus de Insulis

DUTY begins with life, and ends with death. It. encompasses our whole being. It bids us do what is right, and forbids our doing what is wrong. It begins with the upbringing of children. It bids us nurture them, instruct them, educate them, and bring them, by our example, into the ways of well-doing.

Duty accompanies us through life. It goes out of our households to the help of others. The master owes duty to his servants, and the servants to their master. We owe our duty to our neighbour, to our country, to the State. The doing of our duty to all, involves an immense responsibility. No one can lead a true life, unless he feels this sense, and energetically acts up to it.

In human society, social rights necessitate their own observance. When the sense of responsibility is blunted, society goes to ruin. "The race of mankind," says Sir Walter Scott, "would perish, did they cease to aid each other. From the time that the mother binds the child's head, till the moment that some kind assistant wipes the damp from the brow of the dying, we cannot exist without mutual aid All, therefore, that need aid, have a right to ask it from their fellow-mortals. None who have the power of granting aid can refuse it without guilt."

In previous works we have endeavoured to show forth the great virtues of a good example. It is among the most priceless of all things. To set the best example in our power is one of our highest responsibilities. Example teaches better than precept. It is the best modeller of the characters of men and women. To live well is the best preacher. To set a lofty example is the richest bequest a man can leave behind him; and to exemplify a noble character is the most valuable contribution a man can make for the benefit of posterity.

All this requires faith, courage, modesty, unselfishness. Temptations beset all men, but by faith and courage we are enabled to set them at defiance. Duty requires us to be chaste and loving. Justice repudiates all forms of selfishness, oppression, and cruelty. Faith in God contains within it the assurance that good must overcome evil universally. "The victory of good over evil," said Mr. Erskine of Ellon, "is the conversion of all evil beings into good beings; it is making darkness light, and crooked things straight.'"

The best and bravest of men may have moments of doubt and weakness — they may feel the pillars of their faith shaking under them; but if they are the best and bravest, they rise again from their depression by recurring to first principles. We must believe that the universe is wisely ordered, and that every man must conform to the order which he cannot change; that whatever the Deity has done is good; that all mankind are our brethren; and that we must love and cherish them, and try to make them better, even those who would do us harm.

No one can really believe in the system of negation. Negation can do nothing for men. It may pull down, but it cannot build up. It is death to the better part of us. It puts an end to faith and hope. Evil cannot be put down by uttering mere commonplace terms of condemnation; but by real, active, working goodness.

Even science has had its victories in faith. Negation never helped Newton to wrest from nature her secret of the laws of motion. It was in faith that Kepler toiled; and Dalton and Faraday laboured. "Not in scepticism, but in faith," says Professor Pritchard, "the elder Herschel, hour after hour, walked his weary but observant rounds, fed by a sister's hand, and stopping not till he had finished his mirrors, not doubting they would in due time unfold to him the construction of the material heavens. And in a like spirit of a loving confidence his gifted son banished himself to the far south till he had finished the work which his father had begun, and for all ages wrote cœlis exploratis ' upon the escutcheon of their fame."

Negation merely leaves us in discouragement and despair. Everything is doubted — faith in God, faith in man, faith in duty, faith in everything but ourselves and our enjoyments. ' Outside this all is passion, confusion, selfishness, darkness, where the personality is abdicated, and the soul finds no guidance. The worth of our life is to be measured by its opportunities for activity in the path of the Divine laws and purposes; and in that path freedom is to be found — the freedom without which there is no real life for man."

Once, a man lying on his sick-bed asked himself, "Has any good come out of my life? Whose heart have I made lighter? Whose sorrow have I relieved? Whose home have I blessed? What good have I done? Is the world any better for my living in it? " The answers given to these self-questionings were hollow. The man rose up from his sick couch a wiser and a better man. From that time he employed himself and his means in doing good. He found abundant opportunities for well-doing. He only wanted the will and the determination. He found them in the law of God. Religion is but the bond of eternal love. Love, greater than hope, greater than faith, is the only thing which God requires of us, and in the possession of which lies the fulfilment of all our duties.

The sense of Duty smooths our path through life. It helps us to know, to learn, and to obey. It gives us the power of overcoming difficulties, of resisting temptations, of doing that for which we strive; of becoming honest, kind, and true. All experience teaches us that we become that which we make ourselves. We strive against inclinations to do wrong, we strive for the inclination to do right, and little by little we become that for which we strive. Every day's effort makes the struggle easier. We reap as we have sown.

The true way to excel in any effort is to propose the brightest and most perfect example for imitation. We improve by the attempt, even though we fall short of the full perfection. Character will always operate. There may be little culture, slender abilities, no property, no position in "Society;" yet, if there be a character of sterling excellence, it will command influence and secure respect. The edge of our faculties is seldom worn out by use, but it is very often rusted away by sloth. It is fervour and industry alone which give the beauty and the brightness to human life.

"I know" said Perthes, "that a quick imagination is the salt of earthly life, without which nature is but a skeleton; but the higher the gift, the greater the responsibility." To a young man he said, "Go forward with hope

230

and confidence: this is the advice given thee by an old man, who has had a full share of the burden and heat of life's day. We must ever stand upright, happen what may; and for this end we must cheerfully resign ourselves to the varied influences of this many-coloured life.... The consciousness of this mortal life being but the way to a higher goal, by no means precludes our using it cheerfully; and, indeed, we must do so, otherwise our energy in action will entirely fail us."

Youth is the time of growth and motion. It is the Spring of man. The young man goes into the world, and puts out his life in manifold forms. Where he has been duly cared for by his parents, and imbibed a high conception of personal dignity and human worth, he must uphold their honour, and do nothing that they would blush to see. He should cherish profound gratitude to those honest- people who had transmitted to him an undefiled character, and represented centuries of labour and good conduct. "Prove yourself worthy of your parents," was a saying of Periander, one of the seven sages of Greece. The virtues of their generous labours are an image of the dead; with families as with men, it is steadfast perseverance which keeps their honour bright. But if the mind and heart of the youth have not been cultivated, and no blossoms of hope appear, we look forward to his manhood with dismay, if not with despair.

Words and examples always come back to the young, and influence them for good as well as for evil. For nothing — not even a word or example — is ever forgotten or lost. We cannot commit a wrong, without in punishment following closely at its heels. When we break a law of eternal justice, it echoes throughout the world. Words and deeds may be considered slight things; yet they are not temporary, they are eternal. An idle or a bad word never dies. It may come up against us in the future — twenty years, a hundred years hence — long after we are dead. "Every idle word," says St. Matthew, "that men shall speak, they shall give an account thereof in the day of judgment; for by thy words thou shalt be justified, and by thy words thou shalt be condemned."

Evil deeds and evil examples have the same resurrection. They never die, but influence all time. They descend like an inheritance. The memory of a life does not perish with the life itself. What is done remains, and can never be undone. Thomas of-Malmesbury said, "There is no action of man in this life, which is not the beginning of so long a chain of consequences, as that no human providence is high enough to give us a prospect to the end." "Every atom," says Babbage, "impressed with good or ill, retains at once the motions which philosophers and sages have imparted to it, mixed and combined in ten thousand ways with all that is worthless and base. The air itself is one vast library, on whose pages are written y ever all that man has ever said, or whispered, or done."

Thus every word, thought, and deed, has its influence upon the destiny of man. Every life, well spent or ill spent, bears with it a long train of consequences, extending through generations yet unborn all this is calculated to impress man with a deep sense of the responsibility involved in his every thought, word, and deed. "I have read a tract," said Dr. Chalmers, "entitled" The Last Moments of the Earl of Rochester,' and I was struck power-fully, when reading it, with the conviction how much evil a pernicious pamphlet may be the means of disseminating."

Bad books are worse than bad words. Like evil deeds, they mould the thought and will of future generations. The printed book lives, while the author is dust and ashes. The bad author lives for ever in his race. His book continues to disseminate vice, immorality, and atheism. "The art of printing," says Frederick Schlegel, "in itself one of the most glorious and useful, has become prostituted to the speedy and universal circulation of poisonous tracts and libels. It has occasioned a dangerous influx of paltry and superficial compositions, alike hostile to soundness of judgment and purity of taste — z. sea of frothy conceits and noisy dulness, upon which the spirit of the age is tossed hither and thither, not without great and frequent danger of entirely losing sight of the compass of meditation and the polar star of truth."[78]

And again: "Insulated already by opinions, these men are separated from each other still more by interests. Covetousness is their soul. Who among them has a family, a country? Each has himself, and nothing more. Generous sentiments, honour, fidelity, devotion, all that used to make beat high the heart of our forefathers, seem to them like empty sounds.... To calculate is the sole business of these men. Conscience is an astonishment and a scandal."

Thus Schlegel argues about the responsibility of authors. They are responsible for the good they do, as well as for the evil that they inculcate. The leprous book gets into our libraries; it gets into our homes. The books may be very clever. Their style draws the reader on, yet they may be full of vicious thoughts. It was said by Sterne, that "vice loses half its evil when it loses its grossness." But this is a mischievous idea. Grossness may revolt us, but covert abominations, clothed in sprightly words, may sink deeper into our minds. Look, for instance, at the scrofulous novel read by young ladies. It is written in a brilliant style, though it is full of unchastity, impurity, and moral poison. It often begins with a murder, and ends with unchasteness and adultery; as if the objects of these writers were to display the cancerous rottenness of life. The worst of these unbelieving novel writers are English women.

Then, there is the book that keeps one in a state of constant giggling — a sure sign of a shallow mind. Illnatured chaff, sarcasm of the good, praise of the bad, is a frightful sight. How different from the good book, or the good novel! Not the "goody goody" book; but the book that inspires health, and purity, and courage. Lockhart said of his father-in-law Scott, "We may picture to ourselves in some measure the debt we owe to a perpetual succession of books, through thirty years of publication, unapproached in charm, and all instilling a high and healthy code; a bracing and invigorating spirit; a contempt of mean passions, whether vindictive or voluptuous; humane charity, as distinct from moral laxity or from unsympathising austerity; sagacity too deep for cynicism, and tenderness never degenerating into sentimentality; animated throughout in thought,

[78] History of Literature ii. 39.

opinion, feeling, and style, by one and the same pure energetic principle — a path and savour of manhood; appealing to whatever is good and loyal in our natures, and rebuking whatever is low and selfish."

The praise is great, but it is deserved. When Sir Walter Scott, towards the close of his life, was congratulated by Dr. Cheney on the purity of his works of fiction, he answered, "I am drawing near to the close of my career. I am fast shuffling off the stage. I have been perhaps the most voluminous author of the day; and it is a comfort to me to think that I have tried to unsettle no man's faith, to corrupt no man's principles, and .that I have written nothing which on my deathbed I should wish blotted."

The same might be said of Charles Dickens. He was the Apostle of the People. "I have read," said the Bishop of Manchester, "most of Mr. Dickens's works, and, so far as I can remember, there is not one single page, or one single sentence, tainted with any impurity or anything that would suggest a vile or vicious thought I believe that the literature of which he was the author has been pregnant with consequences of incalculable benefit to our people. It has made us see truly simple virtues under rugged exteriors. It has taught us the great lessons of Christian sympathy; and though in all things Charles Dickens is not what we might have desired, or what he might have been, yet we are not his judges. We do not know the circumstances of trial through which his life was passed But I feel that England owes a debt of gratitude to her great novelist for what he has done to elevate and purify the human life where it most needs elevation and purification."

The good book, like the bad book, will live long after the author is dead. A book written two thousand years ago may fix the purpose of a life. The remembered sentiment of the speechless dead may arrest the attention and transform the character. On the other hand, vicious books still lift their voices and urge the young to deeds of shame and crime. The authors speak from their graves, and spread pollution and infamy throughout the world.

A book is a living voice. It is a spirit walking on the face of the earth. It continues to be the living thought of a person separated from us by space and time. Men pass away; monuments crumble into dust. What remains and survives is human thought. What is Plato? He has long been resolved into dust, but his thoughts and his actions still survive.

Bad books are moral poison which continue to disseminate evil. *Litera scripta manet* Mischievous authors, even when in their graves, murder the souls of their survivors, from generation to generation. The good book is a life treasure, while the bad book is a tormenting spirit. The good book teaches rectitude, truth, and goodness; while the bad book teaches vice, selfishness, and unbelief. The authors die, while their works live on. Such a thought ought to give authors a deep impression as to the undying responsibilities of literature.

An intimate friend of Wordsworth has thus recorded his recollections of the poet: — "The last time I saw him, he was in deep domestic sorrow, and beginning to bend under the infirmities of old age. 'Whatever,' he said, 'the world may think of me and my poetry is now of little consequence; but one thing is a comfort to my old age, — that none of my works, written since the days of my early youth, contains a line I would wish to blot out, because of pandering to the baser passions of our nature. This,' said he, ' is a comfort to me; I can do no mischief by my works when I am gone.'"

Before we conclude this chapter, let us give a Fable of Krilof the Russian, which has proved of use to writers of books in more cases than one. It is entitled "The Author and the Robber."

"In the gloomy realm of shadows, two sinners appeared before the judges for sentence at the same time. The one was a robber, who used to. exact tribute on the highway, and had at last come to the gallows; the other an author covered with glory, who had infused a subtle poison into his works, had promoted atheism, and had preached immorality, being, like the Siren, sweet-voiced, and, like the Siren, dangerous. In Hades, judicial ceremonies are brief; there are no useless delays. Sentence was pronounced immediately. Two huge iron cauldrons were suspended in the air by two tremendous iron chains; in each of these one of the sinners was placed. Under the Robber a great pile of wood was heaped up, and then one of the Furies herself set it on fire, kindling such a terrible flame, that the very stones in the roof of the imperial halls began to crack. The Author's sentence did not seem to be a severe one. Under him, at first, a little fire scarcely glowed; but the longer it burned the larger it became.

"Centuries had now gone by, but the fire has not gone out. Beneath the Robber the flame has long ago been extinguished; beneath the Author it grows hourly worse and worse. Seeing that there is no mitigation of his torments, the writer at last cries out amidst them that there is no justice among the gods; that he had filled the world with his renown, and that if he had written too freely, he had been punished too much for it; and that he did not think he had sinned more than the Robber. Then, before him, in all her ornaments, with snakes hissing amid her hair, and with bloody scourges in her hands, appeared one of the infernal sisters.

"Wretch!' she exclaimed, 'dost thou upbraid Providence? Dost thou compare thyself with the Robber? His crime is as nothing compared with thine. Only as long as he lived did his cruelty and lawlessness render him hurtful. But thou! — long ago had thy bones crumbled to dust, yet the sun never rises without bringing to light fresh evils of which thou art the cause. The poison of thy writings not only does not weaken, but, spreading abroad, it becomes more malignant as years roll by. Look there,' and for a moment she enabled him to look upon the world; ' behold the crimes, the misery, of which thou art the cause. Look at these children who have brought shame upon their families, who have reduced their parents to despair. By whom were their heads and hearts corrupted? By thee. Who strove to rend asunder the bonds of society, ridiculing as childish follies all ideas of the sanctity of marriage and the right of authority and law, and rendering them responsible for all human misfortunes? Thou art the man! Didst thou not dignify unbelief with the name of enlightenment? Didst thou not place vice and passion in the most charming and alluring of lights? And now look! — a whole country, perverted by thy teaching, is full of murder and robbery, of strife and rebellion, and is being led onward by thee to ruin. For every drop of that country's tears and blood thou art to blame. And now dost thou dare to hurl thy blasphemies against the gods? How much evil have thy books yet to bring upon the world? Continue then to suffer, for here the measure of thy punishment shall be according to thy deserts.' Thus spoke the angry Fury, and slammed down the cover on the cauldron."[79]

CHAPTER XVI

THE LAST

When darkness gathers over all,
And the last tottering pillars fall,
Take the poor dust Thy mercy warms,
And mould it into heavenly forms.

O. Wendell Holmes

I hear a voice you cannot hear,
Which says I must not stay;
I see a hand you cannot see,
Which beckons me away.

Tickell

O life! O death! O world I O time!
O grave, where all things flow!
Tis yours to make our lot sublime,
With your great weight of woe.

This is our life, while we enjoy it. We lose it like the sun, which flies swifter than an arrow; and yet no man perceives that it moves. ... Is not earth turned to earth; and shall not our sun set like theirs when the night comes?

Henry Smith.

THE young man enters life with joy and enthusiasm. The world lies all enamelled before him, as a distant prospect sun-gilt. But time quickly cools his enthusiasm. He cannot carry the freshness of the morning through the day and into the night Youth passes, age matures, and, at length, he must resign himself to growing old.

But the end is the result of his past life. Words and deeds are irrevocable. They mix themselves up with his character, arid descend to

---

[79] Krilof and his Falles. By W. R. S. Ralston, M.A.

futurity. The past is ever present with us. "Every sin," says Jeremy Taylor, "smiles in the first address, and carries light in the face and honey on the lip." When life matures, and the evil-doer ceases not from his ways, he can only look forward to old age with fear and despair.

But good principles, on the other hand, form a suit of armour which no weapon can penetrate. "True religion," says Cecil, "is the life, health, and education of the soul and whoever truly possesses it is strengthened with peculiar encouragement for every good word and work"

Yet we must all go away; and the place that knew us shall know us no more. The invisible messenger is always at hand, — "the messenger," says Carlyle, "which overtakes alike the busy and the idle, which arrests man in the midst of his pleasures or occupations, and changes his countenance, and sends him away." "Poor Edward," said Balzac, "has been stopped in the grooves of life. He has begun to send his equipages and jockeys on an embassy to the greatest sovereign in the sublunary worlds-death."

It comes to all. We each day dig our graves with our teeth. The hour-glass is the emblem of life. It wanes low, to the inevitable last grain, and then there is silence — death. Even the monarch walks over the tombs of his forefathers to be crowned; and is afterwards taken over them to his grave.

When Wilkie was in the Escurial, looking at Titian's famous picture of the Last Supper, an old Jeronimite said to him, "I have sat daily in sight of that picture for now nearly threescore years. During that time my companions have dropped off, one after another; all who were my seniors, all who were my contemporaries, and -many, or most of those who were younger than myself. More than one generation has passed away, and there the figures in the picture have remained unchanged! I look at them till I sometimes think that they are the realities, and we are but shadows." And yet the time came, when the old monk himself was taken away.

The old men must give way to the young, and these too for men who are younger than themselves. When time has tugged at us long, we cease to do more than vegetate; we become a burden to ourselves and to others, and what is worst of all, we get a longing for a still longer life. "When I look at many old men around me," said Perthes, "I am reminded of Frederick the Great's expostulation with his grenadiers, who demurred at going to certain deaths ' What, you dogs! would ye go on living for ever?"[80]

The great Cyrus had placed upon his tomb these words; "O man! whosoever thou art, and whencesoever thou comest (for come I know thou wilt), I am Cyrus, the founder of the Persian empire; envy me not the little earth that covers my body." Alexander the Great visited the tomb, and was much affected by the inscription, which placed before him the uncertainty and vicissitude of earthly things. The tomb was broken open, and Alexander caused the author of the sacrilege to be put to death.

The only wise thing recorded of Xerxes was his reflection on the sight of his army of over a million of men in arms, — that not one of that

---

[80] Life of Perthes ii, 473.

immense multitude would survive a hundred years. The thought seemed to be a momentary gleam of true light and feeling.[81]

Pericles, at the last moment of his life, said that while those about him were commending him for things that others might have done as well as himself, they took no notice of the greatest and most honourable part of his character — "that no Athenian, through his means, ever went into mourning."

Despair seizes the minds of men whose desires are boundless, and who see at last a limit set to their ambition Alexander cried because there were no more kingdoms to conquer. It was the same with Mahmoud, the Ghiznevide, the first Mahommedan conqueror of India. When he felt himself dying, he caused all his treasures of gold and jewels to be displayed before him. When he surveyed them, he wept like a child. "Alas!" said he, "what dangers, what fatigues of body and mind, have I endured for the sake of acquiring those treasures, and what cares in preserving them! And now I am about to die and leave them!" He was interred in his palace, where his unhappy ghost was afterwards believed to wander.

Thus the poor Manchester manufacturer, who had accumulated an immense fortune, had a pile of new sovereigns brought to him and laid upon the coverlet of his bed. He gloated over and fondled them, feasted his eyes upon them, filled his hands with them, and let them fall in a stream upon each other, thus making music in his ears. When he died, he was no richer than the beggar at his door.

The death of Charles IX of France was a terrible one. He had authorised the massacre of the Huguenots on the fearful night of St. Bartholomew, and was haunted by its horrors during his dying moments. "I know not how it is," he said to his surgeon, Ambrose Parè, "but for the last few days I feel as in a fever. My mind and body are both disturbed. Every moment, whether I am asleep or awake, visions of murdered corpses, covered with blood and hideous to the sight, haunt me. Oh, I wish I had spared the innocent and the imbecile! "He died two years after the massacre, and to the last moment the horrors of the day of St. Bartholomew were present without ceasing to his mind.

Sydney Smith once visited Castle Howard, and stood with Sir Samuel Romilly on the steps of the portico. He gazed around on the beautiful landscape before him, and then at the family mausoleum which was in sight. After a long pause, he exclaimed, lifting up his arms, "Ah! these are the things that make death terrible."

When Cardinal Mazarin was told that he had only two months to live, he paced along his beautiful galleries filled with exquisite works of art, and exclaimed, "I must quit all that What pains I have had in acquiring all these things. And yet I must see them no more!" Brienne approached, and the Cardinal took his arm, saying, "I am very feeble, I cannot see more." And yet he returned to his tribulations. "Do you see, my friend, that beautiful picture of Corregio, and again, that Venus of Titian, and that

---

[81] For the death of Ninus, the great Assyrian monarch, see Jeremy Taylor's Holy Dying chap. I sec. ii.

incomparable picture of Annibale Carracci! Ah! my poor friend, I must quit all that Adieu, dear paintings that I have loved so much, and that have cost me so dear!"[82]

But there are worse things than death. That is not the greatest calamity that can befall a man. Death levels, yet ennobles. Love is greater than death. Duty fulfilled makes death restful: dishonour makes death terrible. "I bless the Lord," said Sir Harry Vane, before his execution on Tower Hill, "that I have not deserted the righteous cause for which I suffer! "When Sir Walter Raleigh was laid on the block, he was told by the executioner to lie with his head towards the east "No matter how the head lies," was his reply, "so that the heart be right."

Once when a great Marshal was about to die, those about his bedside spoke to him, of his victories, and the number of colours which he had taken from the enemy. "Ah!" said the old warrior, "how little avail all the actions which you call ' glorious! 'all these are not worth one single cup of cold water given for the love of God."

Sir John Moore was struck down on the field of Corunna, and the doctor arrived to his help. "No, no! "he said. "You cannot be of use to me; go to the soldiers, to whom you may be useful." The last words that Nelson said were, "Thank God, I have done my duty, I have done my duty! " "My dear," said Sir Walter Scott to his son-in-law on his death-bed, "be a good man; be virtuous, be religious, be a good man. Nothing else will give you any comfort when you come to lie here." "Live well!" said the dying Samuel Johnson.

Kant died at eighty. He retained his powers almost to the last. During his illness he spoke much of his approaching end. "I do not fear death," he said, "for I know how to die. I assure you that if I knew this night were to be my last, I would raise my hands and say, 'God be praised!' The case would be very different if I had ever caused the misery of any of my fellow-creatures."

Kant once said, "Take from man Hope and Sleep, and you make him the most wretched being on the earth. We then feel that life's weary load is more than our weak nature can abide, and are only cheered onward in the toiling ascent of Pisgah by the great hope of yet beholding the promised land."

We have only one way into life, and a thousand ways out of it Birth and death are but the circling of life in itself. God gives us our being, and gives us the custody of the keys of life. We can do, and labour, and love our fellow-creatures, and do our duty to them. "The way to judge of religion," says Jeremy Taylor, "is by doing our duty. Religion is rather a divine life than a divine knowledge. In heaven, indeed, we must first see, and then love; but here, on earth, we must first love, and love will open our eyes as well as our hearts, and we shall then see and perceive and understand."

If we would face the future, we must work on courageously from day to day. It is in the steadfast hope of an existence after death, where tears shall be wiped from every eye, that we are enabled to live through the

---

[82] St. Beuve's Causeries du Lundi ii. 249

sorrows and troubles of this life. A man's true wealth hereafter is the good he does in this world to his fellow-creatures. When he dies, people will say, "What property has he left?" But the angels who examine him will ask, "What good deeds hast thou sent before thee?"

To everything under the sun there is a last. The last line of a book, the last sermon, the last speech, the last act of a life, the last words at death. "Bring my soul out of prison, that I may give thanks unto Thy name," were the last words of St. Francis of Assisi. Hic jacet is the universal epitaph. Then the secrets of all hearts shall be finally revealed — at the last day.

> "Even such is Time, which takes in trast
> Our Youth, our joys, and all we have,
> And pays us nought but Age and Dust,
> When in the dark and silent grave,
> When we have wandered all our ways,
> Shuts up the story of our days;
> And from which grave and earth and dust.
> The Lord shall raise me up, I trust."